## "You have no choice now, miss," said Tante Tillie . . .

Shayna pleaded with them and wept and knew it was no help, had known actually for weeks that it was going to come to this. All the weeks she had scrubbed and Poppa had shouted, she had known. Even with Mamma and Rachel gone, so two less (no—two fewer, she corrected herself) mouths to feed, there was need for more money. Yakov was on strike and wasn't bringing in anything. She had known she would have to quit school and go to work. All right, she would have to go to work, there was no way out of it.

No! There had to be a way. All night long after Poppa told her his decision she lay in bed and thought of it. She had to find a way . . .

# JOURNEY HOME

## JANET C. ROBERTSON

**POCKET BOOKS**

New York   London   Toronto   Sydney   Tokyo   Singapore

An *Original* Publication of POCKET BOOKS

POCKET BOOKS, a division of Simon & Schuster Inc.
1230 Avenue of the Americas, New York, NY 10020

ISBN: 0-671-66885-4

First Pocket Books printing June 1990

10  9  8  7  6  5  4  3  2  1

POCKET and colophon are registered trademarks of
Simon & Schuster Inc.

Printed in the U.S.A.

*For Jonathan and Rachel*
*(in case I forgot to tell them)*

# JOURNEY HOME

## ❧ 1 ❧

*Honour thy father and thy mother.*
*(Deuteronomy 5:16)*

Maybe Shayna Klugerman was the luckiest girl in the world. She stood a moment on the crowded corner of Avenue A and Eighth Street and thought about it, and then she let people push her across the street. Why not? It was a warm May day, and there were so many people who could push; why take any direction at all of her own free will? She decided instead just to clutch at the strap around her schoolbooks and see if the whole world would push her home. Maybe, she thought, if she could leap into the air, as a knight could leap on a charger, the press of the crowd would carry her home to Orchard Street without her even having to use any power of her own at all. Maybe.

She could think of lots of maybes. She could also sometimes (not today, she told herself) think another way; she could think of lots of what ifs. What if something happened and she became like all the other girls on Orchard Street, the girls who had to leave school when they were fourteen and work, the girls who could not finish high school? What if something happened to her mamma and poppa? Brina Rubenovsky's parents died of tuberculosis within a month of each other,

1

and Brina's brothers and sisters were parceled out among relatives. What if that should happen to her? Shayna had even heard how Brina had to go out on the street to find men who would pay her, and now she lived in a flat with other girls who did what she did. Brina was only a year older than she was. What if . . . but Shayna wouldn't let herself think any more of what if.

Now the sun was shining, even here in New York City, and she could feel the sweat starting under her scratchy underwear. Every drip, every push, even every smell of the sweating people around her was transformed into a part of the special cheer of being herself, Shayna, thirteen-and-a-half-going-on-fourteen, in New York City, New York State, the United States of America, the North American continent, the Western Hemisphere, the whole wide world. And maybe, since she and the twentieth century were both in their fourteenth year, there was a mystical significance to it all, one like those unraveled by the Cabalists, those weavers of mystery and mathematics of whom her poppa had spoken. Maybe she would even be lucky enough to live to see it all—a whole century, the modern world—and she might experience it all.

Shayna's dreams narrowed toward reality as she got closer to Orchard Street. Her brown eyes smiled as her brown pigtails flapped behind her; she hurried on, more self-propelled than she wanted to admit, through the teeming, pushing, rushing streets toward her delicious afternoon. She had it all planned. Never mind what if. She would sit down the minute she was in the door, and she would start to read *Rob Roy*. She had carefully hidden it under her pillow when she left that morning, open to her page and ready for her return. Mamma would want to hear more of the story while she ironed, so Shayna would read aloud to her again the description of the great crowd in Glasgow, the pressing, sweating crowd that was so like the one carrying her along.

2

Shayna could just imagine how Mamma would prop up the iron carefully, or maybe put it back on the stove to reheat, how Mamma would look as she swiped at the strand of blond hair that always escaped from under her properly severe *sheitel*, the ritually required wig she had always worn since her marriage to Poppa. (What if Shayna had to wear an old-fashioned *sheitel* some day?) It had happened so many afternoons before, this sharing of the books Shayna read. She knew how Mamma would gasp at the wickedness of the spies in the crowd, how they would wonder together at how alike were the two cities—eighteenth-century Glasgow and twentieth-century New York. Her afternoon was all planned. No what ifs.

She knew how the afternoon would be because that was how it always was. Poppa and her older brother Yakov wouldn't come home from work till later. Her sister Rachel would be out taking care of the little ones. Tante Tillie would be off at work, and Tante Sadie wasn't coming over today. Afternoon was always the time Shayna and her mamma had for themselves—when they were together while Mamma worked and Shayna read her books.

Everyone else she knew, maybe every other girl on the whole Lower East Side, came home to help at the end of school in the afternoon (if they were still in school), but not she. She was different. She was allowed to dream. And she had two whole hours that afternoon before the gathering of the family would put a stop to her dreams. Maybe she should run a little faster and not wait for the crowd to push her anymore. Maybe her mother would be sitting on the stoop in the sun waiting for her. More maybes.

But at #40 Orchard Street only Mrs. Goldstein with her sharp eyes and her pointy chin was sitting on the stoop in the sun. "Good afternoon, Shayna," she said, speaking carefully the English words she had learned, Shayna knew, to fit an occasion to which she would forever be an angry stranger—the simple occasion of afternoon on a stoop in front of a tenement in New York—an embarrassing stranger all too familiar to Shayna.

"Good afternoon, Mrs. Goldstein," she said, hoping to hurry by.

But Mrs. Goldstein surprised her. "Your father is home."

When Shayna said nothing Mrs. Goldstein asked sharply, now in Yiddish, "Is he coughing these days? Is there sickness?"

Shayna already had the front door open, and she clutched the knob's solidity as a sudden cold fear made her gulp. It was as if it was November, not May. She knew that's how things could happen— suddenly. She remembered Brina, and her what ifs came flooding back. But she also knew better than to talk about family, even with a neighbor like Mrs. Goldstein. "No"—she made herself sound positive, insisting on English—"there is no sickness. You know my poppa doesn't cough. But he does come home sometimes if the work is slow, so he can read. He is probably home reading now. You should know"—she searched for the believable in order to conquer her own fear—"how he studies with Uncle Tanchun on *Shabbos.*" There. It was a possibility even Mrs. Goldstein would credit. Under its cover she ducked inside the door.

The thought of that coughing, that terrible coughing, the sickness they all feared, was like a cold wind drawing her up the five flights of stairs, the beauty of the day blocked out, the anticipated idle hours not even in her thoughts as she shoved aside children and refuse, running up the wooden steps. At the top floor she stopped very still, trying to quiet her hard breaths, and listened in the hall outside her door. Listened for the coughing, trying to stop breathing beside the smelly toilet in the hall, listened for the racking sounds she had heard so many times outside so many other doors.

4

But there wasn't any coughing. What could it be then? Why was Poppa home? She tried to reason it out the way she had been taught.

What if he had lost his job? But then surely Mrs. Goldstein would have said that Yakov was home, too. After all, Poppa had been a cutter all these years, he was skilled enough to cut the samples, and Yakov was only seventeen and would be fired first. They worked in the same shop, and the boss would surely fire Yakov (especially after Yakov's union talk) before he fired Poppa. So if Yakov wasn't home, then it couldn't be the job.

Oh, my God, what if it was Mamma? What if Mamma was sick? What if they had called Poppa from the shop because Mamma was so sick she was dying, and Poppa had come home to take care of her. Oh, my God, what would she do without Mamma? With that possibility reason fled.

"Mamma," she called, turning the knob on the door, "Mamma, what's happened? Are you all right?" She heard no answer. She shoved the door open with her books still clasped in front of her.

The room was empty. The sink was empty of dishes; nothing was on the stove. The bed was neatly made up, the bed she shared with her sisters Rachel and Sophie. Tante Tillie's bed was shoved against the wall behind the screen, where it always was. The chairs were drawn up neatly to the wooden table in the middle of the crowded room. It was nearly dark, as usual, in the boys' room, but she could see the empty bed of chairs, all neat, where her younger brother Harry and the baby David slept. Yakov's bedclothes were not on the couch, but tucked away.

Yet even the light in the front room seemed changed. There was the corner with the chair, and the bookshelf with Poppa's books, but there was no space among them for a book missing because he was reading. (So it wasn't what she had told Mrs. Goldstein.)

5

The ironing board was even standing where it always was, but there was no iron heating on the stove.

Then she realized why the room looked different. The door to Mamma and Poppa's room was closed. And now, for the first time, she heard the voices. Her mother and father were in there, they had started shouting at each other there in their room, and she had been so absorbed in her own fantasies that she hadn't even heard them. How could she not have heard them? Of course they had not heard her as they argued.

She stood and listened. Mamma and Poppa were in there shouting at each other in Hungarian. They were arguing in that language she had never learned to understand, and it wasn't just Poppa shouting, Poppa who always shouted when he got angry. The strange thing was that Mamma was shouting, too. Mamma who never raised her voice even to the children, certainly not to her husband, as far as they knew. Mamma was shouting at Poppa.

Shayna dropped her books and sat down with a bump at the table. Something must be terribly wrong. Mamma and Poppa always talked in Yiddish to each other. But when they disagreed, they talked in Hungarian. Now they were not talking; they were yelling in their private language, both of them, yelling and yelling. In Hungarian.

"It will go away. I won't pay attention. I'll read my book." She spoke the words out loud to reassure herself, went over to the bed, and reached under her pillow. Then she went back to the table, shoved aside her schoolbooks, and opened *Rob Roy*.

With the remarkable power that books gave her, she could get away. She could leave Orchard Street and the hot day and the smells and the Hungarian shouting and go back to her maybes. So she went— quietly to cool Scotland, gratefully to the attempted

6

restoration of a royal Stuart to an English throne. No more Hungarian shouting.

Isaac, the children will be home soon. I have to tell them.

Isaac, I am going.

Isaac, it is my duty.

Never mind all that. The truth is, I want to go. I want to go home. I want to see my mother. I want to see my brothers and sisters. I want to see little Mendel, who was only a baby when I left. I took care of him; I loved him. And my oldest brother Pinchas, who was good to me. I want to go home and see them all. More than want; I *must* go.

(Oh, Isaac, don't you remember what it was like there in May? Don't you remember the way the rivers ran in the sunlight and the way the new leaves looked small and green and so promising in the spring? Don't you remember the blue flowers in the woods? Have you forgotten it all? Or, God forbid, was there, perhaps, no place with flowers and trees and a brook near your village? I've never known; you never spoke of home.

There is so much of which you have never spoken. Look outside there. Look at that street. Look at those people. Where is the brook, where are the flowers, where is the tree to have a new leaf? Isaac, it is twenty-five long years; I must go. I am in a prison here, and I *am* going.)

Isaac, remember the fifth commandment. Honor thy father and mother. So would you keep me from obeying the commandment? My mother is perhaps dying back there; she has written that she wants me to come to see her and receive her blessing. Isaac, I cannot bear it any longer. I cannot be forever a stranger in a prison. I am going.

I have always obeyed you, but if you order me to stay, I will not obey you now. I will come back in August, but I am going now.

The family is all here. They will obey you, they will take care of you—your precious sisters, too. They will be here in America. But I must go home. Let me go; don't make me disobey. *Let* me go.

You know I have always been a good wife, and I will be a good wife again. Now I must go home. I am going home. We have six children born here in this new land, not counting, may they rest in peace, the two who died between Yakov and Shayna. Three sons and three daughters, so I have given you children. I have made a home. I will come back to it before the High Holidays. Only I must go now.

My mother, my brothers (the brook and the trees and the flowers) are there. My girlhood is there, there where I was young. Later, you'll see, I will settle down, I will do it all again, again and again to the end of my life. I will be what I should be again—a dutiful wife, a good mother—but now I must be something else. I am also a daughter, and so I must travel far away. I am going. I am going because the truth is that my heart can mend there; it will break here.

What choices can I have? That I do not come back? That I stay there with my mother? What could make me not come back? There is nothing. Or is it a choice that I come back, true, but go to that other of whose existence you do not even dream? Ah—that, at least, is a choice you cannot worry about. That is a choice that is only my own.

Isaac, let me go.

Shayna sat there in the kitchen, so deep in *Rob Roy* that she stayed oblivious to her parents' argument, to the tenement noises, indeed to anything connected with the world of Orchard Street. She didn't even hear the clunk, clunk, clunk of her older brother, Yakov, coming up the stairs. She didn't hear the door open. The perfidy of Argyll lairds in a highland glen, not the routine evening arrival of Yakov Klugerman at a flat at #40 Orchard Street—this was the focus of her attention.

Nearly eighteen, Yakov was tall and skinny, over six feet tall like Poppa, much taller than the other men in the neighborhood. And skinny, his sister would say, like that cigarette now dangling from his mouth. His dark hair was cut short, without the side curls at his ears that would have been the mark of the traditionalist, and he was certainly not growing a beard. Yakov did not choose tradition, when he had a choice, no matter what Poppa said. The skinny cigarette was just another affront to tradition, one that distressed his family, as well he knew. But he liked to distress the family.

"There she is, reading as usual," he remarked to the world in general. Then he spoke directly to his sister, willing her attention. "Don't you know what time it is?" The cigarette dangled ostentatiously from the side of his mouth so she would notice it, a badge of his rebellion and anger.

"How should I know the time when I don't see a clock in this house?" flashed Shayna. "And you'd better hide that cigarette before someone sees you."

She turned her head significantly and nodded toward their parents' room, from which Mamma's and Poppa's argument could still be plainly heard.

"I pay for my cigarettes. They can come out and see it and even learn to like it. I work and earn the money slowly enough, God knows," he drawled, then he removed the offending weed briefly from his mouth and bent to blow smoke in her face. "You are certainly Miss Hoity-Toity today with your book and your strong moral views. Do you have to do everything always the way they say?"

"Shhhh!" she whispered, coughing through the smoke.

Always on the edge of real anger, Yakov's feeling stopped simply smoldering and flared up with a sudden intensity. "Stop with your 'shhhh.' What do I care what they say? Oh, my God, the whole world is unfair. And I don't care what you say either. I give ten dollars a week, nearly all my money, to help with the family. So I'll at least smoke if I want. And do I see you getting ready to quit school and help out?"

"I can't quit yet because I'm only thirteen. I couldn't quit till November. And anyway, even when my birthday comes, I'm not going to quit then either. So there!" Shayna slammed her book down to punctuate the immediate rage he called forth.

"Oh, aren't you?" Yakov's sarcasm was soft but heavy. "Unless I miss my guess, Miss Hoity-Toity, your turn to quit is coming sooner than you think— the minute you're fourteen and it's legal. Maybe that's what that"—he pointed to their parents' room—"is all about."

"I *am* going to graduate from high school. I'm going to stay in and graduate." When she got angry Shayna always started to cry, a weakness that made her even angrier. She brushed the tears from her eyes and tried to speak more slowly and positively. "Besides, Mamma says I can stay in school."

"Oh, Mamma says. But Poppa says you go out and work when you're fourteen."

Suddenly, without warning, he grabbed *Rob Roy* from the table. "What do girls need to read books for all the time, anyway?"

Shayna's tears swam again in her now-horrified eyes as he took the book toward the stove and opened the door. It seemed he would throw it in the fire the next minute. She jumped up and ran toward him. "You give me back that book," she cried. "It's a library book. And you can't stop me anyhow." She had to gulp between sentences and then take a deep breath to try to stop the tears. "Just because you quit and went to work—I'm going to make something of myself, not work in a smelly shop. I'm going to be different from the rest of Orchard Street.''

"Different? Smelly shop? Now we're beginning to hear something.'' He held the book high above his head and spoke for a moment with more conviction than anger. "But if you read anything besides romances, you might find out how to make the smelly shops different, instead of just thinking all the time about yourself.''

For a second Shayna was caught by the fact that his voice was not quite so angry, but then he went back to the familiar theme of all their battles, ready again, it seemed, to do away with her book.

"Get the book for yourself, Miss Hoity-Toity. Let's put something beyond your reach.''

To Shayna's horror, he held it again up high, much too high for her to reach from her five feet three inches, even when she jumped for it. Why was he always like that? What had she done?

"I'm not going to give you anything,'' said the angry Yakov. "I told you—I give enough to this family.''

Shayna was completely in tears with vexation and frustration, and at that very moment the four younger children appeared at the door, surprise registering on their faces at the sight of Shayna and Yakov, at the book high in the air and the tears and the jumping.

Twelve-year-old Rachel was the first to deal with the situation. "What's happened?'' she asked, running to help her sister. "Shayna, why are you crying?'' Immediately she rounded on Yakov, too, pigtails flying. Her normally quiet brown eyes were flashing. "Yakov, stop it! Give her back her book!'' She was a fierce defender, even though she was younger and smaller than either of them. She was usually the calm one, competent to still all their quarrels.

Indeed, Yakov smiled at Rachel, patting her curly brown hair. He lowered the book, shrugging his shoulders. "Ahh, I was only teasing her. Nobody was going to take her precious book."

He glanced at the younger children and saw ten-year-old Sophie and eight-year-old Harry screwing up their faces to cry, too. The baby, David, unsteady on his two-year-old feet, was already in tears where Rachel had put him down beside the door. "Oh, my God, don't all of you start crying," said Yakov. Again his hunted expression returned; he headed for the door. Sophie's blond, childish prettiness, blue-eyed and chubby-cheeked, the beginnings of the approved side curls at Harry's stick-out ears—all of it filled him with jealousy and disgust. "Look, Rachel," he said, "I'm going out. I can't stand it around here. You'll all have to find out for yourselves what's going to happen."

The door banged behind him, and they could hear him running down the wooden stairs. Then the noise stopped suddenly in the room, and the older children who were left just looked at each other without saying a word. In the silence the argument in the bedroom was audible to them all.

"What did he mean? What's going to happen, I wonder," said Shayna to Rachel. She sighed exaggeratedly. "Why couldn't I have a brother who understands something?"

"Oh, Shayna, why don't you try and understand him? He can't help it. It's very hard for him, too. Mamma says it's hard for Yakov." Rachel's large eyes filled with tears now as they had not earlier. But she, too, brushed them aside and asked, "Why are Mamma and Poppa arguing?"

Shayna just shrugged her shoulders before she sat back down at the table with her book.

"Well, I'll peel the potatoes," Rachel said to her. She went and took them from the sack in the corner, found the knife in the drawer, and started to work, standing by the sink.

Sophie and Harry and David settled down peaceably enough, and soon the only sounds in the room were the argument next door and the scrape of Rachel's knife on the potatoes.

At last there was no more shouting to be heard from behind the closed door of Mamma and Poppa's room, and the door itself opened.

"So, Rachel, good, you started the potatoes. Poppa will go to *shul* now, and then we'll eat." Sarah Klugerman spoke firmly and calmly, as she had spoken every day of her children's lives, and all was immediately and miraculously the way it had always been. There was Mamma, her shoulders square and her face strong. Nothing was strange now; there were no more what ifs.

Always, every night, Poppa went to *shul* to be part of the *minyan,* the ten men who said the evening prayers together. He could have said the prayers at home, but Poppa went to *shul* every night to say them. Always, every night, the family ate what there was to eat for supper when Poppa got home.

As he stood by the door, his back slightly bent from standing all his days over the cutting table, Poppa still was over six feet tall. He quickly shifted his skullcap, his *kappel,* off his head with his right hand and replaced it with the fedora he had ready in his left hand. Had she been looking at him in that moment, Shayna might have glimpsed a thinness in his graying hair that went with the hints of gray that were becoming visible at the sides. Otherwise she would not have seen it, because there was never a time in Isaac Klugerman's life when his head was uncovered—only those instants when he changed hats at the door, coming in or going out.

Now he asked the children, "Where is Yakov?"

"He went out," said Rachel.

Every night Isaac looked for Yakov to go to *shul* with him. But nearly every night Yakov wasn't home to accompany him.

13

"Again?" asked Poppa. For a minute, standing there so thin and tired, he looked as if he might say something else, but his hat was on his head, so he opened the door and went out instead. He left Sarah to say it.

Dear God, how do I tell the children? David is only two years old, my baby. How do I say I'm leaving them for three months? For children, three months is forever.

So maybe it *is* forever.

No, it isn't. I'm coming back in August.

But I will have three months for myself; I must. Three months to go back, three months before I am older. Then I can come home.

Now I must tell them I am going.

When Isaac went out the door Sarah was already standing by the stove, tucking that stray piece of hair under her *sheitel* as she got to work. The bustle of her work was the bustle of a normal evening. There was, at the beginning, no difference.

First she addressed her daughters, saying as she did every evening of their lives, "Everything must be ready for Poppa when he gets back. You must never keep a working man waiting for his food. Remember: That's a woman's work."

"Tante Tillie isn't home yet," sighed Rachel.

Now came the difference.

"Good, I want to talk to you before she comes back. Shayna"—Sarah spoke more loudly to get her eldest daughter's attention—"pick up your head from the book. I have something to tell you, and I want it should be said before Tante Tillie comes."

It was such an unusual request that the children all stood around the table as Sarah sat down quickly. She spoke in a trembling, breathless voice, hurrying to get out the difficult words. They listened, Shayna with her book now on the table, her finger holding the

14

place, Rachel with a knife in one hand and an unpeeled potato in the other.

"I will tell it quick, because it is hard to tell what I have to say. It is hard for me to say, and it will be hard for you to hear."

"What are you talking about, Mamma? What will be hard?" asked Rachel.

"Just this." Sarah swallowed, then said it. "I am going away."

Their astonishment was so tremendous that she had time to hurry on before the questions came. "I have had a letter from your grandmother in the old country. It came last week. She's sick." The words now came even more quickly, but they were somehow harder and harder for Sarah to speak. "Your grandmother . . ." She took a deep breath. "My mamma . . . is sick back there. She's very sick, and she wants me to come to see her before she dies."

Rachel, the comforting, thoughtful one, put down the potato and the knife in the sink and went and stood behind Sarah with her arm around her. But "It will be all right, Mamma" was all she could think to say.

Sarah reached up and held Rachel's hand a minute. "Yes, it will be all right. I'm going back to the old country to see my mamma before she dies. That will be all right, because it has to be . . . because I have to go." Now that she was through the beginning, her voice was firmer at the end.

But Shayna just sat in her place, her finger in the book aching, then numb. This couldn't be happening. Mamma couldn't be saying those words. It's simply impossible; I'm not hearing it right, she thought. She couldn't even speak.

It was Sophie, volatile little Sophie, who started to cry right away. "But you can't go!" She began, as usual, in the middle of a sob, "You're our mamma. You can't go away. Who'll take care of us?"

15

Shayna had always felt that Sophie was practical underneath. Now she and the other children turned to Sarah. It was the obvious question for them all. Who would take care of them?

Sarah's voice was steadier as she replied, lifting her hand again to her shoulder to hold on to Rachel's comfort. "That will be all right, because Shayna will take care of you, just as if I was here. Shayna will be the mamma here while I am gone in the old country."

At last Shayna found her voice. "Me, Mamma?" She looked around the table at the sobbing Sophie, at Harry, standing straight and puzzled, at little David, sucking his thumb next to his brother, and finally at Rachel, incredibly having to comfort their mother. The only way she could deal with it was through a book, as usual. "Will it be like a story, like *Little Women*? Will it be like Meg and Jo, and Rachel and I will care for the family like those girls did when Marmee was away?" Maybe Shayna could manage if it would be like a story in one of her books. Maybe.

"Yakov and your poppa will be here, and of course Tante Tillie. And Tante Sadie will come and help." Sarah's words were meant to be reassuring.

Sophie did not stop crying easily. A strand of blond hair caught on her tear-streaked face. "But Shayna can't cook," she wailed, "or do anything to help us around the house. Shayna is always reading a book, and everyone else is at work. Will Rachel have to do everything now?"

They were a lot of words riding on a lot of sobs, and Rachel looked at her little sister with surprise at this sudden defense from such an unlikely champion. Sophie's little pink cheeks were wet and messy with tears.

Mamma's answer amazed them all. "Rachel won't be here to do anything. Shayna will take care of you, but Rachel will come with me. My mamma has never seen any of her new American grandchildren. Now she will see at least one, because Rachel will come with me.''

''Rachel will go where with you?''

Stricken already, Shayna turned to the new voice at the door and saw Tante Tillie standing there, severe and straight and stiff as always. Now she looked even worse than usual, though, it seemed to Shayna. Now Tante Tillie reminded her of a picture she had seen in one of her geography books, a picture of a bird of prey with a large hooked beak, all glittery and poised, getting set to swoop down to where it could gobble up a nest of smaller birds.

Tillie spoke sharply with little puffs between words from coming up the stairs, and she sat down on a chair without even waiting for an answer to her question.

Sophie wailed louder than ever as she told Tante Tillie the news they had all just learned. ''Mamma's going away. She's going back to the old country.'' Then she added a pure Sophie embellishment: ''We'll never see Mamma again,'' and she buried her head in Sarah's side.

The moment's silence gave time for Tante Tillie's first look of astonishment to be slowly replaced by a smile. The smile did not open her mouth, Shayna noticed as she looked at her aunt's pointed face, and it never reached her sharp eyes.

''How can that be?'' Tillie asked. ''How can *you*''— she pointed to Sarah with one clawlike hand, the other leaning back on the chair—''get to go back?''

''I have spoken to Isaac—'' Sarah began, but she was immediately interrupted by Tante Tillie, who never wanted an answer to any of her questions anyway.

''And what right have you to leave my brother? Or to leave your family, for that matter?'' Again she did not wait for an answer as the children looked uncomfortably at Sarah. Even Sophie realized her mistake.

''But not that I'm not glad for you,'' Tillie's sarcastic monologue hastened on. "After all, not all the families on Orchard Street have a Rockefeller in their midst." The sneer that had started as a kind of smile twisted her face. "I find out so late, I see, that poor Isaac, who has worked so hard all these years, had secretly married riches. His wife can even afford the trip back to the old country. And does this Mrs. Fancy Rockefeller have a nursemaid planned for her family, a governess to leave behind so that they all can go walking in the park while she is taking her ocean voyage?"

"What's a governess?" asked Harry, who had been just standing there in what seemed to Shayna his special eight-year-old dignity, trying to follow the conversation while watching the grownups with wide brown eyes. He turned to Rachel, the sister who answered questions for all the little ones.

"Harry, hush now," said Rachel. She let more annoyance than usual into her voice. "You're always wanting to know what words mean at the wrong time." To soften her impatience, she led him to the sink. "You help me peel the potatoes."

Sarah ignored Tillie for a minute and picked up Sophie, big as she was, to cuddle her in her lap while she sobbed more and more slowly and finally sucked her thumb, the way she had when she was really little, settling at last in peace. "Hush now, *zies kind.*" Sarah patted her. "You're ten years old. You can be a big girl now and help your sister."

"What sister?" Tante Tillie's hard voice again broke in. "That one over there with the book? Shayna can't even bake bread. Shayna can't do anything in this house, let alone be in charge of a family. Shayna has never, to my certain knowledge, made a bed or ironed a shirt . . ." Every ounce of her contempt for her niece was trembling in the accusatory hand she pointed toward her.

For once, Sarah answered her back sternly and

without a placating word. "Tillie, baking bread and ironing a shirt don't matter. It is other things that are important, and Shayna can do the important things in the house. She can take care of the family now. Some day she might make beds and iron shirts, even bake bread as you and I do, but taking care of a family is much more than that. So she will be responsible while I am gone. Not you, Tillie—Shayna will be responsible. She has to learn."

"So I suppose I must do all the real work around here, with maybe my sister Sadie to come over from her own home to help me, poor thing, while you take a pleasure trip, Mrs. Rockefeller? I work all day in the shop, and then I come home to slave for you and your six children; that is your plan?" Tillie shook her head, getting in her final word. "I've always said that my poor brother married badly in this new country, before any of his real family was here to help him. Now he has to pay for it."

The words were spoken in the usual self-pitying tone Tante Tillie adopted when talking to the family, but there was a small note of satisfaction in her demeanor as well, which even Shayna could hear. On her worst days Tante Tillie was sorry only for herself, but on her better days—and this, astonishingly, was one of them—her birdlike eyes glittered with being sorry for herself and Tante Sadie and also her brother Isaac.

Shayna gave her head a shake to clear it from the grownup confusion around her and opened her book again. Could Tante Tillie actually somehow be happy that she would have to help more in the flat? Could anyone be happy with Mamma going away? Such questions seemed too hard for a thirteen-year-old to ponder, even thirteen-and-a-half-going-on-fourteen, so Shayna turned back to *Rob Roy* while Sarah went over to the sink and put the last of the peeled potatoes in the pot.

*     *     *

"Shayna isn't lively like a fish; she'll never marry," Tante Sadie had said to Tante Tillie with a shake of her head.

"She can't bake bread yet; she'll never catch a man," agreed Tillie with contempt.

Shayna had heard them. What did they do all day, those two aunts of hers, Shayna wondered. She wondered, and she knew inside her that what they did was sit in the flat all day, huddle in those three rooms, conspiring against her. It didn't matter to Shayna that Tillie worked, sewing in a shop five blocks away, that Sadie was married to Uncle Franz and lived on Avenue D. Inside her, Shayna knew that they sat there all day and huddled and conspired and waited, waited always for their beloved brother to come home to them, Shayna's poppa, whom they felt they owned. Huddled and conspired and waited.

Tillie was getting old and still was unmarried. Sadie was childless. They were already old ladies, Shayna thought, always had been old ladies, wearing old-lady-size dresses, dumpy and beaky with buns on the backs of their heads and long dark dresses, huddled over their endless conspiracies. Isaac was their one love.

What if her aunts won against her?

"Mamma, why are you taking me?" asked Rachel, turning her gentle brown eyes to her mother. "Shayna is older—shouldn't she go?"

"No," said Sarah. "It would not work out. Shayna must stay and you must go. Your poppa and I have decided."

It is not that she is my favorite. If there are favorites, then they are both my favorites, the one with her books and her questions, the other so good and sweet.

But I have a duty to them both. And this is the way

20

to fulfill my duty—to take the younger and leave the elder behind.

Besides, Shayna is so much of an American; Rachel my family will love. And she will be easier.

Will any 'of them understand? But no one ever understands.

After Isaac came home the family ate the potatoes for supper. Grace was said and the little ones tucked in before they gathered again around the table with Shayna and Rachel. Yakov, as usual, was not home.

Sarah spoke first, in the pool of light cast by the lamp placed in the center of the table. Always afterward Shayna remembered the pool of light and the slight breeze coming in from the hot May night outside as her mother's voice outlined the plan. "I have saved a little money every week, and with the help of the *landsmanschaft* I will have the fare to go. It has been twenty-five years of saving from when I first came to this country. For Rachel's ticket, that is a different thing. I will sell my cameo pin that you gave me, Isaac, when we were married."

There was no sound but the breeze in the room as she looked a long time at him after she had said it. He did not reply but at last bent his gaze to the table. So she continued, "With the other, that will pay for Rachel to come with me."

With his eyes still on the table, not on Sarah, Isaac began speaking at last. "The Law says that a woman's place is in her home . . ."

Tante Tillie smiled in self-satisfaction at that, but Isaac raised his deep-set eyes to look at his sister directly as he went on in a stern voice. "But on the other hand, the Law says a child owes a duty to a parent. Sarah is right to go to her mother."

Tante Tillie did not reply.

To Shayna, sitting there, the oddest thing of all was to think of her mother, with the gray *sheitel* and the worn hands, as a child of someone, someone she had never herself seen, someone to whom she owed the duty of which Poppa spoke. Sarah had always been just Mamma, not a separate person with a mother of her own. It was a mystery Shayna did not really understand, felt she might never understand, this mystery of Sarah as a child, Sarah a daughter just like herself. Did it mean that Mamma maybe didn't love her anymore? Her mind turned away from such an unbearable thought. She was a girl who needed her mamma's love.

In a way, she reflected, the evening did seem the same as all other evenings. Poppa was talking about the Law. Tante Tillie had her mean smile all over her face. The little ones were in bed, and Yakov hadn't come home yet. Rachel was nodding now over her homework.

But everything wasn't the same. What if it was never the same again?

"I thought I would come to see you." The English came hesitantly to Sarah's lips as she stood in the cool doorway of the ground-floor flat and let her eyes become accustomed to a darker indoor world after the bright morning sunlight.

David Nathan stood in the doorway before her, the door open and a look of welcome mingled with the surprise on his face. "Come in. Don't just stand here in the door. You know I have no pupils this morning; they're all in school at this hour. I just got up. Come have a cup of coffee." His voice was the same warm, quiet voice she had known for twenty years, since before she was even married.

Sarah walked in and entered another world—one she could surely find nowhere else on the whole Lower East Side. Here there were oriental rugs on the floors and copper pots on the tables—but mostly there was room. That was the biggest difference, the one that hit first; there was room everywhere. A whole three-room flat, and only occupied by one bachelor—David Nathan, who had never married. David Nathan, who taught piano to the neighborhood children, who came here from another world.

She had not come to see him alone for a year, and here it all was, just as she knew it would always be, as if they had met but yesterday. When she closed the door and came into the room she was still a short, square woman with a gray *sheitel* on her head from which that wisp of blond came always sneaking out. Beautiful, no; she had never been more than clear-eyed and smooth-skinned. But those qualities had remained while other, prettier women had coarsened and wrinkled. Her skin was smooth still, and her eyes were clear also, and they looked directly at him.

"Tell me what you've been doing. I send Shayna over for lessons every week, but what have you been up to in all this time that you never come to see Isaac and me?"

"What do I always do?" He shrugged as he lapsed into the pattern of speech of this neighborhood in which he had lived for so long. "I have too many pupils, and only one or two of them are any good. I read Tolstoy and Dostoyevski. I go uptown to see my family maybe once a month. That's what I do—what I've always done."

As she listened to him, taking her seat at his table while he poured the coffee into two cracked cups, she smiled to herself. It was always the same story.

"Why don't you take fewer pupils? You could just suggest that the ones who don't pay might prefer another teacher." She smiled as she said it, because it was what she always said, and she knew what the answer would be.

"But Sarah," he said gently, "what do I do if the ones who can't pay are the ones who *can* play? I may go to the poorhouse, but if I do, I am going to leave behind a student who plays the piano. Money isn't everything, or did you know?''

This was all part of the banter in which they always indulged. He knew well enough, and to his cost, that Sarah Klugerman did not live her life with money as its chief consideration. If she had, perhaps both his life and hers would have been very different. But best not to think of that. Best not to think, ever, of how much he loved this woman who sat before him, best not to think of their years, which were not together, would never be together. She had married another man.

Today, however, seemed to be a day when Sarah was thinking of it. "I was remembering when we first met," she said, looking at him over her coffee with those cool, clear brown eyes.

"You were younger then. So was I." He made it sound short to see if he could skirt it lightly, and he got up from the table to get more coffee from the stove, turning his back to avoid those clear eyes.

"I've always wondered, all these years, what you were doing here then, why you should come to a dance on Houston Street. You came from that other world." She had been seventeen at that dance on Houston Street, seventeen and ripe to love such a man as David Nathan.

He turned back to her and paused with the coffee-pot in his hand. "I never told you the story? I came to see this neighborhood like a tourist. My cousin Julia worked down here at the settlement house, and she told me about the dances. I'll never forget the day she told me about them," he mused. "My family threw the two of us together often in those days, even though we were cousins. Julia and I were probably 'intended' for each other. That day I was sitting on the sun porch of our place in the Berkshires, and Julia came tripping in, telling about her settlement-house work, full of tales of people I could not even imagine, people here on the Lower East Side. I thought it would be interesting to see the strange creatures" —his smile took the sting from the words—"she told me about. I came that first time out of curiosity. Where I came from there was nothing like this."

"So we were strange creatures, were we?" But Sarah spoke without rancor. When you come from elsewhere yourself, as she did, you know about differences. "Well, it seems long ago, and we probably were. In our world, the one we came from, a marriage was arranged between parents. And, God knows, men and women did not dance together. But in this country we had no parents, so we had the dances to arrange the marriages." She stopped, thinking back to that seventeen-year-old night. Then she went on with an important truth, the one she had followed despite love. "Sometimes even the orthodox, like Isaac, came."

"*Sephardim* also arrange marriages. In that other world we, too, have our marriages arranged, but with our own people." (The world of *Sephardic* Jews who had begun to prosper in America hundreds of years ago was indeed different from that of these recent immigrants.) He sat down again at the table and met her eyes at last.

"Did your people never arrange a marriage for you, David? What about this Julia?"

"My cousin Julia married a stockbroker. And I decided not to marry. I told them I would not marry without love, and there was no one—among our people—whom I loved." He was still looking at her. "They accepted my decision. What else could they do?"

To Sarah it seemed that in some families, with some sons, there might have been a lot they could have done. But David Nathan was not so easy; she wondered what batterings his family had tried, to no avail, against that rock of decision. But she would not

25

ask. Already she had come too close to the truth that must never be spoken between them.

"Will you play for me?" Her change of subject was an abrupt relief.

"The piano is not in very good tune." Now the litany of excuses started. "I haven't really got anything in good shape. If I had known you were going to come, I would have practiced something."

"Oh, David. Just play—don't always tell me the same thing. How about some Beethoven?"

"But—"

"Just go to the piano and play for me, David," she said gently.

Sarah settled back in a comfortable tapestry-covered chair that faced him at the keyboard from across the room and waited. He put down the coffee cup and stopped talking, then went over and sat down at the piano stool, as always unable to refuse her anything. The music on the piano was, as she knew it would be, Beethoven.

While he played she didn't close her eyes. Instead, she watched those strong hands skim impossibly swiftly over the keys, and she let the music seep into her bones. The tiredness left, and the questions, and with them her great trouble. Isaac's reproaches, Shayna's fears, even Sophie's weeping—all seeped away to be replaced by the strength of that swelling and receding sound. This music was what David Nathan had given her. Here she could be alone with her secret self, in another world from that of #40 Orchard Street.

Not alone. There was David, his clean-shaven dark face with the incongruous gray eyes, oblivious to her now, utterly concentrated instead on the sheet of music in front of him. His hands moved on the piano, touching it gently and surely, then harshly and surely. His eyes always grew so wide when the hard passages came, as if to absorb the music through a wider surface before translating it into those whorling ripples.

Sarah watched him as he played. And even as she watched, sighing, she knew that she had been right to marry Isaac, who was a scholar. She could brush aside Isaac's daily work, his cutting cloaks in Saperstein's shop, because he did that only for money, and it was not money, of course, that mattered. In his head, in his heart, Isaac was a scholar. In the important times of his life he studied, always studied the holy books— on *Shabbos,* even in the week if the work was slow. She knew that she had done right to marry a man who studied, a scholar of the Law, even one who was poor. She had learned from her tiniest childhood that it was right to marry a scholar.

But still she could not stop being drawn to the flat with all the room and the oriental rugs and the piano and the man with the strong hands and the wide gray eyes who was not a scholar. Still twenty years had not cured the ache that could fill her whole being at the sight of this stranger from another world, at this sound of beautiful music. If she could not have David Nathan—and God knows she could not, she corrected her thought—then at least she had found a way, through him, to music. Despite Isaac's shouting and Tillie's injured remarks, she had music—even a piano at home and Shayna taking lessons, David sometimes visiting and playing that piano.

At first, when Shayna had told her about the piano, she had thought that such a wonder would never be possible. But the family who owned it was moving uptown, and all they wanted was to get rid of the instrument for the moving of it out of their flat. Yakov had been surprised, and Isaac had shouted, but they had cajoled some men from the shop and moved the upright piano down three flights and up five flights, and now Sarah had, if not David (never David), at least music. Music, even a baby whose name was David (although Isaac was his father), and a heart that needed mending.

When the sonata ended she stood up, as he knew she would. "I must go now."

He had never said a word to stop her. "Thank you for coming. Say hello to Isaac and the children for me."

She made her announcement to him then, quickly, not wanting to inflict pain, but knowing it had to be told. "I am going away soon. To the old country, to see my mother, who is very sick." Then, to forestall anything, "But I will be back in August."

"Sarah . . ." His hand went out, but he brought it back to his side without touching her. He had no way to ask anything.

"It's all right. I'll be back in August. Practice something to play for me then. Don't have excuses." She smiled and walked out the door quickly without saying any of the words that could never be said.

Across the world, across thousands of miles of ocean, across nearly all of Europe, an old woman turned restlessly on her pillows. "Water," she mumbled. "I'm so hot. A little water." Her gray hair was damp with fever.

"Coming Mamma," said Chava, her daughter-in-law.

Chava held up the old woman's head while she took a few sips, then lay back exhausted. Slowly the tired eyes cleared a bit, and she smiled, wrinkling her already wrinkled face.

"Chava, thank you. You are like my own daughter."

"Mamma, you will be better soon."

"No, I mean it. My Pinchas married well that time when he married you. Bless you, my child."

Chava turned away in embarrassment, but her mother-in-law's voice was soon querulous again, calling her back. "Is there any letter?" she asked. "Is there any letter yet from Sarah?"

"No letter yet, Mamma," Chava sighed, hating to disappoint her again, "but maybe Mendel will bring one when he comes by this evening."

"If only Sarah will come," said Rivka, feverish again as she lay on the pillows. "If only my little girl will come home to me, then, then I can die in peace."

"You are not going to die, Mamma," Chava insisted, hurrying again to the bedside, tears gathering in her startlingly blue eyes. "The doctor says you are getting better. Don't talk anymore about dying."

"I want my baby, I want my baby," Rivka suddenly cried aloud, weeping and shaking her head, refusing to be comforted. It mattered not at all that it was twenty-five years since she had seen her Sarah—it mattered not at all that Sarah was grown now and married, had children of her own. Rivka cried aloud for her, for that daughter she still missed so sorely.

When her mother-in-law started like that Chava knew it might be hours before she was rational again, before the sadness left her. But Chava knew, too, that she could not bear it either if her own children left her for the new land, left like the dimly remembered Sarah had done when she was still so young, left and never came back. So Chava took Rivka in her arms and tried to comfort her, this old woman who had taken her in and let her marry the widowed eldest son without parents of her own, without any dowry. If this care now was what she owed for that goodness and comfort in her youth, then it was a debt she would gladly pay—to comfort the old mother now when she was so sad and so alone.

She heard the door bang, but it was not Mendel who came into the room on his way home, it was Pinchas, her beloved husband. A sober man of middle height, Pinchas in his fifties gave no hint to the rest of the world of his passion for his wife. That was only expressed to her in his murmured endearments in the dark of night when he could not even see her blue eyes. So Chava knew his love, even if it was a secret love.

"Good evening, Mamma," he said. "Good evening, Chava." He was punctilious and correct, always, her Pinchas, giving precedence where precedence was due.

Rivka did not respond to his greeting but raised her eyes only to plead, "Has the letter come? Has it come, Pinchas? The letter from Sarah?" as she had every day now for a month, always before to no avail.

But to Chava's surprise, Pinchas's face lit up with a rare smile, and he said, "Yes, Mamma, it's come at last. The letter you've been waiting for."

Thus it was from her eldest son that Rivka had the joyful news that not only was her baby, her Sarah, coming home to her, but also the little girl, Rachel, a grandchild she had never seen. Maybe if they came home, she thought, it could be true that she might get well. Such a sight would itself maybe make her well. She sat up firmly in the bed then and said, "Read the letter again, Pinchas, read it to me again. Oh, Chava" —she clasped her daughter-in-law's hand—"is it true? Are my sins forgiven? Is my little girl coming home?"

"What sins, Mamma?" laughed Chava. "Of course it's true, and you have no sins to be forgiven anyway."

"Ah," said Rivka, a brief sadness again clouding her eyes. "Everyone has sins, Chava, everyone has sins to be forgiven. But"—and she laughed aloud— "thanks to God, my baby will come. Thanks to God, my Sarah will come home now."

## ❧ 2 ❧

*Day unto day uttereth speech,
and night unto night
sheweth knowledge. (Psalms 19:2)*

Shayna, Shayna, time to get up." Sarah's whisper, meant only for her, roused Shayna slowly from her sleep. If only high school didn't start so early in the morning.

Isaac and Yakov were already up, the latter waiting impatiently while his father said the morning prayers. Without even opening her eyes Shayna could see him standing and swaying, Poppa with his prayer shawl and his *tefillin* swaying with the morning prayers. It was what all men did every morning, she thought sleepily. (All men but Yakov?) Sometimes she woke early enough to see Poppa take the *tefillin*, little black boxes with ribbons tied to them, out of their special case and fasten them on his arm and around his head, already mumbling prayers as he performed the ritual motions. The Law said of God's words, "Thou shalt bind them for a sign upon thine hand, and they shall be for frontlets between thine eyes." Poppa's ritual was an obedience to that Law.

Sarah was making the morning tea and putting out the last of the bread with some jam for the little ones' breakfast. Tante Tillie was already dressing behind the screen. There were so many of them crowded into the little rooms that when Shayna stirred against Rachel and Sophie, looking sleepily at the mounds of pillows and bedclothes everywhere, she wondered if she were perhaps sailing on a sea of beds. Now, she thought, they were all open and wavy with lumps of people, but during the day the little-boy bed, made from chairs and cushions, would be a bed no more, and Tante Tillie's bed would push against the wall. Only Mamma's and Poppa's bed in the other room and the girls' bed in this room would be left down to be neatly made. Yakov slept on the couch, and so had a bed to himself, but his bed then disappeared during the day, and the bedclothes came out only at night. Beds weren't tossed and turned the whole day long, not ever. The walls might be dark wood, the wooden floor might be scratched from the scraping of chairs or tables or people, but it was all scrubbed as clean and as neat as it possibly could be in Sarah Klugerman's house. The whole rest of the Lower East Side might inhabit a sea of filth and squalor, but the Klugerman family came home each day to cleanliness.

Yakov must have come in late last night, thought Shayna, focusing for a moment on her older brother. I didn't even hear him. She wondered about it for a minute, yawned, and put it out of her mind. She dressed hurriedly.

"Mamma." She startled Sarah, coming quickly up behind her. "Will I have to make the beds and clean everything when you're gone? Will I have to wake everyone?"

Sarah smiled her hurried Friday-morning smile, her arms now deep in the bread bowl, flour up to her elbows. "It won't be waking everyone or the beds that will be trouble, Shayna; don't worry about the beds."

"What then, Mamma? What will happen? When will you come back, Mamma? When will you go? Will it make any difference about my staying in school?"

"So many questions from my usually silent daughter." Sarah's smile, as she kneaded the bread dough in the bowl, was evident, even though she didn't turn around. But Shayna had to say out loud the worries that troubled her this Friday morning.

"Oh, Mamma, please don't go and leave me in charge. I can't take care of them all. You know I can't."

Sarah turned toward her. "You can always do what you have to do, Shayna. I must go back. My mother needs me."

There it was again. The idea of Mamma having a mother of her own. But Mamma was so old. Or was she?

"How old are you, Mamma?" asked Shayna even before she thought.

"Your mamma is thirty-eight years old," came Tante Tillie's voice close behind Shayna. "Old enough to know better than to leave a family and journey across the ocean, one would think."

"Tillie, do you want to eat something before you go to work?" Sarah's voice was even, and she didn't look at Shayna. "Drink some tea, Shayna, before you go to school. Where are your books?"

"All right, Mamma," she said between gulps, "I'm on my way."

She whisked on her coat and headed out the door, stopping there only briefly to say, "But remember that I asked the questions, and tell me the answers this afternoon."

"This afternoon will be nearly *Shabbos*." Sarah turned back to the kneading. "There will be a lot to do. Don't dawdle on your way home."

"Cassie and I will be quick at the library," Shayna tossed over her shoulder.

"Cassie, Cassie, Cassie," muttered Tante Tillie, passing her on the stairs. "Always your friend Cassie. What kind of a name is Cassie?"

A perfectly good name, thought Shayna, but she didn't say it aloud. No, Tante Tillie made her too angry to say anything aloud, or she might say far too much, she well knew. What's wrong with the name Cassandra, anyway, she thought, justifying her best friend's parents' choice. It comes from a Greek myth, and I think it's beautiful. She nodded vigorously to herself. Nothing is wrong with Cassie, especially not her name, she thought, sticking her tongue out at Tante Tillie's vanishing form. Grrr, Tante Tillie made her mad.

Sammy came running from the fourth floor and caught up with Shayna as she clattered down. His side curls waved beside his smooth face under the black hat as he buttoned his long black coat while running down the stairs. "Where are you off to in such a hurry? Hey, wait a second, I'll carry your books to the corner of Avenue A if you'll just slow down a minute. . . ."

But suddenly even Sammy, who had lived downstairs for what seemed like always, was too much for Shayna. She ran down the rest of the flight as fast as she could.

"What's the matter with you all of a sudden? Why is today different from all other days?" he tried to joke.

They were talking so loudly that several heads popped out of doors to hear what they were saying. Shayna skittered down the last few steps, calling, "I can carry my own books. There are *some* things I can do for myself, thank you very much. And who asked you anyway?"

"Oh, mind your own business," said Sammy to a surprised Mrs. Goldstein, who was peering at him around a door. "A person can't even have a private conversation around here without all the neighbors poking their heads out."

"A fine thing for a young man who is supposed to

be a scholar, talking like that to a girl in public, I must say." Mrs. Goldstein had the last word before she shut the door firmly.

Shayna, who heard that slam, knew what Mrs. Goldstein was thinking. On Orchard Street Sammy was that most precious person, a student of the Law, a scholar. Mrs. Goldstein thought that Sammy should not fill his head with foolishness like carrying a lot of schoolbooks for a silly, useless girl like herself. Mrs. Goldstein was even a friend of Tante Tillie.

She deliberately slowed down and handed her books to Sammy wordlessly as he came up to her on the stoop, smiling as she did so in an instantly understood conspiracy at the grownup world. He took them and smiled back, and they were off down the street together, as they had been most mornings that spring. It was only a few blocks before they parted, she headed for Washington Irving High School, he toward the yeshiva. What harm did that morning walk do Mrs. Goldstein, Shayna asked herself.

When Cassie caught up with her, black pigtails flying and catching her breath in gasps (Cassie had short legs and had to run when other people walked), Shayna was still frowning.

"What's wrong?" Cassie asked, skipping a step now and then to keep up with her friend.

"Just grump, grump, grump—it's the way I feel this morning, I guess," replied Shayna. But her smile belied her words.

"Well, it's Friday," Cassie pointed out, "so there's no reason to grump. Anyway, we're going to the library together this afternoon. It's still okay, isn't it?" she added, her round cheeks pink with her running.

"Yes, I warned my mamma I'd be late. . . . Oh, Cassie—don't let me forget to tell you about my mamma this afternoon," she whispered in an undertone as Karen Berkowitz joined them.

But Cassie was obviously off in another thought

and not listening by then, Shayna could tell. It made her smile at her best friend—the way Cassie didn't always listen. She herself didn't always listen either; it was a fault they shared, one of the qualities they had confessed to each other in those long best-friend walks they had taken more and more often recently. She felt that she really knew Cassie and that Cassie really knew her in all the important ways. Like trying to help each other not only with Latin, but with all the hard things that kept happening at home now that they were in high school.

She had told Cassie about Sammy, for instance—how he carried her books in the morning, and how her mother was always commenting on that, like they were sort of throwing her at him, but how it didn't really seem to matter very much to have him around anyway. And Cassie had understood. She had nodded her dark head and looked at Shayna with those wonderful deep brown eyes and understood, even though there wasn't a boy who carried Cassie's books. Cassie had a brother, though, and she said she learned a lot from him about boys.

Shayna was trying to understand that, because she certainly didn't feel she learned much from her own older brother; Yakov only wanted to fight, she thought, not to teach a younger sister. And all he did was work in the shop all day anyway, not anything he could have taught her about. She tossed her head as she dismissed him from her mind and went into her history class. Ancient Egypt was more fun to think about than her brother Yakov.

Yakov wasn't confused. Others in the shop were genuinely confused, but Yakov was sure that he was not among their number. He could see the Cause clearly, of that he was certain. Poppa might say all he wanted to about being grateful simply to have a job, and how one must just do what the bosses said. But that was cant and did not confuse Yakov.

The others who didn't understand, the ones who just went home at the end of the workday, they would never know the way he felt when he climbed the stairs to Kalinsky's room. There he would always find companions waiting for him at the end of the day. It didn't matter that none of them had supper those nights, it didn't matter that he was the youngest, that they were all older than he, because in Kalinsky's room they were all one, all drawn together for the Cause.

The room was undecorated above the rows of chairs and Kalinsky's bed, undecorated except for the carefully lettered signs in English on big pieces of paper hung on all the walls.

WORKERS OF THE WORLD, UNITE!
YOU HAVE NOTHING TO LOSE BUT YOUR CHAINS!

FROM EACH ACCORDING TO HIS ABILITIES:
TO EACH ACCORDING TO HIS NEEDS!

RELIGION IS THE OPIATE OF THE PEOPLE!

Yakov had yelled the one about religion to Poppa only a few weeks ago. Isaac had been trying to get him to come home in the evening with him, to go to *shul* again. But there had been a meeting scheduled at Kalinsky's house that night, and Yakov hadn't gone with Poppa; he was committed to the union now. He was committed to the Cause now. "Religion," he had yelled at Poppa, "is the opiate of the people!"

Isaac had struck his own forehead with his palm in an open-handed upward gesture of contempt and condescension that nearly knocked off his hat. "Oh, so you've taken up the Cause now, have you?" he had said. "Wait till you're married and have a family to feed and clothe, and then see if that's where your faith directs you. You're wrong, and God will see that you learn you're wrong. He always sees." He had shaken his head and looked, for once, more sorrowfully than angrily at him, Yakov thought. "I know," he had said in a low and final tone. Then he had turned and gone to *shul* alone.

But what did Poppa really know? Yakov had learned in the meetings at Kalinsky's how to deal with Poppa's "knowing." It was his rejection of Poppa's ways that had turned him to the Cause, after all. "The first sign of difficulty will turn away the frightened among you" had been the words of the speaker that very night. (Yakov knew he was not among them—those to whom the speaker referred, the frightened—like Poppa, for instance.) "But we must take up the cudgels and do what is needed to ensure the coming of the Revolution."

The speaker's eyes shone. The eyes of each of Yakov's friends that night, sitting there in Kalinsky's little room, huddled in warm overcoats against the cold chill of the last bit of winter, had shone with the vision behind the words. The Revolution. The Cause. The Triumph of the Proletariat.

That night, when the discussion grew technical about what would happen after the state had withered away, coats gradually came off. Some of the group argued passionately for the workers as a group taking over each of the areas of production; others argued just as passionately that a small group be elected from their number to manage industrial progress. From their number! It would be they, not the old men like Poppa, who would have the power in that glorious future when the Cause was won.

As the argument and the night and the room got warmer the talk lapsed totally into Yiddish, despite the speaker's efforts and Kalinsky's urgings to bring them back to English. Why not? Yakov smiled to himself. Weren't they all better arguers in Yiddish?

God knows they had argued at home in Yiddish for years, all of them, before they had ever become involved in the Cause. Argued against the old religion, argued against the old men. Old men like Poppa.

Arguments don't make us confused, though, thought Yakov. They clarify the issues. They are a healthy step toward the Revolution. He spent nearly every evening now at Kalinsky's. He even took a greater part in the arguments himself. What was there at home to compare with this?

By afternoon, when the children came home from school, Sarah had most of the preparations for *Shabbos* completed, and the perspiration was dripping from the tip of her nose if she didn't take a moment to brush it away. The braided *hallah* loaves, smelling of nutmeg and saffron, decorated with a scattering of poppyseeds, were just out of the oven, cooling in egg-glazed twists on the table. She certainly made a good *hallah,* she thought to herself with satisfaction and pride as she looked at the loaves.

Today she had taken some money from the jar over the sink and bought a chicken for dinner. Even if there wasn't meat on any other day, if there was money in the jar, they had chicken for *Shabbos*.

"I wonder if Shayna will remember about getting a chicken," she thought. "I'll talk to her about *Shabbos*." She shook her head. "Shayna is not like Rachel—who knows if she has ever even noticed about the chicken?"

That bird, long since plucked, was now simmering in a steaming soup on the stove. The noodles were all finely cut and drying on the floured board, ready to be popped into the soup at the last minute. The bubbly sound of the chicken soup with its faint aroma of onion and garlic, the bright carrot gleaming up as she took a peek under the lid, gave Sarah great satisfaction. No one could ever say she was not a good cook.

Even when there was little (and even though Isaac never praised it), the food Sarah cooked was good, she knew.

That satisfaction, so often comforting there in her kitchen, did not follow Sarah's thoughts away from the stove, however. She knew that her eldest daughter would be home soon, true, but she was probably visiting her friend Cassie's house on the way to the library. It was good for Shayna to have a friend outside of a book, but Sarah sighed when she thought of Cassie's family. And Isaac did not approve of Cassie's family, as she knew. Isaac, so careful in his orthodoxy, did not approve of people like the Roses, who changed their name as they changed their religion, he would say, according to whim. And Cassie's brother, according to Shayna, was studying to be a rabbi at that Jewish Theological Seminary, a place of which Isaac certainly did not approve. Conservative Jews were like godless Christians to Isaac. If only Shayna had found her friend a little closer to home.

Just then Shayna came in the door and sniffed. "You know, Mamma"—she sounded surprised at her own words—"I think I can make chicken soup."

"Of course you can make chicken soup." Sarah's positive eyes encouraged her tentative child.

"But I can't bake *hallah,* and I've never made a bed in my whole life—Tante Tillie is right about that. And I can't iron either."

"Your Tante Sadie will come and bake the *hallah.* And you can learn to iron and make a bed if you have to."

"But I'll never do it well. You know I won't. Oh, Mamma, why didn't you ever make me do those things around the house? How will I manage?"

Before she could allow herself to falter Sarah made her voice stay positive and strong. "You'll manage because you're the managing kind. You'll do it because you'll have to do it. I learned. You will learn."

Shayna collapsed into a chair at the table. "But Mamma, what if I can't? Yakov will yell at me. Poppa thinks I'm foolish, and Tante Tillie knows I'm useless."

Sarah moved from the sink to sit opposite Shayna for a moment. "Look, Shayna, I came all across the ocean from the old country when I was your age—thirteen years old. I came alone. I had to work shoveling coal in someone's cellar for my two dollars a week and a room in an attic. One time I was so tired I fell asleep in the coal bin next to the furnace. And I didn't know any English.

"But I learned, and I managed, and I grew up, and I married your poppa, and now I have six children of my own. You will learn." She had rehearsed all day what to say. Now her words bored into Shayna. "Remember, Shayna, when you have to learn, you learn. When I come back in three months you will know what you can do."

Who is that wise person speaking? It can't be me. God knows I'm not sure like that.

I told Isaac she could do it. I told him over and over again, but maybe those were only words. I don't know any better now than I knew then.

I remember what it was really like to be thirteen. I remember when I had to come. I remember how I had to leave home. And I remember waving to my mamma and riding in a cart to Budapest with Reb Vershovsky. And that was only the beginning of the journey. I remember the weeping. . . .

No.

Even if I was the only child who was sent away, it was my chance to make a good life in a new country. God knows I took the right chance, and God knows I am going to make this into Shayna's chance.

It has to be right for her. I have to go. She is the same age I was, and she will make it right as I made my chance right. She has no choice either.

*    *    *

41

"But what if I know only what I can't do? Oh, Mamma, it isn't fair—why did you decide to take Rachel with you? She's the one who knows what to do here at home, she's the one the little ones listen to. Poppa always says she's so good, and even Tante Tillie says Rachel will turn out well." Shayna's voice really pleaded, then the look in her eyes grew far away. "Why doesn't Rachel stay home, and I'll go with you? I know about the old country and traveling from my books, and you know how I want to see the world. I *know* I could travel well."

"Rachel knows how to stay, so she must go, and you know how to go, so you must stay, Shayna." It was the kind of argument that would appeal to Shayna, her mother knew, because it had a twist. Shayna liked words with a twist. "Your poppa and I have talked it all out," she went on. "God knows we've argued it all out. I'm sure you heard us." For a moment Sarah looked at her daughter now as she would have looked at a woman who was her own age. "When I leave on the boat next week Rachel will be with me."

"Next week, Mamma?" The reality was too much. "Oh, no, not so soon. Today is already *Shabbos*," and Shayna burst into tears. She felt all alone, as if her mother had really stopped loving her, loved only Rachel now. How could she bear life without Mamma's love? For only a moment she was so jealous of her sister Rachel that she hated her.

Sarah sighed, looked at her again, and reached across the table, putting a hand awkwardly on the bowed head of what was, after all, only a child. "Yes, *shaynheitel*," she said in her softest voice, "cry now. When you are the mamma you must not cry."

Her voice was so quiet and sad that Shayna looked up, forgetting her own misery for a moment. Mamma's look at her was a look of love; she wouldn't let herself doubt it. "Oh, Mamma," she said, "I didn't even think how you must feel. . . . I'll say a prayer that you have a safe journey. And that you come back to us soon." Abruptly her curiosity, that saving grace, surfaced again. "What is her name, Mamma? I never knew Grandma's name."

Sarah sighed again, got up from the table, and went back to the sink. "Her name is Rivka. Now read to me a little from your book while I finish getting ready for *Shabbos*," she said.

It was final now.

Shayna picked up *Rob Roy* and read aloud while Sarah let the words drift over her, thinking of the reader, not of the book. When Rachel brought the children in later to clean up for *Shabbos* they found the usual sight—Mamma working and Shayna reading.

That night after dinner, with the melodies of the special songs the family always sang together on Friday nights still tingling in her ears, Shayna lay in bed and let herself remember her afternoon's brief visit at Cassie's house. It was a special pleasure to savor the visit by herself. With Rachel and Sophie asleep beside her she watched the lights and shadows on the ceiling from the guttering *Shabbos* candles reflected in their brass tray, and those flickering lights merged with her flickering dreams.

Cassie's home was so different from her own. The Roses and the Klugermans might live in the same part of New York, but they lived so differently, Shayna thought. It wasn't just that their flat was bigger—five rooms just for Cassie and her sister and her brother and their parents—and on fashionable East Broadway. It was also more full of light, Shayna decided. In Cassie's house there was light not just from the windows, but from the constant talk, the searchings in words for lights for the mind. And from the books everywhere. Shayna had never dreamed that there could be so many books in the private possession of a single family. There were books lining all the walls in the living room. Shelves and shelves of books like in the library. Some of them were low, but some of the shelves reached up to the ceiling, and they were all filled with books.

The minute Shayna had walked in the door the first time, those months ago, she had been caught up in listening to a discussion about those books. Mr. Rose, a short, stocky man without a *kappel* on his bald head, had been holding a book in one hand as he stood in his shirtsleeves by the windows that faced out into the front. And he had been shouting at his wife (which Shayna had since learned was merely his usual mode of address) that day. Mrs. Rose had been peaceably sitting on a large couch, with one of her legs tucked under her, knitting. Her graying hair was pulled back with a ribbon, Shayna remembered, as if she were a young girl, and the brightly colored blouse she had been wearing hung out of her skirt in a way that, while it certainly looked comfortable, was not the way other mothers dressed, not in Shayna's experience. She had smiled at the girls as they came in that first day and patted a place beside her when Cassie introduced Shayna.

"Sit down, Shayna," she had said, "before my husband's rhetoric knocks you down. Really, Alec," she had admonished him, "your shouts will bring the police one of these days, thinking you've killed me. He's preparing a review," she had explained to the astonished Shayna, who had never heard her own poppa and mamma speak in that manner to each other. "He doesn't seem to like the book." She smiled at her own understatement.

"The author is a fool," said Mr. Rose, still at top volume. "He seems to think the world is made of green cheese. His idea is . . ."

Cassie's father taught at the Educational Alliance,

he wrote for the *Jewish Daily Forward* (even Poppa sometimes read a column of Mr. Rose's out loud to the family from the *Forward*), and he was always talking about ideas. Even the children were named from his ideas: Cassandra and Miranda were the girls—from a Greek myth and a Shakespeare play, for heaven's sake—and Ari was short for the name of an ancient Greek playwright who wrote comedies! (Shayna had never dared to tell her parents any of that part of it.)

Actually, Cassie had confided in her, and Shayna hugged the knowledge to herself with delight, Ari didn't like his name, just like he didn't like it that his father had changed their name from Rosenblum to Rose. Ari had inherited Mr. Rose's tendency to question, but what he seemed to question, Cassie told her, was Mr. Rose. He was studying to be a rabbi now, a Conservative rabbi, and he was a champion of ideas that Mr. Rose was always against. He had told the family last week, Cassie explained in awe, that he was going to use their old name of Rosenblum again, because he was proud of a name that sounded Jewish. And furthermore, he had told them, he was taking the name Arieh, which meant "lion" in Hebrew. That way he could still be called Ari, Cassie said, but now it was for a Hebrew name. He wanted his identity to be all Jewish, he said. He even talked to them about returning to the land of Zion, to *Eretz Yisrael*. It seemed that Mr. Rose argued instead for joining what he called "the mainstream of American culture," according to Cassie.

Shayna had thought even before she'd met him that Ari must be truly wonderful after everything that Cassie had told her about him, and today she had actually gotten to see him for the first time. He had come home for *Shabbos* just when she and Cassie had arrived to drop off Cassie's schoolbooks. She had imagined him before, arguing with his parents about

45

his pride and his Jewishness, fighting for it against their ideas about melting into American culture. But when she actually saw him, tall and dark-bearded and incredibly blue-eyed, he had exceeded her imaginings. She wanted to know more about him then, more about this son of intellectuals who was brave as a lion, and beautiful, it seemed, to boot. Surely even Poppa would approve of such a young man—or would he? There were no side curls, even on a young man studying to be a rabbi.

"Does he talk to them like that all the time?" Shayna asked Cassie after Cassie had told her about the name-changing argument.

"Yes," said Cassie, seeming surprised that Shayna was surprised. "Don't you talk to your family about ideas and principles and things?"

Shayna had thought carefully before she answered. Her father was a scholar, of that she was proud, and there were books in her house (though many fewer), so she was not ashamed of that. But talk? Questions about the books? Greek myths? Shakespeare plays? Poppa read the *New York Times* every day, he even read the *Forward* most of the time, though he said it was "a wrongheaded socialist paper," but he read to tell them things, not to discuss, not to question. She didn't want to paint a false picture of her family, because the wonder of having Cassie as a friend was in the comfort of someone to talk to, someone who understood. So she sidestepped Cassie's question. "I never heard my brother talk that way to my father— just tell him something, I mean. My brother gets mad and yells at my father, but he isn't like your brother." How to explain Yakov? The task defeated Shayna. And she already had to be careful even before she met Ari when she said the words "your brother" to Cassie, and she had to look the other way. His name, his beautiful name, Ari, that Shayna could certainly not say, because she knew she would blush and stammer if she tried. And now that she had actually seen him, her feelings about Ari were too precious to share even with his sister, even if that sister did happen to be her best friend.

She lay in the bed and wallowed in those feelings, staring at the dying *Shabbos* candlelight glowing on the ceiling but unaware of it, as she was unaware of her sleeping sisters beside her or Tante Tillie's snores. Ari, Ari, Ari, she thought. It was the most beautiful name in the world. Of course it stood for a brave lion, not for some Greek! If only she were older, old enough to really talk to someone like Ari, old enough so he might notice her. Some day, she thought sleepily, snuggling herself beneath the covers, some day I'll be old and educated, and then . . .

On Sunday Shayna went out to Hester Street, unbeknownst to either her sisters or her mother, carrying fifty cents she had kept hidden for a long time, ever since Miss Carlton gave her the prize for being first in her class when she graduated from eighth grade. She had stayed up for hours on Saturday night, wrestling with her conscience, .and she had determined at last to spend the money.

Rachel was her dear sister, and Rachel was going away with only one dress. She, Shayna, knew how a person could feel with only one dress. She had one, and Rachel had one. Rachel was a little tall for her age, and Shayna was a little short, so they had always been able to share their clothes before. That had meant that when there was a reason to wear a good dress—on *Shabbos* for instance, or when they went to visit Uncle Franz and Tante Sadie—they could exchange dresses, so Rachel's everyday dress was Shayna's good dress, and Shayna's everyday dress was Rachel's good dress. Only now Rachel was going away with only one dress, and surely there would be reasons she would need a good dress in her travels.

So Shayna had decided she would buy one for her. It had taken a lot of deciding, and a lot of tossing and turning in the bed last night, because she had a thousand other things she had thought of spending that fifty cents on; but now she was on her way to Hester Street.

She headed directly for the corner where she knew Mr. Garfinkel had his pushcart with the clothes. How often she had stopped and looked at those clothes! Well, now. She squared her shoulders and shook her head in a gesture more than slightly reminiscent of her mother's. No use thinking about those other times when she hadn't bought. How about maybe enjoying this time when at last she would buy?

NEARLY NEW, COME AND SEE, Mr. Garfinkel's sign said. But when Shayna got up close to the pushcart to see, the clothes did not seem nearly new at all. And the prices on them! A dress with a big tear in the sleeve, three dollars. A dress with the front stained from neck to waist, two dollars. She was afraid she couldn't find anything for fifty cents, no matter what the quality.

But when she listened for a minute to the women pushing in around her, she began to take heart. Like her mamma in their gray *sheitels,* all of them, but they didn't smell good like her mamma.

A tall one was saying, "Nobody would pay three dollars for a ruined dress. What's wrong with you, Mr. Garfinkel, did you make a mistake here, or didn't you see the torn sleeve? How about I give you a dollar and we call it quits?"

Mr. Garfinkel was a dark-bearded, handsome man dressed in a dark pair of trousers and vest to match over a wrinkled white shirt. His sleeves were rolled up to expose the dark hairs on his arms as he worked. He had a *kappel* on his head. When he answered a customer Shayna could tell that there was a way in which the lady would find it somehow flattering that he was speaking to her. "Look, missis, do you want me to go to the poorhouse? I paid a fortune for this lot. How about two dollars at least?"

"A dollar fifty, and that's my last offer."

"All right, all right, but I'm a ruined man," said Mr. Garfinkel, his cheerful mien belying his words as he pocketed the proffered money and handed over the dress.

Then Shayna heard the tall woman saying to her friend as she hurried away with it, "That Garfinkel! But I know my Froma can sew it up so the tear will never show, and then it *will* be just like new."

"I never thought I'd get more than a dollar and a quarter for that one with the torn sleeve, but look," said Mr. Garfinkel to his wife as Shayna turned back to the cart. And he showed her the money where she was standing next to Shayna, arranging the pile of clothes at the end of the barrow.

"So since when does twenty-five cents extra make a rich man?" asked the impatient Mrs. Garfinkel, fussing to arrange things in a more advantageous way. With her rough ways she seemed to Shayna a very unlikely spouse for the handsome Mr. Garfinkel. "How about a short prayer now," she suggested, "that Leah Morgenstern does come today with the clothes, like she said?"

"Who is Leah Morgenstern?" Shayna found herself asking, so interested now that she forgot she wasn't supposed to be listening.

Mrs. Garfinkel stopped and turned around in surprise and annoyance, then smiled. Her smile transformed her face, revealing the kindliness below that abrasive manner. "Oh, it's Sarah Klugerman's girl, isn't it? Your mother does some sewing for us sometimes. Well, don't be listening to other people's talk all the time! But I'll tell you the answer to your question—Mrs. Morgenstern is a rich lady who lives uptown and brings clothes to us that we can sell."

"Why?"

Mrs. Garfinkel thought a moment. "Probably because she wasn't always a rich lady."

"What was she before?" asked Shayna, sensing a story.

"Questions, questions! She lived here on Hester Street before, and she was like you, only her father had a pushcart once and sold clothes the way Mr. Garfinkel and I do. Then she married a rich man and became an uptown lady, but she didn't forget that here people still need old clothes. So she brings them for us to sell. If you wait here today, you might even see her, because she said she would come again soon, and she usually comes on a Sunday."

"Oh, Mrs. Garfinkel, do you think she might bring something I could afford? I only have fifty cents." Shayna showed her the money.

Mrs. Garfinkel looked at her from head to toe with sharp, appraising eyes. "Fifty cents is not very much money," she said. "And why do you need another dress anyway? Sarah Klugerman's daughter should be saving her money to help with the family."

"It's not for me, Mrs. Garfinkel, it's for my sister Rachel. She's going away, and she needs a dress. . . ."

Soon the astonished Mrs. Garfinkel had the whole story—the first person outside the family to know of the impending departure—and she stood with her hand on her ample bosom in a gesture of surprise. "So you want to buy a dress for your sister, do you? You're a good girl, just what I would expect Sarah Klugerman's daughter to be. God grant her other children should give her equal pleasure."

"But will I be able to find anything?" insisted Shayna, and she blushed as she reiterated, "with only fifty cents?"

"Nachman," said Mrs. Garfinkel, calling her husband away from a just-completed sale, "we have a problem here, please. The little Klugerman girl here needs a dress.''

"So what's a problem? Surely you can see a dress here, can't you, little one?" He practically had to shout above the noise in the street, and Shayna was embarrassed to be singled out in that way.

"But Nachman . . ." and Mrs. Garfinkel whispered hurriedly into her husband's ear.

While she was doing so Shayna saw a sight very unusual for Hester Street. A great big automobile, a shiny black one driven by a uniformed chauffeur, was inching its way between the pushcarts and the staring people, coming along, it seemed, in her direction. On East Broadway, where Cassie and—but she didn't let herself even think Ari's name in public—lived, you might see automobiles, but rarely, very rarely, one like this. And certainly it was unlikely here on Hester Street. Wouldn't her brother Harry love the sight of this one!

"There she is, what did I tell you?" crowed Mrs. Garfinkel, turning to Shayna. "I thought Mrs. Morgenstern would come today, and there she is. Now if you are quiet, you will see something. Just stand here."

Shayna obediently stood rooted to the spot, her eyes wide with the sight of that sleek-looking black car as it pulled up beside the pushcart. Then the chauffeur, his gray uniform with the brass buttons gleaming in the May sunshine, stepped from the car and held open the back door, from which a veiled lady dressed from head to toe in navy blue stepped carefully.

"Please get the clothes and give them to this man, John," said the lady to the chauffeur, and she pointed to Mr. Garfinkel. She didn't look at his wife.

To cover up that slight Mrs. Garfinkel took over the bargaining with the continuing stream of customers, so the noise around Shayna increased, if anything, and she couldn't hear more of the conversation between the lady and Mr. Garfinkel on the other side of the cart. Instead her attention was riveted on the bundle of clothes now passing from the arms of the chauffeur into Mr. Garfinkel's waiting hands. If only there was a dress for Rachel in that bundle. If only she herself could have a dress from a lady like that! It seemed as if the aura of uptown and the uptown world of which she had always heard those enticing rumors—a world of immense riches, of huge libraries filled with endless books, of lovely, ethereal young ladies sitting all day on chaises longues reading and eating chocolates—that whole world would be embodied in a dress from the lady in the chauffeur-driven automobile.

Mr. Garfinkel took the bundle of clothes and handed it over to his wife. Soon the car began to back cautiously away from the curb, still stared at by the crowds that pressed toward it on every side.

"Yetta," Shayna heard Mr. Garfinkel say in a low voice, "get the prices on these fast, and put them high while they can still remember that car."

"Right away, your lordship, because I have so much free time." Mrs. Garfinkel was impatient as ever with her husband. "But one I'll keep a little back," she muttered aside to Shayna with a wink.

"Oh, Mrs. Garfinkel, do you think it could be this one?" asked Shayna, fingering a dark maroon silk with ruffles down the front, made for a woman twice her size, and with an ostrich-feather hat to match.

Mrs. Garfinkel's smile grew wide, but she was kind. "If your sister were a bit older, that might indeed be the perfect choice," she said. "But since she is not yet *your* age"— Shayna reveled in the implication that she herself might wear such a dress—"I think instead this one might be more her style. Is she about your size?" Mrs. Garfinkel held up a beige lawn dress with its own matching lining against Shayna, who nodded wordlessly. Tucks descended in little rows from the high neck to the waist, and there was a beige silk rose at the throat. The sleeves were full to below the elbows, then tucked to the wrists, where they were gathered about cuffs each fastened with a row of mother-of-pearl buttons.

Shayna fingered the fabric, then turned with tears in her eyes to Mrs. Garfinkel. "However can I afford such a beautiful dress?" she nearly wailed. "It would be the perfect dress for Rachel."

"But didn't you say you had fifty cents?" asked Mrs. Garfinkel. "Here, look, I was just going to mark fifty cents on the ticket for this dress," and she showed Shayna (but no one else) a ticket on which she wrote the magic sum.

Shayna's radiant smile and shiny coins were the rewards Mrs. Garfinkel collected, and as she dropped the latter into the cash box she said to her amazed husband, "Stop always with the griping, Nachman; we'll charge five dollars for the maroon number and make it up. We, too, are entitled to do a *mitzvah* once in a while, not only the rich. Why shouldn't we have a chance at heaven like they do?"

But the delighted Shayna heard none of that last exchange. She was already on her way home, the beautiful beige dress folded carefully in her arms. She didn't even have a second to think about how she would have liked a new dress of her own anymore, so intent was she on getting back to Rachel with this gift—truly a new dress that would look absolutely beautiful on her brown-eyed favorite sister.

Leah Morgenstern sank back into the soft upholstery of the Daimler and breathed a sigh of relief. Her trip to Hester Street was over again. Her unseeing eyes on the back of the chauffeur's neck, she let her mind drift away from the confusions such a day always brought. He threaded his way through the crowds and headed the car back uptown. Every time she went through this, she wondered in the end how she stood it, why she did it.

Was it truly necessary to her conscience to bring those extra clothes to Nachman Garfinkel, her father's one-time helper? Each trip to Hester Street was a reminder of the life she had left, the girl she had been. That pretty, pale girl was behind her in a dim past that she surely had no wish to recapture. Now she was a solid, handsome matron, as she liked to think of herself, the mother of three attractive children. Maybe the only reason she took each trip to Hester Street with the discarded clothes was the blessed sense of relief she had as she left again—a reminder of the relief she had felt when that girl she had been had left for the first time on the arm of Aaron Morgenstern.

Or maybe she came to Hester Street because it made her respect Aaron more each time she went back to him—both Aaron and his money, she corrected herself; they had always been behind her devotion in approximately equal shares. Where had been the mistake? Because every time she took the trip to Hester Street a part of Leah knew that there had been a mistake. With her pale girlhood she had left something else behind. She tried to remember her successes now.

Her daughters were growing up, and Norman, the last-born son for whom they had prayed so long, was surely going to follow in his father's footsteps in business. And do better, she thought, smiling, because in America the son could always do better, even better than Aaron, who had come from less and had grown (with her beside him) to so much. True, ten-year-old Norman right now was merely Fraulein Wenzel's charge, but he would go far; his mother was sure of it. Hadn't she herself come far? If the girls, Ethel and Diana, would follow her advice and do their blond hair in the style she suggested, they, too,

54

would go far. She had plans for her girls, too. Already they had finished with the riding lessons and the summer camps and were playing tennis and golf with the boys in their set.

Soon the summer would come (the heat was beginning to reach warm fingers into the car as she rode home), and they would go to the summer place in Jersey that Aaron had bought the family several years ago. This year Ethel and Diana could play tennis every day if they wished, and in a couple of years, when they turned twenty-one—in a couple of years, the marriages she had planned for them . . . But they were not alike, her girls.

Diana, younger by a little over a year, was like Aaron. She knew how to use people and things. Just the day before she and Diana had gone through their clothes as a prelude to Leah's trip downtown. Diana knew how to sort through clothes and throw away the torn, older ones—not throw away, Leah amended, give away. Diana knew what to give away.

But not Ethel—Ethel had always been difficult. Had she herself wished to be difficult like that? Even when the girls were little, playing in the sand on the Jersey beach, Ethel had tasted the mud pies. She had never known when not to do something. Leah smiled again at how odd it was that it was Ethel who had always been the apple of her eye. When Ethel had climbed a tree, or run off down the beach and come home with a dead starfish smelling to high heaven, Leah remembered how she'd swooped her daughter up in her arms and laughed with her firstborn at Aaron's remonstrances, at Fraulein Wenzel's scolding. It had been no way to discipline Ethel's naughtiness, she knew, but Ethel had been such a joy, tasting all those forbidden pleasures that had certainly never been a part of her own upbringing. Where was the mistake?

Diana, Leah told herself, was a good girl—as I was

when I was young. So Ethel was the one she worried about because she was not that same good girl; but even that worry, she thought, was foolishness. There was nothing to worry about, she told herself firmly.

Leah closed her eyes and made herself relax. She had not come this far for nothing. She had always been a good girl, even before her father had chosen her life. She remembered how she had obeyed his orders on that day years ago when he had told her of his choice, that day when he had come home with the miraculous tale of his shipboard contract with the German tailor.

"I promised him," her father had recalled of the man he had met in steerage when they were both on their way to America, "that we would go into business together. He would make the clothes, and I would sell them in the new country. It seemed so simple then. How was either of us to know that Morgenstern would get rich from the making and I would stay poor from the selling?" He sighed. In those days of Leah's youth prices of ready-made clothes had actually gone down as mass production had become cheaper, and vendors like her father had suffered while the manufacturers like Morgenstern had reaped greater and greater profits. Ah, well, as the Lord willed.

"We sealed the bargain with a contract," Leah's father had told her, "that if he had a son and I had a daughter, our children would marry. In the old country things were often done that way—so you were betrothed, Leah, before you were born. His son Aaron has joined the business now, and they will honor the contract."

"Of course you will honor it as well, Poppa," Leah had said, praying for strength to be obedient while at the same time she forced down feelings of rebellion in her young breast. Nachman, the handsome apprentice who helped her father with the pushcart, had never returned her adoration, had barely looked at her when she brought the meals to Hester Street in those days. At least now, she wept into her pillow that night, he would have no further chance to reject her; she was the betrothed of Aaron Morgenstern. She would show her father that she could be good.

Twenty years later she had pushed such memories far enough down in her mind so that she only let herself think how it was the least she could do now to bring old clothes to her dead father's one-time helper. Soon little Norman would come with her and learn about charity. It was out of the kindness of her heart that she helped Nachman Garfinkel—that must be why she came back to Hester Street, she decided. It had nothing whatsoever to do with Nachman himself, handsome as he had remained. And she certainly had never let herself wonder why he had married that clever but unkempt Yetta Leditsky. What did Yetta have now that she, Leah, did not? The least Leah could do was bring them old clothes. But she was always disturbed when she went to Hester Street. Disturbed at the memory of that obedient girl she had been. Why hadn't being a good girl been good enough?

As the car pulled up in front of the house on Riverside Drive Leah was startled for a moment. She thought she caught a glimpse of her daughter Ethel going around the far corner. And it looked as if Ethel was on the arm of a young man. A young man Leah did not immediately recognize. She hadn't remembered that Ethel had an engagement today. Again a vague worry about Ethel threatened her. Maybe something wasn't quite right after all. A headache suddenly materialized behind her eyes. Damn this going back to Hester Street!

"John," she said aloud to the chauffeur, "who was that with Miss Ethel just now?"

"I'm sure I don't know, madam," said John, his face wooden as he held the car door and helped her out.

I wonder who it was, mused Leah, uncomfortable with a feeling that she had seen the man somewhere before, but she could not remember where. All thoughts of Hester Street must pass from her mind now; she must concentrate on finding out what that brief glimpse of her daughter was about. Turning to John, who had followed her up the steps to open the door, she put her request into words. "I want to see Miss Ethel as soon as she returns," Leah said. "Tell the other servants also—she is to be sent to me immediately." She went quickly past the heavily carved brown door, calling her younger daughter's name as she did so.

Diana, indolently stretched out on the sofa in the parlor, didn't actually bother to get up in response to her mother's summons. She just answered, "Yes, Mamma," in her usual absent tone.

Leah stood in the hall, annoyed for a moment, knowing Diana was probably just looking at advertisements for dresses in the Sunday paper. The girl didn't ever seem to want to move unless it was absolutely required.

Handing her hat and coat to the maid, Leah went into the parlor through the double doors. She suppressed her impatience at Diana's sprawled form, Sunday papers spread around her. She had a more important subject to discuss and knew the futility of fighting on too many fronts with this child of Aaron's.

"Who was that with your sister?" she began, speaking sharply. (Leah also knew the value of surprise and did not plan to give up any advantage an immediate attack might hold.) "I saw Ethel leave the house as I drove up. I want to know all your escorts—Ethel knows that perfectly well. Who was with her?"

That evening on Orchard Street Sarah wrinkled her nose at the smell of the disinfectant she was wiping on the inside of the new (secondhand) suitcase. She had scrubbed it hard, and now she would make very sure there were no bugs left in it. It was lying open on the table, a mute symbol to the returning family as they gathered for supper that the next day was the day of her departure.

I have bought the ticket, Isaac.

For tomorrow. Because it's all decided.

Go to *shul,* finish your prayers, don't try still to change things.

(Yes, if I were a better person, maybe I would still stay, but I can't say that to him or to anyone. I have today bought the ticket. Already I have the suitcase. It's light now, a suitcase; my arm will ache with the long journey and the carrying of it.)

But my gentle Rachel will be there to help.

In a few hours, when I have closed the suitcase, everything will be in it. By this time tomorrow I will be gone. Once the ship has pulled away from the dock there will be no turning back. I can't swim. He can't put a rope on me and pull me back. I will be truly gone.

Even if the ship is hell, as I remember, it will be taking me home. I will miss my children, but everything here will no longer be my responsibility, thank God.

The bread is baking to take; the boiled eggs will be cool by evening, even in this heat. The dress is ready to put in, and the shawl I knitted for Mamma, and whatever my little Rachel can bring. If only I had money for a dress for her as well . . .

At least I am taking my sweet Rachel with me to see my family. At least one will meet and know her grandmother and her aunts and uncles. She is so like my sister Chenny was. At least one will see the brook and the plum trees.

I know I'll miss my children. I wonder if I'll miss Isaac. My God, I wonder if I'll miss David Nathan.

What kind of a person am I to have such a question to ask myself?

I have to go. God knows I have to go.

Not until the suitcase was about to be closed did Shayna finally bring out the new dress for Rachel. "I have something for you, Razele" was all she said, and the dress was in her hands.

Rachel stared, simply stared at the delicate fabric, the tiny tucks at neck and sleeves, the little flower at the throat, but she didn't say a word. She stared at the dress, and then she stared at her older sister.

"Don't you like it?" Shayna asked with a sudden flare of anxiety. What if the dress had been to her own taste but was not something her sister would want? What if she hadn't thought enough about what Rachel would really want? "It's because we won't be able to share while you're gone, so you will need a good dress. Oh, Razele, I'll miss you so."

Suddenly both the dress and Shayna were in Rachel's arms, and the two sisters were sobbing while the astonished family looked on. Rachel backed away first, sniffing and smiling. "It's so beautiful," she said, holding the dress up in front of her. "It's the most beautiful dress I have ever seen. And look, it is just the right length."

"How did you get such a dress, Shayna?" Sarah at last found her voice.

"I got it from Mr. Garfinkel in Hester Street, where else? And I paid for it with my own money. It cost the whole fifty cents."

"Only fifty cents? How could that be? Or did you steal it?" asked Yakov, his voice thick with disbelief, ready as always for a fight.

"Of course I didn't steal it," replied Shayna in a righteous tone. "While I was there a rich lady came along . . ." and soon the whole story of the dress had been told.

But throughout the telling Rachel remained silent. Finally she spoke. "But Shayna, you won't have a good dress when I go either, because we won't be able to share anymore. What will you do?"

Shayna worked at putting just the right note of careless unconcern into her voice as she replied, "I'll manage just fine. Who knows? Maybe Sophie and I will be able to share soon."

"Your dress is too big for me. You know we can't share," said Sophie, taking Shayna more literally than she wished.

"You will need something for dress-up, Shayna, something for *Shabbos*," said Rachel in a worried voice, a frown furrowing her forehead. Then she looked again at the new dress, and her face cleared. She smiled at her sister. "Here, you take the flower—the dress is so beautiful it doesn't need a flower to improve it, but the flower will make your dress special if you pin it on for *Shabbos*."

The silken flower was off the dress and in Shayna's delighted hand in a second. "Thank you," she said to her sister, and her eyes conveyed the full extent of her pleasure. The flower and Rachel's generosity in thinking of it combined in her mind suddenly in a comfort. Maybe it would be all right. At least she had made the right decision about her fifty cents.

On that last night Isaac turned toward her on the pillows. He spoke in a whisper. "Sarah, did you go to the *mikveh?*"

She sighed. "Yes."

Then he put aside the feather bed cover and came into her bed. He was always kind, and it was quickly over, the strange stirring thing she had never really understood. He had never spoken to her while it happened, never said a word beyond that first question.

She knew it was her duty, and that it gave him a surcease that he needed. Sometimes she was surprised, because it also gave her a great pleasure, a suddenly blinding flash that left her shaken and amazed, but she never said a word even when that happened. (Perhaps he felt her throbbing then beneath him?) It was an unexpected goodness in her marriage, she thought. Sometimes then, too, she thought of David Nathan and wondered.

What Isaac thought she did not know. He had never said.

This time, when it was over, he did not leave her and go back to his own bed as he had always done in the past. Instead he held her, and she heard him speak, saying words she had never thought to hear from him in all her life.

"Sarah." His whisper was muffled by her hair. "Sarah," he said, "I am afraid."

There came upon her then a great tenderness, like what she felt when one of the children woke in the night with a frightening dream and she was able to be of comfort, a tenderness somehow also mixed with the great pleasure that had just come. She held him as she held a child.

"Isaac, I will come back" was all she said. But they held each other, together in the same bed, for all the hours of the rest of the night.

In the morning she left—a traveler, a daughter going across the sea to visit that mother Shayna had never known. Poppa did not read the article about the ship's departure aloud to them from the *New York Times*.

## ❧ 3 ❧

*Whither is thy beloved gone?*
*(Song of Songs 6:1)*

Hush, now." Sometimes, when Shayna heard herself talking to Sophie these days, she wondered where the words really came from. They sounded like Mamma's words. "Would you like me to tell you a story? If you stop crying, you'll be able to hear it better. Hush, now. It's a wonderful story about Mamma and the old country."

Slowly the sobs stopped, and Sophie curled up next to Shayna in the bed they shared alone now that Rachel was gone.

"Harry, come in so you can hear, too." Shayna's whisper was louder, but carefully not loud enough to wake little David.

Harry crept in and sat on the edge of his sister's bed in the dark.

"If you listen to stories about Mamma, you'll forget to be sad that she's gone, and before you know it the summer will be over, and it will be the end of August, and Mamma and Rachel will be home." Mamma had been gone for a few weeks already; it was the beginning of June.

"Tell us the story, Shayna," said Sophie. She took a deep breath, and the sobs stopped for good.

Shayna used her special story-telling voice: "It's a story about even before Mamma was born. It's the story of how Mamma's mamma and Mamma's poppa found each other. Listen carefully.

"Once upon a time, long long ago, there was a very young girl. She was older than you, Harry, and she was older than you, Sophie; as a matter of fact"—Shayna herself was surprised to find the truth in this remembered tale—"she was just about my age. She lived in the old country in a little wooden house, and one day she went down to the river to do her washing. It was a lovely warm day—"

"Like today was," said Sophie dreamily.

"And she and her friends laughed and sang as they did their washing." Why not a little embellishment? "When they finished pounding the clothes on the rocks (that's how they got clothes clean in the olden days—they didn't have washboards, I guess) they hung them on the lower branches of some trees to dry—"

"I used to think a tree was a large flower." Harry's little voice still held a hint of a question, as if his small experience of trees had left him unsure.

"The girl I'm telling you about decided that while she was waiting for her washing to dry on the tree she would see if her friends were ready for an adventure. Why not go swimming in the river? They all thought it would be a good idea, so soon all the young girls were swimming in the cool water, with the bright sun shining overhead and the clothes flapping on the tree branches to dry, and everyone splashing and playing in the water, when suddenly"—Shayna paused for breath and effect—"suddenly some horsemen on great big white horses came galloping up! They were soldiers going to fight in a war, a kind of revolution, and they were fighting under a famous general—they were members of Kossuth's army, and the year was 1848."

"Was that very long ago?" asked Sophie.

"Yes, very long ago. This is 1914, so that was nearly seventy years ago. But listen. The girls were still swimming in the river when the horsemen rode up, and the girl we were talking about—the one who grew up to be our grandmother, Mamma's mamma (her name was Rivka) —she had long golden hair that was gleaming in the sunlight as they swam.

"She must have been a vision—a happy golden vision—to one of the soldiers, because he reined in his horse and stopped and just gazed at her.

"Then he turned to the horseman next to him. 'Do you see that girl over there swimming—the one with the long golden hair?' he asked. 'Someday I'm going to come back here, and I'm going to find her and marry her.'

"Then, before his companion could open his mouth to speak and say how young the girl was and that he was being ridiculous and how impossible was such a marriage, the soldier spurred his horse forward and went riding on.

"Really," Shayna continued, "it's a story that *really* happened, and that soldier was your grandfather. And that young girl is your grandmother. He was already very old then, much older than she; she was only thirteen. He must have been more than fifteen years older. But that's not the end of the story." She paused for a break.

"Here's how it happened: It was nearly a year later before the war was over, and the surprising thing is that the soldier remembered Rivka with the golden hair all that time, and when he finally could, he came riding back into the little village by the river. It was a miracle, because he found her.

"He went to her father and asked for her hand in marriage. Her father wasn't at all sure that it was the best thing in the world for his daughter to marry a soldier. But, you see, the soldier had been a scholar at the great yeshiva before the revolution, and now he

65

wanted to go back to being a scholar again, and he wanted to settle down because he had had enough of revolutions and of war. After all, wars are very terrible, even when God is on your side.''

"Are wars very terrible even when God fights for the Jews?" asked Harry, who had learned at *heder* about the Maccabees and Bar Kochba and even the great battles of King David and was wondering if he could have a chance to fight in a war some day. He must ask Uncle Franz, he decided. Uncle Franz would know more than his sisters, but he didn't think Uncle Franz had ever fought in a war. He loved his uncle, Tante Sadie's husband, loved going home with Tante Sadie sometimes to see Uncle Franz.

"Hush, Harry, wars are always bad," said Sophie, and she reached for Shayna's hand.

"Remember," Shayna continued the story of the long-ago romance, "that the soldier was much older, so it was especially hard to convince Rivka's father about the marriage. But finally she admitted to her father about the day she had been washing in the river. While she didn't tell him all about the swimming, because he would have thought it was very wrong for a girl to swim, he finally did understand that she *had* seen the soldier before, and that she wanted her father's consent to her marriage with this suitor.

"So her father gave in—because the soldier was really a scholar—and they were married at last. They had nine children, and the youngest of those children is our mamma. And now"—Shayna put a new ending on the story she had heard so often—"that young girl with the golden hair is a very very old lady, and Mamma has gone to see her before she dies. You can see why it was right for Mamma to go. And Sophie has long golden hair now, just like the girl in the story."

Sophie and Harry both nodded and yawned on cue as the story ended.

"Good night, Shayna," said Harry, and he went padding back to his own bed.

"Good night, Shayna," yawned Sophie, snuggling further into bed herself, pleased about her own golden hair.

"Good night," said Shayna. A cool breeze came in the window at last. She slept, and her dreams were all about soldiers on white horses who came to rescue her from complications she couldn't remember; they all had blue eyes and dark beards and bore a remarkable resemblance to Ari Rose. The children slept peacefully the rest of the night. Isaac slept in his own room, alone.

Alone also, in that bed beyond Shayna's dreams, lay her grandmother, Rivka, whose romance, over now, had at least lasted the days of her youth, into her fortieth year. And all these years later she could still warm herself with the memory of that man who had ridden out of the forest above the river to be her lover.

Always Rivka had known that Avrum had minded being older than the husbands of her friends, more than fifteen years older than she was. To her he had always been straight and tall, with an aura about him as if the sun shone perpetually through those trees to limn his every move. To her he would always have that look. When Sarah, the ninth child, was born he was congratulated, as was the custom, but she could tell how he felt—that he detected in the voices of the other men a hint that he was somehow rather old to be having a child. She didn't mind. She didn't mind anything about him, least of all his age. She loved him. To her, even after nine children, he was still beautiful and brilliant, the horseman who had ridden to her through the forest of her dreams. But Avrum—Avrum loved her too much not to mind. He was respected in the village, true, and the other men looked up to him, but still he minded.

Lusty young men, they seemed to Avrum; when they looked at his wife perhaps they wondered that he could still give her a child. Perhaps it was because he could not believe that Rivka herself was forty years old in that year when the baby Sarah was born. For him she still had golden hair; she was still the young girl in the river. The realities of worn hands and sagging breasts were never realities to him. He glared at the younger men even as he accepted their congratulations. Those younger men were like Esau in the Torah, he told himself, hairy and uncouth.

At the end of that summer, when the peasants round about the village had brought in the wheat harvest and there was a hint in the air already of the autumn to come, when the plums were picked and preserved, somehow those damnable young Esaus of the village still had a surplus of energy. They were not much for scholarship, those young men; they rarely spent time in the house of study, especially at the golden end of a long summer. There was blood stirring in them, and they looked around for a challenge, a way to work off the exhilaration of the end of the hot days.

Finally they found it. They decided to have a race on a *Shabbos* afternoon just before the High Holidays in September. It would be a race to finish out the old year, they joked, and the winner could have . . . but they never decided what the winner could have. For them the winning meant less than the running itself. They planned the course from the center of the village to the top of the hill that stood east of their homes. It was an impressive hill, perhaps five hundred feet higher than the village, and the pines on its peak had blocked their sunrises all their lives. On that September afternoon they would see who could run first to the top of it.

Rivka begged him not to run. "They are young and foolish; let them have their fun. Stay here with me," she said.

It was the wrong thing to say; it was precisely their youth and folly that he envied. He could not bear to have those younger men best him at anything. He could not bear to be old and have to stay at home, even with his darling.

So Avrum ran. The race started about three o'clock in the afternoon, when he was usually taking his *Shabbos* afternoon nap. But on that afternoon there was no time for the nap, and he turned aside Rivka's entreaties with impatience. Finding at last that she could not prevail, she did have to stay at home in order to feed the baby, so she did not even see them start off.

Avrum ran quickly through the little street, so by the edge of the village his lungs already felt as if they would burst. Every breath was drawn in pain. By the time he was only a little way up the hill a red haze appeared before his eyes. But when he glanced around the red haze could not block out the sight of the younger men, and the pounding of his heart could not erase the sound of their panting breaths so close behind him. The sweat poured off him, and the way, not quite a mile, seemed to him endless.

It took less than a quarter of an hour, actually, for Avrum to reach the pines on the eastern hill, and he stood among them panting, the victor—but knew too late that it was a hollow victory. As he fell to the ground the smell of those damp pine needles, too briefly breathed, informed him instead that the younger men had won after all; they would live to tell Rivka, his golden-haired Rivka, not of his race, but of his death.

It was a wonderful, brave story, this story of Avrum's death that Rivka had told her children over and over again. The reality had not been wonderful. She was already a widow with nine children by the time she was forty. Nine children, the youngest the baby Sarah. No husband, so no money to buy food or pay the rent to the *goyish* landlord so they should have a roof over their heads. True, her grown-up boys helped; Pinchas was married to his first wife and expecting his own firstborn even before his father had died. But that meant he could not support his widowed mother for long.

When the tailor, Hermann, mean-minded and sallow as he was, asked her to marry him at last, it was the only solution. Of course she had married the first man who offered. She felt it was, after all, a miracle that anyone offered. She even bore him Mendel in years when other women did not bear children. She had had her dream when she was young. Now her hair was no longer golden, and no horseman could come riding up to her dead father's house to spirit her away.

But it was on account of that second husband, Hermann, that she had had to send little Sarah away to America as soon as she could go, when she was only thirteen. He had begun to look at the girl with his small eyes, and he arranged to brush against her in doorways. Once Rivka had even seen his hands reach out and touch her little breasts as he passed her. So Sarah had had to go. She, Rivka's baby, who had comforted her in her deepest sorrow, was sent away. The other girls were married by then; except for the little Mendel, child of her second marriage, Sarah was the last.

In all the years since she had gone away, in more years than Rivka wanted to count, if she even could be bothered to count anything anymore, which she was, God knew, too tired and too sick to do, she thought, lying there propped on her pillows in the moonlight, she had only had letters from her Sarah.

Letters from a golden land, letters chronicling too briefly the life of her little girl grown far away to womanhood, to marriage, to motherhood, her little girl gone so young across the world. If only Sarah, her Sarah, would come home once to see her, she had thought through those years, it would be a blessing to make all the rest bearable. She missed her baby. Sometimes it seemed it had all happened so long ago, it was as if it had all happened to another woman, truly only a story. Sarah was the last shred of the reality of her dead love. Now even the part about Hermann had grown unreal, Hermann who had also died, which was indeed a blessing, because then she no longer had to share his bed, no longer had to hold her breath in pain from his weight above her, no longer had to face that bitter reminder of her old joys.

Now they told Rivka years on the calendar that were not the years marked in her father's house. They told her now that it was 1914 and another war was coming. One thousand nine hundred fourteen since what? What had happened of such importance since the creation of the world to make a new calendar with new years? Surely not, as her sons impatiently explained, simply the beginning of the *goyim*. She smiled to herself at the foolishness of it.

In another war perhaps other soldiers would ride out on other horses, as they had done in her youth, but now in other causes, and her love, her Avrum, was long gone, no longer standing in the shade of the tall trees on the riverbank, no longer darkly handsome in her father's house, asking for her hand. She could even smile and look at her hand, wrinkled and old now in the moonlight, but once he had held it in love. She could smile now and think of her baby, her Sarah, coming home, on her way, coming home.

"Mamma, are we nearly there? What does Grandma's house look like?" asked Rachel, her eyes scrubbing the strange sights. They spoke to each other in English, not Yiddish, because the cart driver, that curious man, knew no English.

"It is a wooden house on the edge of the village. It is square. It was newly painted white when I left—but that was a long time ago, Rachel. Many things have changed here." Sarah stared straight ahead for a minute. "I'm sorry the plum trees have finished blooming, but I've told you about the plum trees." She would have liked to have given Rachel the plum trees in blossom.

"Yes, Mamma." Rachel sighed. Mamma had told her the story many times about how the plum trees here in the old country were so beautiful in blossom. Somehow, in the story, Mamma had been a little girl lying under the beautiful blossoming plum tree, and a ripe plum, delicious with the very essence of summer, had just fallen into her mouth. In a foreign land, Rachel had thought, the trees could bear their fruit and still blossom, all at the same time, and a perfect pitted plum could fall gently into the mouth of a little girl who grew to be her mamma. Now it seemed that the woman sitting beside her, while still undoubtedly her same mamma, was also somehow foreign, somehow very different from the mamma (whom she had left in America, perhaps?) at home.

The change had happened very gradually while they had traveled. Rachel herself had at first been miserable with seasickness on the ship, and Mamma had tended her the way Mamma always did, holding her head while she retched until her whole insides felt as if they would come out, until she had wished she was dead. There had been days on that boat—Rachel shuddered with the memory—when she had wished only to die.

After the ship landed they had stayed with relatives in Amsterdam. Rachel had never known that Mamma had relatives in Amsterdam, but she had still been so fuzzy with the leftovers of her illness that she had not asked many questions. It was all so new—the tall, narrow house by the narrow dirty canal—the newness had frightened Rachel, and she had been quiet in Amsterdam, still rocking from the voyage even on dry land; she had let Mamma do the talking with those strangers.

"We have heard that your mother improves," they said to Mamma in a ponderous Yiddish that was hard for Rachel to understand at first, speaking of the grandmother Rachel had not yet met. Apparently these square, bearded men were distant cousins of her grandmother Rivka.

"I cannot wait to see her," Mamma had replied in a girlish, eager tone that Rachel had never heard her use before. "I have been too long from home," her mamma had gone on, as if home was somehow there in those foreign places that smelled still of the sea.

Already Mamma's words had made a distance for Rachel, and the distance was between a foreign mamma and herself. Mamma became more silent in those days in Amsterdam, with a faraway look in her eyes, while Rachel had talked desperately, volubly, telling the Amsterdam relatives about America, about her home on Orchard Street in New York, about her sister Shayna who was a great reader, about her brother Yakov who worked in a shop, about her sister Sophie's golden hair and her brother Harry's questions, about her baby brother David, about anything that would show them how she belonged in America, not in this old world that had already begun to frighten her so much. Even the food the Amsterdam relatives fed her tasted foreign, was spiced with the South Seas flavor of the islands where their Dutch masters traded. And the relatives seemed quickly to disapprove of her and of her mamma.

"You left a baby?" Mamma was asked by an old woman who shook her head as she asked it.

"I had to come home once before my mother dies," Mamma had said. And Rachel could tell that Mamma had minded their disapproval, their stolid questioning of this journey. She knew how much Mamma was missing the other children, so she wasn't surprised when Mamma had said, as soon as she felt well again, "We leave tomorrow," or that Mamma was very quiet on the last night in Amsterdam.

The train trip to Budapest had been long; Rachel's back ached from sitting up all night on the wooden benches. Her eyes ached from the foreign cities and the foreign mountains that had sped by the windows. Her ears ached, too, from the clatter of foreign languages she could not understand, but in which Mamma had given up her silence, had chattered away happily in words all strange. Chattering away in foreign tongues, chattering with worldly strangers, this new mother of hers.

And now the cart, and no plum blossoms, and a hungry look in her mamma's eyes, ready to devour it all, searching for a square, whitewashed house on the edge of a village somewhere in a foreign land.

All my bones ache.

Maybe, if I sit perfectly straight and don't move my head to look always at the little patches of woods, it will be better. I will not, maybe, feel it so much when we bump over the little wooden bridges.

It is all smaller than I remembered. Everything is smaller. Even the boat was smaller, and thank God the voyage was shorter. Well, if it is maybe smaller, than surely I know it is a perfect smallness, a miniature blessedness, this coming home.

But is it really home? Are these small houses really the large houses I have remembered? The wood is so gray (no longer white), the road is just a rutted track coming into the village here. And who is that old lady on the chair in front there, looking toward the road?

An old lady and two strange men—what are they doing in front of my house? Has Mamma died, and no one wrote to me? Have they moved and I did not know, that there should be strangers there?

Dear God, have I made this journey for nothing? Have I sold Isaac's brooch and left him and my children for a woman who is dead? But . . .

"There it is, Rachel. That is the house where I grew up. That old woman is my mamma. Those are my brothers, those men. And do you see? A rose is blooming by the door."

So why am I weeping?

The cart has stopped.

"Come, Mamma." Rachel's voice is gentle.

"My mother has gone back to the old country," Yakov said to Kalinsky. Without thinking he kicked aside an old shoe that had been lying on the sidewalk. The two of them had come out of a lecture at the Educational Alliance together and headed by mutual consent for the East River to talk—Yakov had thought to talk about Dostoyevski, the subject of the lecture, but it was not so. The night was warm, and the breeze seemed to blow along the river with a beckoning cool that was needed after their evening's warm attention in the auditorium crowded with people. Even Mr. Nathan, the music teacher, had been there. Mr. Nathan was a friend of Mamma's—and of Poppa's, Yakov supposed. He had never thought, until this moment, how strange it was that his mamma had a man for a friend. What if . . . ? But he put that beginning of a question out of his mind.

Thinking of Mamma instead, Yakov suddenly remembered a time, years before, when he had taken a forbidden swim from one of the piers on the East River. He had come home soaked, but Mamma hadn't told Poppa on him.

"The old country?"

"We still have relatives over there," Yakov explained hesitantly. When he talked to an intellectual like Kalinsky Yakov was always hesitant. He had no idea what Kalinsky's background really was—only that he was of Russian extraction. "My mother had to see her family," he explained. Was it an explanation?

Kalinsky was nodding, so Yakov didn't notice the absence in his voice when he said, "Relatives over there? Don't we all?"

Yakov didn't realize either that Kalinsky had deliberately sought out this walk with him, and for his own purposes. Kalinsky had plans for Yakov Klugerman, but, like the fox in the old folk tale, Kalinsky kept those plans for the future. For now it seemed to pay him to walk with Yakov and listen to Yakov and simply show him that he was singling him out. The objects of Kalinsky's plans, unlike those of the fox, sometimes didn't even know when they had been swallowed alive. That way they remained available to Kalinsky, sometimes for years, for reuse for more plans. He looked now across the East River to Brooklyn and he planned. He planned how Yakov Klugerman could be useful, young as he was. Besides, even though Kalinsky assured himself that he acted always on political motives, the truth was not quite that. Something stirred in him, something he never admitted even to himself, when he looked at Yakov. And—he hastened to put that something utterly away— Kalinsky sympathized with Yakov's position in his family.

"I really don't know much about them," Yakov went on, speaking of his relatives. "Probably only a group of old-fashioned people who didn't raise the money to come. I understand it's all a question of economics. No courage," he added. The river, still tidal here, was low now, and it smelled of gulls and fish. Some barges were dim forms waiting in their slips for the next day's sailings. Other boats, however, were moving out there, lights winking in the heat haze. Why, Yakov asked himself, had he gotten on the subject of these useless relatives he had never met? That would be no way to impress Kalinsky.

But Kalinsky was smiling. Yakov had, after all, provided the opening he had looked for. "Not everyone can join the Cause," Kalinsky said, with the implication that present company was therefore special. "Uneducated peasants, for instance. Or those who are still caught up in the old religion. They can't see the necessities in history, the way they are simply part of the class struggle, or even the fact that they can't change things unless—"

"Unless," Yakov interrupted him, carrying on his thought and carrying it further, even though his own words were still simplistic, "unless they finally break away, completely away from the old ways." His eyes shone. "We have to show them how to do it if they can't find it for themselves, don't we? We have to lead the way even for the old ones. You can't wait for them, or you'd wait forever. That's the idea?"

"Right," said Kalinsky, "that's the idea, Klugerman. In your shop you have to talk to the old ones about the union, because of course the union is the beginning." He paused, wondering whether he should play further at this time, then decided to get on to business.

"Saperstein is your boss, isn't he?"

"Yes," said Yakov, flattered that Kalinsky knew it, flattered by the fact that he was walking here along the river with Kalinsky in the cool of the evening. It was as if he had been granted a special meeting all to himself, even as if Kalinsky was his friend. He had not had this kind of friend before, someone with whom he could talk this way. He felt he had risen above the petty surroundings of those piers, that garbage, the city itself, risen to a position of importance now that Kalinsky was maybe becoming his friend.

"Well, watch out that Saperstein doesn't catch you,

or you'll be out of a job," Kalinsky cautioned. "If you're fired, you can't help us organize, and we need your help." He had stopped and turned toward Yakov, allowing himself to put his arm on his shoulder. He looked hard at him with his burning eyes.

For a moment Yakov was embarrassed as well as pleased by Kalinsky's attention, although he couldn't imagine why he should be embarrassed. True, he felt proud to be alone with him, but Kalinsky's arm on his shoulder, his face so close to his own, made him nervous. Kalinsky's breath smelled bad close up, he thought, reminding him of the garbage of the river, not his long-ago sweet summer swim, and then he was ashamed of himself for the thought. This was what he wanted, wasn't it? This closeness, this common dedication to a Cause that transcended his narrow existence in the shop and at home with his family?

He must simply strive to be worthy of the part he was supposed to play, he resolved. He must utterly divest himself then of family ties, ties to the old ways, to old-country thinking. He must only be part of the great new movement, part of the Cause. What possible connection did he have anymore to the old world? He had grown beyond it, away from it. With Kalinsky as a friend he could even change the world.

The world of Aaron Morgenstern was the world Yakov wanted to change, but it had aspects of which he did not even dream. Aaron Morgenstern dreamed of them, because in his own peculiar way he was also a dreamer—a dreamer and a user.

Aaron found himself wishing, one *Shabbos* afternoon, that instead of living the way he had been, he could simply lose himself in a book. (It was, perhaps, the last time in his life he was to dream of that.) He sat at the desk in his study at home and looked at the shelves of books on the wall across from him. The raveled bindings, he felt, were staring back at him in a sort of mute accusation as the dust accumulated on their unturned pages.

When he had taken those books from Leah's father's flat, after the old man died, Aaron had vowed to himself that he would use them. He would find time to study Talmud, time to read. The old man had never found the time; he had been too busy scraping by with the pushcart. But he had kept the precious books, and now Aaron had them. He, too, had promised himself the time, and he hadn't kept his promise. He had said in those far-off days that he would be different from his own father, not always concerned only with money, money and business all the time. God knows his own father also had never been a scholar. So Aaron had promised himself he would take time for books, an old promise. An old promise, an old dream. A Jew's first duty, he had told himself, was to study. He had taken care of the business, he had taken care of Leah, he had taken care of the children, but he hadn't taken care of that promise, and there was still a little of that old sentiment in him to make him feel mildly guilty on a *Shabbos* afternoon.

Why did he remember Leah's father today, the poor peddler with the pushky? Until today he had forgotten sometimes for months, for years, about the promise to the books, but why today had he remembered?

Was it because of what that man Saperstein had said when he had been in the office yesterday? Saperstein had greedy little pig's eyes. There was something somehow unkosher about that man yesterday when he had pocketed the money that had made him no longer independent, made him now part of the larger Morgenstern enterprises. Saperstein had said something about making sure that the employees continued on the Jewish work week—Saturdays off for the *Shabbos* duties, he had said, as if Aaron Morgenstern had needed such things explained. Sundays Saperstein's men would work, he had assured his new boss, but not on Saturdays. Had Aaron come so far from his origins that men like Saperstein felt they had to tell him things about *Shabbos* duties? His use of Saperstein and his business would show that fool how wrong he had been.

Today, however, there was more to Aaron Morgenstern's worry than Saperstein's words, more than his own unfulfilled promise to the books. And that more was a large part of the feeling of guilt he did not want to name. Why should he feel guilty about it? he asked himself.

But the picture kept obtruding in his mind as he stared sightlessly at the books in his study. It was very simple, so simple that to a more experienced man it would have been banal—a picture of a little blond dish with a cute round bottom that beckoned for his hands, a little blond dish named Tina who had smiled at him with bewitching red lips, had leaned forward toward him at an angle that had made his head swim every night for the last two weeks when he had gone to the club on Fourteenth Street. Aaron had begun to dream of Tina far more than he dreamed of being a scholar, even more than he thought of business or buying out Saperstein. His dreams of her were commanding all his attention these days. The books on his shelves would continue to gather dust, his business colleagues would perhaps say more and more of the sorts of things that new man Saperstein had said, but the result of it all was what mattered. The result of the years of Aaron Morgenstern's rise was that at last he was powerful enough to taste those joys of which he had never even allowed himself to dream in the old days—the old days when he had married Leah, that pale girl who had been such a boring wife to him.

Aaron Morgenstern was deciding on this *Shabbos* afternoon that at last he was going to reap his rewards; he was going to take a mistress, and her cute little rump, her pert round breasts, all the joys of her body were going to be his. He could do it all, all that he had never before let himself dream. The business could be run, the household could be cared for by Leah, and he could enjoy himself as he had never enjoyed himself with his stolid lump of a wife, in a way that brought more than a smile.

He stopped smiling only when he thought of Leah—that monument of respectability in the Jewish community, that cosseted bitch who had mothered his children but with whom he would never have to couple again. He had used Leah for what she was good for, given her three children. But that was enough of her. He smiled again. He could have Tina instead. He had earned her.

Why else had he bought out that Saperstein and all the others, why else had he consolidated his manufacturing concerns under the organizational scheme run from his offices? It had not been for mere money, he knew that. It had been so that, undefeated, powerful, he could seek his pleasures in places of which his wife did not even know the existence. Tina's little squeals of delight when he had pinched her as she walked by him at the club, when she had sat on the arm of his chair after her dance was over—those were sounds he had never heard from Leah, sounds that would be magnified and that would reward him at last for his life. Now there was no way he could be defeated by the vicissitudes of the market or the demands of his work force, certainly not by anything Leah could say.

Books and study—what had he been thinking of? This very week, he promised himself, this very week he would set Tina up in her own flat. She might not even know to what uses she could be put, but he would show her. This very week he would have her, all of her delicious body, for his own delectation.

Good enough to eat, that was how he thought of

her. And thinking of her as delicious, Aaron let himself dream how he would someday cover all of her with whipped cream and then lick that cream off every inch of her. It was a fantasy that made his manhood rise as it had never risen when thinking of Leah, so that, unbuttoning his pants and feeling his hard penis, he looked with surprise from his lap to see himself still in his study at home, still surrounded by those old books. He had come far from dusty old books. What use were they?

But in thinking of his plans and his power, thinking of Tina, Aaron did not reckon with Leah. Leah had other plans, and Leah knew of other troubles that lay in wait for him.

But how, Leah asked herself each day, could she tell Aaron of these troubles? Or where had she failed? She knew full well that Aaron would look on what had happened as her failure, and she could not face him until she had somehow come to terms with it herself, organized her approach in her own mind. She was afraid of her husband.

It had all started for Leah the day she had taken the old clothes down to Hester Street to Nachman Garfinkel. If only she hadn't gone, perhaps she could have stopped it. No, she knew that was ridiculous. Because for her daughter Ethel it had obviously started before that day. It was just that that was the day on which Leah had found out that Ethel had been seeing the man. And it wasn't the first time, she now knew, that Ethel had seen him outside the house. She knew it wasn't. But she still didn't know when the first time had been. Was it irrelevant?

Again she brought her thoughts back to Ethel and asked herself where she had failed. She herself had been a good girl. She had married a rich man. He had become much richer. She had been devoted to her children, all of them, and she had been a good mother;

anyone would say she had been a good mother. She had given them everything money could buy— everything, at least, that Aaron's money could buy, and that was not inconsiderable. And she had maintained a beautiful home.

Hadn't Ethel grown up in a home where the Sabbath table was always covered with a lovely damask cloth, where silver candlesticks gleamed beneath the candles she had been taught to light every Friday night? Leah thought how she and Aaron had attended services regularly with the children at the reform temple Aaron had joined. True, the place had made her uncomfortable at first, but she had been determined not to be old-fashioned, and Aaron's business status demanded that they both maintain a certain social position within the community. The reform temple had offered the best opportunity to do that, and she had learned (not without difficulty, she admitted) to appreciate the abbreviated prayers in English, the sound of the organ, the choir singing foreign music. Since the children were brought up in it, the Reform Judaism of the temple was their only contact with the old faith, which (she and Aaron had discussed it) was probably just as well. But Ethel had gone to Sunday school there. Supposedly she had been taught about the importance of Judaism there. Where was the mistake?

It seemed to Leah that her questions only multiplied— leading to the worst: Why was Ethel, her favorite daughter, breaking her heart? How could she face Aaron with this news about his eldest child? How could she face the family? How could she face their friends, the other members of the temple? That the daughter of Aaron Morgenstern should be going about secretly with a Christian! It was still hard for Leah to formulate those words, even in her head, even though she had known it now for weeks.

She went back instead to the most difficult problem: How could she tell Aaron and still protect Ethel? He would be furious; he would blame her. He always blamed her for things that went wrong at home. Home was her province. He expected her to take care that nothing went wrong there. Their marriage was based on that kind of bargain.

And he would not be able to stop Ethel—not Ethel. In one way, Leah let herself reflect only briefly, Ethel was better than she, Leah, had been. Ethel did not let Aaron rule her completely, as Leah's father had ruled Leah. She had always had a will of iron, this first child of theirs, and Leah had made sure that she had always been indulged. Even Aaron could not stop Ethel, Leah hoped. He must see that young people did what they pleased these days, and there was nothing their elders could do to change it. Maybe even Aaron couldn't change it.

Ethel said she loved the man. Leah had once had a glimmer of what it might be like to love a man, long ago when she lived on Hester Street and Nachman Garfinkel had been her father's helper. She might have been young then, but she remembered it. Of course, her father had told her then, to forget love. She had obeyed him. Could Ethel be protected from such an order now? Leah wrung her hands, knowing her own lack of courage, bred from years of obedience.

And it was Aaron's fault more than hers. He had been the one who brought that young man home for dinner the first time, hadn't he? He had been the one who had introduced this whole possibility into their midst. And just because he had thought the new buyer for Bonwit's was such a go-getter! He had wanted a chance to talk to him, and since the young man had come to his office late in the afternoon, he had brought him home to dinner. Why hadn't he taken him out to one of those clubs or restaurants or whatever they were instead of bringing him home? It might never have happened if he'd only taken the young man to a restaurant.

Aaron's fault. But, she sighed, the result of Aaron's ironclad rule. If he was home rarely otherwise, Aaron was home each evening at seven o'clock for dinner. Who cared that he went out later in the evening? He had told Leah that his father, the one who had started the business, had always come home for dinner during his childhood, so he thought it was a worthwhile practice. Aaron did what his father did, and he said "It is a worthwhile practice" very often, Leah knew. His father still followed the practice, varying it since Aaron's mother had died only to come to their home on Sunday evenings and to Aaron's sister Jennie's home on Friday evenings for *Shabbos* dinner. Jennie lived close by her father and was more old-fashioned in her observances, so he went to her home for *Shabbos* dinner. Her husband was in the business, too.

Which would be worse to Aaron—Leah turned it over in her mind—the fact that he was not Jewish, this boy of Ethel's, or the fact that the girl had done it all in secret? Which would Aaron mind the most?

"Why didn't you tell me?" she had asked aloud, her first question to Ethel when she had finally found out the bitter truth.

"How could I tell you?" Ethel had countered. "You wouldn't have understood. You don't understand now." She had been crying even as she spoke.

"But we've always been so close," Leah wailed, herself in tears standing over her accused daughter. Why didn't Ethel know how much she hoped for her?

Ethel and Diana had looked at each other then, not at her. Diana had been sitting idly in the parlor as usual that day when Leah had finally accosted Ethel with the truth, which she had wormed out of one of the servants. Neither girl seemed to have the feeling that morning that they had, in fact, been close to her, and they seemed surprised to hear Leah say such a thing. Children never seemed to know how you felt.

"James is a business friend of Daddy's," insisted Ethel. "Why shouldn't I go out with him?"

"Why shouldn't you go out with him?" Leah remembered having sputtered. "Why shouldn't you?"

"Yes, why?" asked Ethel. She had stopped crying by then.

Leah had controlled her own rising hysteria in order to reply with the obvious answer. "Because he is not Jewish, that's why."

"Oh, so what?" Ethel had said. "What difference does that make?"

As Leah had fallen onto the velvet-covered sofa she had begun to have her real questions, the ones she still could not answer. How could her firstborn injure her in this way? Had her whole unhappy effort at life been somehow wrong? My God, she asked herself still, where did it go wrong? Haven't I given my children a Jewish upbringing? How could my daughter ask me such a thing—"What difference does it make?"

"This will kill me," she had moaned that first day. Then, practically as an afterthought, "This will kill your father."

"Don't you care about me at all?" Ethel had countered. "Don't you and Daddy care that James and I love each other, that we want to be married?"

"Married! Has it gone that far? And you didn't even tell me you were seeing the man! Love! Married!" Leah remembered how she had broken down completely at that point. "What am I going to say to your father?"

"James will talk to Daddy," Ethel had said, and Leah could tell that she was struggling to sound grown up. "That's the proper way to do it, he told me. James knows about the proper American way," she'd added with pride in her voice.

But that threat—that the young man would talk to Aaron—was what had finally pulled Leah up and made her face the crisis. "No, he won't," she had said, looking at Ethel till even she finally quailed. "I will talk to your father. If he has to hear such news, let me be there to break it to him, not some stranger. He should hear such a thing only from family. I warn you, Ethel, don't let that young man talk to your father." There was no way that some stranger's interference was going to threaten the whole carefully constructed fabric of her life, not ever. And, perhaps more important, it had now become clear to Leah that no stranger was going to hurt this child of hers, however mistaken she was. What did the man really want, coming among them like this? God alone knew what Aaron would do to Ethel if he heard this from a stranger.

"Yes, Mother," Ethel had finally had to say. Even lovely, impossible, stubborn Ethel had finally had to say "Yes, Mother." Despite her own fears, Leah still ached for Ethel when she thought of the tone of those words.

"It will be the death of him," Leah had told her daughter another day, referring to Aaron. Then she realized what she had said and had broken down that day, too. "Death, that's what it will be. You know that, don't you? We will have a dead daughter. Our oldest child—we'll mourn for you—we'll sit *shiva* for you, and you will never be mentioned in this house again." There were truths even Ethel would have to face. She would have to know the extent of what her father was capable of. Leah felt as if she was revealing a gigantic secret; she must now reveal Aaron to his daughter. It was the secret from which she had always wanted to protect her children.

"Mother, what are you talking about?" the girl had asked then.

"You don't even know the old ways," Leah said.

"You and your reform temple. When a child marries outside the faith, that child is dead, don't you even know that? The family sits *shiva*—mourns for seven days—in the home, with the mirrors all covered with black. Don't you remember when your grandmother died?"

Her voice had sounded like the tolling of a terrible bell in her own head, which still tolled every time she thought of what was to come when they faced Aaron. It had tolled for her in some ways since her wedding day. Was there any way to protect her daughters—at least Ethel—from a lifetime of its sound?

Diana had been utterly still that afternoon, looking from her sister to her mother.

"But Grandma was so old-fashioned—you and Daddy aren't like that," Ethel had insisted.

"You don't know your father," Leah whispered in reply. She could say no more.

Ethel and Diana had looked at each other. They hadn't spoken, but Leah could see from that look that Ethel had heard her words, but—true to form—had resolved against them, despite whatever fears she had. She had courage, that one. Diana had heard her words, but she would never do such a thing as Ethel contemplated. Diana was the kind of coward Leah had always been, she had to admit. Diana would even, perhaps, be Aaron's comfort in this trouble. Where was comfort for her? Would Ethel have to be dead to her now, after Aaron was told? Would all the mirrors be covered with black?

She had to develop a plan with which to deal with Aaron. Out of the whole course of her own life she had to salvage at least Ethel.

"I do everything around here, me and my sister," Tante Tillie snapped.

"My own hands are full as they can be! Stop complaining at me all the time." Unplanned, Shayna's words just tumbled out of her mouth.

"Wait till your poppa comes home" was Tillie's ominous threat at that. "He'll know how to deal with the way you lazy about."

And it was true that Poppa was harsher and stricter than ever these days. But Shayna felt her hands were indeed full. There was the washing, the scrubbing, the endless cleaning of floors and walls and sink and stove. There was shopping and bargaining for whatever they could afford for food. There was hauling it up to the fifth floor. Mostly there was planning when to do it all and what to do first and what to leave out because she was still in school in June and there were still mountains of homework as well as all the rest of it. Why did Tante Tillie always have to turn on her? It wasn't fair.

And Shayna missed her mamma—oh, how she missed her mamma. There was no one she could talk to now in the afternoons, no one to defend her, no one to remind her that she would be different, that she would finish school, no one to tell her that she could make something of herself. Heaven knew her aunts and her father didn't think so.

And the little ones! They missed Mamma also. David started to cry now in the other room, and she ran in and picked him up. Actually, though, he was such an easy little boy to care for. She sat him down on the floor (thank heaven she had just washed it!) and gave him a pot and a spoon to play with; he looked sadly around for only a little while; soon he was banging happily away. He left off to toddle to the door when Sophie and Harry came in from outdoors.

But Sophie had fallen and torn her dress, and Shayna knew with just one look at her that a flood of tears was lurking right behind her eyes, held in for the five flights of stairs but ready to erupt at the sight of Shayna. She distracted her quickly.

"Tante Tillie has made lovely noodles for soup, Sophie," she said.

"Don't think, just because you say something nice now, that I'll forget what you said before," whispered Tante Tillie at the same moment.

As she said that a memory suddenly came unbidden to Shayna's mind. She remembered the times that Mamma had praised Tante Tillie's cooking in front of the children. Had Mamma, too, bitten her lip while she listened to bitter words from Tillie, then turned around and said something nice? Mamma always said something nice. "I wonder if she thought the angry thoughts I think," said Shayna to herself. How did Mamma manage?

Then she shook her head with that quick gesture of Sarah's and cleared it. It came to her that Tante Tillie always spoke her bitterness and became more and more bitter as a result. Mamma must have felt angry and bitter, too, sometimes, but she never put it into words. Where was all Mamma's bitterness? Where could her own go? Sometimes it was ready, lying there in her stomach, to choke her with gall. Was that why Mamma had gone away?

Again she shook her head. Well, there wasn't time for it now. She made a mental note that she would have to get out a needle and thread later and sew up the tear in Sophie's skirt, mercifully forgotten now as the children gathered David into playing house with them.

## ❧ 4 ❧

*For precept must be upon precept,*
*precept upon precept;*
*line upon line, line upon line.*
*(Isaiah 28:10)*

Sophie"—Shayna interrupted the children's game—
"don't forget we have to get the milk. You and Harry
will have to go, because I haven't got time. You can
push David in the carriage and finish your game later."
Every week they got free milk from the Nathan Straus
Milk Station in Tompkins Square.

"Aren't you going to come with us, Shayna?" asked
Sophie, her eyes round. "How could we find it alone?"

"Oh, Sophie, you've got to grow up sometime. I
know it's a long walk to Fourteenth Street, but Poppa
and Yakov will be home before we know it, and their
supper must be ready." No matter how much help
the aunts were, how much cooking they did, this was
still her responsibility—to be sure the meal was on
the table when the men came in. Poppa often stopped
at *shul* on the way from work, and Yakov might not
even come (she never knew for sure these days), but
if she went for the milk, she just might not be home in
time. "No, I can't come today. You're big enough to
do it, you know the way," she encouraged Sophie.

For once, to Shayna's relief, Sophie was ready to cooperate. "Come on, then, let's start," she said, shrugging her shoulders. She scooped David up with more competence than usual and clattered bravely down the stairs, with Harry cheerfully following behind. Harry was not going to complain about an adventure if Sophie led the way and Shayna said they could go. He could tell Uncle Franz about it, he thought. Harry always saved up things to tell Uncle Franz.

Shayna calculated that they would be back just before Poppa got home. She'd have the supper all ready. The soup was on. There was still *hallah* left from *Shabbos*. She'd even been able to finish all her homework during study period today. It seemed that the teachers gave less homework now that the close of school approached with the end of June. Truth to tell, she admitted to herself, she had wanted some time alone; and, with Tante Tillie and Tante Sadie downstairs having a chat with their friend Mrs. Goldstein, she could sit down for a few minutes and read her book. (Work had been slow for Tante Tillie— she had been home two days this week—which always meant less money and more mean words.) It seemed such a long time since Shayna had had a few minutes without the children crowding around or the work to do or the aunts snipping at her, so her luxury was precious. She turned the first pages of the new book she'd borrowed from the library, *The Three Musketeers,* and D'Artagnan's arrival in Paris whisked her away from any thought of milk, children, or supper.

The eight Nathan Straus milk stations were scattered all over New York City, funded by the Jewish philanthropist who had decided that pasteurized milk was the answer to infant mortality, perhaps to all the diseases of the poor. The papers were always full of controversy about Mr. Straus's notions, and Poppa always read them articles from the *Times* about this milk station or that one opening or closing. But luckily, the one in Tompkins Square, which they had always frequented (located as it was at the edge of the part of town where so many of their old-country compatriots had settled), had not closed. Closer ones had, and Mamma always said it was just as well to keep going to the one they knew.

Now, by the time Sophie had gone only a few blocks she was feeling very important, walking along toward the milk station with Harry, the two of them pushing David in the old wooden carriage. They each held a side of the handle, and it bobbled along gently enough so that David nodded off to sleep, lulled by the motion even more than he was fascinated by the noise and activity around them.

Crowds pressed against the carriage, grownups hurrying back and forth through the street, on and off the sidewalk. The pushcart men they passed stood beside their loaded carts hawking their wares.

"Hats for sale! Find a nearly new hat to fit. Hats for *Shabbos,* hats for work, all kinds hats for sale," one sang out lustily. Sophie and Harry even stopped the carriage for a moment, and Sophie watched a woman try on a hat with a cloth bird on it as passersby fingered soft felt and inspected long feathers.

"Old clothes, buy your old clothes here, old clothes!" shouted another man by another loaded-down cart.

"Look, Harry, maybe that's the cart where Shayna bought the dress for Rachel. Remember the story she told us about the beautiful rich lady?"

Harry was busy with his own thoughts and didn't reply, but as they walked along Sophie's mind was full of that story again, and she mused on about the lady who had come with the automobile and handed over the dresses that Shayna had described. She couldn't remember the lady's name, if Shayna had ever told it to her, but Shayna was such a good storyteller that she could just see it all—she'd make her tell the story again, she decided. "Do you suppose she really did live here once, and do you suppose her father really did have a cart once on Hester Street? But how did she ever get an automobile on Hester Street?" (The streets seemed far too crowded for that.)

Still no reply from Harry, but Sophie didn't notice. Her imagination bounced up like a spring with the sight of the old-clothes cart and her memory of the rich-lady story, so she paid no attention as they passed the food vendors a little further along—the carts with old apples and spring cabbages, the carts with potatoes and carrots—filling nearly the whole middle of the street. People continued to push and shove by the children to buy things, and they shouted to each other as they went. The noise was nearly deafening between the roar of the voices, the honking of motor cars in the distance, and the clatter of horses and carts.

Still David continued to sleep, so Sophie was off in her own private dream, just putting one foot in front of the other. Maybe someday she could sit in the back of a beautiful automobile, driven by a chauffeur such as Shayna had described. Maybe some day she could have lovely clothes to give away.

Maybes, like Shayna had maybes. But not like Shayna's maybes.

Harry's dreams were different. At eight, Harry was more different than anyone in his family realized. Not that they realized much about him because, being good all the time, and smart besides, he was the child who had never commanded much of their attention. He comforted himself for their lack of interest, for being so near the end of a line of six children and yet not in the baby position, in a way none of the rest of them had ever thought of: He pretended he didn't belong to the Klugerman family at all, that instead he was really Tante Sadie's and Uncle Franz's little boy. They had no children, so Harry had reasoned it out that they must have at least one, and he loved them, so he was the one.

He thought about it a lot, what it would be like to live with them all the time and be their only child, how he would make Uncle Franz proud of him by doing so well in *heder* (Poppa never even seemed to notice how well he did), and how he would grow up to help Uncle Franz in his dry goods store. There was no way anyone could ever help Poppa with anything. Poppa didn't need help; Uncle Franz did. It was a small step in his dream to the idea that he really belonged with his uncle and aunt instead of where he had been put. Like if the angel who had brought him—Sophie said angels brought babies—had just made a little mistake about which branch of the family he was put with, putting him by mistake with the Klugermans instead of with Uncle Franz and Aunt Sadie.

Abruptly, scared a little by what he had been thinking, Harry came back from his reverie. He tried to get Sophie's attention, tugging at her. "Where are we, Sophie?" he asked. "I don't know where we are now, and we've been walking for so long my legs are tired."

Sophie stopped the carriage with a bump. "Let's sit a minute," she said, called back from her fantasy as well. When she looked around, to tell the truth she wasn't quite sure where she was either. She needed a few minutes to get her bearings.

As they had plodded along they had passed block after block of houses, all exactly like their own. All the houses were four or five or maybe six stories high. All the fire escapes in the front looked a lot the same, with wash hanging out on some, with children playing on others. There were pushcarts in every direction. There were little boys running and darting back and forth between the grownups, playing games. There were serious old men like Poppa with side curls and black hats, carrying books in their hands. There were mothers sitting on the stoops or on straight chairs in front of the tenements talking to one another, stopping their talk sometimes to call out for a little girl or a little boy, who would come reluctantly back and stand for a minute obediently on the stoop, only to dart back into the crowd the moment the mother turned to speak again to a neighbor.

All of a sudden, as she looked for a stoop to sit on, Sophie thought of her mamma. Where was Mamma? On remembered Thursdays, Mamma had been home, and Shayna and Rachel had gone to get the milk. Shayna and Rachel had sometimes taken her with them, it was true. But they were older; they knew the way to Tompkins Square. It was such a very long way, Sophie thought. And Mamma wasn't waiting at home at the end.

Now Mamma was gone, and Rachel with her. Even Shayna was busy all the time. So she, Sophie, had to find her way through all the forest of streets to Tompkins Square to get the milk, and she hadn't even remembered to feel sorry for herself yet as she had walked along. Now she felt sorry for herself for sure, because now she was lost.

Harry beside her was nearly in tears, and David would wake up soon, and where were they? She decided to shake her head to clear it, not knowing how much a part of the women of her family the gesture had become. She tried to think.

She ticked off the streets in her mind. Had she crossed Rivington Street? Or had that been Delancey? When she came to think of it, had she gone on straight, or had she turned anywhere? Was she heading toward the bridge, for goodness' sake? She realized then that she had just walked along, with Harry clutching the other side of the carriage, and she hadn't really thought what direction she was going. She could even have been going in circles, for all she knew! Now it was getting late, and she had better get her thinking cap on very quickly, or Shayna would begin to worry at home.

"Sophie, are we lost?" came Harry's tearful question at that very moment.

"Hush, and don't cry for nothing." She made her ten-year-old voice firm and important. "Of course we're lost for a minute, but I know how to find ourselves, so don't worry." Her own words gave her confidence—she couldn't cry herself if Harry was already about to cry—because she was the one in charge. All of a sudden, then, she *was* in charge; she knew she could find her way again. "It's not important that we don't know where we are right now, Harry," she said. "Because we'll just go to that corner and look at the signs, and they'll tell us where we are. Then I'll know how to go. Come on." She gave her brother a tug, and they both pushed the carriage to the corner. It was the corner of Houston and Clinton streets.

"We've gone out of our way," said Sophie, breathing a sigh of relief, "but only a little bit. So if we just cross here, we'll go up Avenue B and be on the right way. We can go home on Avenue A." Even though they must have wandered off their path some, the solution was plain. Sophie was surprised at herself. It seemed that she already carried a kind of map of New York in her head. She had always thought only grown-ups did things like that. Maybe growing up was going to be fun after all.

Harry's eyes were wide open as he looked at his sister. Where was weepy Sophie, the sister who was always crying?

"There, there, David," he said, reaching to tuck the little bit of blanket around the still sleeping baby.

He was no longer cold and afraid. He spoke to the little one to show that he, too, had an idea of where they were. The crowds might be thicker than ever now that the afternoon was wearing on, but Harry told himself that it was an adventure, and that they knew where they were. He could tell Uncle Franz about it next time he went to see him. It would be one more way to help him be Uncle Franz's little boy.

Shayna put *The Three Musketeers* down reluctantly and went to get out the dishes. She felt the beginnings of what must be housewifely pride, she thought. Tonight there would be more than just bread or protatoes. There was going to be lovely soup as well, with noodles in it. Soup was usually only for *Shabbos,* but today there was soup, and it was just a Thursday. She smiled about her remembered bargaining for the soup bone at Mr. Liebermann's butcher shop on the way home from school. Tante Tillie and Tante Sadie may have grumbled, but they had made the soup and the noodles. Now she "mustn't keep a working man waiting," in Mamma's words. Maybe two working men. Maybe Yakov would be home.

"Where are the little ones?" asked Tante Sadie, coming in from her chat with Mrs. Goldstein. "Haven't they come back yet? I have to get back to your uncle right after your supper, as you know." A look of annoyance creased her face. She was taking some of the soup home in a pot for Uncle Franz's supper. "I don't know why you sent the boys along anyway," she said. "Harry is too little for such a walk. And David!" She snorted.

Shayna didn't reply as she put the bowls on the neatly laid table, but she felt a little guilt mixed with her annoyance. What if . . . Still, Tante Sadie was always *kvetching* at her for not treating Harry right. You'd think he was something special the way she carried on about him. "Harry's so bright, you don't pay attention to Harry," she mimicked her aunt's voice in her mind. Now "Harry's too little to go for a walk." If Tante Sadie had her way, Shayna thought, Harry would just sit in the house and look at his Hebrew books all day, probably not even attend *heder,* so he wouldn't ever be out of someone's sight. Luckily, except for all his questions, Harry was nearly as easy as David for Shayna to take care of.

"Is our good soup going to be ruined because you sent those children out for the milk and they're still dawdling on the way?" asked Tante Tillie, drawn upstairs by the necessity of turning up the flame under the soup pot.

"When Poppa and Yakov come home, then we eat," said Shayna evenly. "The children will be home by then."

"Yes, Mrs. Rockefeller's assistant," said Tante Tillie with her sneer.

But even Shayna was a little surprised that they weren't home yet. Then she heard feet clattering up the stairs. "That will be the little ones now," she said. But she spoke with a question in her voice, and in a second she heard the door open on the fourth floor and knew that it was just Mr. Pincus who had come home from work. It wasn't Sophie and Harry and David.

Soon there were other sounds on the stairs, and this time the feet came up and up and up, past the fourth floor and to their own. "Now they're coming," she said.

But again it was not Sophie and Harry and David who came in when the door opened. It was Poppa. And behind him (tonight of all nights) was only Yakov.

Isaac looked tired as he came in the door, and his sisters rushed forward solicitously, one to take his coat, the other to hand him the *kappel* to replace his outdoor hat. After washing his hands he went to the table immediately and broke off a piece of bread

99

before he spoke or sat down. His lips mumbled the prayer over bread as he put some salt on the piece, and then he was ready to preside at dinner.

"Well, come to the table," he said, just as he did every night. He put salt on another piece of bread and at last looked around the room for the first time. Tante Sadie was staying for the meal, so she slipped into her seat while Tante Tillie ladled out the steaming broth, making sure that an extra portion of noodles went into Isaac's bowl. After all, he was her brother, and he was the poppa. Shayna sat down at the end of the table. But there were the empty chairs.

"So where are the others?" asked Isaac, his eyes on Shayna.

But Tante Tillie answered from over by the stove before Shayna had a chance to open her mouth. *"She"* —Tante Tillie pointed at Shayna with the ladle—"she sent them out for the milk, and they haven't come back. It was late for them to go, and now they're just taking their time to come back, good-for-nothing children."

"Oh, Poppa," said Shayna, and her eyes filled with tears she could not help. "We've been waiting and waiting. I did think they were old enough. Sophie has been with Rachel and me so many times, and I thought she could find the way. But now they must be lost. Maybe I did send them too late. And I guess I shouldn't have let them go without me." She stared at the soup in front of her, choked with responsibility and misery.

"Why did you have them go without you?" Isaac's voice was stern and harsh. "They will be punished for being late, and you . . ."

Tillie was already nodding her approval, but Tante Sadie seemed to hesitate before she smiled at Poppa. Shayna thought with resentment that Tante Sadie would probably find a way to save her precious Harry from punishment, especially if it was a beating with the strap.

"I want to hear your reason first," Poppa continued.

"She has no reason," burst out Tillie. "She makes all her plans just to suit herself, so she can sit and read those useless books all afternoon. That girl just suffers from too much schooling."

A frown appeared on Isaac's forehead at the mention of Shayna's reading, dark wrinkles below his skullcap. "Answer me yourself, Shayna. You are in charge of the children. Your mamma said you could manage them. If your sister and your brothers are gone, why did you send them? Why didn't you go with them? And have you been reading instead of taking care of the children?"

Shayna knew she had to look up from the soup bowl in front of her. She had to answer. Even if she was afraid of Poppa's frown, she had to answer. He had always been fair, she told herself, even if he was so harsh, so he would listen. "I stayed home because I wanted to be sure that supper was here for you and Yakov when you got home. Mamma always said it must be ready, that was a woman's job." She took a breath and went on to tell the rest of the truth. "Tante Sadie and Tante Tillie made the soup and the noodles, yes, but I did the rest." She hesitated. "And yes, I did read my book for a while, but then I got the supper." It sounded flimsy even to her own ears, knowing as she did that her aunts had done the cooking, and there had not been very much "getting" left for her. But it hadn't sounded flimsy in the afternoon. She searched for a distraction now. "Perhaps you should eat your soup, Poppa, before it gets cold. I know they'll be back soon. . . . At least I think I know it," she added under her breath.

The frown stayed. "All right," he decided, "I won't waste good food. They may be back soon, and then we will know why it has been such a long journey, I suppose, just to get the milk. Sit, Tillie"—he gestured to his sister—"sit and eat the good soup."

For a while the only noise in the room was a slurping of soup and a plopping of noodles. Shayna barely touched hers, however, because she was busy listening for that other sound—the sound of feet on the stairs. She glanced occasionally to the bedroom door, on the back of which, she knew, hung her father's strap. Even if it was her fault, she knew that Poppa would beat the little ones this time, maybe not even her, because they were the ones who were late, and she was in charge. It was just possible he wouldn't beat the one in charge, but . . . it was her responsibility to take care of the little ones, not just the meal, and the little ones weren't home. Where were they?

And then another thought came to her—Yakov was home for dinner, and he had not yet said a word against her. Shyly she looked up at him. She caught his glance, too, going toward the bedroom door, and he seemed to have a listening look in his eye, as if he wondered about Sophie and Harry and David. Or was he just remembering the strap himself? Yakov had been beaten many times over the years of his childhood. Poppa had certainly never been light on the strap with Yakov. They all expect me to be right all the time, thought Shayna resentfully, just because they expect me to have taken over for Mamma and always make the right decision. What if this time I didn't?

Finally, just as Isaac drained the final bit from his bowl, there was at last a clattering of feet on the stairs. At last the door opened, and at last the three children came rushing into the room.

"Where have you been?"

"What happened?"

"Where is the milk?"

"Harry, are you all right?" (From Tante Sadie, of course.)

"What took you so long?"

Shayna, Yakov, Tante Sadie, and Tante Tillie tumbled out their questions all at once.

But Isaac's voice rose above theirs. "Wash your hands and come to table," he said in his sternest voice. "Eat! Then we will see what you have to tell."

Sophie was the one who lifted David into his high chair after that, and then she and Harry sat down at their places without a word. Tante Tillie put the bowls of soup before them silently, glancing up at Isaac's set face after she did so. Then they ate. Everybody waited. It seemed to take a long time. There were potatoes after the soup. A very long time.

"I wasn't lost," said Sophie in a wobbly voice as she finally finished her last bite. "At least I wasn't lost for long, because I knew where I was."

"Sophie found our way," said Harry, done a moment later, his eyes and smile wide with pride in his sister. Maybe now his words would protect her. "We sat on a stoop, and she figured out to look at the sign on the corner, and then she knew the way. We put the milk bottle in the carriage with David, because it got so heavy to carry. Oh"—he yawned—"we walked a long way."

David, too, was already nodding to sleep.

"We will say grace now," said Isaac, as if he had not heard, and began the prayer after meals. When he finished he turned to his ten-year-old daughter. "And where is the milk now?"

Sophie's hand flew to her mouth. "Oh, Poppa, we left it in the carriage in the hall downstairs." Her face started to crumple into the tears familiar to all the family. "I knew I'd forget something."

Isaac rescued them momentarily from the prospect of Sophie's tears, however, with his next words. "You did well to find your way," he said, rare praise. "Now, though"—his frown reappeared—"go find the milk." He paused only momentarily. "And then it is the strap—for all of you."

Shayna, her stomach knotted, at last lifted her eyes from her place and looked her father full in the face.

She knew that pleading would be useless, even if Poppa was not being fair. They had not done anything wrong, except that they had lost their way. But Poppa cared the most that they had been late for supper, for which they must be punished. He probably didn't even care that they were safe. And she herself had only tried to do what was right. But she was responsible, and Poppa didn't believe in letting anyone off. The strap was waiting after all.

Absorbed at that moment by her own fear of the pain to come, Shayna did not see her aunts. At Isaac's words, Tillie, smiling, had turned her gaze to Sadie, but even she knew what would be in Sadie's mind at the mention of a beating with the strap.

Sadie is four years old and she is cold. It is the coldest winter anyone can remember—she heard the old people say it—but that doesn't help or hurt her, wrapped as she is in her own cold. Her small hands and feet ache; she sits hunched in front of the stove like a little old lady. Her sister Tillie comes in the door of the tiny hut with tears streaming down her red cheeks.

"Oh, Sadie," she says, "the fire is nearly out. Where's Mamma? How will she light the stove if there is no more fire?"

Sadie turns her face toward her older sister and shakes her head, wise beyond the possibility of only four years old. "I'm cold, Tillie," she says.

Tillie stands beside her, watching the last embers in the stove, and puts her arm around her small sister. "Mamma will bring some wood," she says. The wind whistles in through the cracks between the boards of the wall so that the ashes glow briefly.

It does not occur to either of the little girls that their father might bring warmth. He is off on one of his mysterious grown-up business trips. No one knows when he'll be back, and no one expects that it will help when he comes. He is, to the little girls, a large, furry shout of a man, and he will not warm them when he comes. They are afraid of his touch.

"Where's Isaac?" asks Sadie, speaking of their older brother. She can see her breath in the air with the question.

"He'll be home from *heder* soon," Tillie replies. "Don't worry, Sadie"—she tries to reassure her— "he'll find wood if Mamma hasn't." Isaac is already their warmest hope. They know too well the possibility that their mother will not help. Mamma is ill and weak herself—she is probably at their Tante Minnie's now, but she couldn't expect anything as big even as a stick of wood from her mean sister; even Tillie understands that. At least, she hopes, perhaps Mamma is beside that fire. Maybe she is warming herself at Tante Minnie's house. (Tillie secretly admires Tante Minnie, whose house is warm. She has learned already to admire and emulate mean Tante Minnie.) After Mamma warms herself by Tante Minnie's fire, maybe then she will go for wood before she comes home, Tillie reasons.

It is getting dark by the time Isaac enters the door. There are only a few glowing ashes left, and he can see his little sisters sitting as close to them as they can get, wrapped in ragged little coats, their little fingers sticking out of the holes in the only gloves they own, babushkas on their heads. They turn to him expectantly, but to no avail. He did not think to stop for wood, and now it is too late and too dark to go to the forest at the edge of the village to look for any. *Heder* lasts late on winter afternoons.

He aches to help them, though, because he is warmer than they are, and he is older, twelve years old, nearly *bar mitzvah*. He has to be the man of the family often now when their father is away. But how to warm them all on that cold winter afternoon?

"Come on," he responds to their expectant faces.

"It will be all right. We can all just get in the bed together until Mamma comes home. It will be warmer under the covers."

He is right, of course. The three children's bodies under the covers warm each other as they lie close together. Isaac is the warmest, so he lies in the middle and rubs the girls' arms and backs and legs. He makes a kind of game of it, and after a while they feel so much better. What heaven to be warm, to have a wonderful brother like Isaac to warm them.

At last, when Mamma does not come home and there is no supper, the three children fall asleep, their arms around one another. When their father comes home he finds them in the bed together. Mamma does not come home, not ever again.

She had been so tired, she had just lain down for a minute before she came in with the wood she had collected out beyond the last of the houses. (The wood must have been heavy, they all understood it was heavy, but later they couldn't understand why she hadn't fetched the children to come out and help her instead of tiring herself that way.) Anyway, Mamma had lain down next to that pile of sticks she was gathering to keep her stove warm, and on that cold night it had been too easy to fall asleep forever there, a black-coated blot on the clean snow beside the forest path.

No one found her till the next morning, when the whole village awakened to screams from the little hut. Reb Rasnowski's wife Malkah finally went over, because the children's screams went on so long. She found them cowering in a corner, with their raging father (she told everyone later that he was just a huge mad bull) standing over them and beating them with a large strap, beating and beating as if he had completely lost his reason, and shouting as he beat that they were sinners, perverted sinners to be in bed together, and he would scourge their sins from the world. The three terrified children were holding their hands in front of their faces, bleeding and screaming from the strap. It was a terrible sight, Malkah said, and the mother nowhere around.

Malkah ran home and got her husband, and he and several other men were finally able to pull the crazy man and his strap away from the children. It was only then that Malkah's son, sent to fetch the day's supply of wood, came rushing in with the tale of the dead woman near the edge of the forest.

Now, even in America, when Isaac just spoke of a strap, his sister Sadie was sick in his house. She left before he took it from behind the door. Shayna did not know the story behind her Tante Sadie's look; only Tante Tillie and her poppa knew. But each of the three had learned a different lesson from that terrible morning in that cold hut. What Sadie had learned was fear and loss and a desperate need to be safe. Tillie, on the other hand, had reinforced her knowledge of the rightness of mean Tante Minnie's ways, which kept one warm. And she had coupled this with a consuming adoration for her brother Isaac. But what Isaac had learned was that even in caring for his family he could fail, and he could be left alone. What did he know but to turn to the strap when the little ones were threatened? Of all of this Shayna understood nothing. All she could see was that her Tante Sadie went away and did not rescue anyone from the beating Isaac gave them.

Uptown, another daughter was preparing for a battle with her father. Ethel Morgenstern, despite all her money, started far back of the line from which Shayna Klugerman began. She was unused to defeat or discomfort, untouched by a strap. Even now, her mother knew, her father might not bring out the strap, but there could be worse things than the strap. For Ethel, it was perhaps most telling that her mother Leah was not Shayna's mother Sarah. She had been taught other lessons. The one her father would want her to learn was about how she must not feel what she felt.

Ethel was in love. She adored James Olson as only a first love is adored. Her lover was totally unsuitable, according to her mother, but that, she told herself, was so far just according to her mother. Perhaps Daddy would see it differently. True, Daddy had never been her champion in the past, but surely he could not think the way her mother had said he did. He must like James, she was sure of it, and then everything would be all right. After all, it was Daddy who had introduced her to James in the first place. It was only necessary now that Daddy be told about their love.

But that was the crux of the problem at the moment. Mother was going to tell him—perhaps soon—and Ethel had to inform James of that fact. About what her mother had said concerning James not being Jewish—that Ethel was not going to tell him. How to tell him about Mother's plan was her problem now.

"I spoke to my mother about us," she finally just said the words, looking at him with adoration over their teacups in the dining room of the Plaza Hotel. "I told her that we were in love, that we wanted to get married."

"Ethel!" James put down his teacup with such a bang that it clattered and splashed a little on the saucer. "I said that I would speak to your father when the time was right. It's too soon quite yet. . . ." He stopped speaking when he saw her look of consternation. "Not that it's not all true, my darling," he added in a tone that any woman with more experience than Ethel would have recognized as doubtful. "But is it really time yet to tell them?"

A waiter had come forward with the clatter of the

cup. He interrupted them, asking, "Is there something I can get you, sir?"

James had recovered himself. "No, thank you," he
said. "Unless . . ." He looked at Ethel.

"I don't want anything more," she said, her lips
trembling as she spoke.

The waiter retired, a barely noticed frock-coated
presence in that oak-paneled dining room with its
large windows looking out toward Central Park. There
were other sounds of clinking china as other couples
put down their teacups on other saucers. Their move-
ments were merely less abrupt than James's had been,
so that other waiters did not come over to them.

"James"—Ethel tried to keep the worry from her
voice—"have I done something wrong?" The last
thing she wanted was to betray her lack of sophistication to this beautiful, wonderful man.

"Of course not, my darling," he hastened to reassure her again. "It is just that I had thought we would
have more time before your parents or anyone needed
to know. I wanted more time while the way we felt
for each other"—he smiled, showing his even white
teeth—"was just our little secret—before the rest of
the world was brought in on it." He knew the dimple
in his chin showed to advantage when he smiled; he
had practiced the expression in the cracked mirror
over the bureau in his boarding-house room.

She smiled then, too, conquering her momentary
concern. She loved that dimple. "My mother and
father are not the rest of the world," she said then, as
cheerfully as she could. "They'll be glad for us—you'll
see."

James did not say to her that of course he did not
see. He was still working to plan a strategy that
would win over the parents of this silly young girl,
this suddenly available rich young girl who had appeared so fortuitously in his path. He must win them
over, he told himself, because Ethel Morgenstern was

the chance he had been looking for ever since he had come to New York. There were not many ways in which someone like James could meet a girl as rich as Ethel Morgenstern.

It was unfortunate that she was Jewish, and these Jews were hard nuts to crack, he knew that; but the possibilities that went with Ethel Morgenstern would make up for any difficulties. And salesmanship had always been one of James's strongest points. He would just continue to woo her, he had figured, and eventually, he thought, her parents would come around. He might convince even himself of his feelings for her. That was, perhaps, his saving grace. He could not see that there was anything to lose by continuing the affair, even if she had spoken to her mother already. Now things would be more out in the open, that was all. He told himself it would work out.

The Plaza was such a calm place that their discussion did not create any disturbance. Ethel let herself absorb the calm and trust that emanated from the quiet of the people around her and James's knowledge of what to do in circumstances she had never before encountered. She continued to look at him with innocence as they finished their tea. This was such an American place, she could tell herself, without any of the tensions that were part of her own background. And her parents had certainly never been to the Plaza.

Although she had never admitted it to herself, Ethel had always been a little embarrassed by her parents. It was not that they had Yiddish accents like her grandparents. It was just that there was a way they were still so tied to the Lower East Side. She couldn't put her finger on the way, but it embarrassed her. If they had left all that behind, why should it still have to tie her, too, so that she couldn't have James, whom she loved? Why must she have the pain with which her mother had threatened her? She would not have it.

Rachel was learning painfully about a world she had never known before. She was rarely alone, for instance, in what to her was a new world—the old country. There were always people around. Even when she went out on an errand to a shop or a neighbor's for her grandmother, Rachel was not alone; her Tante Chava or her cousins went with her always, wanting, they said, to show the little American the way through the streets of their world.

It was all very different from her imaginings of Mamma's stories, and too often it frightened her. She pushed her fears way back into her heart, however, and tried to be all that would please her mamma and her grandmother.

On the afternoon when she went with her cousins Blumeh and Nomi to buy the tea, she was beginning to succeed, she thought. It was such fun to have new cousins, dark-haired girls a few years older than she but about her height, with kerchiefs on their heads, who still skipped along the cobbled streets with her. She barely noticed what she thought of as their shyness. So what if when they came out of the Jewish section of the town toward the little shop at the edge of the square, that then Blumeh and Nomi stayed close to her side and kept their heads down, hurrying along?

"Want to race to the corner?" Rachel asked them, trying to jolly them back to their previous carefree ways. "Come on," she bragged, "I bet I can beat you."

"Not here." Nomi, the elder of the two, pulled at her sleeve.

"Just come quickly," said Blumeh. "Later," she added.

It was only then that Rachel saw the gang of boys

across the street and began to sense what could be the reason for her cousins' hurry.

"Dirty Jews, dirty Jews," the boys started to shout. They looked very big to Rachel. Big and threatening. She saw one of them actually pick up a stone as if he was about to throw it, but luckily they got to the shop at just that moment and hurried inside. It had happened so quickly that Rachel barely had time to be afraid at first.

And once they were safely indoors the girls said nothing about it. Nomi just politely asked the storekeeper for some tea. He handed the packet to her when she put the coins on the counter, then looked more closely at the three of them. He asked Nomi a question in rapid Hungarian and pointed to Rachel, who kept her eyes on her cousins, of a sudden afraid again.

"He wants to know if you're American," Blumeh whispered to her in Yiddish.

Rachel looked at the storekeeper in surprise as Nomi confirmed his guess. Was it all right to be American? How did she look American? How could he tell? Suddenly she felt very exposed in this place full of strangers.

At that moment one of the boys from outside swaggered in. He spoke to the storekeeper and pointed at the girls. Rachel caught the word "Jew" and turned to Nomi in sudden panic, but Nomi just shook her head quickly and kept her eyes down. The storekeeper was speaking curtly to the boy, and then he even held the door open for the three girls to leave the shop.

For a moment Rachel hung back, not knowing what to do. Neither inside nor outside seemed safe.

But Nomi pulled her along. "Don't worry," she said to her in Yiddish. "He told them not to behave badly to an American. They won't do anything now."

This time as Rachel followed her cousins she kept

her head down, too, and walked quickly in the same held-in way she'd seen them walk before. She did not breathe freely until the clattery cobbled streets gave way at last to the quiet dirt lane leading to her grand-mother's house. It was safe at Grandma's; she wanted to be safe.

Later she looked for comfort, not telling of her fears. "Grandma," she said, "Mamma always tells me stories, but it's the same stories over and over again. I want to know some different stories so when I go home I can tell Shayna. My sister Shayna loves stories," she confided. "She reads all the time." Sto-ries were safe; they were comforts.

Her grandmother smiled. "I don't know how to read," she said. "I wish I had learned, but I was not taught."

"Maybe that's why you have so many stories," said Rachel.

Always, while they talked, Grandma's hands were busy, except when she stopped knitting and dozed once in a while. Between the dozes her knitting nee-dles flew so fast they were blurred, so that Rachel almost couldn't see them. Already there was a sweater for little David, and the one for Harry was nearly complete. She had taught Rachel to knit in those short weeks, too, but Rachel was very slow at it. The needles seemed to stick together or bang into each other all the time when they weren't supposed to. Her first laborious casting on had to be done over four times, and Grandma Rivka had laughed one of her rare laughs at the three rows that had to be redone this morning.

"Why didn't your mamma teach you to knit?" she asked Rachel.

"I don't know," said Rachel. "Why didn't you, Mamma?" She turned to Sarah, standing by the stove pouring a glass of tea.

"I wanted to keep you good-tempered," laughed

Sarah. "I knew how you would feel while you learned; you were too good to waste on knitting."

Rivka smiled. It was a sensible answer, the kind of answer that reassured her that Sarah was really there; the same Sarah who had gone away all those years ago was the Sarah who had come home to her. Six children she may have had herself, but she was still the same Sarah, still sensible, still smiling.

Not six children, she reminded herself, letting the knitting fall briefly to her lap. Eight children. Dear God, why that for her Sarah?

"Tell me," she said then, forgetting Rachel there in the room, "tell me about the two children who died." She herself had so little time; she had to ask the questions now.

But this Sarah could not bear, and knew she could not. She missed all the children who were alive so much; it was more than she could bear to think of the two babies who had died.

Yet her mother waited, so she spoke as briefly and firmly as she could. "Tell Rachel a story now, Mamma. Why remember the sadness? They were babies. They died. But I have six strong children left (God grant they should be healthy). Never mind that time. Tell a story now."

Even you I cannot tell, Mamma. Even you.
I can't forget, I can't remember.
Pain I can't forget, terrible pain, and Isaac's eyes.
But I cannot remember what they looked like, those little ones. God help me, I cannot remember.
Could it have been God's punishment for my thoughts of another man?
It is all part of what I have come here to tell, and now I stand here with the pain and cannot tell it, even to you, Mamma. I miss my babies.

"Yes, Grandma," said Rachel, struggling with what seemed to her like twenty needles, each seven feet long, "quick, before I drop a stitch, tell a story." She looked up while her smile warmed the room.

Shayna found herself in the middle of what seemed to her a series of battles with her poppa. Then suddenly, when she announced that she would be singing in the chorus at the graduation concert, she was in the middle of something that might end in the strap. Not in the middle—at the end, because Poppa's mind was already made up, as usual. She had told him the chorus would be singing Haydn's Lord Nelson Mass.

"I won't let you sing, and that's final," he shouted.

"You can't just forbid me for no reason," Shayna found herself saying. She had learned at least to try to force him to state his reasons. "I'm thirteen years old. If I were a boy I would be *bar mitzvah* already. And Mamma . . ."

Luckily for Shayna, no one else in the family was home to hear the argument between them. The children were out playing in the last of the long late-June evening; Tante Tillie was sitting again on the stoop with her friend Mrs. Goldstein; Tante Sadie had gone home to Uncle Franz. Her aunts would have taken Poppa's part, of course. She didn't even bother to question why—she knew the answer to that, could just hear them in her head, talking the way they had talked ever since Mamma left:

"Why does a girl need to go to school for so long?"

"Shayna should be out of school."

"Shayna should be helping at home now that Sarah is out of the way."

"Isaac, we want to talk to you about Shayna's future. . . ."

She knew full well how much future she had if Tante Tillie and Tante Sadie had their way! It wasn't fair.

She could hardly believe her eyes now as tears began to stream down Poppa's cheeks. "Oh, Shayna,

how can you even be thinking of singing in a Catholic
Mass? You're Jewish. Why don't you simply know,
without being told, that a Jewish girl can't do that?"

"I'm no longer a child," she answered, still hotly.
"And it's not as if it's in a church; it's a school
concert." She tried to moderate her voice because
she had never seen him this way. Poppa weeping!
"Why can't I do it? It's only the chorus, not a solo."

"Chorus! Solo! Church, school! What difference
does that kind of thing make? You are a fool! How
can a daughter of mine be such a fool? Why don't you
know? When I was a child in the old country people
threw stones at me on Easter—those same Catholics,
those *goyim* whose music you want to sing! You
know about the pogroms, you know about *goyim*.
Oh, Shayna, it is because you are a Jew. How dare
you question it? That is enough reason, even in
America."

Nevertheless, to Shayna's surprise, he did not beat
her for the very thought of it. It seemed to her sometimes that he might try to beat her very thoughts out
of her, but, to her surprise, this time he didn't. Of
course, he did not let her sing in the Lord Nelson
Mass at the graduation concert; but she could comfort herself, she thought bitterly, that this time she
didn't get the strap.

If only she wasn't so alone. But in August, she
reminded herself, Mamma would be home. She could
look forward to that.

## ❧ 5 ❧

*And Abraham said ... I will speak.*
*(Genesis 18:27, 30)*

No," Poppa said, "no boats."

"Oh Poppa, please," begged Shayna. "Please let me go. Cassie's father and mother said they'd look after me. Please let me go. Just this once," she pleaded, "let me do something the other girls do."

Isaac looked at her hard. "No boats," he repeated.

Why wouldn't he let her go? It was only a Sunday outing with a group from the Educational Alliance. Mr. and Mrs. Rose were going to take Cassie and Mira, and they had extended an invitation through Cassie for Shayna to come, too. It sounded like heaven, a day on the river on a boat, mysterious and wonderful to be sailing on the cool Hudson through a summer breeze with such a group, all of whom were probably like the Roses. On the voyage they were to hear a lecture about "Religion and Science: The Meaning of Darwin's Theories for the Believer," but she hadn't told Poppa about that part of the program. She didn't talk to Poppa about scientists like Darwin. Poppa's scholarship, Shayna had already learned, had to do with the Law and the Prophets and commentaries about them. He read those books, he memorized

117

everything about them; he did not ask questions to which Darwin might have an answer, so she never talked about Darwin. Now what he was objecting to, of all things, was boats.

"Would you let me go if it was a walk or a train ride?" she reasoned.

He considered. Then he must have realized that he was considering in front of his daughter, and that wouldn't do. "No boats," he said again, but his position had weakened as far as Shayna was concerned.

"Mr. Rose said this is a boat with all the latest safety features," she pressed him. (Mr. Rose had taken her aside to advise her the last time she'd gone home with Cassie.) Usually she would not have dared to press, but this time she had a feeling that pressure might actually accomplish her end, and she wanted so desperately to go. "Mr. Rose told me to say to you that it was not at all like the *General Slocum.*" How had Mr. Rose known that Poppa would object, that she should mention that ship's disaster, which might be the root of his objection? "The *General Slocum* didn't have enough lifeboats or the right kind of life jackets, Mr. Rose says. That's why all those people died. Mr. Rose says that the people from the Educational Alliance have checked carefully about the safety measures on the *Susan and Bertha,* and everything is in order. Really, Poppa—they checked. Mr. Rose said so."

"More than a thousand people died on the *General Slocum,*" insisted Poppa.

"But this is different," Shayna reassured him.

"Different, different, it's always different for you," said Isaac impatiently. "I am tired of this Mr. Rose of yours." He hesitated, then went on. "And who is supposed to take care of the little ones while you go off on this boat trip?"

Shayna had a feeling then that she was winning, and she had her answer ready. "I know you'll be at work, Poppa, but I asked Tante Sadie if it would be all right if she took the little ones, and she said yes."

"Your Tante Tillie can't help her on a Sunday," insisted Isaac. "She also will be working on Sunday."

Tante Tillie, like Poppa and Yakov, worked for a boss that gave *Shabbos* off instead of Sundays, to accommodate the large Jewish majority in the sweat-shops. Anyway, Tante Tillie could never have been persuaded to say she'd take the children so Shayna could get away for the whole day. She hadn't been part of the answer.

"Yes, Poppa, I know," said Shayna, "but Tante Sadie said that even though Uncle Franz is open on Sundays, he wants to see the children. So she will be glad to have them home with her." Actually, Tante Sadie had taken a lot of persuading, because the only child she was really glad to have was Harry, and she had not wanted to take Sophie or little David, but in the end, in order to get Harry, she had capitulated and said she would take care of the others for the holiday as well. Holiday, she had said, for Shayna, but not for herself, with all the work she would have taking care of three children. And she had said a lot more, but she had at last given in, in order to get her precious Harry for one day, as Shayna had guessed that she would.

"Well," said Isaac, beginning to capitulate in turn, "if Sadie said it would be all right . . ."

"Yes, Poppa, she really did," said Shayna eagerly.

"I will let you go with this group for the day. But I want you home before dark, do you hear?" he insisted.

"Of course, Poppa. The boat is supposed to be home at four o'clock in the afternoon, so I will be home to see to supper. Really I will."

It was important that Poppa feel sure about the time. Ever since the disaster when the little ones were late with the milk, time had become the thing he insisted on with Shayna. Now she vowed to herself that nothing would keep her from having his supper on the table when he came in on Sunday evening. If Tante Sadie brought the little ones back late, after supper, that was her lookout, but Shayna herself would be back. She was not going to risk the strap again, and there was no reason there should be any trouble; Mr. Rose had told Cassie the schedule, Cassie had told her, and she would be able to be responsible at home.

"Thank you, Poppa," she said as he turned from her. She really was grateful, and it did not come too hard to say thank you to Poppa for this permission, even though most of her conversation with him did come hard. Poppa was not an easy man to talk to, and he was always so careful about his rules.

Like his rule about the extra chair at *Shabbos,* she thought. Poppa always said there must be an extra chair, an extra place at the table on *Shabbos,* in case there was an unexpected guest. After all, the prophet Elijah, who would herald the coming of the Messiah, might come disguised as a *Shabbos* guest to the door of any Jew. That was a lovely idea, but for Shayna it was ruined by the fact that Poppa had a rule for it. She always felt that Poppa would not welcome a stranger with fuss and delight, as one should welcome an unexpected guest, but would simply say to the prophet Elijah, standing there at the door of their fifth-floor flat at #40 Orchard Street, "Oh, yes, come to table, we have a rule for you." Why should Elijah choose such a place to bring his wondrous news? No, Poppa would be difficult even for the prophet Elijah to talk to, Shayna thought.

But what did she need to talk to Poppa for? Only to argue, it seemed. But Mamma would be home at the end of August, and Mamma also didn't talk to Poppa much. When she came home, Shayna could talk to her again. It was another way she and Mamma were alike. In the meantime, summer was here, she could talk to Cassie, and she was planning a riverboat trip on Sunday with the Rose family and no responsibilities, just fun. A whole lovely day of fun, just for herself.

Actually, that thought made Shayna feel a little guilty. She promised herself that in the summertime she would take the children for a special trip, too. Maybe she could take them for Sophie's birthday in July. Yes, she assuaged her brief guilt, that's what she would do—save a little from the grocery money and take the little ones somewhere for a day trip for Sophie's birthday so they could have some fun.

She lay in bed that night and thought about her own anticipated voyage. For once she didn't have to worry about the little ones. In the weeks since Mamma had left it would be her first long time without them. She let herself dream about how she'd spend the day.

In order to meet Cassie on Sunday morning on East Broadway so they could walk to the boat together, Shayna really had to move quickly. The working members of the family were off very early as usual, and she and the little ones were right behind them down the stairs. She had decided that there would be no slipups in the schedule today, so she would take them all the way to Tante Sadie's house on Avenue D, then come back to meet Cassie and go to the boat. In order to do it she fairly flew the carriage through the streets, with Sophie and Harry panting and running alongside her as she dodged the pushcarts and the people on the way.

"Slow down, Shayna, please," begged Sophie.

"Come on, Sophie, you can move faster if you want to," countered her hurrying sister. "Tante Sadie and Uncle Franz are waiting for you. We don't want to be late."

Harry, the one who really didn't want to be late, ran ahead as much as he ran beside the carriage and then doubled back. His dark hair was soon plastered to his head with sweat, and he was panting with delight as much as with exertion.

Not Sophie. Sophie liked to dream along at a sensible pace, and she thought this whole early-morning run wasn't for any goal she particularly wanted. "My feet hurt," she complained.

"What's your favorite thing in Uncle Franz's store?" Shayna was inspired to counter. Maybe if Sophie thought about a favorite thing at the end of the journey, she'd move faster. Shayna was not going to miss that boat if there was any inspiration that could prevent it.

"Embroidery thread," said Sophie immediately. She always had an immediate answer to what she wanted. "Maybe," she puffed, "Uncle Franz will let me pick out some skeins of thread. They're such lovely colors."

It had worked. "What do you want to make?" asked Shayna, relieved to have found the antidote to Sophie's dawdling. If Sophie would just want something, her sister knew she'd move to get it.

"I could make something for Mamma, for when she comes home," said Sophie. Mamma had taught her to embroider with cross-stitches, and she really enjoyed the work. Shayna had never learned, and not even Rachel was good at embroidery, so it was Sophie's special talent. She would make a special present for her mamma with it. When they finally arrived at Uncle Franz's store on Avenue D Sophie was actually smiling.

"What have you been running for?" Tante Sadie accosted them immediately. "Harry looks exhausted," she said, looking at him first. She turned to Shayna. "I'll bring them home at the end of the day, and it won't be running all the way," she said.

"Thank you, Tante Sadie," said Shayna hurriedly. "Hello goodbye, Uncle Franz," she called in the door to her uncle, who looked up in surprise from his ledger at the odd greeting.

But his face immediately began to smile when he saw his favorite nephew come past her into the store. "Hello, young man," he said to Harry.

He and Tante Sadie didn't even pay attention as Shayna ran off.

Sadie followed Harry in, pushing the carriage to one side and picking up David. She shook her head to her husband. "Shayna had them run all the way from Orchard Street," she said. "I don't know what that girl is thinking of. Not her duty to her brothers and sisters, that's clear."

"I'm the only sister at home now," spoke up Sophie, going up to Uncle Franz, "and I guess Shayna was in a hurry." She felt she had to be loyal to Shayna, at least a little. Duty done, she said then, "I love your store, Uncle Franz" by way of greeting.

Her uncle thought she was a pretty child to be so enthusiastic. "Look around, look around," he urged her. A merry man (at least until recent experience had confused his innate optimism), Franz naturally responded to her cheerfulness.

"Can I stay in the store with you this morning and help? Please, Uncle Franz," begged Harry in turn, and he knew the answer.

"Of course, young man, of course," said his uncle. He brushed the hair back from Harry's forehead. "I can use your help. We need to move the shirt collars today, because there is a new delivery of lace coming in—the jobber will bring it later."

"I'll put David to sleep in the back," said Sadie, "and then I'll be in to help." Actually, she knew her husband didn't need anyone this morning—there were no customers at the moment. But if Harry was going to be in the front of the store, she, too, wanted to be there.

Sophie wandered past the row of housedresses on a

rack, toward the notions on the rear of the counter. She loved going toward the back of the store, where the bolts of cloth stood. Here was the sheeting, and here the blankets were piled. It was the part of Uncle Franz's store that always smelled cozy to her.

"Why are there these funny letters on the price tags?" she asked, peering more closely at one on a shirt that had been left on the counter. "Why does it say SR here beside the price?"

"All the tags have letters," said Uncle Franz. "It's our code. Then when people come and bargain about the price, we know what something cost us, so we don't go too low. We can't afford to go below our costs, or we wouldn't make a profit."

"A code?" asked Harry, coming up to where Sophie was holding the tag in her hands. "What kind of a code?" A code sounded like an exciting idea.

Uncle Franz looked around. "Since there are no customers here, I'll tell you," he said. "We have a special code, *nacht geshir,* for the prices."

Sophie and Harry giggled. *Nacht geshir* was the Yiddish for "chamber pot."

Their uncle smiled. "We picked a phrase we could spell with ten different English letters in it. Each letter stands for a number. N is 1, A is 2, C is 3, H is 4, T is 5, G is 6, E is 7, S is 8 (we just leave out the second H), I is 9, and R is 0," he explained.

"So SR stands for eighty cents," said Sophie, who had been calculating.

"Yes," said Uncle Franz. "It helps to know how to spell the way we spell." His conspiratorial smile took them both into his confidence.

"Wow," said Harry, "it really is a secret code. How did you figure out to have a code, Uncle Franz?"

"All stores have codes," said Franz. "But they all have different ones. You've just never looked hard at the price tages before, so you've never noticed the little letters. I even did it in the old country."

As both children looked at him in admiration Franz thought to himself how little they knew about the old country, about all the world that had shaped him and their Tante Sadie, had even brought them together. To the children, he realized suddenly, he was probably quite old—to them he was, perhaps, elderly. It made him smile, remembering that he had once been a child who thought a man of thirty-five was an old man. And Sadie, of course, was younger than he. Did they think of her as old, too?

Sophie was standing now at the counter looking at the embroidery skeins and wishing, Franz could tell. "Do you think I should embroider a pillowcase for Mamma for when she comes home?" she asked aloud. Her uncle had stopped paying attention to her, however.

Sadie was off putting David down in the back where they lived behind the store, and Franz and Harry were absorbed in transferring the collars to a higher shelf so that when the lace came in it could be displayed more prominently.

When Sadie did come back, Harry was busy arranging some papers of pins next to the place where the lace was going to be. She watched him for a moment. Then she spoke to her husband. "Franz, that child is so tired; he is neglected at home. Even my brother Isaac pays so little mind to him."

"Sadie . . ." began Franz. He hated to see her start about Harry.

"I know he sends him to *heder,* which he didn't do with Yakov for long, but Yakov had no mind for it—there wasn't any sense in spending the money for his education. Yakov is only a troublemaker, a good-for-nothing. Harry," she insisted, "is special."

Franz had to agree. "He is very smart," he said.

"Sometimes I feel like I should just put a red *bendel* around all of him," said Sadie.

"Sadie," said Franz, "that is a ridiculous superstition—

125

protecting someone from the Evil One with a red ribbon. Remember, Harry has a mother and father of his own.''

"A mother!" Sadie said hotly. "Some mother—going away for months and leaving the children. And what about that baby I just put to sleep in there? Would any decent woman leave a little child like that? If I had children of my own—"

"But you don't," he said shortly. "You don't have any children of your own, and these are not your children." It was a discussion that could end only one way. "What Sarah and Isaac do with their children is their own business." In his distress he was speaking loudly enough now so that Harry heard him and came to stand beside him. He knew that they were talking about him.

"Sometimes I wish I was your little boy, Uncle Franz," he said.

Both his uncle and his aunt started. It was as if their own dearest wish had at last been spoken aloud, even though neither of them had ever admitted it to the other. They had always talked around it, talked about how Isaac and Sarah's children were treated, made veiled references to how they would do if they could do, and never actually said what they thought. Now Harry had said it. It leapt into the eyes of each of them as they looked over him at the other. If only they had a child . . . if only Harry was really their little boy . . . They both started with shame and guilt.

Franz denied the momentary dream. "You have parents of your own, Harry," he said firmly. "You are a good little boy, and you have your own mamma and poppa. Your Tante Sadie and I will have children of our own someday." He allowed himself to touch the child's head as he spoke. "Then you can come and tell them how to be good, too."

"But I want to come visit you always, Uncle Franz," insisted Harry. "Couldn't I stay with you for a while, at least while Mamma is away?'' It seemed to him that Mamma had been away for so very long already that it might be forever, and maybe he really could be the child he dreamed he was—living on Avenue D with Tante Sadie and Uncle Franz, an only child and beloved son.

Sophie came from her end of the counter. She had heard Harry, and she didn't want her younger brother to go anywhere without her. ''Harry, don't be silly,'' she said firmly. ''You can't stay here forever. We would need you at home, and you wouldn't be there. Besides, all your friends are on Orchard Street.''

Harry sighed. He did have friends on Orchard Street, but he so wished to be able to be Uncle Franz's little boy. Now maybe they didn't want him.

Tante Sadie had stood by quietly. Unexpectedly, she supported her husband and Sophie.

''You have to be a good brother, Harry. Sophie is right—you must stay at home.'' She cast her mind then for a way out of this suddenly feeling-laden talk. What did their mother do to distract the children? Then she remembered and spoke quickly. ''If you want, I'll tell you a story—the story of *my* brother, who is your poppa, when he was a little boy, and then you will learn what a good brother is.''

''That's a good idea,'' said Uncle Franz, also relieved to have the painful conversation come to an end. ''Go in the back with your Tante Sadie, both of you, and she'll tell you stories. I have business to get to.''

Both children loved stories, and no one had ever told them a story about Poppa, so they followed Tante Sadie willingly. It certainly seemed that she was different at home on Avenue D than when she was at their house. She even told stories.

On the way to the back, though, Sophie stopped again by the embroidery thread.

''Take three skeins, go ahead, pick them out,'' said

127

Uncle Franz impatiently. "And here is the cloth and a hoop for the embroidery."

"Could I have a needle, too, please?" asked Sophie in a smaller voice. She sensed the tension still in the air, and she didn't want Uncle Franz to be annoyed with her. But it would be such fun to embroider while she listened to Tante Sadie's story.

"Yes, of course," said Uncle Franz. He rummaged beneath the papers of pins that Harry had been arranging and handed her a needle that had an eye that was just large enough, but not too large. Mamma had taught her to separate the six strands of embroidery thread and use two at a time for most stitches, three if she had to make a heavier line, but that only very rarely. It was important to have a needle that would take two strands, but thin enough not to leave a large hole.

Sophie smiled her thanks to her uncle. He went back to his place behind the counter, thinking again that she was a pretty child with that blond hair, and when she smiled she was more like her mother than her father (her father that saint, according to Sadie). He knew how Sadie thought of her brother Isaac. And in all fairness, Franz sighed to himself, he had to admit that Isaac had been good to his sisters. Of their childhood in the old country Franz knew little, only that they had lived with an aunt—Sadie had said the aunt's name, Minnie, always with distaste—after their mother had died when Sadie was young. But he had been told often enough about how Isaac had come ahead of them to America, had saved the money to send for them, had brought them over as soon as he could, had provided a home for them when they came. Sadie would undoubtedly tell that story to Franz's niece and nephew. It was such a different story from Franz's own that he still wondered how he had become connected to the Klugerman family. Wondered, but knew. Knew, even, but did not understand, and felt always lonely when he thought of it all.

In the old country Franz Cantrovitz had been a peddler, and when he had come to America, what was more natural than that he should be a peddler in the new country as well? Back there he had peddled tin pots and all manner of household supplies—threads and cloth and shoelaces and knives—that might possibly sell from house to house in the poor villages through which he traveled. Mostly he sold to Jews; sometimes he sold to *goyim* as well, but poor people, nearly all of them. At first he had taken goods in trade, not sold only for cash, because who could afford even the small prices he charged? Trade, cash, it made little difference in those first years; he had what to eat, and sometimes a decent roof over his head. It was nobody's fault but his own that he wanted, always wanted something more.

In the houses where he went with his goods, sometimes tired housewives, exhausted from the vain effort to keep clean a tiny house and put bread in the mouths of too many children, would exact a price from the peddler, not only he from them. It was an easy price; they would sit him down and read him their latest letters from relatives in the Golden Land, talk to him while he rested his feet and drank a glass of tea, talk about the Golden Land. But it was the letters that changed his life, that focused Franz's desires. For gradually it was borne in on him that the listening was not really a price to pay, but in fact the letters could tell him of the something more he had always wanted. He listened and he learned.

He found that he wanted to go there, to America, to the Golden Land from which the letters came. It did not matter that some of them told of hardship and disappointment. Hardship and disappointment he understood, but he ignored such missives, really listening only to the message of the happy ones, the ones who made it sound as if the streets were literally paved with gold, as if it was really a place of dreams, the America of his most cherished visions.

Once he had seized on the idea he began to save. Oh, how he had saved! He ate only a crust, he haggled with renewed vigor, he squirreled away his hoarded coins in a tin box with a key that he kept always on a string around his neck. His customers found him harder than they ever remembered, always wanting to take cash, no longer willing to take items in trade. Cash, cash he insisted on, cash for the ship's ticket, for the ship to the Golden Land. He was a peddler with a purpose.

Never before a religious man, then Franz prayed three times a day, prayed as a good Jew, because he had what to pray for. He had wanted something more, he had found what it was that he wanted, now he was saving his money to get it. Prayer might help as well. He came to know the houses of prayer in all the villages on his route, but beautiful altar cloths, silver Torah decorations—all passed unseen before his eyes, which were closed in prayer—prayer for his goal, prayer that went beyond the prescribed ritual and cried out to God for his America.

Three years later, in that America at last, perhaps it was his habit of prayer, now firmly ingrained, that had finally married him off. What else could explain it? He had been a poor peddler in Hungary; though he was still poor, as God well knew, here he was a married man, the proprietor of his own shop, in an America that, if not the paved-with-golden-coins land of his dreams, was still, thanks be to God, America. So why didn't his prayers bring him children?

Prayer had brought him, in the first lonely, terrible months, to the small *shul* of the Hungarians who had come from his section of the old country. He had found his little comfort there, coming faithfully to make up the *minyan* every evening. He knew it was not necessary to pray in the *shul* in the evenings, but a *minyan* of ten men always was maintained in case (God forbid) there was someone saying the mourner's *kaddish,* someone who needed a *minyan.* Franz Cantrovitz always came to *minyan* on those cold days of his loneliness; it happened that Isaac Klugerman also came every evening, and it happened that Isaac Klugerman had an unmarried sister (two unmarried sisters, but Franz only learned that later).

Isaac had brought his sisters over from the old country, Isaac had even saved up a little dowry for one of them by the time he met Franz, and Isaac had been looking for a husband for the sister who was older—Tillie was her name. He had explained it all to Franz as they came out of prayers and walked along together. A peddler listens when a man with a dowried sister talks to him. He even walks a little out of his way to hear the brother of a sister with a dowry. And of course he accepts the invitation to supper to meet the unmarried sister on a Friday night.

Franz Cantrovitz did all that. He accepted Isaac's *Shabbos* dinner invitation. He sat in the empty chair at the *Shabbos* table. He ate Sarah's good chicken soup. But that was when he found that there were two sisters. He wanted the younger one, Sadie, not the elder, Tillie, who was not kind to her little nieces and nephews. He wanted a woman who liked children, because he liked children, and why else would one get married except to have children?

"Does your sister Sadie have a dowry, too?" he asked Isaac after dinner while Isaac walked as far as the corner with him. Franz wanted the dowry—he wanted finally to stop being a peddler with a pushcart; he wanted a store, and he needed the dowry money for the stock.

Perhaps taken aback by the directness of the question, Isaac answered, "It is best to marry off the elder first. She is not so old, still good for childbearing." He tried to bring the conversation back to an honorable beginning. "Are you interested in a wife, Cantrovitz?" he asked.

"I am interested in a wife," Franz replied carefully. "But I must be sensible about marrying."

"What could be more sensible than a woman with a dowry? Tillie is good as a worker, as you know, and she can take care of a home—she did so from the time when she was young, ever since my mother (may she rest in peace) died in the old country."

"Yes . . ." Franz hesitated. "But perhaps your sister who is younger might have the dowry if there is a man who is interested? Because then a man might be more interested," he added, again carefully.

As far as Franz could understand, of such a conversation (was it truly the result of prayer?) had come the dowry that had bought this store where he sat behind a counter in America, married now to Sadie Klugerman. But that conversation was five years ago, and there were still no little ones of his own—only those children of Isaac to cheer him as he grew older. He didn't understand how it had happened that he was here on Avenue D with a shop of his own and a wife of his own (and no children of his own). It was perhaps wrong to hate Isaac Klugerman. Hadn't Isaac been good to him?

"Did you like him?" Sadie had asked her sister Tillie after that long-ago *Shabbos* dinner.

"He was all right," said Tillie doubtfully. "But he isn't very tall. He isn't even as tall as I am."

It had been understood among them all that of course Mr. Cantrovitz had been brought to meet Tillie. She was the elder sister, the only one who would be considered in such a case.

"I didn't think he was very ambitious. And he is not a scholar," she added.

"He seemed tall enough to me," said Sadie. She looked down at her brown dress, nervously pleating a little with her hand. "You will have to marry someone. We can't stay here forever," she added, glancing at Sarah, who had just entered the room. It seemed to Sadie that if Tillie did not marry, her own turn might never come. She was then in her late twenties; she needed to marry.

"If only there was someone as tall as Isaac," said Tillie wistfully.

"Height isn't everything." It was Sarah who interrupted.

"Oh, you," Tillie said. "You only say that because you are married to a tall man like my brother. You do not seem to appreciate—"

"Tillie," Sadie said in warning, "I am sure that Isaac has other friends. Perhaps he will find one who is taller."

"You must tell him how you feel." Sarah was obviously being careful to be correct. "There is, after all, the dowry he has prepared and saved for. He would not want to give the money to a man you did not like."

Tillie didn't like Sarah's unspoken implication that the dowry was the most important consideration, not her own desires. And Sadie could tell that Tillie was angry when she spoke. "Why did Isaac marry *you* without a dowry? A dowry is natural for a good man to want."

"He married me without a dowry because we were both greenhorns," Sarah sighed, placating her. Isaac would be furious if he ever found his wife in an argument with his sisters. "Perhaps he would be wiser now. But I did not have a dowry as you do."

Tillie smiled at this reiteration of her own good fortune. "And he has begun to save for one for Sadie." She added fuel to the flame, coming to her sister's defense before any defense was called for.

Sadie continued to pleat her dress nervously. She felt as if the years stretched endlessly before her, years of arguments, years of endless piecework in another woman's house, years of another woman's children, never her own.

"Yes," said Sarah, "I know." She didn't say more, but Sadie could hear behind her words her unspoken complaint. We go without what to eat, Sarah must be saying to herself, so you can have your dowrys. Will there be enough money for Shayna and Rachel and Sophie when their turns come? a mother would ask herself, Sadie knew. But Sarah did not say it out loud. Sadie was sure she was right, though; they couldn't stay under this roof forever.

Later, when Isaac came in from his walk with Franz, he repeated the question Sadie had asked. "Well," he said to Tillie as soon as he had changed his hat, "did you like him?"

His inquiry had, of course, been expected by Tillie, and she considered it, looking at her brother. If she said that yes, she liked this Franz Cantrovitz, she would probably be married to him. Then she would move away from Isaac and his wife, as Sadie suggested, and live with that little man. Why was she always given such bitter choices? He was a poor peddler, but her dowry might make him able to open a store, true. But what would their lives come to? Only that she would live back of a store with this Franz Cantrovitz, who was short and not a scholar, and she would probably have lots of children. And never see Isaac.

Why had Isaac married? Surely he could have brought them over sooner if he hadn't wasted his money on marriage. It was the only deed of her brother's with which she had ever found fault. Why hadn't he waited for her to come to keep house for him in this new country? Now she had to work in the shop every day because Sarah was here to keep the house. Someday, Tillie even caught herself reasoning on occasion, someday Sarah will die (she knew, from her own experience, that mothers died), and I will keep house again. I will take care of Isaac again, as he took care of Sadie and me when we were little. She smiled a secret smile.

But Franz Cantrovitz? Did she want to marry Franz? Now the very thought made her ill. Of course she didn't want to marry him. Someday, she told herself, someday she would marry, perhaps, but she couldn't think of it now, when Isaac stood there before her. Not such a little man. "He is well enough," she replied carefully, not wanting in any way to denigrate the kindness of her brother in thinking of her, "but he is not very tall. I am afraid I am too tall for him."

Isaac looked at her sharply. "The height would make no difference if you felt he was the right husband. I don't want to force you to marry a man you do not want, tall or short." He bestowed one of his very rare smiles on his sister. "If you do not want him, we will say no more about it."

"Then," said Tillie, looking him in the eye as if there were no one else in the room, as if they two were all alone, "I do not want him. I will wait for a taller man." She smiled, too.

"I wonder," Isaac began again the next afternoon, after the *Shabbos* noon meal, "I wonder if he would really want to take the younger. . . ." He seemed to be speaking his thoughts out loud. "He is a good man, and pious, the kind of man I would want for my sister, but he needs a woman with a dowry." He turned to Sadie, sitting again and looking at her lap as she creased the pleat in her skirt between her fingers.

At that moment Tillie saw her own solution. If she pretended generosity and gave up the dowry to Sadie, then she would be rid of Sadie here in Isaac's house. She would be the only sister left.

Sadie did not look up. She colored, however, under

her brother's scrutiny, and thought about what he said. And she began to hope.

Later, when she married Franz, Sadie never told him any of her hopes. She never told him a word about her abiding desire to have children, to have a home of her own, to be a mamma who kept her house warm. To tell might mean to love, and it had never occurred to Sadie that she would love her husband. She loved her brother, she loved her sister, she loved her unborn children. (Why could they not be born into the world for the love she had waiting for them? She had to guard her love until they came.) Perhaps Franz did not really expect love anyway; he did not need to understand. And to love Franz was a thing of which Sadie was very much afraid. Perhaps she needed to be safe even from love.

When Shayna finally reached Cassie's house that breathless morning after dropping the children off at Avenue D, her friend was sitting out on the stoop waiting for her.

"Ooh, I'm glad you got here," Cassie said. "I was beginning to wonder if you'd make it."

Shayna flopped beside her, perspiration beaded on her forehead. She wiped her head absently with her sleeve. "Oh, what a day," she breathed. "I ran all the way, and I'm boiling."

"Come on in then for a minute," said Cassie. "Mamma will give you a glass of water before we go."

Shayna toiled after her gratefully. Mira met them as they entered the door, calling in to her parents, "Shayna's here, Shayna's here at last, so we can go now."

Mrs. Rose was putting the last of the food into the wicker picnic basket as Shayna entered the kitchen with Cassie, so it was Cassie who got the drink for her. Mrs. Rose looked as cool and unfussed as always. She had wrapped herself in a light wool shawl with a bright purple print to go out. "I'll need this on the boat, I expect," she said. "I suppose you girls wouldn't think of taking anything warm?" She asked it but smiled when they merely looked surprised.

To Shayna Mrs. Rose, as always, seemed like a varicolored mother bird, not exactly real. Besides, the girls, warm as they were, took the notion of extra warmth as simply another oddity of grownups. They certainly didn't want shawls on such a day.

Cassie's father called from the living room, "Are we finally ready, then?"

"Yes, Alec," said Mrs. Rose, going into that parlor and handing him the picnic basket. "You can put your books in here." She smiled. "I know you can't leave them, even for a day. Mira"—she turned to her youngest—"call your brother, and let's be on our way."

Shayna's knees turned to water. Was Ari coming with them for the day? She didn't know if she could bear such happiness. What must it be like for Cassie and Mira to have a brother like Ari, to take it for granted that he would come on a family outing with them, spend time with them whenever they or he pleased?

"Hello, Shayna," he said, seeing her as he came into the room.

"Oh, Ari," said her mother, "surely Shayna is old enough so you might call her Miss Klugerman now that she's in high school."

"Oh, Mamma," he mimicked her. "Surely I can call Cassie's best friend by her first name without giving offense."

The whole family turned to Shayna, who found herself blushing. A typical family discussion in the Rose household again, but this time it was, embarrassingly, centered on herself! None of them seemed to agree with the others about this or about anything, and luckily she didn't have to answer. She followed them down the stairs, having gulped her drink, to the sound of their voices arguing about whether or not she was "Miss Klugerman" yet, for goodness sake! It was a relief that they didn't wait for her opinion—she wouldn't have known what to say.

The *Susan and Bertha* was nearly full of holiday makers when they boarded, and all the families on the boat seemed to be busily talking and laughing in much the same way the Roses were doing. Gradually, as they had walked along, Shayna managed to get over her embarrassment about her name; and, realizing at last that nobody much was paying attention to her, she could just enjoy the delicious feeling of being there without responsibility.

For the rest of her life, she thought, she would remember that morning. She might even forget Cassie and her parents, but she would always remember this—what it was like to be walking along with Ari Rose, what it was like to board a boat with Ari Rose, what it was like to stand by the railing and look at the receding shoreline with Ari Rose. Salt air always would smell to Shayna like that day, because that was the day when she had first noticed its sour, garbagey scent, because she had first smelled that smell while standing next to Ari Rose, looking at the Statue of Liberty in the distance in this wonderful summer when she was thirteen-and-a-half-going-on-fourteen, on the *Susan and Bertha*'s river trip for the Educational Alliance. It was a day not to be forgotten.

"Have you ever been on the river before?" Ari asked. Cassie had gone off somewhere with Mira, and the two of them were somehow still standing by the railing.

"No," said Shayna. "But my mother has gone on a boat back to the old country," she volunteered, surprised to find herself even able to talk to him.

"Cassie told me," he said. He took a pipe out of

his pocket and put it in his mouth as Shayna watched. He struck a match on the railing, cupping the flame carefully in his hand as he brought it to the pipe, because the breeze was stiff. The boat was now fully on its way around the tip of Manhattan Island into the Hudson River, the Statue more and more visible. Several careful indrawn breaths later, the pipe adequately lit, Ari turned back to Shayna. "Have you ever seen the Statue of Liberty before?" he asked.

"Just in pictures," Shayna replied truthfully.

"Neither have I," he said. "I didn't expect it to move me so much, though, because I've seen those pictures so often." He really looked, to Shayna, the way she felt, choked with tears.

They stared at the great lady silently.

"My mamma told me how wonderful she looked when she came here," said Shayna. It was ungrammatical, but she knew that he would understand. "Even with Ellis Island still to come, my mother loved the Statue of Liberty."

"I wonder, though," reflected Ari, "if America really is the answer for the Jews." As always, he was questioning an idea. Shayna was enthralled as he went on. "I've been thinking more and more about Palestine."

"Palestine?"

"A homeland for the Jews in Palestine, like the Torah tells us we will return to one day."

"My poppa says that we mustn't think like that now. He says that we will go back to Jerusalem only when the Messiah comes on a white horse and rides through the golden gate into the city. In the meantime, he says, America is the best place in the world for the Jews. It certainly is better than the old country," she added.

"We were all brought up on that promise of the Messiah on a white horse," said Ari. "Yes, even I was," he went on, seeing Shayna's disbelief. It seemed impossible to her that Ari Rose, standing beside her and smoking his pipe as they talked, could possibly have been brought up on any of the same stories she had heard. He seemed to be out of a story himself, a bearded, pipe-smoking god of dreams with blue eyes and a beautiful way of simply leaning on a boat railing to look down at the passing river below. Surely he knew truths, not stories.

"I heard a rabbi talk the other day about Zionism," he said, "and he made it really sound possible. The return, I mean. The return to *Eretz Yisrael*. Hard, but possible."

"My poppa says—"

"Cassie told me that you and she went to a lecture by Miss Henrietta Szold one time," he interrupted her, "so I know that you've heard about it before."

Shayna was uncomfortable for a minute, remembering the afternoon in early spring, even before Mamma left (why was she dating everything in her mind by when Mamma left? It wasn't as if Mamma was dead; she was only away. . . . She was going to come back after all), when she and Cassie had gone to Miss Szold's lecture. When she had come home and told her mamma about it even Mamma had been scandalized. It was shortly after that her poppa had spoken about the Messiah coming on his white horse. She believed Poppa, didn't she?

Even Yakov had scoffed when she had talked that night about Miss Szold. He didn't exactly side with Poppa, of course, but he didn't agree with Shayna's interpretation of the lecture. How could she ever explain to Ari Rose about that? The discussions in the Rose family were so very different from what occurred around her own family table. At home she had told about going to a lecture; Mamma had gasped, Yakov had pooh-poohed, and Poppa had told them what it said in the Torah. (Or in the Prophets or somewhere. It didn't matter; he still told it, and it was

140

the Law.) Then there was no question any more about the truth, because Poppa always knew the truth, and that was that. And he had forbidden her to go any more to Zionist lectures or to waste her time on Zionist foolishness. Was talking to Ari Rose a disobedience to Poppa's injunctions? No, she rationalized, why should it be? She was not at a Zionist lecture; she wasn't wasting her time. All she was doing was listening to her best friend's brother tell her about things that interested him.

And talk they did, for the rest of that memorable morning, until Mrs. Rose found them and took them off to the bench where she had laid out their picnic of boiled eggs and lovely bread and butter. To Shayna's starry eyes the bread and butter from the Roses' house indeed looked lovely, and it tasted delicious. Especially because there was thick brown *lekvar* to spread on top, the prune butter that had always been only a very special treat in the Klugerman household, one she had only eaten a few times before. Here it was at a picnic!

"The lecture will take place shortly," said Mr. Rose, wiping the last crumbs from his mouth and stretching himself with satisfaction. "Really, on a day like this I can't believe anything those pessimists among our Russian friends say about the possibility of war. How could there be a war in a world this good?" He grinned at them all, willing them not to disagree.

Shayna did not know what he was talking about when he mentioned the possibility of war.

"I saw Mr. Morgenstern on board," he went on, changing the subject.

"Mr. Morgenstern?" Now Shayna's ears did prick up.

"Aaron Morgenstern is one of the major donors who support the work of the Educational Alliance," explained Mr. Rose. "He's a clothing manufacturer—that's where his money comes from."

"My brother says that the Jewish manufacturers are just as bad as the *goyim*—worse even, because they exploit their own people." Shayna found herself surprised at her own words.

"Is your brother a socialist, then?" asked Ari, smiling.

Shayna was confused. She hadn't intended to say anything at all, and she didn't really know what Ari's words meant exactly. Luckily, however, her confusion was covered by the interruption of a little girl who came toward their group ringing a bell, followed by a man announcing that the lecture was about to begin in the main saloon and urging all who wished to attend to find their seats in that room.

"I don't think I'll go," said Ari. "I have no real wish to hear another discourse on religion and science—it's the kind of thing I've heard before, I'm afraid."

Shayna and Cassie looked at him, impressed. The rest of them, except for Mira, were picking up the leftovers and stowing them away in the picnic basket.

"Well," said Cassie positively, "Shayna and I are curious, and we haven't heard it before, so we'd better get going and find our seats."

Shayna followed her friend with only a twinge of regret. The heady wine of her morning's talk was probably enough for the rest of her life, she thought. Besides which, if this was a topic about which Ari Rose had heard before, she wanted to find out what it was all about.

The ship's lounge was crowded, even though it was a "main saloon." It was not such a very big room for a crowd like this, because so many of the passengers had wanted to hear the lecture. She and Cassie sat down next to Mr. and Mrs. Rose just as the formalities began.

"Before today's speaker starts," said a short, clean-shaven man with glasses who had signaled for quiet, "I want to introduce to you the two people who have been most responsible for today's trip, Mr. and Mrs. Aaron Morgenstern."

The audience applauded politely as, behind him, a very well-dressed middle-aged couple stood and bowed. Mr. Morgenstern, stout in his dark business suit with the gold watch chain visible across his front, exuded the very essence of American success as it was envisaged by most of his audience. He spoke briefly, saying only that it was a privilege to share in the good works of the Educational Alliance, and that he looked forward to hearing the interesting lecture planned for the day. His wife, in a silk dress and broad hat, sat smiling beside him.

Shayna's eyes were bright with interest as she looked at them up there on the platform, because she was thinking that right that very minute she had on the flower from a dress that this very Mrs. Morgenstern had given the Garfinkels to sell. There she was again, Leah Morgenstern, the uptown lady.

"I have something to tell you later," she whispered to Cassie.

"Okay," Cassie nodded.

"Ssshhh," said Mr. Rose as the day's speaker was finally introduced.

It never occurred to Leah Morgenstern, sitting there on the platform, that some pale girl out in the audience could possibly know anything about her, could possibly feel some kinship with her because of a flower from a dress she had given Nachman Garfinkel. Now she composed her face into a listening look as she turned toward the speaker, even though she had no intention of listening to the speech. She had something serious to think about; she would let Aaron do the listening while she tried to organize her mind.

She glanced briefly at her husband. Here he was on

a Sunday, sitting with his stomach sticking out beneath that gold watch chain, not at work. But that was only because it was a kind of work for him to be here, too—part of his philanthropic activity, as he would have said in his pompous way. He would not be spending a Sunday with her or the children otherwise, because—he would say—of the pressures of business. Yet, she reminded herself, business was what she had always wanted him to care about, after all, what she herself had cared about. Beside the children, of course. Now with a possible threat to Ethel she had found this new strength to care about more.

Part of what nagged at her mind was that she was not totally sure that he was exclusively involved with the business these days. During the last week, for instance, Aaron had been out every night after dinner. She had tried to get him to stay home, she had told him there was something they must discuss, but he had gone out anyway. He had seemed to her subtly different, too, in a way she could not understand. Here she was, burdened with the difficult problem of protecting Ethel despite her *goyish* boyfriend, and she could not capture Aaron's attention even long enough to tell him about it. The most ridiculous part of his conduct, from Leah's point of view, had been that in some indefinable way he had looked happy, happier than she could remember. Somehow that worried her most of all. Why was Aaron happy?

But why, she asked herself, should she be worrying? She did not think it could be a woman; he'd never seemed very interested, thank God, in that side of marriage. It must be something to do with the business. That was all he had ever cared about, and each night when he went out he told her he was going to business. He was probably earning his money in some new way, and that was what was making him

144

happy. It did not matter—who but she and the children could be the beneficiaries of his happiness?

Soon, however, she must capture his attention, must tell him about Ethel. She was sure the girl was still sneaking out with that young man, no matter how closely Leah tried to keep tabs on her. Only Aaron would be able to put a stop to it. The big question was what would Aaron do? She would have to tell him soon. Whatever this new business concern, he would have to take one evening and listen to her, and it would have to be soon.

As the speaker finished Leah smiled and applauded.

Shayna's applause was more enthusiastic than that of the dignitaries at the front of the room, because she had really been listening to the lecture. The idea of rereading scripture—the Torah itself—in the light of Charles Darwin's discoveries! The idea that there might be a way to reconcile scientific knowledge with a modern interpretation of religion! Might there be a way then to know the things she had learned in school and still be a good Jew? She certainly could not tell Poppa what she had heard, but there was an uncomfortable part of her that needed to talk about it with someone.

She looked at Cassie sitting next to her, her eyes also glowing with the ideas behind them. Could she talk to Cassie? But what did Cassie think about the orthodoxy Shayna's family practiced? So busy with what she thought of the Roses, it was the first time Shayna had stopped to consider what the Roses, even Cassie, must think of the Klugermans as a family, the Klugermans with their set rules and ways. Did they think of her as pitiful and benighted because of her family's unscientific, unmodern life? Were they in some sense sorry for her? Shayna shrank inside at the thought. The afternoon's speaker, after the morning's talk with Ari, had filled her with questions, but she couldn't be sure that she wanted to talk to Cassie about her questions. She didn't want to hear even her best friend speak against Poppa's way, even though she herself might question it all.

As the boat pulled into the dock she stood aside from her hosts, her mind full of those questions, feeling very alone. It seemed that nothing was as simple as she had thought from her books. There were new questions every day, and she was alone with trying to find the answers. She hated being alone. But where could she turn to ask? Who in her family had ever thought the thoughts she thought? Certainly not Poppa; she dismissed that possibility. And yet she could not expose him by talking to Cassie about her disagreements (were they really that?) with Poppa. There were more and more things, she suddenly felt, looking at Ari, that she found it hard to talk to Cassie about. And the idea that Cassie might be her friend just because she felt sorry for her . . .

When she did part with the Roses it was with heartfelt thanks, however, because she wanted to be happy with her day, more than happy with the warm feeling in her as she watched them into their house and then walked the rest of the way home. And she felt grateful, when she arrived at #40 Orchard Street, that she was on time to make supper before Poppa got home; Mr. Rose had been right about the schedule for the day. She was tired, but she was on time. Maybe the rest would work out, too. Maybe.

But Poppa had not changed. The hard thing to learn was that Poppa did not change. And he was always going to be hard, Shayna thought.

After Sadie brought the children home that evening she did not linger. She was surprised at herself, but there was something that was pulling her home, and she went with the pull, back to Franz, without staying to talk to her brother. It was the first time that she could remember that she did not stay to see Isaac before she went home. Always before, the place where she had felt safest was in Isaac's house. Yet after her day with the children, tonight she wanted to be safe home with Franz.

Walking through the streets in the sunny June evening, she felt actually happy without understanding too well why that should be. She had taken care of the children, they had been good, Harry had even given her a quick hug before she'd left him, and Sophie had reached up and kissed her. Those were reasons to be happy, yes, but they could not explain the way she felt. It was as if during the past weeks of helping to care for them the children had melted an icy shield inside her, leaving her with the curious lightness of heart she felt as she went back to Franz that evening. Perhaps the oddest thing about her happiness was that she did not want to question it. She just wanted to breathe the softness in the air, to listen to the relative quiet of the streets, now echoing only with a few late-playing children, deserted at last by the pushkies that had crowded them until this hour. She just wanted to feel the way she felt without questioning for a change. Sadie felt young and free. Perhaps she had never felt that way before.

When she came in Franz put the CLOSED sign in the door of the store. She smiled at him because he said she was home sooner than he had expected. He seemed pleased.

"It's a lovely evening," she said. "We could sit for a little outside. We could put two chairs on the sidewalk." She had never suggested such a thing before.

He was obviously surprised, but he brought the chairs.

The store was on the east side of the avenue, so when they sat in front they could see the few clouds changing color over the buildings across the street as the sky gradually became a dark blue, then took on a pinkish tinge, finally even glowing orange before the sun sank completely. The buildings became black silhouettes against it as the world at last darkened. Sadie and Franz watched the close of the day without speaking, just sitting there next to each other in front of the store. She had never felt more content.

At last Franz spoke. "Come in, Sadie. You will be chilly if the breeze comes up."

For a second she wanted to stay outside, not to lose the last of the day in case her strange happiness should fade with the night, but then she stopped wanting that and wanted instead to follow him inside. Suddenly Franz seemed inexpressibly dear to her as he carried those chairs into the store and led her to their own flat in the back.

"Let's not turn on the light," Sadie said. "Let's just go to our room in the dark." She was shocked at her own words, but silently Franz took her hand to guide her around the furniture, and suddenly they were in their own room. It was mysterious to walk without any light. The whole evening was mysterious, but she had decided somewhere in her not to question the mystery.

They stood beside their beds in the dark, which was now complete, and Franz turned toward her and kissed her. Sadie was in his arms, just like the young girl she had felt herself to be this evening, and she did not question how she felt there and what she did next. She just put her arms around him and kissed him back, there in the dark.

"Oh, my God, Sadie," he said then, and his breath seemed to come in a new way as he ran his lips along her cheek but did not draw away from her. "I love you so," he said. "I want you so much." He had never said such words to her before.

Now for the first time in the years they had been married such words had lost their power to frighten Sadie. What he wanted, she found she wanted. Why question the melting in her heart? Why ask where it had come from? She did not question any of it, she only kissed him. And then she started to take off her clothes.

I love you, too, Franz, she whispered in her heart, but how he could have heard the whisper she did not know.

He must have heard the thought, she reasoned later, because he seemed to understand. Even as she fumbled with her buttons he helped her, kissing her all the time there in the dark and touching each of the parts of her that he released from her clothing until the two of them stood at last naked together, locked in a new embrace so that all of her skin could feel all of his warm skin against her. He was hairy in places where she was smooth, but that made him suddenly dearer to her, so that without thinking what she was doing she kissed his chest and his beard, and without thinking what she was doing she moaned with the pleasure of those kisses while he arched his back and thrust himself up at her.

Somehow they were on her bed then, touching each other all over with hands that raced over each other's bodies because they had never before felt the way they felt on that night. Always before Sadie had lain passive beneath him, always before it had been quickly over. That late June night, however, for the first time in their married lives, she and Franz really made love to each other—hands, then kisses on breasts, on hips, on places they would never even have thought to touch before that night—caught in a passion they did not question. Something happened to them there in the dark of that June night, and there was no questioning when he finally entered her, no questioning as she pulled his hips against her and wrapped her legs around him, moaning with the pleasure that she wanted, wanted so much that she actually shouted there in the dark when he brought her to a climax she had never before dreamt of, a climax he himself achieved just moments after, with her still shuddering beneath him while he kissed her deeply with his tongue inside her mouth as she had never dreamt he would.

It was then, as they lay there spent together in the dark, that Sadie said out loud what she had only whispered in her heart before. "Franz," she said, "I love you very much."

She did not question why she had finally said it out loud. Perhaps it was just that there was room in her heart for love that night. From such love, she thought briefly as she drifted into sleep with her arms around her husband, might even come a child. It was something she could no longer question there on such a night. She knew at last that it was not only necessary that she love her unborn children. She had always done that. The secret was that they must be born from love, from such a love as she had found on that dark June night together with this man in her arms.

## ❧ 6 ❧

*Behold, the nations are*
*as a drop of a bucket. (Isaiah 40:15)*

What's wrong with me? Shayna asked herself. The pain seemed to start in her stomach, then settle into her thighs, causing her to act very peculiarly. She had been walking back from her piano lesson with Mr. Nathan when it hit. First she saw Cassie across the street. Then, just as she was about to cross over and talk to her, she realized that the tall man walking with her was Ari. Just Cassie's brother, after all. So why hadn't she crossed the street? Why the pain? And why had she run into Mr. Sandowsky's shop and hidden herself behind the fat lady near the pickle barrel?

Why? Had Cassie seen her? How could she possibly explain her action? Why didn't she want to talk to Cassie? Was it just Ari who had scared her? Why should he? And why the pain? She panted behind the pickle barrel, unable to understand herself. Herself or anyone else. It seemed as if her whole life was questions, not answers. About so many things.

Like earlier today, when she had been playing the Czerny exercises, her piano teacher Mr. Nathan had been so abstracted. He even sat and read the *New*

*York Times* while she played. She apologized for her lack of practice. She explained that it was hard to find time to practice the piano now that her mother was gone. That last had finally brought his attention.

"Have you heard from your mother?" he asked abruptly.

"Not yet," Shayna said. Mr. Nathan was a friend of her parents, she knew, but he had never inquired that way for Mamma before. "We're looking for a letter any day now," she explained.

"Let me know if you hear," he said, glancing again at the paper. Then he put it down, but he was still peculiar. "I'm sorry I was impatient. Play the piece again, and we'll see what we can do."

Imagine a grownup who apologized when he was abrupt! Even Mr. Rose never apologized when he shouted around.

"Maybe you'd play it for me?" Shayna asked timidly. "If you play things, sometimes it helps."

"No," he said. "You try it once more, and then I'll show you. Work on getting the rhythm in the right hand more even. This will be a way to get in a little of that practicing you missed." He smiled, but it was as if he was smiling at someone else.

So she had played the piece through, but then it didn't seem that he was listening after all, because there was a long silence when she was done. He seemed to be looking at her, but she could tell that his mind was somewhere else. Really, Mr. Nathan was peculiar.

A knock at the door seemed to wake him up. He took the newspaper and put it away. "That'll be my next pupil," he said.

Shayna took up her music on cue and went to open the door. She always liked walking through Mr. Nathan's rooms and looking at the furniture, slipping her feet along the pretty patterned carpets. "Good-bye," she called as she let Lizzie Moskowitz in.

But oddly again, his reply came from right behind her. Usually he stayed in the piano room, didn't come to the door like that. "Good-bye," he said. "Remember to tell me if there's any word from your mother." He waved Lizzie in, but Shayna could feel his eyes on her, really on her this time, all the way down the hall.

Oh, well. Grownups.

Then, when she had seen Cassie and Ari and the pain had started, she had done such a peculiar thing herself, hiding. Now, as she tried to fade from view behind the pickle barrel the pain receded, and she was left without an explanation that made sense. Sour vinegar and dill, fat ladies pushing toward the counter, herself utterly unnerved —no sense at all. When she dared to look through the plate-glass window of the shop she saw no sign of Cassie or Ari, so she headed home alone with her miseries. When she arrived the letter was waiting.

The address was written in Rachel's perfect penmanship, there were funny foreign stamps on it, and the postmark was from her grandmother's town. Putting down her music, she tried to conjure up what it must look like, this town she had never seen, this house in it, the house of the grandmother Rivka she had never seen. But she could only shake her head; the romantic stories she had heard didn't fit with a faraway actual house where her mamma was tending a sick old real lady who was maybe dying.

She picked up the envelope and held it to her nose. Maybe it would have a little of the smell of Mamma about it. But no, it was just a letter with a papery smell, sort of dirty from all the places it had been, but there wasn't any smell of Mamma. Then she was angry at herself for thinking like that. What smell had she expected? Mamma always smelled of onion and garlic and kosher soap. Even when she squeezed a little lemon juice on her hands (if they had a lemon!)

or put salt on them to wash off the smell, she still smelled of onions and garlic. But not now, now she wouldn't—she probably wasn't cooking now, thought Shayna. Mamma was traveling now, so she wouldn't smell the same even if Shayna could be with her right close up.

Still fingering the unopened envelope, she tried, instead, to imagine how Mamma had looked—in her long skirt and coat, with a scarf around her neck and a hat on her head—as she had seen her last. But the picture in her mind was getting a little blurry; it was hard to think of it. She could barely remember anything except, with a sudden start of tears in her eyes, the scratchy feel of the coat when she had hugged her mamma good-bye, and the softness of Mamma's cheek.

Would her mother fade away now and not be remembered, just because she had gone to the old country for a visit? It was a scary thought. Shayna concentrated instead on remembering that Mamma would be back at the end of the summer—in August—and then everything would be exactly the same again. She would stick to the comforting thoughts, not the scary ones. What if . . . ?

Bravely, she put the letter back on the table. She couldn't open it because it was not addressed to her. The address was to the whole family, the Isaac Klugerman family, #40 Orchard Street, New York, New York, United States of America. It was certainly a long address. And Poppa would say when it should be opened. He was the head of the family. When he came home for supper he would say when they could open the envelope. There was no reason to be afraid, she comforted herself again as she picked up her book.

Later, when Isaac came in with Yakov, they were both talking at once and did not even see the letter on the table to which Shayna tried to direct their attention. Isaac put the *New York Times* right on top of it, covering it up, and said, "Look now what is in the paper."

They recognized the urgency in his voice, Shayna and Tante Tillie and Tante Sadie, noticed that he had not come in ready for dinner, and they peered at him. "What is it, Isaac? What has upset you?" asked Tillie, the first to speak.

"There will be bad times now in the old country, you mark my words. Now you will know to thank God we have come to America," he said. "Pray hard"—he turned to Shayna—"that your mother and sister come back to us soon."

Afraid suddenly, Shayna read the headline aloud. "Heir to Austria's throne is slain with his wife by a Bosnian youth to avenge seizure of his country." Was that what Mr. Nathan had been reading in the paper this afternoon during her piano lesson?

The women looked blankly at one another. "But what does it mean, Poppa? Has something happened to Mamma?"

"Nothing has happened to Mamma—yet," said Yakov, answering before his father, and he, too, sounded very troubled. "What it means is that the Archduke Francis Ferdinand has been shot in some little town in the old country. He and his wife. They were shot by a young man of the people, though, apparently a young man with progressive ideas," he added defensively, obviously wanting Poppa to hear what he said even more than to answer their questions.

"Yes, yes," said Isaac with impatience, "but it means much more than that. I will try to explain. The emperor of Austria-Hungary, Franz-Joseph, is a very old man—" he began.

"You must have learned in school that Austria-Hungary is a big empire, Shayna," interrupted Yakov again. "The village in the old country where Mamma and Rachel are staying is there—you know that much at least."

How odd, thought Shayna. It's always been just "the old country" to me. Maybe sometimes I knew it was Hungary, but I never connected it with the real places I learned about in geography, or with a real emperor.

"The man who was supposed to rule the empire after the emperor died—the heir to the throne"—Isaac pointed again to the headline—"has been killed by someone. Someone climbed up on the running board of the heir's automobile as he was driving in the street and shot him. And what it means is that there may be a war in the old country."

"Oh, no," said Shayna, voicing her thoughts aloud now, because now she understood why the men were so upset, maybe why Mr. Nathan had asked those questions about Mamma. If there was a war in the old country, then her mother and Rachel might be hurt.

"When will the war start? Didn't you see Mamma's letter here? Maybe it's about this same thing—where is it now?" She scrabbled under the newspaper, at last bringing the envelope forth triumphantly. "You can read it to us, and then you must write to Mamma and Rachel and tell them to come home right away, right now, not to wait till August to come home." Suddenly she was giving the orders. She looked frantically around again, ready to do something at once. "Where is a pencil and paper? How long will it take for a letter to get to them?" Her questions were a call for immediate action; she would delay only to listen to Poppa reading the letter, and then she would look in the drawer for a pencil and paper for him to write the reply.

"Shayna, Shayna, when will you learn to think first instead of always rushing to do first? I will decide what must be done, not you." Isaac was impatient and tired as he took the letter from her and prepared to deal with its contents. For a moment it seemed to

Shayna that she and Poppa might argue even in front of the rest of the family, even before the letter.

"Isaac," said Tante Tillie, roused to speak at last, "will there surely be a war in the old country now?"

"Tillie, I don't know 'surely.' But the paper says it is a possibility. The paper says that everybody in all of Europe has been affected. The German kaiser is very concerned as well, because he was a friend of this archduke who was shot, it says. He's worried that the Russians will be more powerful now, and the Russians are worried about the Germans, and the French are worried about them both. God knows what the English think! The important thing, Tillie, is that none of it is good for the Jews. And none of it points to peace."

"America, America—I thank God every day for America," said Tante Sadie like a prayer. She shook her head. "I remember what it was like in the old country. The dark forest . . ." she said, and she shuddered.

It struck Shayna, when she looked at her aunt, that even though Tante Sadie was talking about it, she seemed unconnected to the news, as if she was seeing another picture.

Sadie went on bitterly, "There was no *New York Times* in our village, was there, Tillie? Nothing there but fear, and maybe the cossacks, and nowhere to go to hide with no money."

"We would be there still—or maybe we would be dead already—if you hadn't sent for us, Isaac," Tillie said, turning to him. "I'll never forget that. Your wife was a fool to go back there. She should never have gone back."

But mention of Mamma had again brought Shayna to speech. "Read it, Poppa," she begged, pointing to the letter. "Please read it quick." Fear stabbed at her, different from the pain she'd had earlier. But in the midst of her fear she was grateful that at least her brother Yakov was there. He was older than she was. She was, thank God, not the eldest. Then she asked herself why Yakov's presence should matter so much to her—was he that much more grown up? How could he help get Poppa to do anything?

When Yakov arrived at the meeting that night the atmosphere was thick with smelly sweat, loud with political harangue as Meyer London's possible candidacy for Congress was discussed. No one was even mentioning the assassination of the archduke or the possibility of war.

"My God it's hot in here," he greeted Kalinsky. "It's even worse than my house, and I came away because I thought that it would be cooler. All they can talk about is this shooting, but they don't understand anything important about the implications of it."

"Take off your jacket and roll up your sleeves. I have cold tea to drink over by the sink." Kalinsky was solicitous, putting his arm around Yakov's shoulder as he guided him in that direction. But he, too, did not seem to want to talk about the possibility of war. Young as Yakov was, he knew that the fact that he had recently been put in charge of organizing a couple of the smaller shops—including Saperstein's, where he worked—had been a mark of attention. Maybe Kalinsky could see potential in him, whatever his gawky exterior. Yakov knew himself as specially marked for favor and felt that maybe Kalinsky was right and there were decisive moments ahead of him, times of leadership where he would not fail the Cause. He knew but did not know also that in a funny way Kalinsky had a liking for him. Well, he thought, putting that aside, what mattered was the Cause.

"There's someone new I want you to meet," Kalinsky went on, shepherding him across the room, away from the purely Party discussion. "She's here to find out what we're doing and coordinate it with the girls who work in some of the shirtwaist shops and aren't yet organized. Dora Schneider is her name. Even though she's only been in the movement for a short while, she understands the need for organization." He flattered Yakov as he motioned to someone in the corner. "Dora, come over here and meet Yakov Klugerman, who will know something about the problems you are having in a small shop with older people."

Yakov looked in the direction Kalinsky was pointing, and in doing so he saw Dora for the first time. She certainly didn't look like everyone else there. It was not just that there were rarely women at their meetings, but that this woman was different from the women he normally saw, mothers and sisters.

Her hair was bright orange and stood out in curls all around her head, not severely tied back, not covered with a modest kerchief. Indeed, there was nothing at all about Dora Schneider that brought the word "modesty" to mind, and yet she was no beauty in the way that Yakov had always thought of beauty before. He had entered his eighteenth year with a vision of beauty as dark hair, as lazy eyes looking provocatively from under long dark lashes. Beauty had meant undulating hips and a large bosom above a tiny waist. The only thing of beauty this apparition walking toward him seemed to possess was the tiny waist. But already, before she was halfway across the room, he realized that he would have to discard his old notions, redefine his categories. Immediately they were only the immature imaginings of the youth he had been before that warm summer evening.

Because that night he felt that he was not a youth anymore. Whoever she was, this Dora Schneider, she was the most beautiful woman he had ever seen, and he was suddenly a man who knew it. Her skin was very pale, and dotted with freckles. Only a fool would think that freckles were not desirable when he could see what freckles did for Dora. They added dots to the stark whiteness of the skin, they informed the color of the hair, they pointed up the sparkle of those green eyes.

Her arms were bare below the short sleeves of her low-necked blouse. The drawstring that held in the neckline covered not the large ample bosom of his imagination, but two well-outlined little apple-like breasts. He immediately found himself wondering what it would be like to take little bites out of them and was ashamed even as he stammered out his "How do you do, Miss Schneider," and felt her cool hand in his. He had not felt as happy and as stupid ever before in his life, not both at the same time.

She was very thin, and the gathered cotton skirt that fell to just above the floor had not far to go from her waist, it seemed to him, because she could not have been even five feet tall. He looked around in astonishment at the other people in the room, but they were all talking and shouting and sweating still as they had been when he entered. How come? How could they be the same? He was no longer the same; he was now on a different plane. He was no longer Yakov the organizer; he was Yakov the enchanted.

"How do you do, Mr. Klugerman?" she replied, and she looked up more than a foot, directly into his eyes. No glance through lowered lashes; no demure and modest gathering of a shawl about her shoulders. In fact, she took the shawl from her arm and threw it on a nearby chair. "It is certainly a hot night, isn't it?" she said as she did so, and the frankness of her look and the ease of her words disarmed him completely.

"Would you like some cold tea, Miss Schneider?" he asked, forgetting to be stupid and shy with someone who could look him in the eye even if she was a tiny thing.

"Yes, and please, let's sit down. I can't stand having to bend my neck up anymore to look at anybody. I wish I were six feet tall, but"—and she shook her head in mock sadness—"since I'm not, and you are, let's sit down to talk. I came this evening because I want to do what I can to amalgamate my little organization with the larger aspects of the movement," she continued, using the important words they had all recently been learning, "and I want to find out what's happening elsewhere, so I'll know where we fit in."

Yakov handed her the tea in a glass that had felt cool when he filled it at the sink but was already warm by the time he brought it across the room. "I work in a small shop, but we are trying to make sure that even the men—the people," he corrected himself, "in the little shops are part of the union now."

Soon—at least it seemed soon because she was so easy to talk to—he had told her all about his shop. He told her about his talks with Kalinsky and Edelmann and how he had learned about the Cause. He told her about how Saperstein, the boss, had reacted, and what the problems were with the new immigrants who would work for next to nothing so they could earn some money—problems she had, too.

He told her about his father, who didn't believe in the Cause, didn't believe in anything, it seemed, but strict observance of the Law according to the rabbis, who didn't understand any of the important values of social justice in this world, who only had legalistic quibbles about unimportant ancient sacrifices that no longer applied to the modern world. He told her about his feeling that there had to be a right way so that the workers would not starve, so that the man down the street from him would not starve, so that the rats would not bite little children, and so that they could all go to the mountains for a week in the summertime. He told her all the things he had thought could come in the future, all the ideals lying behind the bitterness of his manner, all the hopes he had somehow never told anyone else before, certainly no one in his family.

He told her because she listened. He felt that he could talk forever to those green listening eyes. The heat of the room, the smell of the sweaty workers after a long day, the noise of everyone else talking and arguing and planning, the frightening news of the possibility of war in the paper this afternoon—all of it ceased to matter to Yakov, who felt as if he were drowning in Dora's green eyes. At last there was someone he could talk to, someone who finally knew him for what he was—not for his rebellion, as his father did, not for his hesitant positions on Karl Marx as Kalinsky did, not for his bitterness as his sister too often did—no, Dora Schneider was listening to the real Yakov Klugerman, and he was cool and quiet and kind because she understood.

While she sat there and listened Dora saw a tall, thin young man with an earnest voice that warmed to his subject. He was clearly not going to mind the way she looked, which was a blessed relief. She was so tired of being judged for flyaway orange hair and bare arms, so tired of all the people who did not seem to be able to get beyond her skinny frame's inadequate shell to the reason for the flash they saw in the eyes. She dressed the way she did to draw attention in this world of convention to which she felt condemned. And here at last, she felt, was someone who understood— who understood injustice, who saw beyond the deliberate fence she had constructed around herself, who was in fact willing—no, eager—to join her in changing the world.

Her experience sitting for twelve hours a day in front of Yankelman's sewing machine, her fears about the wooden stairs and the terrible, stuffy, crowded room in which they worked—all were reflected in the eyes of this Yakov, and the terrible unfairness of it all was there as he talked, not just a plan for a world in some indefinite future, but a way to do something now, soon, because the future was too far ahead to be waited for.

She found herself talking to him, too, then, about the impossible demands the boss had made, and the way they had no time in the day for a meal if they were to sew the quota of clothes he had in mind for them. She even told Yakov about the way there was no toilet without passing the boss and having him pinch you on the way. She told him of her shame at the ignorance of her parents, people who could not read or write but lived, she felt, more like animals than human beings, never changing. She told him of their blunted acceptance of all the world she wanted to change, their utter stolidity in the face of that world's cuts. And Yakov listened, and his brown eyes looked from under dark brows with understanding.

She wanted to touch his arm then, noticing the dark hairs where his shirt cuff was rolled back from his wrist, wondering irrelevantly if those hairs were smooth or bristly. She couldn't understand her desire at first, because she had just met him, after all, he was a few years younger than she; surely it was their minds that were so very much in tune. Why then did her understanding seem to extend to her body—why did she feel as if she had gooseflesh on such a hot night?

Finally, when each had told the other about their work and the shops and their hopes, they looked around in a daze and saw that they were nearly alone in the room. Kalinsky was yawning as he came toward them, and Dora stood up and gathered her shawl about her precipitately.

"We have been talking," she said, and the light in her eyes seemed to dare Kalinsky to presume in any way. She didn't know why his look made her suddenly afraid. "Mr. Klugerman has told me a great deal about the work you are trying to do. Now I must go. Tomorrow is another long day."

"I'll walk you part of the way," said Yakov. "We

go in the same direction," he added, knowing already that it was of necessity the truth and wondering why he was excusing himself to Kalinsky. "Good night," he said quickly.

Kalinsky sighed as he gathered up the dirty glasses and watched them leave. It had been an extremely hot night, and he wasn't sure that much had been accomplished after all, but if they could get Schneider and her girls to come in with their group, maybe their efforts would gather momentum, maybe those above him would see his abilities. So he had probably been right to use an idealist like Yakov Klugerman for the bait. Yet he was worried as he watched the two of them go. He was worried, but he made himself put aside the worries, because they had to do with a part of himself he never thought of in any conscious way. He told himself that if he baited his hook with Yakov, and he snagged Dora, it was for the Cause, and nothing personal must interfere with the Cause, not ever.

Aaron Morgenstern had brought the paper home that day, but he had read it with only half his mind. He seemed to do everything with only half his mind at home, because what awaited him after his duty dinner with his family was all that mattered to him now. He barely glanced at Leah and the girls these evenings. He would leave them shortly, and he would catch the trolley car on Broadway (he was careful not to use his own automobile and driver) to ride down to the apartment where his mistress Tina was waiting for him. That was what mattered.

Nevertheless, the archduke's assassination and the banner headlines about the possibilities of war did engage half his mind, and even that half was enough for him to make some tentative plans he thought of during his trolley ride. (Leah had tried again to get him to stay home tonight—she said she had something to discuss with him. Was the woman already suspecting something? Luckily he could wave the paper at her and tell her that there was a meeting at the business to discuss the implications of the news.) He tried to while away the time on the car before he would be with Tina by thinking of what he might have said if there really had been such a meeting.

The obvious first step for a business like his if there was a war was to lower costs so that profits could be higher. (Even if there wasn't a war, that was always Aaron's first concern.) But there were even greater profits to be made, perhaps, if this war really happened. His shops manufactured garments. Soldiers' uniforms were garments. It would be necessary for many new soldiers to join the army if a war came, and they would all need uniforms. The Morgenstern concerns could make those uniforms, necessarily at lower costs than other firms, could underbid others and still make vast profits, especially if costs were brought down.

So what the possibility of war meant to Aaron was that wages must be lowered, not raised, in order to reduce costs as soon as possible so that he could take advantage of the coming opportunities for profit. His workers would have to conform to these new demanding circumstances. He smiled with satisfaction. Soon enough, if the United States became involved in a war, people would be pointing out that any threats of strikes to raise wages would be unpatriotic. And even though all this was only happening over in Europe, it could well be that the United States would get involved. He hoped so as he thought of the money to be made. It would at least be prudent to hold the line on wages in preparation for that eventuality. Anyway, it was always prudent to hold the line on wages, Aaron thought contentedly, and he stepped off the trolley to walk the rest of the way to the building where he had set Tina up.

That was the last thought he gave to the possibility of war that night. In a certain sense, Aaron Morgenstern was out of control of his life. In a certain sense—and he had not yet begun to be frightened by the fact of it—his infatuation with Tina had gained control, and he was turning into a fifty-year-old marionette whose strings were pulled by a former dancer with big breasts and a plump bottom, who was not stupid, as Aaron would one day learn if he ever tried to get rid of her. The strings she held were going to be made of steel by such a time; Tina would see to that. She was, in fact, the only person he had ever met who was more expert at using people than he was himself.

In Aaron Morgenstern's house the next day there was an unnamed tension that had nothing to do with the assassination of the Archduke Francis Ferdinand. Upstairs with her sister, Aaron's eldest child, Ethel, felt that tension, and it fed her determination. How could her parents really stop her, she asked herself, from marrying James? She would count on Daddy, she had determined, still not understanding her mother's wishes to protect her. Daddy had never stopped her before, and she wouldn't be stopped now. But she did feel the tension in her mother, and she gritted her teeth for the coming battle.

"Diana," she asked her sister, "what can I do? They want to ruin my whole life."

"How should I know?" Diana was trying on her new summer clothes one after the other, standing in front of the full-length mirror in their room. The sun streamed through the long windows, glowing on the pile of silks and cottons that lay draped over the love seat. "Hand me the georgette, would you?" she said, not turning around, but removing the shirtwaist she was wearing and preparing to slip on the lighter one.

"Di, please," begged Ethel, "please listen. I love

James Olson. I can't bear it if they won't let us get married." Diana had to listen.

"Love, pooh!" was all Diana said. She seemed to think there were more important things to think about. "An overblown infatuation, that's what it is," she went on, then she changed the subject. "I need to decide what I'm wearing to the tea dance on Thursday. Really, Ethel, you're so intense." She examined her mirror image carefully. "I think I should wear a lacier camisole under this one, don't you? Undergarments make all the difference in the warmer weather."

Ethel looked at her sister vaguely. Then she realized that if she concentrated and commented on the clothes now, she might eventually focus Diana's attention on herself. She had determined on a new plan, for which she needed Diana's cooperation. "Yes," she agreed. "The effect would be better with lace underneath. Why don't you try mine—the one I got Mary to fix for me? It has eyelet." Usually she hated to have Diana wear any of her things, but maybe her sister would be grateful and listen to her. Besides, Ethel wasn't really interested in camisoles, just in James Olson. Giving up a possession was minor in comparison to what really mattered to her.

"Thanks," said Diana, removing the new shirtwaist and the offending camisole. She stood half naked then, admiring her young breasts in the mirror. She jounced them up once, then leaned forward to look closely at herself. "Do you have any hairs on your nipples?" she asked her sister matter-of-factly.

Ethel had gone across the room to the bureau and opened the top drawer. She paused with the camisole in her hand, her back to Diana.

"I don't know what you can be talking about, really, Di," she said. "You have no modesty at all." She turned around and walked back across the plush carpet, keeping her eyes down so she wouldn't see her sister's body. She held out the camisole to her but still did not raise her eyes to Diana, who had turned toward her.

"You've always been a prude, Ethel," Diana said, laughing. "What's wrong with saying 'nipples'? Even men have them, you know." She put the camisole up in front of her to see its effect. "Even at summer camp you never got undressed in front of the other girls. What are you going to do with your precious James?"

"It's called modesty, not prudery," retorted Ethel. Let Diana think her a prude; she herself knew better. On that wonderful afternoon last week when she and James had gone back to his boarding-house room after tea they had been alone together, and that modesty of which she had spoken to her sister had given way, blissfully given way to the most beautiful melting feeling she had ever known, as if all of her had become a lovely lake, moving beneath the hand of her lover at first with little ripples, then in great deep whirlpools of drowning pleasure. She blushed at the memory, and at the feeling the very thought seemed to produce now between her legs.

"Besides," she insisted, sitting down again on the green velvet chair in the corner, "James loves me." He wouldn't have touched her that way if he hadn't loved her, would he? He had told her that he loved her just last Sunday afternoon.

Diana's back was to her, and Ethel had a glimpse in the mirror of high young breasts, full but not pendulous, as her sister slipped on the camisole. (From where she sat no hairs were visible. Diana must have been joking.) "James says he has always admired reserve in women," she continued, assuming the innocence her sister expected and that was indeed natural to her.

"Well, some men want a peek at something else, thank God," said Diana, buttoning the shirtwaist and admiring herself again. She smoothed the skirt over her hips. "There!" she said with satisfaction. "That's much better, see?" and she pirouetted before Ethel.

"It looks very nice," admitted Ethel.

"Do you really think so?" Diana asked, her eyes back on the mirror. She clearly was still not sure. "I wish I had rescued that silk flower from last year's lawn dress before Mother gave it away. It would go awfully well with this." Her mouth turned down at the corners momentarily, but then Ethel could see her catch herself as she turned back to her. Mother had always said that they must watch the expressions on their faces because they might freeze that way. (How could your expression freeze? Would it mean you turned into a statue, like that game they had played when they were children?) Diana even said a kind word. "Your James *is* very handsome," she ventured.

Here might be the opening for which she was waiting, thought Ethel as her eyes lit with pleasure. She smiled. "He is, isn't he?" she agreed.

Diana looked critically at her again, though. "You really look quite pretty when you smile like that, Ethel," she said. "Only you don't do it very much. You're always going around these days looking like some kind of a scared rabbit."

"Didn't you think it was scary the way Mother talked about disowning me, pretending as if I was dead?" countered Ethel. "And it's weeks since she said she'd tell Daddy about us—when will she get it over with?"

"Oh, don't worry so much," said Diana. "Daddy's never paid that much attention to us in his life; why should he go to the trouble of pretending that we were dead? Anyway, that sitting *shiva* she talked about would take him away from the business for seven whole days—he wouldn't do that," she went on. Diana was practical.

"He did it when Grandma died. Mother was right about that."

"Yes, but that was because Grandpa did it. But he won't do anything like that now, for heaven's sake! You're worrying a lot for nothing."

"Do you really think so? That's what James says, too." At last Ethel had Diana's full attention.

"Have you seen James again?" her sister asked. Clearly it seemed to her amazing that Ethel was continuing what she must think of as a ridiculous affair in the face of all the objections. But she should know that Ethel had always been brave. Yet in her own mind Ethel knew that her sister was surprised to find her so full of sticking power now, when the stakes appeared to be higher than ever before. Perhaps, Ethel thought, she could capitalize on the fact that Diana was interested in gambling even though she never took risks herself.

"I didn't see him," she lied carefully. "I wrote him a letter, and I had John take it downtown and deliver it after he dropped Daddy at business yesterday," explained Ethel.

"Wow!" Diana said, forgetting herself for the moment. She read novels, and the heroines of the novels did brave things like that. She herself never would; Diana knew that. What if someone had caught Ethel or read the letter? In the years of their growing up it had always seemed that Diana would have the lover, not Ethel. But the clandestine correspondence impressed her.

"But I have to see him. A letter isn't enough. I just have to see him," said Ethel, "before he speaks to Daddy and everything is ruined."

"Maybe everything won't be ruined, even if he gets to Daddy before Mother does," Diana offered.

"No," said Ethel in her most positive tone. "Mother will be really furious now if she doesn't get to tell Daddy. She's the one who might ruin everything. Oh, why can't they just leave me alone and let me marry the man I love?"

"Does he have any money?" Diana was practical again. Money had always been at the root of everything their parents had done; they had sensed its importance all their lives.

Now Ethel dismissed it. "Money? Who? James? I don't know," she said. "What difference would that make? I'll have money. And he has a good job," she added in his defense. "He's a buyer for Bonwit's, and he's sure to rise. That's why Daddy brought him here in the first place."

Diana looked critically at her, perhaps seeing (it made Ethel squirm) a self she refused to look at. Ethel could tell that in Diana's eyes she might be adventurous, but she was still a little too plump, not attractive in any conventional way. And she didn't pay enough attention to clothes. And Diana was right that James had no money.

Diana took a firm tone. "Ethel," she said, "maybe you ought to be cautious about this. Maybe he's just marrying you for your money. Mother always has such awful tales to tell about men who are fortune hunters," she added in her most self-righteous way.

"Oh, Mother was a fortune hunter herself, if you remember." Ethel was irritated by the turn the conversation was taking and wanted to get it back on track. "She didn't have anything when she married Daddy. You remember her stories about Grandpa's pushcart? We were supposed to laugh at how funny it all was, and we were supposed to think how romantic she was, but when you really think about it, she was just a poor girl downtown with no money, and she was lucky enough to marry a rich man. Anyway, that has nothing to do with James and me," she insisted. "Nothing at all." Really, Diana had it all wrong. She never seemed to have any pluck. "James and I love each other, and we're going to be married. It's not at all like Mother and Daddy." Had Daddy ever touched

171

Mother like James had touched her? Had Mother ever felt the way she felt? It was inconceivable.

"You won't be married if Daddy says no," Diana countered, "and he'll say no if your James hasn't got any money, Jewish or not."

"But why should Jewish matter so much?"

"I don't know about that part," her sister replied. "They never seem to have thought it mattered so much in the past. But the money will matter—you'll see—and they'll cover it up with the Jewish business."

"Do you ever wish you weren't Jewish?" demanded Ethel. "I surely do. I wish I weren't Jewish, and I wish I were poor, and I don't see why Mother and Daddy won't let me marry James."

"Oh, well," said Diana, losing interest and turning back to the mirror. Those were not her wishes. "I don't know what I can do about it anyway."

Here was as much of an opening as Ethel could hope for. "Actually," she said, raising her eyes to meet her sister's in the mirror, "there is something, Di. I'm going to write another note to James, so John can take it tomorrow morning. I'm going to suggest a place for us to meet. I've thought and thought about it, and if you and I were to encounter him by chance while we were downtown doing some shopping in the afternoon—I mean you and I together—even if people saw us, who could object? Will you help me?"

"Help you?"

"All you have to do is come shopping with me. Tomorrow is the day Mother goes to visit Aunt Jennie, so she won't be able to come shopping, and the two of us could go alone. Then when James meets us you could just find something you had to look at in another part of the store for a while, couldn't you?" At last she had stated her plan, and it sounded workable, even to her own ears. Since last week—she must have suspected something, or one of the servants must have told—her mother had not let her out of the house. "Please, Di?"

"I might do it," said Diana, concentrating still on the mirror. "By the way"—she was trying to make it sound casual— "do you think your brown faille skirt would look good with this?" She whirled then and faced Ethel.

It was a test, and Ethel knew it. "Yes," she said, meeting her sister's eyes. "Actually, I think it looks better on you than on me. Why don't you just take it for yourself?"

"Take what?" came their mother's voice as she walked in the door. She never knocked at doors.

"Oh, Ethel's been a sweetie and given me her brown faille," answered Diana. "But Mother," she went on, "don't you think it would be fun if John drove us downtown tomorrow afternoon so we could look for something for Ethel to replace it? We'll be going to Jersey soon, and . . ."

"Well," Leah began, "I don't know about tomorrow. I have to go to Aunt Jennie's tomorrow."

"Oh, please, Mother," cooed Diana. "Just this once let us brave the stores on our own. Ethel's been so nice to me, and I want to help her pick out something. We're old enough."

It worked.

"All right," Leah consented, "I'll arrange for John to take you in the car. You can drop me at Aunt Jennie's on the way. And about that other matter, Ethel," she added, looking at her daughter, "if you're still thinking about it . . ." She hesitated, but Ethel didn't stop her. "I'm going to talk to your father this evening. His temple board meeting has been canceled, so I know he'll be home tonight. He's been so busy lately."

Ethel's stomach seemed to rise in her throat, and she felt momentarily faint. Nevertheless, she didn't lower her gaze. If only she could see James before tomorrow! If necessary, she vowed to herself, they'd simply run away together when they did meet. Her parents couldn't stop her. She counted on James's love no matter what, no matter what her father said.

At last, Leah thought as she left her daughters, her girls were behaving the way sisters should, not bickering all the time the way they used to. They looked so pretty there together among the heaps of clothes—maybe she should arrange to have their portraits painted. Mrs. Loeb had told her at the Sisterhood meeting that she was having her girls done in pastel. Maybe Ethel and Diana could be done in oil. With little Norman, too, of course. Well, perhaps, she reasoned, since they were being so nice, she was right to let them go off shopping on their own. Anything to distract Ethel, who still seemed to be stubborn.

This evening, at last, she would talk to Aaron about the girl and this frightening romance. If only her courage didn't desert her. Clearly Ethel didn't understand how she was trying to find a way to protect her. The child might as well have a shopping trip to comfort her after her father's wrath descended upon her, because descend it would—no matter how Leah put it to him. There might be no more talk about marriage then; she was afraid that was true. Aaron would see to it. Why couldn't she save Ethel, she thought yet again, wringing her hands.

"Aaron, I must speak to you," she said to him as they readied themselves for dinner. He was in his study, as she knew he would be, and she had walked in without knocking.

"I have to go out this evening—" he started to say, putting her off.

"No, you don't," she insisted. "Not tonight. Your meeting has been canceled. And I must talk to you."

He sighed and looked around like a cornered animal, but he gave her his attention.

Maybe it was that open display of how he wished to be far from her that made her abandon any subtlety when she talked to him. Whatever it was, in her search for courage she told him the whole thing so suddenly that all he was able to do at first was stare. But then, when he had caught his breath, he shouted at her his shock and disbelief.

And with his shouting they were immediately in the midst of a fight. Leah thought afterward that she would always remember the explosion of his "No!" which, even though she had expected it, had startled her by its vehemence.

"Not no," Leah said, in a milder tone than she would have thought herself capable of in such circumstances, "yes." She kept her voice down in the vain hope that the servants would not hear. She felt her courage melting as she faced him. "I cannot help it, but it is the truth," she added, beginning to know, surely and with despair, that there was indeed no way to protect Ethel. "I wouldn't tell you such a thing if it were not so." And then she repeated it, because in a way he did not seem to understand. "Ethel is in love with a *goy,*" she said again. "That is the truth. I wish it weren't so, but it is." She sat down in a leather chair and prayed for him to speak as if he cared.

But he shouted again. "You undeserving bitch! I've devoted my whole life to you and those children, and now you have the nerve to saddle me with this as well! First you bear me those two damn daughters, and then, finally, after you at last produce a son, you still give me trouble over your girls."

She merely looked at him, not knowing what to say next. It was worse than she had feared.

"Love!" he shouted then. "Love!"

If she had been a more thoughtful person, Leah would have wondered why it was the idea of Ethel's being in love that seemed to cause the worst explosion. She hadn't yet told him that they planned to be married. It was as if love was the thing his daughter should not be allowed to have, the thing he would not give her. But Leah was not so understanding, so she simply kept on staring at him. She had known he wouldn't take the news well, had known his anger would be directed at her, she told herself, feeling nausea rising in her throat.

All those years, he reminded her at the top of his voice, since he had raised her from her depths, fulfilled his family obligations, and she still couldn't keep up her side. Not only had she produced two stupid, useless daughters, he repeated, but it was beyond her to manage even those daughters. Thank God for little Norman. (At least Norman was a point in Leah's favor.)

"He's what Ethel wants, Aaron." She went on desperately with her statement of Ethel's interest, trying to ignore her husband's words. She had to tell him the rest. "She wants to marry him," she said. "So I had to come to you."

"Marry him?" Why did he seem to be reduced to mere spluttering at that point? "Marry a *goy?* She actually said she wants to marry him? But that's impossible. I simply will not allow it!" Then he summoned Ethel.

As she sat waiting for her daughter to enter the room Leah tried to tell herself that he was hoping to reason with the girl. Maybe he would just reason and shout at her but not act. She breathed a prayer.

"Don't be afraid, Ethel," he began; Leah could tell he thought he was being noble. "I have been talking to your mother, and she has told me an astonishing thing. I've called you in here to see what you say."

Ethel stood silently by the door at first, her hands clasped in front of her, held tightly together to stop their shaking.

Then the girl found her voice. "If what you mean is about whether James Olson and I are in love and wish to get married," she began, raising her eyes to look at her father with a defiance Leah had never expected, "yes, it's true," she said.

"But Ethel," Aaron said in as silkily persuasive a tone as he could muster through his anger, "you know that's impossible."

"Why?" The question was stark but ready.

"Because the man isn't Jewish, of course," said Aaron. "Really, dear," he couldn't resist adding as he turned for a moment to look murderously at Leah, still sitting there quietly in her leather chair, "didn't your mother explain it to you?"

"Yes," Ethel admitted, "Mother said that. But honestly, Daddy"—she looked at him then in a way that was clearly designed to remind him of the little girl she had once been—"I don't see why that should matter. We love each other. I want to marry him. Really, Daddy, I want to." Her face was as appealing as that child's had been years before when she was denied a piece of candy. But Ethel was no longer a child.

"You want to?" His pretended patience snapped, and he was shouting again. "You want to? And you think 'want to' is reason enough? Well, let me tell you, young lady, 'want to' is not reason enough for sin, and it is a sin to marry outside the faith." Leah could see that now he had chosen to be the God of Wrath. She knew his roles. He chose only certain parts to take in his dramas, she thought bitterly. He would tell himself that he was, after all, only doing a father's duty, telling her about sin.

But suddenly a note that sounded final came into his voice. "No one will be able to say that the daughter of Aaron Morgenstern has married a *goy*, no one," he shouted. He moved toward the girl with his hand raised and actually slapped her across the face. It was the first time he had ever struck her. Later, when she thought about that blow, Leah supposed it was just that it was the first time he'd ever *bothered* to strike his eldest child.

"Ethel"—Leah knew she surprised him by breaking in at that moment—"go to your room!" What did she fear? Something primitive she hadn't known about him, perhaps, because Aaron looked so wild that her first instinct was to protect the girl from further physical harm. Herself he might beat; not her Ethel. Ethel left them then, weeping.

It wasn't until she was gone that Aaron spoke a plan aloud. And then he simply informed Leah of it. She listened in pain, her heart gone out the door with the girl.

"You will pack immediately," he said, "and you and your daughters will go on a voyage to Europe for the rest of this summer. We will not be opening the house in New Jersey after all."

"But . . ." Leah began, then she shut her mouth, because at least he was not hitting Ethel anymore, and he was not hitting her as hard as she had feared he would. Of course he did not need to explain. "Thank you, Aaron" was her bitter last word as she crept from the room. If only Ethel would not blame her! She had honestly tried, but she had not known any way against Aaron. She was all too aware of her own weakness.

After she left him there was still no connection in Aaron's mind that night—none until much later—between the necessity of his family's European trip and any possibility of war. When the connection came to his mind they were already abroad. He didn't care.

It was so hot that night that Isaac had taken his jacket off and even rolled up his sleeves. All the windows were open, and still the air did not stir. He read the letter out loud to them again after they had finished eating, when Yakov was no longer home to hear it.

*My dear family,*

*Rachel and I are well, and the journey is over at last. I am having Rachel write this letter because her writing in English is better than mine, but I am telling her what to say.*

*When we came here, Mamma was much better than I had dared to hope. She was even well enough to be sitting outside the house waiting for us. Pinchas, my eldest brother, was with her, and my half-brother, Mendel, who was just a little boy when I left, is now a grown man and was there as well. He had his baby before I came. They send their wishes for your good health and good fortune, as do all the members of the family.*

*There are roses in bloom here now, and other flowers, for the summer is very warm. We have even been gathering mushrooms in the woods, Rachel and I. Perhaps there will be plums on the trees before I leave to come back to you. The peasants are cutting the hay in the fields outside the village. It is much as I remember it. I will tell you more when I see you, children, about what it is like.*

*My mother is in better health than I had expected. Her eyesight is not good, however, and she is still so weak from illness that she can only be up for a few hours a day. Pinchas's wife, Chava, was living here and taking care of her while she was so ill. I do not know how long her recovery will take.*

*Now that I am here, I am helping, of course. Rachel is a big help, too. She learns different ways.*

*I hope this letter finds you all well. Please*

*give my regards to Tillie and to Sadie and Franz.*

> *Your wife and mother,*
> *Sarah Klugerman*

*P.S. Everyone admires my new dress. Shayna, you would be proud to see me.—Rachel*

"But does Mamma know about the shooting of the archduke, Poppa?" asked Shayna, still afraid.

"How do I know what she knows and does not know? This letter was written two weeks ago—long before there was news of any archduke," he replied impatiently.

Shayna took a breath against her father's annoyance and went on anyway. "But if she doesn't know, we have to write to her now we have finished supper, and tell her to come home right away."

"Shayna, Shayna, always so impatient. I shouldn't have told you what it said in the paper. Now we simply have to wait and see what happens. Probably nothing will happen."

"But you said before—"

"I said probably nothing would happen!" The heat had combined with his usual impatience, and he shouted.

Still Shayna persisted. Something in her told her that she had to persist. "But should we take a chance, Poppa? Shouldn't we do something right away? What can we do except write? So we should at least do that."

"*All right!*" He stood over her now, yelling in earnest, then turned his back and spoke more calmly, though with barely tamped intensity. "I will write. But you have to understand. Writing won't do any good. Your mamma will come home when she planned, she won't come home sooner." He turned back and sat again at the table. "That will be soon enough," he said with a sigh. "She will come back in August. Now it is the end of June. So in two months she will be home. Pray she at least doesn't have this heat over there in the old country! Tillie, was it ever so hot there?"

"Will it never get cool? Will there never be a breeze in this prison?" Tillie replied with a question.

Indeed, all day long the heat had risen up through the house and beaten down through the roof, and the Klugerman flat on the fifth floor had become hotter and hotter. Shayna had tried to forget it so far that evening, however, because she was concentrating on the talk of war and the need for a plan of action. Suddenly she realized how hot and sweaty she felt, and she looked at the flushed faces of Sophie and Harry and made a decision.

"David has finally gone to sleep, Poppa, and I am going to take the children up on the roof to find a breath of air." She turned to Tante Tillie. "Do you want to come?" she asked, even though she wanted nothing so much as to escape from both Tante Tillie and her father. She had even seen Tante Tillie's usual smirk when Poppa said that Mamma would not come home soon. Poppa never caught his sister looking that way.

"You go ahead, Tillie," said Isaac. "You will feel better. I'll stay here with the baby and write to Sarah. Maybe Yakov will be back soon anyway."

"No, Isaac, I will keep you company. You should not have to stay alone with a baby."

"Come on, Shayna, come on," said Sophie, already standing impatiently at the door, and Shayna tried to conceal her relief as she took Harry's hand in hers and went with them.

When they got up to the roof and felt the air all three of them were suddenly lightheaded and cheerful, Shayna for the first time in hours. They had a quilt with them, which they spread out so they could sit on it. For a while they just sat, letting the barely moving air touch them, enjoying being away from Isaac's anger, Tillie's sanctimonious disapproval.

"When I grow up, Shayna, I'm going to live on a roof all the time, where it will always be cool and there will always be a breeze," said Sophie.

"But how will you like the breeze in winter?" asked Harry, ever willing to put in a question. "In winter it's cold, remember?"

"I don't think I will ever be cold again either, Harry, because I will have my rooftop in a place where no winter comes, and no hot summer either, where the air is always just perfect," said Sophie, dreaming already as she laid her head on Shayna's knee. "And I will have a big beautiful automobile to drive through the wind, and ten dresses to flutter in the wind, and a hundred scarves to float in the cool air . . . all of different colors." Sophie's eyes shone briefly in the moonlight, then she closed them.

"Sleep up here for a while, Sophie." Shayna smiled as she patted her sister's golden head. "Have sweet dreams."

"Oh, for goodness sake!" said Harry, clearly disgusted with the turn his sisters had taken. He stood by the edge of the parapet, then said, "I'm going to find a boy to play with. Girls make me sick."

Shayna let him go, feeling cool and quiet now. She tried not to think about trouble for a little while. It was useless to dwell on it. No amount of thinking on a hot night would bring that archduke back to life or resolve her father's annoyance with her about writing to Mamma. What if there was a war? What if Mamma was still in the old country when this war came? What if their letter was too late to bring Mamma home before it happened? What if Tante Tillie and Tante Sadie convinced Poppa to take her out of school when she turned fourteen? If she let herself think about her what ifs, the world held frightening possibilities. But so far things were going all right with the children, so far she was caring for the family, and at the end of August Mamma would be home, and her what ifs could be banished to the land of dreams. Except for that one time when the little ones were lost, she was doing pretty well at being in charge.

Idly she looked around at the neighbors who were up on the roof to catch the evening breeze and smiled at the little boys running around. Harry could manage all right. She found herself wishing that one of her own friends from high school lived in this building so she could have someone to talk to. Her back ached a little from sitting still with Sophie's head on her lap. But there were no other girls her age up there, only boys, and she didn't want to talk to Sammy tonight, even if he should turn up. Sammy was okay, but he looked as if he was going to grow up to be just like her poppa, and she didn't want that kind of man for herself when she grew up, no matter what the older women said.

What could she talk about with Sammy, after all, even now? The children? The cooking? All the questions she had and couldn't ask? Or could she talk about the war that might come? She had a feeling that Sammy wouldn't like domestic topics; maybe he wouldn't understand about this business of the archduke, and she didn't really know if she could explain it.

Cassie would understand. Relief flooded Shayna as she realized that the archduke was something she could talk to Cassie about. She would not have questions about talking about the archduke with Cassie. She had forgotten her crazy hiding behind the pickle barrel that very afternoon when Cassie had passed by. Instead, for a moment her thoughts rested with envy on Cassie. Cassie had probably spent the whole afternoon, the whole evening, talking to her parents about the shooting of the archduke. Maybe, Shayna hypothesized, again not remembering who she had seen in the street that day, maybe Ari had come home for the discussion, maybe the Roses knew whether there would really be a war, maybe they even knew that. Maybe Mr. Rose truly understood the news, maybe he knew what to predict from it. Maybe, if she visited Cassie tomorrow after school, Mr. and Mrs. Rose would tell her that it was going to be all right. Maybe Ari would be there. Maybe—and then she remembered—maybe she would stop feeling so peculiar. Maybe . . . She shook her head. It was too many maybes, and she knew it. And somewhere at the back of her head her what ifs persisted as well.

She looked up at the moon and wondered if Rachel and Mamma, all the way over there in the old country, were looking at the same moon that night. Or were they even able to look out at the moon at all? What if there were clouds? What if they couldn't get onto the roof of their building? Or what if they were asleep in bed and couldn't see from under the covers? If only they could see the moon, if she knew they could see that same moon, then there was a connection. . . .

She was surprised to find a tear cooling her cheek, dropping onto Sophie's golden head.

## 7

*Train up a child
in the way he should go.
(Proverbs 22:6)*

There was no school anymore in July, and Shayna felt that her protection had been taken from her. School was her safe fortress, and each day of Mamma's absence she had gone to school in the morning knowing that she went to a safe place where they valued her for the things she did well. She learned well, and school was where she could do that. At home it was different. She had learned Hebrew, was even good at it. But according to Poppa, her learning wasn't necessary—might not even be good—for a girl. Boys should learn. Men should learn. It mattered to Poppa that Yakov did not learn, but he had sent Harry to *heder* to learn; in a few years David would go. Shayna's learning didn't count. And when she learned Latin and mathematics in school Poppa felt it was useless. Could she ever win with Poppa? Now that school was out, was there anywhere she could turn?

Cassie and her family had gone to the mountains for some weeks, so even Cassie's friendship wasn't there to anchor her, and Shayna felt more and more alone as each day passed. Now there wasn't even the hope that she could see Ari on the street (even if she hid when she saw him), because now handsome Ari wasn't even in New York.

And she found that she was really pressed down by worries. What if there really was a war? Would Mamma and Rachel be safe? They had no more letters after that first one, and it sometimes seemed to Shayna that maybe Columbus had been wrong—maybe the world was flat after all, and Mamma and Rachel had sailed off the farthest edge of it. They were truly gone now that it was summer, and with no school and no Cassie, Shayna was very alone.

On *Shabbos* morning she sat in the curtained-off part of the *shul* with Sophie, wondering why the two of them had even bothered to come. They didn't have to, after all (it was another thing that women didn't need to do), and it didn't seem that Sophie would ever be interested. Besides, Shayna found that she herself wasn't listening to the chanting. The wandering of the Jews in the desert, however appropriate to the hot morning—the laws about them, too—just couldn't seem to hold her interest. Luckily, Poppa and Harry weren't close enough to peer at her and see her head begin to nod. She closed her eyes and smiled that at least Tante Tillie was spending the day with Tante Sadie and Uncle Franz. There would be a little peace when they got home. Peace? she asked herself, shaking her head awake quickly, peace despite the rumors of a coming war in Europe reported daily in the papers? Peace despite no more mail from Mamma? She hoped peace, but it came to her, sitting there, that she herself could have no peace this *Shabbos* unless she had someone to talk to, so she made a resolution to find that someone.

It took time. After the *hallah* and cold eggs at noon Shayna began to wonder if Poppa would ever take his *Shabbos* afternoon sleep. Finally, when she had just about given up hope, he leaned back in the chair and put the handkerchief over his face at last.

"I'm going to rest until Uncle Tanchun comes," he said in the tired Saturday voice he had used even when Mamma was home. Tanchun, his closest friend, was an honorary uncle to the children. He came over every *Shabbos*.

"For my rest I'm going to sit outside and wait for Yakov," announced Shayna, knowing that her brother usually came home for the beginning of *Shabbos* afternoon, even if he would be off again later on. Yakov had seemed a little different these last weeks; maybe she could talk to her brother.

"Sure," said Poppa, colloquial and agreeable for a welcome change.

Isaac smiled wearily beneath the handkerchief, sweating in the summer *Shabbos* heat, and thought about "sure," this word he had said to his daughter. How wonderful it would be to go back to the days when he was so sure! There, in the old country, how sure he had been! He had sat in the little *shul* till late in the night, chanting passages from the Talmud, the accumulated sure wisdom of the past. He had worked long and hard days to accumulate the money to come to America, the Golden Land he was sure he had wanted to enter. He had been so sure it was a safe land—of cities far from the dark forests that menaced his village. (How could Sarah go back to those terrible trees?) He had been so utterly sure that America was far from his father and at last a safe place.

His refuge now was only in sure speech. No one but he knew the forest of doubts rooted under so much of what he said. Doubts about his arguments with Shayna, this child his Sarah had left to manage his home. Doubts about his arguments with Yakov, that disappointing firstborn son who broke his heart daily—now with the trouble he was causing in the

187

shop. Yes, today Isaac felt he could rest, but what would he say on the day when Mr. Saperstein confronted him (as he surely would) to ask whether Yakov was behind the recent union agitation? Saperstein was the boss. What could he say to the boss that might save his son on that day?

For himself, he knew he would not join a union. He had thought of it when he was young, working on a machine in the row of operators who sewed for next to nothing when the season was on and the business was good enough to hire them, who earned less than that nothing off season. The garment trade was seasonal if it was anything. When the orders came in for the fall season, for the winter season, for each of the seasons, then there was work, work, and more work. But after the orders were completed, before the next season's work started, there was nothing. The machines stopped. The workers were without jobs, and they were not paid when the jobs were gone. In the slack times Isaac had indeed thought of joining the union when he was young and desperate to find a way to earn the money that would bring his sisters here to a city no longer golden but harsh and real and poor (yes, all those bad things, but never as bad as what they would leave behind—of that he was still sure). He had thought of the union then, when other men had come whispering to him, whispering of shorter hours, whispering of a dream. Ah, the seductiveness of those whispers—he knew what Yakov heard.

But he had stopped thinking of the union when he'd seen Sarah for that first time at the dance and knew sureness again. She had smiled, and in Sarah's smile was the safety of all the world. He had never really understood why she had smiled on him, but she had, and that sureness had stilled the whispering. Or was it marriage and responsibility that had changed his dreams? Or his obligation to bring his sisters over as he had promised? Or the birth of his children? For suddenly he'd had a family to support. He didn't listen to whisperers, he didn't go out on strikes then. He took care of them all as he had always meant to do, as his own father (he tried to make himself think "may he rest in peace" and failed) had never done.

With work he had risen. He could tell himself now that he had risen to become a part of the business that was really necessary to Saperstein. He was always the last fired when orders were slow; he was always the first hired when they picked up again. Saperstein wouldn't ever get rid of him for good now; he needed him. Isaac was the chief cutter now, he worked on the samples the salesmen took to sell in the big stores. And now Saperstein's shop had become part of the larger Morgenstern manufacturing concern, so he was necessary to Morgenstern, too. Isaac had worked hard for this toehold in an unsure world. Now in season he made good money, and he could comfort himself that off season he had time to study sometimes.

Time sometimes. Some sure thing! If his family could have seen his face then beneath the handkerchief, would they have understood the frown for disappointment, for the doubt he felt that any part of it had been worth doing after all, or would they have simply thought he was angry as usual? That's what they saw—his sure anger—but he knew that they didn't guess at any of its roots in this swamp of doubts.

Didn't Yakov see that it would be impossible to win against such big men? That a man's only hope was to consolidate a position with his own skill? No, Yakov only saw Saperstein; he did not see what was behind him. The union might achieve a few successes with littler men, Isaac would grant that, but not in the shops that were part of the bigger enterprises— they couldn't win there. They were fleas to Aaron Morgenstern. If they started to parade about with signs in front of Morgenstern's place, he would crush them between his thumb and the nail of his index finger, snap them in two like fleas. But how to explain that to Yakov?

A fool. His son was a fool. And Shayna was a fool. She had seen that Leah Morgenstern—had seen her twice now, she said, which was a strange coincidence— but she didn't know about such a family. They only used the poor; they were not people who cared at all. Isaac stirred in the chair, his shirt wet with the afternoon's accumulated perspiration. It was no *Shabbos* rest to think all the time about such things.

Thinking inevitably brought him to Sarah. About Sarah he was truly not sure. He knew she had smiled on him that lifetime ago. He knew, too, that she had left him now. She had every intention of coming back, he believed that. As was her duty, he firmly reminded himself. But would she really come? What if there really was a war? What might happen to her if she was over there and a war came? And would she return anyway to a life he knew she suffered, from that world of which she spoke with such longing and love? He could not feel as she did, but he knew how she felt. Felt. He felt then, in reality, a stirring in his loins from the thought of her. All these years, and the very thought of her still did that to him! He made himself quell it with his mind before it grew to prominence in his body, moving again in the chair. It was a long time to be without a wife, when you were used to a woman. Women, though, were not like men, although sometimes lately he had wondered about his sisters—Tillie, who had never had a man, and Sadie, who was still childless although she had been married to Cantrovitz for five years now. But he could be sure, he realized, about that one thing anyway—women didn't need it like men did. (Yet there in his mind the doubts sprouted again, remembering those times when Sarah had shuddered beneath him in the dark.)

He sat up deliberately and removed the handkerchief from his face, putting it on the arm of the chair. He must have been sleeping to allow himself such dreams! He took a book from his shelf and put it on the table, willing himself to the study he knew could cancel his doubts. His friend Tanchun would find him already involved in their work, the only work allowed on the holy Sabbath day. He could lose himself in a book, of that he was truly sure.

Shayna took herself out into the summer sunshine with her flower still pinned to the throat of her dress. The last time she had worn that flower, she thought, was the Sunday of the boat trip with Cassie and the Roses. When Mr. Rose shouted it was not like Poppa's shouting. And Ari . . . But it was partly because of ideas like Ari's that she was starting to have all these questions.

Now her timing was perfect; just as she settled herself on the warm step and rested her chin on her hand Yakov appeared around the corner.

"Hey," she called, "don't go up. They're all asleep, and besides, it's hot up there. Sit a minute with me," she said, patting the step beside her because she was determined to be friendly to this impossible brother of hers. (Cassie got along with her brother; she would get along with Yakov.) For once there weren't other people on the step; all of them seemed to be taking their naps inside today, so she and Yakov had the whole stoop to themselves.

"What do you want to talk about?" He seemed to welcome the new pleasantness of her approach and made an attempt to fall in with her plan. "You look like a balloon ready to burst. What's the matter? Are the children too hard to manage? Or are Tante Sadie and Tante Tillie getting on your nerves? Or maybe," he teased mildly, still ready to be good-humored, "Rob Roy has fallen into the hands of an evil band?"

Shayna was diverted from her purpose momentarily. "I didn't know that you knew anything about Rob Roy," she said. "I thought you never read anything." She looked hard at him. "Anyway, I'm finished with that book."

"There are lots of things you don't know about me, little sister," said Yakov as he took a cigarette out of his pocket and started to light it.

Instantly she was upset, and the afternoon threatened to erupt into one of their regular battles. "But Yakov, it's *Shabbos*—you can't light a cigarette on *Shabbos*," she said.

"Watch me," he said, and while she looked the cigarette was lit and in his mouth. No lightning came out of the sky to strike him dead. "Poppa's asleep, and you won't tell," he said.

Shayna was further upset at his casual assumption that she would not tell Poppa than about his breaking the Law. But she found herself blurting out, "It's that kind of thing I want to talk about. Why does Poppa always say that the Torah is right? Sometimes it isn't right. And Poppa's not always right."

Yakov looked at her sharply, then took refuge in a puff of his cigarette. "For instance?"

"For instance . . ." Now she was ignoring the cigarette completely in her eagerness to have someone, even her brother, hear her. "If God made all the world in the six days before he made *Shabbos*, how can they tell me about evolution in my biology class? Or, for instance, if God is always good, like we say in our prayers 'I have never seen a good man forsaken or his seed lacking for bread,' how come the Karlovskis' little Froma was bitten by a rat and died? Mr. Karlovski is a good man, but he's so poor, and they have so little—you know they do 'lack for bread.' And if the Messiah is going to come on a white horse, how come Miss Henrietta Szold, and Theodore Herzl for that matter, said we should make our own promised land in Palestine? Or if God is so good, how come there might be a war in Europe when Mamma and Rachel are over there?" At last she paused for breath. "I can't ask Poppa any of this. I've tried. He wouldn't even let me sing in a school concert—you can't ask *him* questions."

"No, you can't ask our poppa. I know that." Yakov paused, reasonable in the calm of a *Shabbos* afternoon instead of angry. Then he sighed. "But I don't always know the answers either. Oh, Shayna, they aren't easy answers, and it's so warm out here." He stretched his legs, not wanting to rush into argument for once. "Just sit a minute and feel the warmth without the questions. Poppa won't like you to ask so much."

The feeling of the rough, warm step beneath him, the hot sun above, rushed deliciously through his body, and he was momentarily distracted, thinking of Dora. He wished he was with her, but he wished that all the time. Besides, hadn't he told himself that he wouldn't get involved with family matters anymore?

Shayna's warm body didn't stop her mind. She went on anyway. "Yakov, I know you go out to work, and you stay out all the evenings. I know you don't go to *shul* with Poppa. You're the only person I can talk to about anything now that Mamma's gone. Please."

He came back to her in a short burst of his usual annoyance. "Shayna, I don't know everything, for God's sake. I quit school to go to work because Poppa made me. He said I'd never be a scholar . . . and he was probably right." He took a breath, shook his head with decision, then went on. "In the shop, though, it's different. In the shop I work next to Edelmann, and sometimes we talk. The lint is so thick in the air in there these days, I think our words can't get through the fog of it. And the boss watches closely, because he doesn't like the 'operatives' —that's what he calls us—to talk to each other. Then we go to meetings after work, and we talk more. But we don't talk about pie-in-the-sky ideas like Zionism. And we read, too, if you must know. But we don't read bourgeois novels by Sir Walter Scott or Zionist foolishness by Theodore Herzl. We read about the future of the oppressed workers of the world. We read Karl Marx. In the future, in spite of people like Poppa, religion will not be used as a whip to tie down the workers to very little pay and very long hours. Religion is the opiate of the people."

He felt anchored by the slogan, anchored to a possibility that he could help even his difficult sister, that this particular family tie might bring another convert to the Cause. "Think of it this way: Why does Mr. Saperstein, the boss, get rich? Why does Aaron Morgenstern, the owner, get very, very rich? Why do the capitalist countries of Europe, where all they think about is the amassing of riches, threaten each other with war, like it says in the paper? My friends Edelmann and Kalinsky say that there have to be answers to questions like that, that there has to be a day when the workers will have enough money so that their families need not go hungry, so a good man like Mr. Karlovski doesn't have to weep in his flat because his wife cannot buy flour for *hallah* and his little child is bitten by a rat. There has to be a day when the workers of the world decide on peace, when . . ."

Shayna sat marveling at the sudden flood of eloquence pouring from the mouth of her silent, bitter brother. But now he was not bitter; now his eyes shone, fastened on a future he was trying to expound, a future with answers perhaps, for questions she had not yet even thought of. Was this what Ari Rose had meant when he inquired whether her brother was a socialist?

Timidly she asked, interrupting Yakov, "Does Poppa know what your friends Edelmann and Kalinsky say?"

"Yes, Poppa knows." Yakov's voice dropped back

to the flat, acid tone she knew so well. "But Poppa doesn't like it. He says the old ways are the only ways. Poppa says"—he spoke sarcastically—"that God will provide for the poor of the world in His own time and His own way. Just like the Messiah coming on a white horse will be God's way of leading us into the promised land. We can't have any questions about God's way, according to Poppa. He won't even join the union. How can we fight Mr. Saperstein and the bosses if Poppa and the old men like him won't even join the union?"

"The union?" He was getting to questions in which she wasn't really interested, questions very far, it seemed, from her own problems. Where had her own questions gone?

"They say that we don't understand how hard it was to get a job when they came here, and how grateful we should be just to work and not to be in the old country. Poppa says that young people always want to rush things. But he's wrong; a union is right, and we have to organize, we have to band together for all the workers. Marx said, 'Workers of the world unite; you have nothing to lose but your chains.' " Again Yakov was anchored. He crushed out the cigarette on the step beside him, hurrying in a rush of words to explain it all to Shayna. He was able to talk to Dora; why not talk to his little sister?

But for Shayna even the idea of acting against Poppa again, after all his shouting at her, was too much. She certainly didn't want Poppa to beat her again with the strap, either. She had questions, yes, about what they told her in school and what Poppa said, but this next step—the step of going against her poppa and actually doing something no matter if he forbade it, not just yelling that she wanted to do something he had forbidden or of which he disapproved, actually doing it anyway—that was a step she couldn't face yet. She went over it in her mind as Yakov went on talking.

Yakov wasn't helping, she thought uncomfortably. Mostly he was just being scary. Scary was what she was trying to get away from by talking to him; it wasn't fair of him to make it worse.

After all, she comforted herself with her reasoning, when Mamma had left Mamma had made it clear that Poppa would be there for her to turn to. Even if she, Shayna, had been left in charge of the children and the household, Poppa was still the head of the family. Poppa had maybe even been right when he beat them with the strap, she tried to convince herself, wincing at the memory. He might have been right about her singing in the concert. (Was he right about saying that a war might come?) Besides, Poppa was a man who studied Torah. Why, right now, Poppa was upstairs waiting for Uncle Tanchun on this *Shabbos* afternoon, waiting to study as he did every *Shabbos*. How could Yakov say anything about actually going against a man like Poppa? She forgot for a moment that she herself could not talk to Poppa, had indeed talked to Yakov. Well, if she had, she had been wrong to do so.

Yakov drilled more words into her thoughts. "Even you have a lot of questions, Shayna. Even you can't think in the old way. You just said you don't think Poppa's always right. But what are you going to do about it?"

It was too much for Shayna to take in all at once. Somehow, her talk with her brother was not working out the way she had thought it would. Where were all the comforting answers she had expected him to give? And then another part of her, far down, wondered why, if she had simply wanted comforting answers, she hadn't, after all, asked Poppa—or even the teachers in school.

Hard answers . . . She had come to Yakov, perhaps, for hard answers. But at the top of her mind she had thought she would talk to him about biology and God and the rats, about the Messiah on the white horse, about the coming of a war, maybe even about being allowed to stay in school and graduate, and he would just explain how it all fit into the ways she had learned from Poppa and Mamma and . . . From Mamma? Could Mamma have been wrong? She shook her head in sure rejection of that idea, sure at least of Mamma.

"Oh, damn!"

Shayna looked up in shock as the words and the crash broke the *Shabbos* peace. They came from the corner of the block, just past the second house down from where she and Yakov were sitting. With the voice and the noise a black suitcase came skittering out on the sidewalk, and an odd, long, three-part wooden stick behind it. Then a tousle-haired young man was suddenly stretched behind the suitcase and the stick, practically flat on the sidewalk. From where Yakov and Shayna sat on the stoop they could see the young man sit up, ruefully brush off the sleeves of his brown suit with grimy hands, then finally stand and brush the rest of himself off, rubbing his knee, which clearly hurt. He picked up the suitcase, which they could see was heavy, in his right hand, and he carried the funny three-pronged stick in his left, heading deliberately toward the two surprised young people sitting on the stoop of #40 Orchard Street.

"Hello. Sorry if I swore a little there. I tripped and dropped all my equipment. Mind if I sit down and have a look at it?"

Before they could say a word he simply sat down on the step below Yakov and Shayna and started to open his suitcase.

"But don't you know it's *Shabbos?*" asked Shayna. "Don't you know that you shouldn't be carrying things

197

today? No wonder you tripped. Who are you? I don't think you come from around here, do you?''

The young man turned and smiled up at her, a smile that lit up his face. His features were regular, and his face was flushed. He had thick glasses on, but she could see that the smile even crinkled the corners of his eyes. "One question at a time, please. First of all, my name is Henry C. Jones. The C. stands for Clayton, so it's really Henry Clayton Jones."

"How do you do," said Yakov, thrusting out his hand. He had met many strangers at Kalinsky's.

"How do you do, I'm Shayna Klugerman, and this is my brother, Yakov," said Shayna, speaking up boldly and even shaking Mr. Jones's hand because she didn't know what else to do when he held it out.

"And you're right, I'm not from around here," said Mr. Jones in answer to her last question. "I'm a stranger in this part of the city, but I've come here because I think it's one of the most interesting parts of New York."

"The Lower East Side interesting?" Yakov's bitterness had returned. "Why should it be interesting to come and see poor Jews who can barely struggle to put bread in their children's mouths? Or is it interesting to see only poor working people?"

"It's interesting to see the people I've always heard of as 'the people of the Book,' " said Mr. Jones gently. "And maybe if I can show these people"—he put up his hand to stop Yakov's coming protest, "yes, with their poverty and work and pain . . . to the rest of New York, then maybe something can be done to make things better here."

"Show people? What do you mean, show people?" Yakov's interest was caught.

"With this." As they had talked Henry C. Jones had been unpacking his suitcase. In it were a camera and plates—a whole set of photographic equipment. "If it's not broken, that is."

198

He inspected each part of the camera and the dark glass plates that went with it while they watched in fascination. "Thank heaven, only one plate is broken," he said at last. "Next time I fall I'll have to be lucky again."

"But what's that?" asked Shayna, pointing to the long stick that, on closer examination, was three sticks fastened together at one end.

"That's what tripped me up at the corner there. It's the tripod, and it's always getting in the way of my awkward feet. It has three legs where I have only two, so it has the advantage of me and has been the cause of my downfall more than once." He smiled as he got up from the stoop and started to set the tripod up on the sidewalk. "Do you see that fire escape over there?" He pointed to the third floor across the street.

They nodded.

"I'm going to take a picture of it."

"But why would anyone want to take a picture of Mrs. Horowitz's fire escape?" asked Shayna in surprise.

Henry C. Jones ignored her at first. He put the camera carefully onto the tripod, screwing the apparatus tightly together. Then he got the black cloth out of his suitcase and made a little tent with it over the camera and his head. His voice was muffled when he finally answered. "There is beauty in unlikely places, Miss Klugerman," he said.

The grown-up form of address pleased Shayna, reminding her of the discussion with Ari and the Roses. (If only she'd been able to talk to the Roses today instead of to Yakov. If only she could ever talk to Ari Rose again.) She looked across the street at the fire escapes again, to see what she had been missing. If she kind of squinched up her eyes, she thought, the fire escapes made a crisscross pattern against the side of the building, which wasn't as apparent if her eyes were wide open and she could see the mountains of buildings on all sides. She tried it both ways. The ironwork itself was lacy at this distance. This strange young man was right. Concentrating on one place and blocking out other things did change her point of view. "They're a bunch of triangles lying nearly against each other up the side of the building—only you can't see all three sides of any of them!" she said in surprise.

There was a mechanical clicking noise, and Mr. Jones's head emerged from under its black tent. "They are at that, Miss Klugerman. If you look at things a new way, they stop being so familiar, don't they? You begin to see something new."

While he spoke Mr. Jones turned his camera around.

Yakov had so far said nothing. Now he asked, "What are you going to photograph next?"

"If I may, I am going to take a picture of Yakov and Shayna Klugerman, sitting on the stoop in front of #40 Orchard Street on a Saturday afternoon."

He looked at the two of them, and he had to laugh at the contrast between their expressions. Yakov looked so pleased, and Shayna looked so scandalized.

"But it's *Shabbos*, Mr. Jones, our Sabbath," said Shayna before her brother could speak.

"Miss Klugerman, I am not a Jew. It is not my Sabbath. But even if it were, I would take photographs."

Shayna's sharply indrawn breath was enough of an answer. Still, she and Cassie had non-Jewish friends in their high school class, she knew *goyim,* so she did try to explain. "You know the Ten Commandments," she said primly. "The fourth one says to remember the Sabbath day, even for you, and to keep it holy." She sat up straight and sure. "We can't help you break a commandment."

But the astonishing Mr. Jones smiled again, undeterred. "I'll take care of the salvation of my own soul," he said. "Don't you worry. Besides, part of my salvation is to come down here and take pictures." He was obviously self-conscious as he said that last, and he went on quickly. "Let me explain a little bit to you. I work on the *New York Tribune*. I know how important pictures are in getting the news to people, though—pictures tell better than words. We have photographs in a special section of the newspaper every Sunday. Who knows—maybe someday there will even be a way to have photographs printed in the regular part of the newspaper every day. So if I can show people all the parts of this city in pictures, well, then maybe they'll begin to understand all the things that are still wrong . . . that still need to be done in New York. For me"—again he spoke uncomfortably—"for me this is a rest—a Sabbath—from my everyday life, coming down here to this part of the city and taking these pictures. Other days I take pictures of parades or of fire engines or of debutantes. Believe me, this is a Sabbath."

As he talked Mr. Jones went behind his camera again, under his little black tent, so his words were somewhat muffled. Shayna and Yakov had to strain forward to hear everything he was saying.

"I never knew anyone who worked on a newspaper before," said Shayna. Her curiosity surfaced. "How did you get a job on a newspaper?"

Just as she finished asking the question there was a puff and a click, and the photographer emerged from behind his camera.

"I know you don't approve," he said, holding up his hand before the outrage in Shayna's face. "Perhaps your brother can explain to you that you've done nothing to violate your Sabbath, what you call your *Shabbos*." His smile was kind.

But there wasn't time for Yakov to say anything, and Shayna's tears were about to burst forth because just then she saw Uncle Tanchun come around the corner. Surely he would see the photographer and tell Poppa of their sin. Even Yakov looked at Uncle Tanchun with distress, and she could tell he was glad that the cigarette was long out of his mouth. He kicked at the stub surreptitiously.

But Uncle Tanchun's mind seemed a hundred miles away as he walked quickly toward them with an abstracted air. Maybe he wouldn't even see them after all, thought Shayna. In the meantime Mr. Jones, oblivious to their distress, was unfastening his camera from the tripod, putting his equipment away.

Uncle Tanchun merely darted a glance at him as he brushed by the suitcase on the steps. But he did look more closely at Shayna and Yakov, who had risen hurriedly at his approach. *"Gut Shabbos,* Shayna. *Gut Shabbos,* Yakov,"* he said.

*"Gut Shabbos,* Uncle Tanchun,"* they chorused, Yakov for the moment as meek as his sister could possibly wish.

"Don't speak to *goyim,"* said Uncle Tanchun, nodding in Mr. Jones's direction and using Yiddish for the unexpected admonition. Then he went in the door and up the stairs to Poppa while they looked after him in surprise.

"I'll be back to see you," said Mr. Jones after Uncle Tanchun had disappeared. "Next time I'll come on a Sunday if I can. And I'll bring you the picture," he added.

"Thank you," said Yakov.

"Oh, no," said Shayna at the same moment, then she clapped her hand over her mouth. Uncle Tanchun had said not to speak to *goyim,* and here she was the next minute speaking.

Mr. Jones smiled and waved as he left.

Watching him go, Shayna felt that the whole afternoon had not gone the way she had planned. She had more than questions now. Now she had all these doubts at the surface of her mind, she thought, and it would be hard to push them back down. And now, even without meaning to she had done something which she could never tell her poppa. She had broken the Sabbath commandment. For the second time that day she found herself glad that at least Tante Tillie wasn't home. Somehow, she knew that Tante Tillie would have seen into her that afternoon.

"Tillie," Sadie was saying to her sister as they warmed themselves in the *Shabbos* afternoon sun, "Franz and I have been talking." Actually, Sadie had not been feeling very well that morning, but that was not what she and Franz had talked about.

"So *nu?*"

"So Franz has a friend," Sadie began tentatively, put off at once by Tillie's sharp look. "Don't jump on me. Just listen."

"I'm listening," said her sister, but her brow was dark. Not again, she thought. Not again with the friend and the matchmaking! (Especially not now, with Isaac's wife gone, when I am the woman in his house.) She watched the crowds hurrying by as Sadie talked.

"Well, really listen this time. It's a widower. His children, though, they're all grown up. They're married and live away from home, so there wouldn't be someone else's children, which I know you object to." Sadie stopped a minute and waited, but there was no reply.

Why am I talking like this? she asked herself. Tillie won't have him—she won't have anyone. Here I am, the one who wants the children, and I am comforting my sister that if she marries she doesn't have to bear them? Why is God so unfair? Now that I have found this new feeling with Franz, will God at last stop being unfair?

"I'm listening still," prompted Tillie. (Actually, it wasn't as bad as usual. What was the catch?) "What's wrong with this man?" she asked aloud. "Is he a cripple? Blind? Come on, Sadie, tell the truth. Surely there is something wrong with this friend of your husband." She always referred to Franz as "your husband," never by name. It helped to make it clear how she thought of that short man.

"No, Tillie," sighed Sadie, "there isn't anything wrong, really. He isn't crippled, he isn't blind. He's just a friend of Franz whose wife has died, and he wants again a woman in his home."

"Is he poor? Is it for the dowry?"

"No, he's a businessman who makes good money. He was pleased to hear about the dowry, of course" —she was trying to be scrupulously fair—"but it isn't the dowry he's after. He just wants a wife. He has heard of you from Franz, and he'd like to meet you. It's really as simple as that, honestly it is." There, her duty was done.

"Meet me?" Tillie was again on her guard. "In the old country—"

"I know about the old country, Tillie," Sadie stopped her, "but this is different. In America a man sees his bride. He meets her and talks to her."

"Bride? What bride? I'm not so easily a bride," insisted Tillie. She kicked a dirty cigarette stub off the step.

"I know, I know. But I thought you would not mind just meeting him, so he is coming over late this afternoon to speak with Franz and take a glass of tea. You won't have to say anything, just see him. He knows you're spending *Shabbos* with us."

"I don't know," said Tillie, but it sounded as if not doubt but decision colored her words. They were moving fast this time, she thought. "I have to be home with Isaac before dark, even on *Shabbos*."

"Tillie, it isn't dark till late now that it's summer," Sadie insisted. "You can see this man and be home early enough. It won't kill you to see him, and I've promised Franz that you would at least think about it."

"You promised? But you hadn't even told me."

"Tillie, it is not always simple with Franz. Do this for me. All I'm asking is that you stay the rest of a *Shabbos* afternoon and see this man. That's what Franz wants. Please. That's all—I promise. Just see him."

"Oh, all right." Tillie's sigh was exaggerated for effect. "For you, Sadie, I'll see this widower, this friend of your husband. But I won't like him."

It was simple to Tillie; she wouldn't like the man because she knew she would not want to be married. With Sarah gone she had Isaac; who would choose marriage instead of Isaac? How could Sadie herself have done that? Tillie sometimes caught herself wondering these days, if there was going to be a war. If so, was there really a chance that her sister-in-law might not be able to come back from Europe? Maybe she, Tillie, could stay then always with Isaac where she belonged.

On *Shabbos* night Rachel had a nightmare. Maybe it was caused by the sight of the twisted candle heralding the beginning of the working week. Maybe it was the smell of the spices on that Saturday night, passed from hand to hand as her Uncle Pinchas said the *havdalah* prayers. Whatever it was, Rachel found herself in a drenching sweat in the middle of the night, clinging to her mother and shaking with fright.

"It's all right," Sarah tried to reassure her. "Just tell me the dream, and it will go away."

But Rachel couldn't tell her. It was too frightening to tell about. She shuddered there in Mamma's arms, trying to calm herself, trying to tell herself it was only a dream, but the terror stayed. It lurked still inside her, still to be dreamed another night and another, another nightmare and another. Even Mamma couldn't help with her fear here.

It was the cossacks. They were huge men in great furry coats who came to the village in the middle of the night with long swords, riding their sweating black horses through the little winding streets. They dragged her from her bed. They dragged all the villagers from their beds and killed everyone in the cobblestoned street while she watched and soundlessly screamed as Mamma and her grandmother and her uncles and aunts and all her cousins were killed, until she stood there alone as they came toward her. They were unspeakable—they did unspeakable things—she couldn't tell of them aloud—they were barely men at all. The old country was full of those cossacks in her nightmares, and she couldn't escape them.

In the morning, when she woke to the bright day, she couldn't believe she had been so afraid. She wanted to be sensible then; she listened diligently to the stories her grandmother told her to comfort her. She blocked out the whispered cossack tales from her cousins, and she tried to forget the frightening gangs of boys in the streets. She decided to stay close to the house, which now seemed her safest protection.

Aaron Morgenstern bundled his family onto a ship bound for France one afternoon very shortly after their revelations to him about Ethel's ridiculous love affair. Even with so little notice he saw that they had managed to pack several trunks of clothes to take—and all those clothes despite the fact that Leah had informed him that they would be using their time in Paris to have their wardrobes made for the next winter.

Of course, Aaron didn't kiss any of them good-bye. He was merely thrilled to see their backs. Not only had he done his duty as a father, he told himself, but the result of their going would be that he could devote more time to Tina, could spend all his evenings with her, could live practically continuously in that new world of pleasure he had recently found. The only remaining task he had concerning his family was to get rid of James Olson.

That would be ridiculously easy. The right people owed Aaron the right favors. (They always did.) Aaron could arrange for James Olson to disappear into the hinterlands without making any trouble. Then, for all Aaron cared, he could prey on some other man's innocent daughter. He simply called Murray Lichowsky in Chicago and had him hire Olson. (He used his connection at Bonwit's to arrange his firing.) Then he decided to summon the young man to his office and confront him to make sure he understood *all* the conditions of this change in his life.

"My daughter has told me of the fact that you have proposed marriage to her," he began.

"Mr. Morgenstern"—the young man's sweat filled the room with the smell of his sudden fear—"I didn't exactly—"

Appalled, Aaron realized at that moment that the fellow might actually be trying to back out of it, might actually say that Ethel had misunderstood him. This was the extent of his daughter's foolishness! This new view of the situation smote him with yet greater fury. A greasy horror like James Olson he could take pleasure in dismissing.

"You will never communicate with my daughter again," he thundered, as if the perfidy of the whole male sex resided in this one exponent of it. "Be grateful," he concluded, "that you are not going to be blacklisted throughout the garment trade. That far I will not go this time." (He had thought through the rumors that might start with such an extreme measure and reluctantly decided against it.) "But," he continued, "*my* products certainly you will never deal in again!"

The young man actually made no protest, simply slunk from the room after Aaron's tirade. He was obviously relieved that his fate was no worse than the one of which Aaron informed him.

Aaron decided that he would never tell Leah of that

scene, at least not until such a narrative might serve some purpose. He did not bother to inform Ethel, because he did not care. Europe was too good for them all, though, he said to Tina as they lay in bed that night. (He had told his mistress the whole story.)

What Tina thought she did not say. Her protection was still, at that point, completely at Aaron Morgenstern's whim. She worked hard so that he would feel he used her well.

Sarah watched Rachel, raising her head frequently from the bread she was kneading, black bread for weekday family fare. Rivka sat asleep in the rocking chair by the window. When Rachel seemed at last to be over whatever it was that had wakened her in the night Sarah sighed and sent her out for some water. Maybe the child's time was starting now, as it did for all women.

The air was stifling in the little room, and the only comfort on a hot summer day was in sitting where a breeze might possibly light. Old as her mother was, Sarah knew she had been glad of the heat coming so early this summer. She saw her smile in her sleep. Sarah smiled also, then bent again over the dough, pushing with the heel of her floury hand, kneading in a gesture so familiar that it required no conscious thought. The baby, Mendel's little one in his cradle, laughed up at her as he saw her pick up the dough and slap it against the table.

She laughed with him, so they laughed together and woke Rivka, who smiled more widely to see her daughter and her youngest grandchild, these two who had not even known each other a few weeks before, laughing together on a hot summer day in her own home. Rachel came in the door carrying a heavy bucket from the well and saw them there laughing. She tried to blow the wisps of her hair off her sweaty face, then gave up and laughed at herself, suddenly comforted. She put the bucket down gingerly, using both hands.

"Do you think it's as hot at home, Mamma?" she asked.

"I am home, *zies kind*," said Sarah after a moment's consideration, and for that moment she was sure of it. She did not see the fear return to Rachel's dark eyes.

So much fear already for Rachel, and there was not yet, for her, even the rumor of war. To such a place, far from any large city, the rumors would come slowly. But when they came . . .

## ❧ 8 ❧

*He increaseth the nations,*
*and destroyeth them. (Job 13:23)*

All the last hot week in July Shayna waited in dread
each night for Poppa's return from work with the
*Times* in his hand. Each day it seemed to her that the
news was more frightening than it had been the day
before, and she thanked God that now it was only a
month till Mamma was due home. The heat in the
apartment, the strap hanging threateningly behind the
door, Poppa's more and more frequent bursts of
temper—all seemed a part of the frightening message
the paper was conveying, the daily clearer message
that Sarah and Rachel might even yet, in the little
time that was left of their journey, be caught in a war
of which they had not dreamt when they left home.
To Shayna, the geography lessons she had painfully
committed to memory in school had a terrible rele-
vance as the end of July approached. Politics and the
possibility of war were her daily companions. Where
could she turn now for help?

On Monday, July 26th, the headlines said: RUSSIA IS
MOBILIZING HER ARMY; BERLIN AND PARIS MOBS FOR WAR.
The question of war seemed to hang on whether the
great countries over there (they were no longer sim-

ply "the old country" to Shayna now that they had taken on terrifying individualities) would honor treaties they had made a long time before. The Triple Entente—England, France, and Russia—might actually end up fighting the Triple Alliance—Austria-Hungary, Germany, and Italy. Then Mamma could be right in the middle of it, because she was in Hungary.

That Monday there was a story headlined FLEEING WAR COUNTRY; there was even an editorial that began, "The only hope of peace seems to be an awakening of the German conscience. . . ."

"You will see now," said Isaac, showing that editorial to Tante Tillie, "the world will come to its senses now, because the paper is right; in Germany there are men of conscience who will not allow this to happen. The Germans are reasonable, perhaps the only hope of Europe. They can stop those Russian cossacks."

But then on Tuesday the paper said, AUSTRIAN TROOPS INVADE SERVIA, and even Isaac could find no comfort in that day's editorial on Kaiser William II: "From the effects of a great war Germany would not recover in forty years, Europe would not recover in forty years," wrote the *Times*.

By Wednesday, July 28th, the hopes held out appeared slim. AUSTRIA FORMALLY DECLARES WAR ON SERVIA; RUSSIA THREATENS, ALREADY MOVING TROOPS; PEACE OF EUROPE NOW IN KAISER'S HANDS.

Then, when Poppa brought the paper in on Thursday, he handed it to Shayna without even telling her where to look. His face was gray. He looked on the table for a letter, but it was only out of habit. When he saw again that there was no answer from Sarah he sat down suddenly, his head in his hands, not even asking for supper. The large headlines did not look worse than they had in the previous days of that week, but Shayna took the paper from him with quick

211

fingers. She spread it flat on the table and started to read.

In a paragraph quite far down in the lead story she finally found the words that must have made her father look so defeated that afternoon. "At the German steamship offices and also at the French line it is stated that in case of an outbreak, all boats would be taken immediately into government service." There it was: all boats—an ocean separated Mamma and Rachel from them, and there would be no boats, no ships to cross that ocean, even if they could get through the war to a ship. Mamma was lost from them back there in the old country, far, far from a ship, utterly lost.

"Poppa." Shayna couldn't believe the irrelevancy of what she heard herself say as she put down the paper, but she could not let herself take in what it said. "Poppa, I am going to take the children Sunday to Coney Island. I have saved a little, and I am going to take them for a treat. It will be Sophie's birthday, and when Mamma comes home next month—"

"I should never have let her go," said Isaac, not even replying to her. "The Lord forgive me, I should never have let her go."


After Aaron Morgenstern scanned the *Times* he went to his desk to write a letter. Mechanically he dipped his pen in the inkwell and prepared to scratch out his required pages in the hour before his meeting with the shop bosses. But what was there to say? And, in fact, would a letter ever find his family, ever even leave these shores on the day when the *Times* itself threatened that shipping to Europe might be cut off "in case of an outbreak"? In case of? He shook his head. He was a businessman; he knew war was now a certainty.

With that certainty in mind he could safely indulge himself with brief conventional thoughts. Would he be able to see his wife safely home? His daughters returned to his roof?

Then his true feelings surfaced. Did he want to have them? The carefully woven threads of Aaron's previously orderly life felt knotted and tangled in his mind. He stared again at the blank writing paper before him, looked up again. What did the *Times* mean, no ships would sail? But he knew what the *Times* meant.

It was only a few weeks earlier that his family had sailed away. Now a war? No ships? What was he supposed to write to them? He lowered his eyes again to the writing paper. Still no words came to him. The truth was that he was glad there were no ships. He was glad because if his family did not come back from Europe, then he could spend all his free time with Tina. He would have no duties at home, no time that, for the sake of appearances, he must spend with Leah. His daughters had completely receded from his mind.

To hell with them all, he thought suddenly, and he was only vaguely guilty at the thought. He no longer seemed to find the desire to do anything that might assuage that vague guilt. He had stopped caring about many of the things he persuaded himself he had dutifully cared about in the past. He was involved in the present.

"George," he called at last to his assistant, looking elaborately at the gold pocket watch he drew out for George's benefit.

"Sir?" George was gratifyingly respectful beside him.

"I haven't time to write this letter to my wife." He looked again at the watch. "Please think of something and typewrite it for my signature." It had come to that.

George nodded.

"And get through on the telephone to someone in

213

Washington—find out what the arrangements will be for the mails if this war gets serious. Oh, yes," he added, as if in afterthought, "and what arrangements are being made for American nationals abroad." Even a Jewish firm could have connections in Washington.

"Yes, sir," said George.

"Why my brother is letting you do this I do not know," said Tante Tillie on Sunday morning as Shayna prepared to take Sophie and Harry for their outing. "It is foolish, maybe even dangerous, and when I get home from work I will tell him that he should not have allowed it." She jammed her hat on her head. "I wish I had spoken up last night," she said as she slammed out.

Shayna did not say a word to her in reply.

"When can we go, Shayna, when can we really go?" asked Harry, impatient and eager for adventure as ever.

"As soon as Tante Sadie gets here. We have to wait for Tante Sadie to come take care of David; I've told you a hundred times," Shayna answered, exasperated.

"Shayna, why do I have to wear all this itchy underwear? It's so hot! Can't I wear a little less underneath my dress? Nobody will know if they can't see it," wailed Sophie.

"Certainly not," said Shayna, speaking sharply to her sister. "And I will thank you not to discuss it further," she added in her most grown-up tone, nodding significantly in Harry's direction.

She wondered if perhaps this expedition to Coney Island on a Sunday was going to be more than she had bargained for. She decided to keep her strictest watch on Sophie and Harry, and to do things just the way they were supposed to be done. Just because this was a special day was no reason to relax her watchfulness. Mamma always insisted that they be dressed properly no matter where they were going. She would try to do it like Mamma, she decided.

The very thought of Mamma filled Shayna with anxiety for a moment, and her stomach knotted up. If only they would hear from Mamma again soon, they could all stop worrying. What if the ships did not take passengers? What if there was no way for Mamma and Rachel to come home? What if they were caught in a war? What if . . . but it did no good to speculate. She resolutely tried to put the thoughts out of her mind and concentrate instead on the day ahead.

Harry was standing with the door open, looking out in the hall for Tante Sadie. "Here she comes, here she comes!" he shouted at last.

"Harry, keep your voice down," said Shayna sharply. "Do you want everyone in the world to know our business?"

But Harry ignored her. He even greeted Tante Sadie with a hug when she came in the door. "I never thought you'd get here," he said to his delighted aunt. "We've been waiting and waiting."

"And why should you be waiting? If you would stay where you belong instead of this foolishness, you would not have to wait at all," she reproved, but mildly. She was mild with Harry, as always.

With a flurry of thank-yous and good-byes to David, the three who were going were soon out of the house, and even Shayna allowed herself to skip a little as they went down the street toward the train that would take them to Coney Island. She felt the warmth of the sunshine and was suddenly again thirteen-and-a-half-going-on-fourteen and glad of it. She took her brother's hand and her sister's hand and ran a little, saying, "Come on, hurry up. We've got all day to go, but it's getting late."

Maybe everything would be all right after all. Maybe.

She felt confidence welling up with the sunlight. Why not maybe?

The accident happened on the roller coaster. Shayna's stomach always churned at the remembrance of it, and she could never forget any of the terrible details, not all the years of the rest of her life. Sophie and Harry had insisted on going around a second time; they loved the feeling Shayna had found that she hated, the long pull up to the top of the hill in the little car, the pause with a view over the ocean and the rest of the amusement park, and then the heart-stopping descent with the wind pulling your cheeks until they flattened against the bone and how you suddenly felt as if you were floating absolutely free, with no control over your own motion. Shayna hated no control.

Harry and Sophie had screamed with delight the first time around, while Shayna bit her lip in terror when she got out, all atremble. They begged and begged.

"I can't," she said, telling the literal truth.

"Oh, Shayna, don't always be a spoilsport," said Harry, full of the slang he was hearing from the other riders.

"No, Harry, I just can't." Her voice was final.

"Well, then let us go without you," begged Sophie eagerly.

"Of course not."

"Oh, please, Shayna, please. It's my birthday." Sophie strove to persuade her, close to tears.

"Well, kids, what'll it be?" asked the ticket man, stopping beside Shayna.

She made the decision in a hurry, unable to resist the pleading in Sophie's eyes, and wanting to let them have their fun. "Oh, all right," she said. "Just this once you can go alone. But hang on and do just as the man says. Don't take chances!" She had to shout the last words because the car was already beginning to slide away.

She stood beside the spiderweb structure and watched to see them whenever she could. But they swooped over the top of the hill to her right immediately, and all she could hear were delighted screams along with the rumble as they went down the first slope. It wasn't the worst one; that was on the other side of the structure, thank heaven, so she wouldn't have to see that. Which was just as well, she thought, because it had been so awful, and she still felt sick just thinking of it. Why couldn't she enjoy it instead of being afraid?

She began to walk off to the left so that she could see the children when they came around the last bend. She walked slowly, because they wouldn't be around for a while, and she noticed a worried look on the face of the ticket taker as she went, or at least she remembered later that she'd noticed it, afterward. Had he seen something going wrong?

In the distance she heard a song. A pro–German crowd, inflamed by the news of the war in Europe, had gathered in the park somewhere, and they were singing. She didn't catch the words then, but the whole scene always popped into her mind years later when she heard the song again and shuddered automatically at *"Deutschland Über Alles."* Now more happy screams came through the air, mixed with the smell of popcorn and summer heat.

What happened next seemed to happen in slow motion, but at the same time all at once. The cars came swooping down the last hill from Shayna's left as the singing swelled in the distance. There was a slight curve about halfway down the hill, and as it came the ticket taker was shouting above the music, "Hold on, I told you to hold on!" at the children in the front car.

One of those children had let go and had her arms

spread out as if to embrace the wind. At the curve the child seemed to lift right out of the car and continue on a path of her own, not rounding the bend with the rest of the passengers. She floated through the air toward the ground, her golden hair streaming behind her, and her arms still outspread, like wings, balancing her as she flew. She screamed as she hurtled through the air, the same happy scream as the other riders. She landed nearly at Shayna's feet, a crumpled bird on the hard ground. It was Sophie.

At home little David woke up from his afternoon nap in a puddle of sweat, crying. Tante Sadie sat in the next room with her eyes closed and waited a minute to see if the cries would continue. There wasn't any reason to rush in, she thought; he would come to her if he needed her. Indeed, when she opened her eyes, there he was at the door, sniffling. He toddled to her.

"Tant' Sadie?" he said, climbing into her lap.

So many afternoons since Sarah had left the little one had climbed into her lap when he awoke. And he wasn't even Harry! This child was always messy, and he never smelled good, and his cheeks were red and fat. But to her surprise, every afternoon her arms went around him anyway, and she rocked back and forth and held him till his sobs subsided. And listened to herself in wonder.

"Hush, now, David," she said. "Everything's all right. Everything's all right."

Is everything all right? she wondered as she held him yet again, murmuring her surprising words of comfort. Is everything all right? Why have I missed my time of flux this month? she asked herself. Why? She thought of the nights in the bed with Franz in the late spring. Is everything, dear God, finally, at last, going to be all right?

*   *   *

Shayna knelt beside her sister Sophie and looked first for blood. If there wasn't blood, she reasoned, then Sophie wasn't hurt. If you're hurt, it bleeds. There were plenty of bleeding scrapes and scratches, but no large bloody places, so maybe it wasn't so bad. But why was the child lying there so still? Was there more blood underneath her? Maybe, she thought, she is hurt underneath, and that's why she isn't making a sound. Or maybe she is just getting her breath; that's why she's so still, it's just her breath is knocked out.

"Sophie, Sophie, are you hurt?" she kept whispering helplessly. She wondered later how she'd known not to move her.

"Do you know her, miss?" asked a shadow that materialized above her.

"It's her birthday," answered Shayna. "She couldn't get hurt on her birthday, do you think?" and she found herself crying there on the pavement.

The next minutes were a frantic blur. Somehow the singing had stopped, and before she knew it there was a crowd of people around Sophie, who was lying so still on the ground. Harry got through, though, screaming all the time. "She's dead! She's dead! Oh, Shayna, Sophie's dead! Oh, oh, oh!"

"No, of course she isn't dead, little boy," said a clean-shaven man who stood near them. "I'm a doctor. Mind if I take a look?" he asked no one in particular as he bent over the still child.

He put his ear on Sophie's breast and then looked up quickly and spoke directly to Shayna. "She isn't dead. It's just that she's hurt. *She isn't dead!*" He had to shout the second time because Harry's wails were so loud.

But the shouting got through enough finally so that Harry began, slowly, to quiet down. Nevertheless, a cold feeling under Shayna's ribs was settled there no matter what anyone said. Maybe if she hadn't felt so

219

strengthless, so like a jelly, she could have caught Sophie—why hadn't she caught her? Why had she let her go in the first place? Why had they ever come to Coney Island? Why oh why didn't she know anything to do to make it better?

Suddenly a policeman was there, too, and they were putting a stretcher under Sophie very carefully, and now she was moaning as they lifted her and started to carry her away.

"Does anyone know this child?" the policeman was asking.

"I do. It's my sister," said Shayna, gulping to get control of herself. "Her name is Sophie Klugerman, and she lives at #40 Orchard Street in New York."

"Where is your mother, little girl?" asked the policeman, looking around.

Shayna's heart sank even further. Oh, Mamma, where indeed? "She isn't here. I brought my sister."

"No parent present," muttered the policeman, writing in his little notebook as the stretcher bearers moved along.

"I mean," said Shayna, desperately trying to think of a way to explain, "it's all right—I'm supposed to be taking care of her. It's all right"—she reached for conventionally correct words—"because I'm thirteen-and-a-half-going-on-fourteen, and my mother is visiting my grandmother today." It was true in a way, and she knew enough of the world to know that the policeman would understand a story about a mother visiting a grandmother. (A mother visiting a grandmother across the ocean in Hungary, a country that was part of the Austro-Hungarian Empire and that was now at war—that he could never understand. Oh, Mamma!)

"Sister in charge," he continued to write. "But look, miss, I'll need your father's name. We have to get hold of your family in case something is very wrong. They will need permission if they have to operate, for instance, and you're too young to give it."

"Operate?" For a minute Shayna thought she might throw up.

"Just if they need to, you know," said the policeman, realizing how pale she had turned.

But Shayna was already recovering herself. "Where are they taking her?" she cried. "Where are they taking Sophie? Stop! Stop!" she shouted, breaking away from the policeman and running after the stretcher. It was headed toward an ambulance with a large red cross painted on the side. No matter how sick and weak Shayna felt, she knew she had to stay with Sophie. Her shouts created enough consternation in the crowd and in the stretcher bearers so that they did stop and stand beside the ambulance with their burden until she caught up with them, Harry clinging to her skirt.

"Next of kin?" asked one of the attendants.

Shayna nodded.

"You can ride along, then, if you want."

At that moment Sophie moaned again and opened her eyes at last. "Shayna," she said, "oh, Shayna, I hurt myself. My arm hurts so much. Don't go away, please." Then she closed her eyes again.

"Don't worry, Sophie, I'm here," said Shayna, so relieved to have heard Sophie's voice that she started to cry again. "It will be all right," she said, voicing a conviction she was far from feeling as she climbed into the ambulance with Harry.

It was the first time either Shayna or Harry had ridden in an automobile of any kind. For a few moments they both stopped crying and nearly forgot their troubles in the wonder of it. "It goes like the wind," said Harry, holding his hat.

"And the breezes feel cool," answered Shayna. Then another stifled moan from Sophie on the stretcher settled that cold feeling under her ribs again. "Will it cost money in the hospital?'' she asked the attendant. He seemed a youngish man with wide-set eyes, skinny for lifting such heavy stretchers.

He glanced directly at her, sitting straight in her dark, patched, and nearly outgrown dress. He said, ''You must ask the doctors, miss. But don't worry. Many people can't pay.''

''If only my father doesn't find out!'' said Shayna.

''I'm afraid he'll have to find out,'' countered the young man. ''That little girl has probably broken something in her fall.'' He shook his head. ''You can't hide that.''

''Broken something! Do you mean she might never get better?'' asked Shayna, nearly in tears again. She had never had any dealings with broken limbs.

''No, no,'' he said impatiently. ''But if she has broken something, she will have to remain in the hospital, or at least have a cast or a sling.''

''How do you know?'' asked Shayna.

''I'm studying to be a doctor,'' answered the young man. ''I'm a medical student. This is just my job to make money in the summertime so I can go back to medical school in the fall.''

''Where do you go to medical school?'' Shayna's questioning continued. Any conversation was a welcome distraction.

''New York University,'' said the young man, surprised to be asked.

''New York University.'' Shayna tested the sound of it. ''Maybe I'll go there when I finish high school.''

But she had no time for further talk about universities or medical schools, no more maybes, because they had arrived at the small hospital, and confusions were all around her. The attendants carried Sophie in on the stretcher, but in what seemed like no time at all she was actually standing up beside a nurse, looking a little dizzy and obviously in pain, but at least able to stand. They had washed all her scrapes and cuts. Then she was gently put back down on a bed.

"I think," said a doctor to Shayna, "that her left arm is all that's broken; maybe she has a slight concussion—and she has lacerations and contusions, of course." He shook his head. "She's a remarkably lucky child. It could have been a whole lot worse. I'm surprised—"

"Does she have to stay in the hospital?" interrupted Shayna. In her experience, everyone who stayed in a hospital was there to die, and she was terrified of the hospital for Sophie. If she could just get her home . . .

"I don't think so," said the doctor. "I would like to be able to speak with your parents, however, about the treatment."

Again Shayna felt cold beneath her ribs. First she tried being quiet. Maybe if she didn't answer, he would stop talking about parents.

"How can I reach your family by telephone?" the doctor persisted.

"We do not have a telephone." Shayna tried to say it with dignity, but her voice shook.

The doctor looked at her hard and seemed at last to realize that she wasn't going to give him any more information than was absolutely required.

"Is your father at work?" he asked. Maybe she was Jewish—the doctor knew they worked on Sundays.

"Yes, of course, in Mr. Saperstein's shop," she replied.

"Well, then, perhaps your mother is home and could be reached through a neighbor."

Shayna found refuge again in the sentence she had trotted out for the policeman. "My mother is visiting my grandmother." A truth that would satisfy him was added: "My grandmother doesn't live in New York." Explanations were so complicated, she knew they would be impossible.

Other patients were clamoring for the doctor's attention. This case was taking too much time already. Defeated by the unforthcoming Shayna, he turned to the nurse. He said, "Why don't we just mark the child down as an orphan for the records and go ahead? I haven't got all day to sort this out."

Shayna's tears stung behind her eyes when she heard the tone of voice and his words, but she couldn't think of anything else to say, and she was feeling very much like an orphan at that moment. She knew herself incompetent to deal with it any other way, so she simply waited patiently with Harry in the little curtained-off room, surrounded by the smell of carbolic, and wrung her hands when she heard Sophie's moans. At last the doctor came back to her.

"I'll let you take her home now," he said. "But be sure this cast is examined in a month, and tell your mother to have a doctor check her if she seems confused. I hope the concussion isn't serious, but it might be." Sophie stood beside him looking very confused and pale indeed, but she was standing, even if her left arm was thick with plaster and she had a sling around her neck to hold it up.

"Golly, Sophie," said Harry in admiration, "does it hurt a lot?"

Luckily, Sophie decided to be brave under the gaze of her little brother. "Not too much," she answered in a shaky voice.

"Thank you, doctor," Shayna remembered to say in the rush of leaving. She didn't dare say anything about the possibility of money, and she was grateful that he simply said, "You're welcome," and turned away.

When his nurse looked at him in surprise as the children hurried out the door he shrugged his shoulders. "It wouldn't be any use," he replied to her unspoken question. "People like that haven't any way to pay. I just hope they get the little girl to another doctor if she needs it." He turned to the next patient.

By the time Shayna got the children home Poppa was already back from work and very angry that they were late. Of course, there was no way to keep any of it from him. When he saw Sophie's cast and heard that she had broken her arm falling from a roller coaster, his rage was even greater than Shayna had imagined it would be. He blamed it all on her. The strap came out from behind the door, and not for Sophie or Harry at all this time.

Shayna swore to herself as the terrible thing came down time after time, smacking, cracking, raising welts on her back that didn't go away for days, that she'd never forget that beating. She hated her poppa. He never understood anything that mattered. And she knew something that she had not known before about her mamma. Mamma had been wrong, after all. That was the part that broke Shayna's heart. Mamma had thought that Poppa would help her somehow, but Poppa would never help her, not in any way that mattered. Poppa would never understand. Mamma had understood, but Mamma was gone. What if she was never coming back? Poppa beat and beat Shayna, and the soreness was for much more than the beating.

Sarah and her sister-in-law Chava took a whole day together, just the two of them, to go to the town of Tokay. They were able to get a ride from Pinchas's factor, who was passing that way on his further journey to Budapest. The plan was made the evening before they went, more casually than Sarah would have expected.

"I have spoken to Pinchas," Chava told her, breezing in after the evening meal as she had often done since Sarah arrived, finding time to sit with them in the long twilight after her own chores were finished. Rivka would sit on the rocker, Sarah and Rachel at the chairs at the table, and Chava sat with them, slim and smiling. "He says we can go to the market tomorrow with Laban Camovitch, who will be passing that way. You'll come, won't you?"

"But there's Mamma," Sarah began, never having thought that Chava would really get permission from her husband for this trip.

"Go, *liebchen,* go," said Rivka, smiling in the lengthening shadows. "Rachel will play with her cousins and help her old grandmother if I need her. Go and enjoy."

"I will, then," said Sarah after only a moment's thought. "You are kind to think of taking me." She looked over at Rachel, trying to use the last rays of light on her knitting. Her scarf was nearly a foot long, and already there were fewer and fewer rows that had to be ripped out and done again. It seemed she was mastering the task at last. "You will be all right?" she asked Rachel.

"Yes, Mamma," said Rachel. "I will be with Grandma." What else had she come this summer for except to be with her grandmother? "Maybe Blumeh and Nomi will come over," she said. It was only for one day.

The day itself was one of those winey summer days containing just a hint of a later season in dry, cool air. A breathlessly blue sky shone over the two women as they rode along, maintaining a decorous silence with the uncomfortable employee.

Every once in a while he addressed a remark to them. "I hear," he said as they passed yet another vineyard, "that the grapes are setting well. It will be a good year for the wine, God willing."

"Everyone is concerned about the grapes at this time of year," explained Chava to the American Sarah. "Throughout the Tokay region the weather is watched closely, and the grapes more closely."

"I remember about the grapes," Sarah answered,

seeing the size of the vineyards strangely shrunken from her memory of them. "But surely it is only the *goyim* who may grow them?"

"Yes, only the *goyim* may grow them," replied Laban Camovitch, as if she had addressed him. "But, of course, we can buy and sell." Pinchas's business was the buying and selling of grapes and wine.

They lapsed into silence again as the road wandered among the hills to the lower elevations where every south-facing slope was covered with vines, then dipped into the river valley where fields of grain were still green.

"It is a beautiful day," Sarah said, closing her eyes and breathing deeply.

The other two smiled at each other as if they had arranged her country tour between them and were even responsible for the bright glisten of the sun on the wet rocks in the river. When the cathedral tower of the town showed above a patch of trees Chava was quick to point proudly to it, although she herself had never entered its precincts.

"I must leave you here," apologized the factor when they came close to the central square near that tower. "I cannot go further with the cart today."

"Thank you for bringing us," Chava said. "We will be quite all right now." She helped Sarah down and waved him off. "Pinchas says he is good at his work," she said of him to her sister-in-law, "but he certainly sweats a lot. I am glad he has gone."

Sarah smiled at her. It was the first time she had seen Chava as the proud wife of an important man. She guessed that Pinchas was important, to have employees who went on long journeys for him. Chava had a right to be proud of her husband. Even if he wasn't a scholar, Pinchas used money he made in his business to be a benefactor of the community, which counted, she thought, pleased with her brother. She surprised herself then, finding in her own heart a moment of pride in Isaac, her husband who was a scholar.

She stepped quickly out of the way of a farmer leading two cows into the square. Behind him came a crowd of peasant women, all in bright skirts and blouses embroidered with flowers. Suddenly Sarah and Chava were in the thick of a group of people, swept along into the square by the colorful crowd all coming to buy or sell. It might have been only a middling market town, but it certainly was a busy one that day. The swirling scene was enlivened for the two women by an accordionist seated on a box in the middle of the square, surrounded by a circle of peasants who tossed coins every time he finished a selection.

"See?" said Chava in excitement, pointing to his fur cap. "He's a Russian. Oh, if only he had a dancing bear!"

Again Sarah smiled. "At least some of the people are dancing," she volunteered. They stood and watched a while, but not for long, because they did not have a coin to waste, Chava said. Sarah would have listened longer, drawn as she always was to music, but these were sad tunes, many of them. They reminded her of David Nathan so much that she sighed aloud. And how desperately she missed her children at that moment—they would have loved this scene. Her eyes teared momentarily.

Perhaps that was the reason Chava pulled her along to the rows of booths set up at the end of the square near the church. The flower sellers had one section, with the fish men beside them, the heady scents of the blooms competing with the stink of the sea. The potters and weavers were ranged across an open area, each booth covered with cloth that flapped in the breeze, threatening to fly away from the flimsy poles that held it. It was to the weavers that Chava headed, and her bargaining for her dress length consumed the better part of an hour.

In the meantime Sarah drank in the colors and smells of the rest of the marketplace. New York was bigger and noiser, she knew that, but here the sight of the vine-covered hills in the distance above the curving stucco facades of the buildings was a comfort to her, mitigating the crowding of the people with the promise of air, of cool, tree-shaded banks by the river. Oh, how she loved these hills of home, she thought.

By prearrangement of which Sarah had known nothing Chava met the wife of the rabbi, also in the town for errands that day, and they rode part of the way home with her. She was a voluble woman, chattering all the way, so they were glad when she dropped them off a mile short of their destination, saying she wished to visit her married daughter in the opposite direction from the one in which they were going.

"We are fine, *rebbetzin*," said Chava. "Do not concern yourself. We will enjoy the walk. Our cheeks will be pink, which will please my husband."

As the *rebbetzin* went off in her little cart Sarah thought how different was this world where a husband might be pleased with pink cheeks. Would Isaac be pleased with any such thing? He had never told her so.

"I know it seems strange to you," began Chava as they walked along the rest of the way on the rutted road to the village. "Me being the wife of the eldest son, saying such things. It wasn't what you expected, was it?"

"What should I expect?" Sarah's question was mild. "I was only thirteen when I left for America—Pinchas was still married to Roza then. And you were my age. I couldn't expect." She thought again of how different this all was—of the kinds of talking she had done over the years with the women who were her relatives in America—Isaac's sisters. The contrast made her smile. It was not a pleasure to talk with those bitter women. Chava it was a pleasure to talk to.

"Let's sit a minute and rest," she suggested as they came to a gently sloping bank beside the road. "I'm glad you married Pinchas, you know," she added. "You are good to him, and you have been very good to my mother. I won't forget that. You have brought joy to our family." Her eyes filled with tears as she said it, which embarrassed her. She turned away a little as she settled herself on the grass.

Chava wasn't looking at her closely, however. First she put down the bundle with the new dress length, then she sighed as she collapsed on the grass. "I'm hot carrying that," she said.

"I'll take it the rest of the way," offered Sarah. "I'm sorry—I should have thought to say so."

"No," smiled Chava. "Not that hot. And I'm so happy about it that I could hug it to me the whole way even if I sweated all over it. I've been saving a long time, you know," she explained.

"The egg money is slow?"

"All money is slow." Chava lifted her eyebrows and nodded.

"I thought Pinchas . . ." Sarah began, then she let the sentence hang because she was embarrassed again, thinking that maybe her brother was ungenerous with money. Perhaps he did not have as much as she had thought he did. Could it be that Pinchas did not give back the joy that Chava had brought him?

"I didn't ask Pinchas. Oh, he would probably have given it to me if I had. But I wanted to earn the money for a new dress myself." Chava looked down at the bundle lying below her. "I had this idea that I would like to have a dress, and I didn't want to be grateful to anyone for it—I wanted it to be my own." Her smile was wide. "Now it will be."

"I know," said Sarah. The two of them were able

to sit together in silence for a while. Sarah knew how Chava felt; she was here herself because of money for which she didn't have to feel grateful to Isaac. She had sewn for the Garfinkels and for others, bringing home bundles all the years of her married life. She had saved. This journey, then, was really her own, paid for with her own savings. She knew how Chava felt. . . . Then she caught herself thinking the impossible, as she had begun to think it more and more consciously ever since she had come home. If only she didn't have to go back. If only August would not come.

But it was coming soon. And she could not tell Chava such thoughts. Besides, there were the children, and to them she did want to go back. Isaac, though . . .

"Tell me about how you met your husband," said Chava, lying back on the grass. "Tell me of your life."

So Sarah told her about the dance where she had met Isaac and even mentioned the name of David Nathan casually in her telling of those days. She told of how she had chosen Isaac because he was a scholar, and therefore the correct choice. But when she mentioned David Chava looked at her with a sudden understanding, and Sarah changed the subject quickly to her children. Much as she would have wished to say words about her ever-present ache of the heart for David, for love, she had never said them to herself, so she could not articulate them, even to this good woman.

On the next Friday night, however, when her youngest brother Mendel came with his wife and family to make *Shabbos* in his mother's house, she did try to say something about her reluctance to return to America. She had just that afternoon received Isaac's letter, which had taken nearly a month to follow her. She had read it alone when it had come. It was, actually, only the second letter she'd received. But it wasn't at all like the first. This letter was different.

The first letter had been all about the family. He had said that the children were well and that little David seemed to be growing taller every day. Sadie was coming every day to the house, he said, as they had planned. With the summer, of course, Shayna would be able to stay home from school. Such domestic details the first letter had contained, and a few words about each of them. Of course, he hadn't said that he missed her, but she hadn't expected that. She had been just as glad that the first letter had contained no real news, because she hadn't wanted to hear anything but just what he had written—that all was well, that they were getting along fine.

It was this second letter that distressed her, tore her with questions, even though he had asked no questions in the letter. Why did he have to need her so?

"Sarah," Mendel began in the middle as they sat late in the evening after *Shabbos* dinner, his wife off nursing the little one and Mamma already asleep. They had sung themselves somnolent in the warm evening air, so his words were all the more startling. "Sarah, Pinchas says it looks as if there is going to be a war."

She wasn't really listening. "War, Mendel?" She asked it automatically, with only half her mind. Why couldn't she relax, why couldn't she just enjoy the evening leisure after the long day of *Shabbos* preparation? Why think of the letter? For the letter, too, had mentioned the possibility of war.

"Yes, I was talking to Pinchas," Mendel went on, "and he said he has heard from a wine merchant in Vienna who sent a newspaper. It looks as if it will be a long war. Of course, he could be wrong, he says, but it means bad times, even here in a little place like this."

"Bad how?" She asked questions because it was the way to find the beginning. "Perhaps Rachel should not hear this, Mendel?" She hesitated, remembering the child's nightmares. "Shall I send her off?"

Rachel sat in the corner, no knitting in her hand because it was *Shabbos*. She listened, hoping her uncle wouldn't send her away, and at the same time afraid that he wouldn't.

But Mendel ignored Sarah's questions and went on with the middle of what he was saying. "Pinchas says it may be a pretext again for the cossacks to come down on us—the Russians are maybe going to use it as an excuse to invade."

She was suddenly up and attentive. "The cossacks? Oh, my God! When the cossacks?" Praise God, there had never been a pogrom in her own childhood, but Sarah's memory of the terrible slaughtering of Jews described in the headlines Isaac had read from the *Forward* in 1903 after Kishinev, of the slaughters in headlines time and time again read aloud with horror in safe America, tinged her voice. It was too late to send Rachel out of the room. The child's eyes were already wide with fright.

"The emperor's alliance with the German kaiser is our hope now—you know how well the Germans have always treated the Jews. As a matter of fact, Sarah, that's part of what I want to ask you about—"

But she interrupted again. "The Germans will fight the Russians? But surely then it will not be here, but in the north?" She was still muddled.

"Pinchas says that might be the way of it, but frankly, Sarah, I'm very worried. I know this is no way to talk on *Shabbos* evening, but I need to talk to you. When are you leaving? You must leave, of course, before war comes. You are an American citizen—you can go to America."

\*       \*       \*

Leaving? But I was not thinking yet of leaving. I was thinking only of staying maybe even a little longer than I had planned, just until Mamma is really stronger, just until . . .

I don't want to leave.

And Isaac has written also of the possibility of war, and he, too, has asked me to come home.

Home?

"But I can't leave Mamma yet, sick as she has been," Sarah protested. "As a matter of fact, I might be able to stay a little longer than I had planned. My ticket is for the twenty-fifth of August from Amsterdam— that is only a few weeks now. I had thought perhaps I should put it off a little, just until September, until I'm sure Mamma is completely better. It is now already the beginning of August, and . . . God forbid, of course, that the cossacks should come, but a war?"

"Mamma is well, Sarah." He tried to be gentle. "She is as well as she is going to be—she is just old." He changed the conversation a little when he saw the pain in Sarah's eyes. "Pinchas and I have been thinking about America, Sarah, we've been thinking about going—"

"To America? That's a long way to make Mamma go, Mendel, and anyway—"

He interrupted her hesitancies with impatience at last. "Yes, yes, Sarah, it's a long way, and Mamma obviously cannot go, but that is beside the point—I want you to tell me about America. Pinchas says that his buyer's cousin lives in Chicago, and he writes that everything is very different in America. You never have said much about it in your letters, Sarah, but he says that Jews don't have to be afraid in America."

"Afraid?" She looked at him. "I have told you that we are poor there, Isaac and I. He works very long hours, and so does my son Yakov, and still we are very poor. And we are afraid, too—we are afraid that

Isaac could lose his work. We are afraid of sickness. We are afraid when there is so much talk about strikes and unions. Oh, yes, it is the same; we are afraid in America, too."

"Yes, yes," he impatiently dismissed her protests, "I have read in the newspapers here, too, of strikes and unions. But that isn't what I mean, Sarah. It is another kind of fear I mean. Is it true, for instance, that you never have to fear anyone like the cossacks there? That Jews are like others in dignity in America?"

Rachel was still listening, sitting absolutely still as they talked.

Sarah answered him slowly because she had not thought of such things in a long time. She listened with surprise to her own answers. "The cossacks—no, the cossacks are not there," she said. "There are sometimes troubles with the Irish or the Italians, but it is not like, God forbid, the cossacks. And yes, Mendel, Jews are like other people in America . . . in a way. It is against the law in America to harm someone just because he is a Jew."

"Yes, yes, I have read that, too, but does the law mean anything there?"

"Well, not always, but does the law mean anything always for a Jew anywhere?" She smiled. "But the law is there, and some Jews have good jobs and grow wealthy. They say some Jews are even friends with people like the president of the United States. Some Jews can get elected to Congress; maybe a Jew could even be president. That's what they say there. It is a strange place, America," she mused, "and a Jew can be what he can be there."

"They say? Who says these things, Sarah?" he prodded her.

"They say them in the night school where you go to learn to be a citizen. I went there and heard them— even the women go there. And they say such things in the schools where the children go—where Rachel goes."

235

Rachel said, "Yes—it is true, Uncle," confirming Sarah's words.

"Do you think I should leave here after this war—it cannot last long—and go? Do you think I should go to America?" he asked, not noticing the child.

"Ah, that is another question," Sarah replied in a troubled voice. "I could not tell you what you should do. It is not so simple to go as you think. I have, perhaps, told you only the good parts. It is not like Budapest. There are no trees or flowers. Not anywhere near where the Jews can live in New York. It is as if the whole world has never seen a green thing. You forget the trees and the flowers there, Mendel, and you miss them. It is worse than you imagine to miss them."

"Yes, yes," he said again impatiently. "But the fear is not there. What do the trees and the flowers matter? And after all, I have a skill. I am a good tailor; I could get work there. Then, perhaps, we need not be so poor as you say."

"Oh, Mendel, there are many tailors in America. I would like to have you near me, but it is not so simple as you think, and simple things matter more than you imagine that they will. It is a long way from home. One does not come back easily."

"As you say, Sarah, as you say," he pacified her, belatedly remembering the fact that it was *Shabbos*. "We will have to think about it. It cannot be now. I have talked to Pinchas, as I told you. Not to the rest of the family. And if this war is over quickly, as Pinchas says—I mean he says it might be over quickly—why, then perhaps first we will move to Vienna, or even to Berlin, to earn some money and try the life of the city. Pinchas could go on ahead, because of his business connections. . . . Yes, that is what we might do, we might move to the city someday. . . ."

Now a light came into Sarah's eyes, and she became eager. "If you move to Vienna or to Berlin, you can move even sooner. It is not so hard to get to those places. Perhaps you could even take Mamma. . . . Perhaps there would be a doctor there who could help her. . . . There are many Jews in Vienna and Berlin—even Jews who are doctors." She was caught up for a minute in a plan that sounded so sensible, that could satisfy his ambition and would not expose him to what she had failed to explain. There were dangers he could not understand.

That evening Yakov and Dora came out of the lecture together, hand in hand. It had not been the best speaker they had ever heard, but they'd waited patiently for him to finish, waited for the time when they could leave, their own time. Every night, if there was no gathering at Kalinsky's, they went to a lecture or a poetry reading at the Educational Alliance, getting through the long summer twilight hours that way until the dark, until their own time.

They crossed the street wordlessly, passing the library to hurry toward their bench in Seward Park. It was dark; no one was on their bench. It waited for them.

Wordlessly Yakov turned to Dora and kissed her, bending over her creamy face, knowing her green eyes were closed in the dark as she returned his kiss. Their tongues found each other and she moved against him, pulling him down beside her on the bench. He knew he would never get enough of exploring Dora's mouth, Dora's breasts whose nipples seemed to reach for his hands. He groaned with his aching desire for her, and her little moans of pleasure at his touch came to him with her mouth still fastened to his.

He wrenched himself away at last and spoke. "I can't bear this," he said, his eyes closed for a moment as he struggled for control. "I have to be alone with you." His voice was urgent. "I want you so. Where can we find a place to be alone?"

"Alone?" Dora's eyes were open then, and he could catch the flicker of reality in them, reflected from the faraway lamplight. "There isn't any place to be alone." Still, her touch made it clear that it was her desire as well as his that would be assuaged only in that future solitude he sought.

"We have to find somewhere," he insisted, reaching for her again. "I can't stand this, I really can't."

"I know, my love, I know," came her soothing murmur. "I want you, too. We'll find a way. I love you so much."

"How?" His hands were on her again.

"I *have* thought of something," Dora acknowledged hesitantly after a few more kisses. Was she too bold in her thoughts? She took courage from him and went on. "When the holidays come at the end of September, I think my family are planning to go away to visit my aunt and uncle in Passaic. Then—"

"But that's more than a month from now!" Yakov's groan was despairing. It was already the beginning of August.

"Yes, it's more than a month from now"—Dora laughed softly as she covered his face and neck with fiery little kisses—"but it's not never." She found his mouth again. "Now kiss me," she insisted, "because I did think of something; it will happen. And because I'm the smartest woman you've ever met. And the most beautiful."

He kissed her smile with delight then, because she was indeed his only love. If he couldn't have Dora always and completely, he thought, he would die. And already he knew it was not just her body he wanted. That he would have, they could plan the way to be alone in a few short weeks, but he knew that even that would not be enough.

Later that evening Yakov walked home the long

way after he dropped off Dora; he had to think. He had to think about Dora, because now he knew consciously, even though the calendar said it was such a short time since they had met, that he was in love, that with Dora was his life. Dora and the Cause. Sometimes it seemed they were one entity in his mind—that freckled, redheaded, skinny little bundle of energy and beauty and wisdom, of devotion to what he believed in, and the belief itself. He resented every moment that he had to spend away from her, even the moments of the day when he worked in his shop and she worked in her shop, all those wasted moments when he was not near her, when he was not touching her. He wanted her—all the time.

Was it really possible that she could feel as he did—that she could want as he did the closeness of arms always around each other, of mouths kissing, loins pressed together? She said she wanted it. Even that thought was enough to make him hard so he had to stop walking a minute and turn toward a fence, leaning against it until the cast iron bit into his face and turned his mind with pain. And standing there, when he thought again of cupping those little round breasts in his hands, pinching those little hard nipples between his fingers, he couldn't walk on. The tightness in his groin just wouldn't go away, a physical swelling of the intensity of his imaginings. Would they really be able to be alone together at last? It seemed to him that to spend his life without Dora—his whole life—would be to spend it in perpetual loneliness, surrounded by strangers.

Because, he thought, as he resumed his walking at last and headed toward Orchard Street, everyone else in the world had become a stranger to him. Or perhaps always had been, and now he simply knew his aloneness. In that short summer since he had met her Dora Schneider had become for him the only person in the world who could complete him and make him

239

whole. And not just his body, he thought, though God knew how he wanted—needed—that. But it was more than that. All the rest of the world—even Kalinsky, even his family—were other, he told himself. Dora and he together were one.

Maybe it would be good, like the affair of Alexander Berkman and Emma Goldman, of whom he had read. They were separated many times, but always they were together in the Cause. (He chose for the moment to ignore the fact that their cause was somewhat different from his and Dora's. Dora's energy and intensity were like what he had heard of the young Emma Goldman, and perhaps he could emulate Berkman's early conviction and bravery as well.) Maybe it could be for them as it was for those famous lovers.

In a few weeks, near his birthday, would come the strike, he knew. Then, he reasoned, it could all be very simple. He would marry Dora, and then he would have her forever. Not just when her family went to Passaic, but forever. He stopped still with the vision. That was it—he would marry her. Why hadn't he thought of marriage before? It would be simple. All he had to do was ask her.

But when? When should he ask her? Doubts suddenly sank his heart. It was so soon; maybe he was only imagining her response in his own eagerness, he thought, forgetting the evening already in a sudden sea of doubt. Perhaps, too, she didn't want something so conventional as marriage. Maybe he should wait until after the strike, until after the holidays, when they would be alone together. First they would be together in the strike, in the Cause; that was it, he decided. Then he would ask her.

In the beginning of August, and for the remainder of that week when the war broke out in the rest of the world, Rachel was busiest bottling plums. Work actually made the war news irrelevant. The ripe fruit wouldn't wait, even for a war, even for her fears.

The heat that summer had made the fruit ripen early, and each morning she went out and picked baskets of purple plums from the trees near her grandmother's house and brought them in warm from the sun. The smell of the sweet fruit cloyed at her all day. When she pricked the smooth skins the juice stained her hands with a purple that never seemed to wash out, not during that whole week they were busy with the plums.

She learned from Sarah how to pit the fruit with a quick push of her thumb after it was washed, and how to stir it in the large pot with the sugar and as little water as possible.

"Don't let her put too much sugar in," said Rivka from her chair by the door. "Sugar costs money, and the fruit will be sweet."

"Do you want to taste and see if it's all right, Mamma?" asked Sarah.

"No, I never taste," she replied. "I can tell from the smell. It smells good," she went on, encouraging her granddaughter.

"Oh, I'm so hot," said Rachel as the steam rose from the large pot, turning her arms red.

"Here, we'll change jobs," said Sarah. "I'll stir a little while. You pit."

"The important thing is to keep stirring," Sarah went on from her new position in the cloud of steam. "It will burn otherwise."

Rachel wiped the sweat from her face with the edge of the apron.

"Don't drip in the bowl of fruit," laughed her grandmother. "This is the first year I've only watched when the plums were done. From the time I was a little girl I did the job with my mother. Why haven't you taught Rachel before?" she asked Sarah.

"We do not have plums like this in New York,"

answered Sarah. "There are no trees to grow plums in New York. There may not be any in all America, for all I know."

"No trees? But it is the city. What did you expect? You must buy the plums in the city." Rivka sounded positive.

"One must have money to buy, Mamma. Isaac does not see the need for plums."

"Oh, well, he is probably right. After all, it is a lot of work and heat, the plums every summer." The old woman hesitated. "You have said that Isaac is good?"

"Yes, he is good." It was the truth, and she knew it. She had married him for his scholarship, true, but also because he was a good man. She had not married David, who was not a scholar but was also a good man. She had been taught how to decide from her youngest years. Why must she still feel such pain from that right decision? And this secret wish to maybe stay always in her mother's house? "But I've missed the plums. . . ." was all she said.

"How sweet the steam smells. If only I could drown in this time. Never have to go back. Drown and stay in this sweet time.

But how could I explain it to Rachel? Already she is afraid. Oh, Rachel, you have been gentle from the beginning. Your very coming into the world was kinder and better than the pain I had with the others.

And you learn about pain soon enough, *zies kind*. You will grow to be a woman and learn. I cannot add to that.

Will it never end, the pain? Why do I go over and over it, opening old wounds? If I could explain to Rachel, if I could explain to Mamma, the story of it . . . (the story of how I was seventeen and went to a dance and met two men there, and one I loved, but he was above me and a musician. Whoever heard of a musician? The other loved me, and he was Isaac the

242

scholar, whom I married. But it is also the story of how I find myself unable to forget the first one, David, who may have loved me—I never knew for a certainty if that was so, and now I will never know, because I did not marry him. To him I did not bear my children.) If it is all reduced to such a story that can be told, it sounds so small a tale. Maybe I can find a way to bear it and get beyond it if I can tell it, maybe find a way home—for, small as it may sound, it has even followed me here, where I came to escape it.

Yet even with that story I cannot tell there is still the fact of my beloved children, whom I did bear to Isaac, and whom I do miss now so dreadfully.

So how can I stay? But how can I go?

Rachel lifted her head from the pitting and smiled at her grandmother. "I'm glad Mamma brought me," she said. "Now I'll tell Shayna about bottling plums when I write to her." She sighed. "If I'm not too tired to write the letter," she added, knowing nothing of ships that might not sail to carry such a letter.

The dark brown thickness and the sweet smell, turning slightly acid, filled the room as the steam billowed. All three of them, even Rivka sitting by the door, were red-faced and dripping before the afternoons were over that week. Rachel felt for days that her right thumbnail was redder than it should be, even after she had scrubbed and scrubbed at it. And her hands smelled of plums for a long time. She always remembered the plums with pleasure. But for Sarah, ever afterward, the scent of ripe plums was the scent of old pain.

## ❧ 9 ❧

*For the Lord thy God*
*is a jealous God. (Deuteronomy 6:15)*

Now what are you doing, Miss Lazybones?" Tante
Tillie came sneaking up behind Shayna, who was
sitting at the kitchen table with the newspaper propped
in front of her, anxiously scanning the war news and
trying to decipher the daily maps of the eastern and
western fronts.

"Oh, I didn't hear you come in," Shayna said,
folding the *Times* as quickly as she could.

"Don't look so guilty, miss. I knew you would be
reading."

"But Tante Tillie, the Russians are—"

Tillie went right on, paying no attention to the war
news. "And I bet that the supper has still to be
made. I come home from work exhausted, and the
supper has still to be made. What I don't do around
here . . ."

"Oh, Tante Tillie, it's so hot, can't you please—"

But Tillie rounded on her before she could finish.
"Can't I please what? Don't you think it's hot for me,
too? What do you think it's been like in that shop all
day in an August heat wave? You and your fancy
mother aren't the only people in the world, you know."

244

"I finished the potatoes. There's nothing else anyway, so why are you yelling at me?" Shayna suddenly shouted even louder than her aunt had done.

"Oh, so the perfect temper finally gives way, does it? I knew you'd turn on me one day, you vicious little thing!" Tillie screamed. Her breath smelled bad, and she spit her words at Shayna. "Well, your mother isn't here to protect you now, so we'll see what your father says when he comes home and finds how you talk to me. We'll see if he doesn't use the strap on you again. After all I've done for you . . ." She stopped a moment, as if the enormity of her goodness to Shayna and the children was beyond her ability to catalog. Then she finished with the conclusion Shayna always knew and always feared from her mean aunts. "What you need, young lady, is some training in the home, not all this fancy-schmancy reading all the time. What you need is to quit school in November on your fourteenth birthday and do some work for a change!"

Shayna turned away and bent to straighten a pillow on the bed. To show how Tante Tillie was scaring her wouldn't do, and anyway she was so hot and uncomfortable that she wanted only to lie down. She knew if she continued to argue it would just get worse. If only there was a cool place she could lie down.

Tillie, however, didn't believe in letting her niece escape. "Turn around and look at me when I talk to you," she demanded. "I don't intend to talk to the wall." She seemed unwilling to let go of her favorite theme. "And remember—you will have to go out and help to earn a little money too when your birthday comes, miss. I'm not talking idly. No matter what Mrs. Rockefeller said, your father is the one who decides. And I think he will agree with me that there must be an end to your foolishness. Time enough for a great girl like you to finish in that school and begin to help the family. If you don't know how to run a house, the least you can do is go out and help to earn. No more school for you, miss, after November, and no more of that everlasting reading, either.''

To Tante Tillie's satisfaction the tears began to run down Shayna's cheeks. Soon she was sobbing.

"Please, Tante Tillie, don't say anything to Poppa about school," she begged. School would start in another few weeks. What if because of the war in Europe Mamma didn't come home? What if Mamma never came home and she couldn't finish school?

It was Tillie who turned away now, and busied herself with setting things out for the meal. She sniffed once in contempt as she did so. And she had a last question. "Where are the little ones? Have you lost them again?''

It was certainly one of the days when a small part of Shayna wished that she had indeed lost them, so she felt a twinge of guilt as she answered, "Tante Sadie took them home with her for the afternoon. Just Sophie and Harry. David's napping in the other room."

"Sadie took them again?" Tillie shook her head. There were mysteries about her sister Sadie that she simply did not understand these days. "Why do you make your aunt take care of them when you're home and perfectly able to do it? Shirking, that's it, you are always shirking."

"Tante Sadie said Uncle Franz had to meet someone uptown, and she also had to go somewhere, so Sophie and Harry could take care of the store for half an hour before Uncle Franz got back—they've helped before."

"Why didn't she ask you? You're older."

"Oh, Tante Tillie, I don't know," sighed Shayna, then she instantly regretted her impatience. Mamma had never shown Tante Tillie impatience.

But Tillie only glared at her this time, too hot to yell yet again. Where had Sadie needed to go?

\*　　\*　　\*

There weren't any customers at first, and Harry was feeling bored. He opened the cash register the way Uncle Franz had shown him, standing on a small stool to see into it.

"Let's see how much there is in the till," he said to Sophie.

She was at her usual favorite place, fingering the embroidery threads with her good hand.

"Okay," she said absently, "you go ahead."

Her cast was itching in the heat, and she wished she could take off the sling that was so hot around her neck. Shayna had washed it for her again last night, but it got hot and sweaty every day. Her arm no longer hurt, but she had outlasted her notoriety in the neighborhood, and now having a broken arm was becoming just a misery without compensations. She wished that she could have gone with Tante Sadie to the doctor to have the cast taken off, but it wasn't time yet, and besides, Tante Sadie had said that the doctor she was going to wasn't for casts. Sophie had loved being the center of attention for a while. But no one noticed her anymore, and now she had even had to come over here and help in the store. It wasn't fair.

"Eighteen dollars and fifty-seven cents," said Harry. "Wow! That's certainly a lot of money."

"More than *chai*," agreed Sophie, also impressed. *Chai* was the Hebrew word for "eighteen," and the same word meant "life," so *chai* was an important number.

"Look, Soph," Harry began, stepping down from the stool and leaving the drawer open so she could come and look for herself. "Would it be all right if I went outside for a little? There's no one here, and it's awfully hot."

He was hoping to pick up a marbles game if he was lucky. He had brought a couple of good ones in his pocket. Maybe he'd make some new friends over here in Uncle Franz's neighborhood. It was all part of his plan to come here and live with Uncle Franz and Tante Sadie. Even though they had told him it was not possible, he still had hopes. He'd heard the grown-ups talking about whether Mamma was stuck now in the old country till the end of some war, and if it lasted until school began, he had a feeling that maybe . . .

"Go on," Sophie said to him. She sighed. With a broken arm she was not going to be able to run around or play outside the whole rest of the summer, so Harry could go. She knew how to make change better than he did anyway.

Harry didn't need to be told twice. He went out, banging the door behind him, and left her alone. She settled into Tante Sadie's chair near the bolts of fabric. If only she could embroider, it would help to while away the time, but even that was not possible because of her arm.

"Good morning. Is Mrs. Cantrovitz here?" asked an old lady who was somehow suddenly standing beside her. Sophie rubbed her eyes, realizing she must have dozed off for a second. She hadn't heard the door.

"No," she said, remembering her job. "May I help you?"

"I'm wanting a skein of this blue wool," the woman said, bringing out a sample after some rummaging in her large bag.

Sophie tucked the blue piece in her sling, then went surely to the drawer with the wool in it. She opened it with her left hand.

"Is this the right color?" she asked, holding out a skein she had compared with the sample. She handed them both to the customer. "You'd better take it to the window to check," she went on.

"It is," said the woman gratefully after a moment's inspection. "You're a smart little girl."

"I'm Mrs. Cantrovitz's niece," said Sophie, proud of it. She had that, at least, to be grateful for. "Tante Sadie always says that blue is the hardest color to match."

"How much is it?"

"Ten cents," said Sophie, looking at the tag.

"I'm an old customer," began the woman, "and—"

"In that case," Sophie went on, having heard the bargaining in the store on other occasions, "perhaps" —she looked at the letter S on the tag and remembered Uncle Franz's code; S stood for eight—"I can give it to you for eight cents," she finished.

The woman handed her a dime, and she went to the till, which was still open, and gave the woman the two pennies that were there. Now there was eighteen dollars and sixty-five cents, she noted with pleasure. She was doing her job. Because of her cast it was easiest to leave the cash register drawer open.

The woman left as two men entered the store. Really, if customers came in so fast, Sophie found herself hoping that Harry would come in soon, too.

"May I help you?" she asked importantly from behind the counter. She felt she was running things well.

One of the men smiled at her and came over. "I'm looking for a shirt," he said. The other man waited by the door.

"We have several prices," said Sophie.

"May I see them?"

"Certainly," she said. She opened the lowest shirt drawer. It was over by the dress rack at the far end of the counter. She brought the shirts to him where he stood.

"How much are these?" he asked.

"Forty-nine cents," she replied.

He fingered a shirt. "Do you have something better?" he asked.

"Yes," said Sophie. "We have sixty-nine-cent shirts

and ninety-eight-cent shirts.'' Thank heaven she had paid attention when Uncle Franz was dealing with the customers.

"May I see them?"

Sophie took the one she had out and put it back in the drawer, then reached for the higher drawer with the sixty-nine-cent shirts. She got one out and handed it to the man. "If you want to look at this," she said, "it will take me a minute to get the more expensive ones. They're on the top shelf."

She got the chair and put it behind the counter so she could climb up. It was complicated to reach for the box of ninety-eight-cent shirts with her left arm. Everything always took longer because of her cast, and she hoped the man wouldn't be impatient. He seemed to be shuffling his feet before her as if he was. She was still on the chair, with the box in her hand, when she heard the door open. She turned her head to see who had come in, and what she saw was the same two men, but they were leaving. The shirts were still on the counter. And in the same second, with a sick horror, she realized that the till was still open, and it was empty. The money was gone.

"Stop, thief!" she screamed after them, getting down from the chair as fast as she could, even dropping the shirt box on the floor in her hurry. She ran out the open door screaming, "Stop, thief! Stop, thief!" at the top of her lungs, nearly bumping into Harry, who had come back after all. "Did you see them?" she cried, still running. "Follow them, follow them. Oh, Harry, run after them quick—they stole the money! Stop, thief!"

Harry took up the cry and tore off after the two running men, who were dodging among the crowds. Sophie had to go back into the store; she couldn't leave it untended, she knew, but what worse could happen? She was crying. This was surely the most awful thing. Eighteen dollars and sixty-five cents, and they had taken it all! What would happen to her? She thought she would just die. Could Harry catch them? Would anyone help him? And what would Tante Sadie and Uncle Franz say? What would Poppa say?

But it was Sophie's heroism, Harry's heroism (that, to the children's delighted surprise, was Tante Sadie's version!) that Poppa and Tante Tillie and Shayna heard about over the potatoes at supper. Because Harry had nearly caught the thieves. Nearly enough, since his shouts and his chase had, in the end, actually prompted the policeman at the corner of Houston and Avenue D to catch them. Harry and Sophie had told the story, and the men had been arrested. The policeman had even written down Sophie's name, and Tante Sadie said in a hushed voice that Sophie would have to appear in court. She would be a witness at the trial, said Tante Sadie.

So Sophie was again a heroine. Everyone felt sorry for her again—poor little girl with her broken arm, and such a terrible thing had happened to her—even Mrs. Goldstein was nice to her the next morning. Motherless now, too, everybody said, shaking their heads. But that was the next morning, after the fire.

Yakov was the one who warned them of the fire. He was coming home from an evening with Dora when he heard a roll of thunder in the distance. Perhaps, he thought, there would finally be some rain to relieve the everlasting heat. He happened to look up from the street as he turned the corner onto Orchard Street, and it was then that he saw the flames.

Later investigation by the firemen and the neighbors seemed to indicate that in fact the fire began in Mrs. Pincus's fourth-floor kitchen. Why Mrs. Pincus should have left a pot boiling on the stove after she and her husband had gone to bed, no one was ever able to discover. The night was stifling already. It was hard to imagine someone leaving extra heat escaping on such an August night, when there was not a breath of air even at ten o'clock in the evening. But somehow, as far as anyone could tell, Mrs. Pincuses' pot had been left boiling, it had boiled out, and then it had turned red-hot.

When the storm's first breezes came the pot had caught a wisp of curtain that had chanced to blow in the direction of the stove. By the time the thunder and lightning were wakingly loud from across town, across the Hudson River, the Pincuses' curtains were burning, the window frame had caught, and tongues of fire were reaching for the rest of the fourth-floor kitchen. The flames seemed to leap out of the open window on the fourth floor, and the sight of them made Yakov forget Dora, forget romance, forget the Cause, forget everything but a primitive panic that galvanized him to action.

*"Fire, fire, fire!"* he shouted as he wrenched the front door open and ran into the building. "Wake up, wake up, wake up! Everybody wake up! *Fire!"* he continued to scream as he took the stairs three at a time. The smoke on the fourth floor was rolling out from under the Pincuses' door. He knew that the Pincuses' flat was right below his own, and his whole body seemed to turn light with fear as he ran up that last flight and burst into his own apartment.

"Wake up, wake up, wake up!" he puffed, his voice seeming too soft to his own ears. "Shayna, Poppa, Tante Tillie, get the children. *Hurry!"* He screamed it, running into the little bedroom and grabbing David up as he came.

"What is it, what's the matter?" asked Shayna, looking in surprised sleepiness from her bed. "Yakov, what are you screaming about?"

*"Fire,"* he said still shouting, still with that desperate sense of inadequacy. "Look, the smoke is even coming up through the cracks in the floor. Hurry,

252

Shayna, take Sophie. Poppa, Poppa, for God's sake get up and come."

For the first time in his life the closed door to his parents' room was not a barrier to him. He wrenched it open to find Isaac stepping into a pair of trousers and reaching for a shirt. "Don't stop to dress," said Yakov. "Hurry, all of you."

Tante Tillie had risen at first in silence but stood still now with tears of terror streaming down her face, rooted to the floor beside her bed, looking down at the smoke that rose beneath her feet. "Isaac, Isaac," she wailed, "we're all going to die. The fire, Isaac, the fire."

Meanwhile, Shayna grabbed Sophie's good arm and held her close. She felt more dazed than frightened as she, too, smelled the fire. She went to the door of the apartment first and reached for the knob. She gasped then, drawing back instinctively. "Yakov, it's warm. How did you come up here?"

"The flames must have gotten to the stairs," replied Yakov, truly frantic. "Stop crying, Tante Tillie, and take David while I look out and see if the fire escape is all right."

But it was Isaac who reached for the little boy, because Tillie still remained rooted to one spot.

"Come on, it's okay here," said Yakov as he went out the window onto the fire escape. "Just don't look down. Pretend it's a game, Shayna, and don't ever look down. There, Tante Tillie," he went on, coaxing her, "you can do it. Just follow Shayna and the children." He pushed Harry along. "No, Poppa, you go first, and then I'll go."

For Shayna, that journey down five levels of the fire escape—past what seemed like endless flaming windows and screaming people, stepping over the bedclothes of those tenants who had been spending the night out there, down, down, endlessly down—

253

was accomplished in what later appeared to have been a complete daze. "Hush, Sophie, it will be all right, just watch your arm, it will be all right," she kept crooning to her sister, who trembled with fright. But she herself did not feel a thing. She just went mechanically down the fire escape and did as Yakov had told her; she did not look down.

Twice Tante Tillie stopped behind her and screamed, but Shayna heard the screams as she would have heard them in a dream. They aren't real, she thought, none of this is real. It's all a story that we're playing out, I'm a thirteen-year-old girl in an exciting story, and in a little while we will be on the street, safe at the end of the story.

She heard the bells of the firemen down below her when she got to the second floor, and the whole world seemed lit up.

"It's all right, little lady," a kind Irish voice said beside her, and someone helped her down the last few steps. "Don't cry, miss, it's all right. Here you are, safe and sound."

Shayna hadn't even known that she was crying, so she turned to thank the tall fireman. But suddenly his face got all wavy in front of her, and a black cloud seemed to rise from the ground, enveloping her in darkness before she could get the words out.

The next thing she heard was the same fireman's voice with its Irish lilt: "There, there, you're all right, wake up now, it's all all right. Hey, someone, dump some water on her head. . . . There you are, that woke you, didn't it?"

He seemed very kind as she sat up spluttering. But it didn't help. "What happened?" she gasped. "Where are the children?" She was instantly afraid. "Oh, my God, I lost the children in the fire? Where are the children?"

"Your mother probably has the children, miss, so just relax. It's all right."

"My mother is gone," she gasped, and the enormity of her words made her weep afresh. "I was supposed to take care of the children. And now I've lost them?" Her eyes were wild, searching the crowd until at last she spied Isaac standing near the fire engine. "Poppa, Poppa," she called in desperation. "I've lost the children." But with all the shouting and the noise of the fire fighters, Isaac did not hear her call. She felt so frightened that she thought her voice was making no sounds, just like a terrible dream she had once in which she called and called without sound, called and called for help, and there was no call that could be heard. "Poppa, Poppa," she tried fruitlessly again.

She struggled to her feet and stood in her night dress, shivering despite the heat of the summer night. Her hands kept twisting before her as she searched blindly around the crowd for the children, never able to focus on anyone except her father, who couldn't hear her.

"Look, young lady, tell me then, how many children did you have to take care of?" The fireman's voice was still patient, if his tone was becoming a little exasperated.

"Three," Shayna mumbled, dazed and still terrified.

"Look, little lady." He spoke slowly so that she would be able to comprehend the words. He knew from long experience, it seemed, how hard it was for people who had been wakened by a fire in the middle of the night to take in what was said to them. "Look— one, two, three!" And he actually pointed to Sophie and Harry and David, who were clinging to Shayna's nightgown. Yes, even David was there beside her, having been somewhat unceremoniously dumped by Sophie's side when Isaac had reached the bottom of the fire escape.

At last Shayna focused her eyes. "One, two, three," she repeated, counting aloud for the comfort of it, at last with a voice that made sounds. "One, two, three," she shouted then, in tremendous relief. And she began to cry great choking sobs as she gathered her brothers and sister in her arms. She hadn't failed this time, after all. *"One, two, three!"*

And then she began to laugh. It was hysterical laughter, but Poppa was furious when he found her there laughing. He didn't understand. But at least he didn't beat her. Yakov, standing behind him, looked very far away.

Later, much later, Shayna learned that the firemen had managed to contain the fire enough so that only the Pincuses and another family on the fourth floor were burned out completely. Of course, if it had not been a hot night, so that the windows were open, they would all have been killed by the smoke. Everyone was able to get back into the house eventually, thank God. Where would they have gone? And how would Mamma have found them when she got back if they'd had to move?

Leah Morgenstern had written a couple of letters to Aaron, and after the mails stopped she sent a cable weekly to his office. She made sure that the cables were cheerful.

She and the girls had several weeks at the Ritz in Paris before the hostilities began to interfere with their plans. (And at first they were able to ignore the war, since it was not close by.) Their Paris shopping was the sort of thing Leah put in her cables. She never put in her worries about Ethel.

Ethel was not consulted by her mother or her sister about any of their plans. But Ethel did not talk to them either, so they had both given up talking to her. Ethel's silence was not a subject on which Aaron received any cables. He did not hear from his wife about how Ethel barely spoke to them at all on the whole journey over, barely spoke all the weeks they were in Paris.

Diana and Leah talked to each other, and they talked often about Ethel as the weeks went by, because Ethel was their problem. She did not seem to improve. She was not interested in the glamorous doings of Paris at all. Diana complained to her mother that Ethel did not even care about the beautiful clothes they managed to have made despite this ridiculous war. Ethel just went through the fittings without commenting on the silks or the embroidery, lifting her arms mechanically when she was told to do so, turning like a puppet when the seamstress pinned the hems. You'd think—and the younger daughter spoke of it resentfully to Leah—you'd think that Ethel would be over her stupid love affair by now; it was more than a month ago, wasn't it? Tragic, soulful looks were certainly boring.

Then, after they'd been in Paris a while, the mails stopped. They sent the cables to Daddy, but they never heard from him. There weren't mails for weeks and weeks, so Diana thought it was understandable that Ethel hadn't heard a word from James Olson either. And even if she had, Leah would have confiscated the letter, Diana knew, because Daddy had said Ethel was never to correspond with him in any way, not ever again. Her mother always obeyed Daddy's wishes in important matters. So why did Ethel remain so endlessly silent? Her looks made Diana nervous, so nervous that they were one thing she and her mother did not discuss.

"What are you thinking of, Ethel?" Diana finally asked her sister one day. "You're always so quiet."

Ethel gave her a look in which even Diana could see the agony. "I have a lot to think of," she said quietly. "So much that I'm not sure I can live with it." Diana certainly did not tell her mother of that short conversation.

And Leah never spoke of how her heart bled for her child. The shopping, the clothes, the luxuries their money bought—all of it was dust in her mouth when she looked at the pain in the eyes of her beloved daughter. Would Ethel ever get over this blow?

While Shayna worked at scrubbing the smoke stains, Sophie was often with her indoors. She sat with her cast resting on the table as she watched Shayna work. Glancing at her, Shayna tried not to feel jealous of her little sister, but it was hard. Why did Sophie always seem to land buttered side up? Yes, she said to herself, Sophie was lost, but then she was found. Yes, Sophie was hurt and had a broken arm, but Sophie would soon be well, and anyway now she was a heroine because of the thieves. Shayna herself was so often in the wrong, and Sophie was a heroine.

At least Sophie seemed to be trying to be more grown up, to be company for her, Shayna told herself. She was trying not to complain about how hot and itchy the cast was. And she was scared sometimes about her coming appearance in court, even though the time had not yet been scheduled. Shayna could tell she was scared when she said, "I'm eleven years old now, you know, Shayna." It did sound grown up. "When Mamma comes home," Sophie declared, "I'll tell her about things myself. You won't have to tell her. It wasn't your fault."

"Sophie, we don't know when Mamma's going to be able to come home now, because of the war." Shayna tried to put patience into her voice, as she had each time Sophie had spoken of Mamma's return. "But she'll be proud to have a brave eleven-year-old daughter when she does come," she remembered to add. (Maybe, she tried to tell herself, it wasn't anybody's fault, any of it.)

But that was hard to feel, at thirteen. Mostly Shayna felt crushed, crushed and jealous of anyone whose lot seemed easier, even her little sister. It was as if the grownups of the world—even the grownups far away in Europe—had all ganged up on her. Her aunts had certainly conspired against her. Her poppa could not hear or understand anything she said. What matter whose fault? The world wasn't fair! There were days at the end of that summer, many days, when Shayna hated the whole world.

"Do you think Mamma will find a ship and be home in time for your birthday in November?" Sophie persisted. "Tante Tillie says that when you're fourteen you'll have to quit school and go to work to help out. Do you think Mamma will be home by then?"

"Oh, Sophie, I hope so, because I don't want to quit school," Shayna said. That much she felt she could say to Sophie; no more. And she was less and less sure that Mamma could rescue her if she did come.

"But Tante Tillie and Tante Sadie were talking to Poppa, and—"

"If Mamma's here, I won't have to quit. Mamma said I could graduate from high school." Shayna said the words, even though she was no longer able to feel them. Now Mamma was in a faraway place where there was a war, and who knew if she could find a ship to come home? Who knew if she would still think the same way when she did come? Shayna knew that she herself had changed from that sure-of-herself girl she had been when Mamma left. Maybe Mamma would change, too.

"But if Poppa says—"

Shayna's patience finally snapped. Even her own sister didn't understand. "I'm too hot and tired to listen to this, Sophie," she said. "And no matter how much Tante Tillie and Tante Sadie and Poppa say, it doesn't matter. I'm going to finish school." Her words spoke a bravery she wanted to feel.

"Well, your birthday isn't until the middle of November, so don't start yelling at me now," replied Sophie, trying to soothe her.

The problem wasn't Sophie's problem, after all, Shayna reflected. She had probably just been offering up a kind of grown-up gossip as she had heard her elders do.

"Why don't you tell me a story, Shayna?" Sophie changed the subject.

"Okay," said Shayna, agreeing easily because she was glad of an excuse not to think about the most pressing of her worries for a minute. Jealousy aside, she needed Sophie, wanted to stay friends with her little sister. She certainly didn't want to argue if she could avoid it. On the other hand, the war was uppermost in her mind. She'd tell a story about the war. "Did I tell you the story I read in the paper about a terrible curse"— she made her voice as scary and mysterious as she could—"that was put on the old, old man who is emperor of Austria?"

"What curse?"

"Well, it seems that long ago, many many years ago, there was a great countess, the Countess Karolyi, in Austria, or maybe it was Hungary, I forget which, and they're both part of the same empire—I mean they're ruled by the same emperor, and—"

"Yes," said Sophie, impatient in turn. She wasn't interested in facts, just stories. "But what do you mean a curse? Tell about the curse, Shayna, not the empire."

"Listen a minute then. This Countess Karolyi had a son—I think it was her only son—who fought in Kossuth's army in the Revolution in 1848. You remember I told you about how our grandfather fought in Kossuth's army?"

"Yes, but what curse? Come on, Shayna!"

"Well, this son of the Countess Karolyi was put to

death by the emperor for helping in that insurrection—I like the word 'insurrection,' don't you?"

"Shayna, stop teasing and tell me the story."

"Well, the son had been put to death, and the countess was so angry and sad that she put a curse on the emperor. The curse was that he should live to be very, very old, which sounded like good luck, but the bad luck was that the emperor should see all his family stricken, those closest to him dying in shame and disgrace, and his children going astray and wrecking their own lives and the lives of others. It was a terrible curse."

"But that was a long time ago."

"Yes, but that emperor is the Emperor Franz Joseph who is still there now; he *is* a very very old man, and part of it has come true already, and more of it is coming true nowadays. I mean, for instance, a long time ago one of the emperor's sons, the Archduke Rudolf, died in very mysterious circumstances with a woman named Marie Vetsera in a hunting lodge at a place called Mayerling, and no one knows quite what happened, but he wasn't married to the woman, and it was certainly shame and disgrace, just as the countess's curse had predicted. And nowadays, with the assassination of the heir to the throne at Sarajevo, which has plunged the whole of Europe into a war, the paper said it sounds as if the Countess Karolyi's curse on the emperor's family is really coming true."

"Do you think that a curse like that can really come true, Shayna?" asked Sophie after a minute's contemplation. "Do you think that's really the way things happen? I mean, could someone bring misfortunes on another person really? Because maybe that's why I hurt my arm and the thieves came and everything. . . ."

It was a moral for her story of which Shayna had certainly not thought, and if she had thought of it, was it to Sophie that she would have applied it? But they never had a chance to discuss who might have cursed whom and caused what, because just then Poppa came in, and both girls knew better than to continue talking about such things when he was in the house. Would he believe a foreign countess's curse could cause all their troubles? Shayna knew he would not. And he was always angry if they talked too much.

Yakov skipped stories about people like the Countess Karolyi when he sat poring over the war news in the paper, waiting on the stoop for Moish on *Shabbos* afternoon. "It's cooler down here," he said through the cigarette dangling from his mouth when, on his arrival, Moish collapsed beside him. "And anyway, my father is upstairs. We can't talk in front of him."

"No," agreed Moish, draping his short, thin form over two steps. "I heard him shushing the other men yesterday when they were talking about Morgenstern."

"He's always scared when Morgenstern's name comes up," said Yakov.

"Yes, but telling the story about how his wife and daughters have gone away to buy Paris gowns," Moish insisted, "while we sweat in one of Morgenstern's shops to make American clothes that aren't good enough for the likes of the big boss—that kind of story helps with the organization."

Yakov nodded. It had infuriated him to hear it, and he had spread the word eagerly until Poppa had started hushing everyone. He let himself imagine for a second how Dora would look in one of those gowns he had seen described in the paper—she would look lovely.

Moish loosened the tie he had worn in deference to propriety and the Sabbath day, not knowing for sure Yakov Klugerman's attitude about such things. "I don't know when I've been so hot," he said. Indeed, the sweat was dripping down his sallow cheeks, and the back of his jacket was wet with it. He didn't smell too good either, thought Yakov, but then he realized that he was probably no perfumed prizewinner himself on such a day.

"At least the sun is not on this side of the street now," they both said at the same time, then they laughed.

"I think we ought to talk a little about the strike plans before we get together with the girls," said Moish, coming quickly to the purpose of his visit. "I mean, we should have a plan before we discuss things with them. There are some things I want to go over with you first." Moish had been a union member for several years; he was the experienced older hand.

"What things?" asked Yakov, eager to learn.

"Well, first of all, you know that with the shirtwaist workers involved, it will be a bigger splash. Ever since that fire at the Triangle Shirtwaist factory, where all those girls were killed, anything with girls is a bigger splash, but we have to be sure that we get publicity. It's important for the newspaper people to be there if strikebreakers come, for instance." He hesitated. "We can count on Dora Schneider to hold the girls together, can't we, even if the bosses bring scabs and they try to cross the picket line? You know her better than I do—how do you think she'll act if scabs really come?"

"What do you mean, act?" asked Yakov. It was suddenly more complicated than he had thought it would be.

"Yakov." Moish was not succeeding very well at being patient with his inexperience, that was clear, and it embarrassed Yakov. "Sometimes I can't believe how innocent you are! Remember, there may be violence. What I'm asking you is do you think Dora can hold them together if there's violence on her picket line?"

Suddenly Yakov's mind filled with a horrible picture. It seemed he could actually see Dora hurt, hurt terribly, blood covering that red hair, matting it down, streaming over the freckled face he loved, over the breasts he touched with ecstasy, over the thin white arms that disdained the covering of a shawl even on cooler evenings at the end of summer. Violence? Dora? He shuddered.

"Hold them together?" He tried to keep his tone even despite the stab of fear in his gut.

"Will she have the courage if they come with clubs, for instance, to continue the picket line, to hold out? Or will she break and run?" Moish's voice was hard and loud.

"Oh, Dora has courage, don't you worry about that," said Yakov, determinedly dismissing his worries from his mind. He had known that there would be people crossing the picket lines. After all, this was for the Cause, wasn't it, and he knew that Dora's belief in the Cause was true and unshakable. His own was true and unshakable, too. What they were planning was right, what they were doing was right, it was a matter of high purpose, and he had better concentrate on the important things Moish could teach him, not allow foolish visions to color his mind. Dora was brave like Emma Goldman. She could take care of herself, couldn't she?

"Good—then, about arranging to get newspaper publicity for our efforts . . ." It was as if Moish was ticking off items on an agenda he had been given. (By whom?) "Do you think you could get in touch with this guy you met who takes photographs for the *Tribune*? You remember his name, you said. Because if we can be sure when the scabs will arrive, we could have him there with his camera all set up, and then he could give us the coverage we need. I think the coverage would be best if the violence does hit the girls, don't you?" Moish hurried on. "I mean, people care more if they see girls getting hurt in the pictures—then they'll be bound to see our side."

"But how can we possibly know when the scabs will be called in or where they'll go?" asked Yakov, dull again with noncomprehension. For some reason he was feeling sick to his stomach. He wouldn't allow himself to think why. But he did wonder if Alexander Berkman was sick before he shot Frick in the Homestead strike. It didn't help to know history if he didn't know important things like that.

"Dora and the girls can stage something that will force the issue, perhaps—no, that won't work. . . . I know," said Moish, suddenly glowing. "I know Morgenstern will probably do it, but just in case, we can secretly hire some scabs ourselves and arrange the confrontation to suit our own convenience." He wanted Yakov to think that he had just hatched the idea that moment. (It was only later that Yakov reflected on what a good actor Moish was, or was it that Kalinsky had coached him well?) "That way we can, if we want, work it all out to our own timetable."

"But that's wrong!" said Yakov, forgetting his apprentice position. "I mean"—he tried to correct the tone of it—"if we could settle it peacefully, isn't that better? And what if our people get hurt? Wouldn't that be our own fault?" His father, he knew very well, would be crossing his picket line, so was he turning violence on his own father? What did it mean "*our* people might get hurt?" Why wasn't it simple anymore?

"What counts?" Moish asked, carefully going back to the theoretical. "What counts is the Cause, right?" He led Yakov through the steps slowly, with the patience he had not previously displayed. "People's individual bodies and lives are only instruments for use to further the Cause, to achieve the goal, right? So if a few people get hurt, what does that really matter?" It wasn't only acting; he did believe it, and his eyes did burn with conviction more than the afternoon's warmth could account for. "Yakov," he went on, "you have to remember the main point. What counts is the Cause. That's all that counts."

Yakov wished he could catch some of the warmth of the belief. "But using women like that . . ." he began; his stomach hurt again.

"Are you going to let a little thing like this upset you to begin with? Remember, this is just the beginning for you. 'The ends justify the means.' Keep the ends in mind. You have a future in the movement; don't forget that either." Moish played lightly on the ambition he knew was part of Yakov's motivation.

"But . . ."

His mentor switched to a conciliatory tack. "Look, Yakov," he said, "I understand how you're feeling. But the fact is that this is the first strike you've been involved in, isn't it?"

Yakov nodded. He had to acknowledge his inexperience. But his sickness wouldn't disappear. Why hadn't Kalinsky been the one to talk to him? Kalinsky was more his friend than Moish.

"Well, then, you're concerned in a way you'll learn not to be so concerned the next time around. Just watch—you'll see, it will all come off like clockwork, and the trouble will be minor. But"—he hesitated, then decided he'd better say it—"you'd better not talk to Dora too much about being nervous."

Yakov's mouth opened to protest, but Moish waved aside his unvoiced thoughts. "Yes, yes, I know that you have a feeling for her, but you have to remember that your personal feelings are less important than the Cause. Speak to Kalinsky if you want to hear it from authority," he offered.

"No, of course . . ." Yakov shook his head, still trying for the sophistication he did not feel. Besides, he knew that if Moish said that, then Kalinsky would have nothing new to add.

"Well, then," Moish finished, "just be sure to tell Dora when we have it all arranged what will happen—

so she'll know when the scabs are coming and how to do the best for the newspapers. It's very important to have photographs in the papers, not only stories. And be very sure she doesn't tell anybody else who actually employed these scabs."

"Can't we count on the bosses to produce the scabs, though? If the strike lasts long enough, won't that happen anyway? And wouldn't that be better?" Yakov asked his questions rapidly, in a last-ditch attempt to change Moish's mind. He felt he was wrong to try, but at the same time he felt it, the words came out of his mouth.

But Moish was adamant, and since he was in charge of the final set of plans for Kalinsky's group, Yakov had to be content with a patient reiteration of the need for timed publicity that would do the greatest possible amount for the Cause, staged at the most useful moment. Why had he ever met that damned photographer?

He tried first to put his own fears, that terrible picture, out of his mind. He had always thought of the Cause only in glorious terms. He would think of it that way again. He started by making himself think again of Berkman. Even if Alexander Berkman was afraid, he went out to shoot Henry Frick. . . .

But that *Shabbos* afternoon, after Moish left, Yakov sat for a long time with a pain in his gut, wishing that he had never seen Kalinsky in his life, then cursing the damned war in Europe. He even found himself wishing for a moment that his mother was home, although what she could have done he did not know.

Sarah, of course, knew nothing of what was happening to her children or her husband in America. She missed them more than she had imagined possible, and she worried more and more as time went on, but she could not know. After the war had started no mails had come any longer from that far-off place.

There were no more letters from Isaac. She sat one day in August staring out of the open window, unable to concentrate on the sleeve she was supposed to be mending. Finally she turned to her mother, who was dozing again in her chair.

"Mamma," she asked, "do you think I should go to Budapest like the paper said?"

Rivka, waking from her rest slowly, looked blankly at her. Each day now she woke with more difficulty from her short naps, found it harder to take in what was said. Each day now Sarah's departure became more imminent, a departure that seemed to Rivka to be following so close upon her daughter's arrival. To what did she have to wake up?

"You remember, Mamma," Sarah spoke slowly, "because of the war, our tickets on the boat back to America are not good, or we would have left already. And now Pinchas brought a newspaper that says that the same thing has happened to many American citizens in the war zone. But the paper also says that American citizens should go to Budapest to see the American consul to get help for going back. Should I go to Budapest, Mamma? Or maybe"—she hesitated—"should I stay longer here now, until this war is over? What do you think?"

Rivka's sigh came, bitter with that acceptance of life she had so bitterly learned. She did speak her little hope, however, just once. "I wish you could be here through the High Holidays, of course, but . . ."

Why did I ask and want her to decide?

I am the one who has to decide. And I must decide soon.

Isaac expected me at the end of August. I know him. Even if the ships are not going, somehow Isaac expects me. Even if our tickets are no longer good, somehow Isaac expects me. I promised, and he expects me. I promised.

And what now is this fantasy I have constructed of a life here? I am no longer young—it is no longer, after all, a choice I have.

I cannot desert my children. I ache for them already. They are still little. Shayna will need me.

And David . . . which David?

Ah, David is the question I will not have to face if I do not go back. (David's music, David's hands so sure on the piano keys, David's eyes.) Will I ever hold David as I have held Isaac?

No.

I will go back to the old life, not to a new life where I have a new love in my arms. Even if my heart breaks from wanting, I will go back to the old.

No.

And it is true I cannot stay here longer. I cannot live always in another woman's house, even if it is my mother's house, even if it is the home I have missed so terribly. And I cannot any longer be only a daughter. That time has passed. I see that with my own daughter here.

But if I go—when I go—I want to go myself, not be dragged. Not Isaac's letter pulling me (not David's eyes pulling me), not even Rachel's fears pushing me. Pull, push.

No.

I have married Isaac, I have borne eight children to him, I have the pain of my dead babies, I have a life. (David Nathan has only been a dream.) No.

I will have to go back. After all, do I really want to stay? Indeed, America is my home now, and even if it is a lonely place and not the Golden Land, I have tasted its good parts, too.

"You are probably right, Mamma," said Sarah. "I must go to Budapest. I have a duty to Isaac, and there are my children." She smiled at Rivka, who could see that the smile was different now, was only in part the smile of the Sarah her mother had welcomed home just a few months before. But also Sarah nodded, making her decision, and brushed her hair back under her *sheitel* before going back to her mending.

"I will always be glad I came," she said, threading carefully through the tangle of possible words, "but war or no war, I must go back to them—I know that is right. And I miss my babies."

When Chava came in she could see the acceptance of that reality in Sarah's eyes. It seemed to be less pain for her than the indecision at which Chava had guessed—less pain, some peace. The choice had been made.

# ❧ 10 ❧

*Out of the mouths of babes
and sucklings hast thou ordained strength.
(Psalms 8:2)*

Somehow Shayna finally got through the days to the opening of school, but throughout the rest of her life she could not remember the end of that summer at all. She blocked it out. She found August and September 1914 in history books she read later in her life and was surprised that they were so full of incident and portent in the world at large. For herself those months finally contained only one fact—the fact that her mother had not come home—and that fact had nothing to do with time. A month more or less—she would have laughed at it if she had any laughter inside her, because if Mamma was gone forever, what did a month more or less matter?

It was the scrubbing that convinced her first. It seemed, while she scrubbed the smoke-blackened walls of the apartment, that she would never get it all clean. Tante Tillie was gone all day at the shop, Sophie went outside with the little ones, but before school started Shayna felt as if she would never get out of the house herself again.

She started each day thinking that Mamma was coming back, then scrubbed reality into her heart as each day wore on. Mamma had promised to come home way before the High Holidays, which would start the third week in September. But they'd had no letter; Mamma was not coming. What would Mamma think, Shayna found herself asking, when she saw the damage? It seemed that it would be impossible to wash away the marks of the fire, even by the holidays. The days were very hot, so that the walls seemed still to burn at her touch. The smoke was everywhere, and everything smelled of it. The stairs outside were so charred that at first she was afraid to walk up them, but the owner said he would come and fix the worst of it, according to Mrs. Goldstein. Mrs. Goldstein always seemed to know everything the owner was going to do. The owner was invisible to Shayna and to everyone else in the building. Even when he finally came they never saw him, but one day some of the treads on the stairs were replaced. Some, not all. So enough char remained to track in and track in and track in, to scrub and scrub and scrub.

Poppa complained about the mess every night and shouted at her because it was not yet clean. She hated him for shouting all the time. His shouting at her did not clean the dirt or erase the smell, and she was doing the best she could, the best that was never good enough for Poppa. Of course, it also wasn't good enough for Tante Tillie and Tante Sadie.

And anyway Mamma wasn't coming home.

Each day was no longer to be anticipated, because each day made it only surer that Sarah was not going to come back, to be back as she had promised. What good were promises in a war? Shayna even caught herself wondering what good was a mamma who couldn't rescue her from her aunts and Poppa and the endless smoke. She scrubbed her anger onto those filthy walls, and neither her anger nor the dirt would go away. Poppa could voice his anger with his shouting, but she had no voice for hers, didn't even want to let herself think of being angry at Mamma, who wasn't coming back, only was impotently angry at Poppa and Tante Tillie and Tante Sadie.

For some people, she knew in her anger, getting home from Europe was easier. For some people who were rich. She read in the paper that when war came some people were able to find their way home without too much difficulty, if they were in Western Europe or if they had money. For those in Eastern Europe, for those who were naturalized citizens or who were poor, coming home was more complicated, less sure, as Shayna well knew.

The United States government, according to the paper, sent an armored cruiser, the S.S. *Tennessee,* to Europe with a cargo of gold so that citizens who found themselves in countries at war could get the money they needed. The banks of Europe, of the countries at war, were in monetary crises of various kinds, and the cargo of gold enabled Americans to cash their now useless checks on American banks. Americans who had checks. Not like Sarah and Rachel Klugerman. Shayna knew that her mother and her sister had no checks.

She read in the paper—though Poppa showed them the articles less and less often these days—about the gold ship. She also read in the paper that the steamship lines had invoked a small-print clause on the backs of the tickets they had issued. That small-print clause that said the companies were not liable for cancellation of passage "in the event of war." Cancellation of passage. So Mamma's and Rachel's tickets were canceled now.

At first Shayna had had a surge of hope when the armored cruiser had sailed with the gold for stranded Americans. Poppa laughed bitterly at her hope. But there were some American liners that were pressed into service to bring people home, and even when they heard nothing Shayna kept hoping that a miracle would happen. She scanned the lists of returning passengers printed in the paper. By the end of August the paper said that the gold was on deposit for Americans who were refugees in Europe. Then, a few days later, her hope sank at the headline: SOME PLANS TO RELIEVE AMERICANS HAVE MISCARRIED. A later article said that naturalized citizens who had bought German Line tickets for a cheap visit to relatives were now destitute. Destitute. That was Mamma and Rachel, not just a word in a newspaper. Cancellation of passage, destitute, Shayna thought, scrubbing and scrubbing at the smoke stains.

So some days she felt cut off from hope of her mamma, on her own. She thought then of how Mamma had come to America when she was thirteen. Had she, too, felt cut off from hope here alone on this side of the ocean? There were so many ways, Shayna thought, that her secret self and her mamma's secret self must be alike. At least that made her feel closer to Mamma.

Would Mamma know that "Americans anywhere on the continent can, by applying to the nearest embassy or legation, get in touch with people in this country, can get money if they need any, and can get transportation and passage home if they want it"? All right, it said so in the *New York Times,* but Tante Sadie and Tante Tillie said there was no *New York Times* in the old country. What was there? How would Mamma know, even if there was something to know? Two months since they had heard, then three months, and still no letters, no word. It seemed clearer and clearer to all the family that Mamma did not know, had not gone to any embassy or any consulate. No one in the family had much faith that a poor Jewish woman and her daughter, even though they were naturalized citizens of the United States—no, one was native born, after all—could possibly be rescued by any efforts of the United States government. Governments, said Tante Tillie, simply would not bother with little people like themselves.

None of them had faith except Shayna. Sometimes. At least for a while, she insisted that all citizens were alike in the eyes of the government—she had learned that in her civics class in high school. All citizens, naturalized or native born, rich or poor, she insisted. Insist, insist, scrub, scrub, but there were no letters, there was no word. More and more she was sure that the whole grown-up world had ganged up on her.

Yakov laughed at the possibility that what he called the capitalist machine could care about individuals without money. He was hard and bitter in those days; he was on strike. Poppa shouted especially about the strike, which made Yakov come home less and less. Mamma was gone, Rachel was gone, Yakov was being driven away by Poppa. Didn't Poppa want any of them? Did he even want Mamma?

Shayna wrote a letter in her head:

*Dear President Wilson,*

*I am sorry to bother you at such a busy and difficult time of your life, but I know you will care about the problem of which I must tell. My mother and my sister, Sarah and Rachel Klugerman, who are citizens of the United States, made a visit to family members in Europe this summer, and now that there is a war over there they cannot come home.*

*We have not received any mail from them since July. Is there any way you could help us trace them and bring them home, away from the war?*

*Thank you for taking the trouble to read this.*

*Sincerely,*
*Shayna Klugerman*

She wrote it in her head, but she didn't dare to send it. Poppa would have been angrier than ever, and Yakov, God knows, would have laughed at her. They thought her ways of wanting always to *do* things were wrong—Poppa said "unseemly." Even Yakov thought that these days, although he was the one who had talked to her about doing things. Why was he, too, against her doing? Of course, she couldn't tell her little sister Sophie about the letter she couldn't write.

So if she didn't actually write the letter, couldn't write it, was it somehow her own fault that Mamma wasn't coming home? It all went endlessly around and around in Shayna's mind, around and around, scrub, scrub, and suddenly it was time for school to start, and there were only two months until her birthday. Her birthday would be on November thirteenth. She would be fourteen years old, and it would be legal for her to quit school. What if she had to quit school because Mamma wasn't coming home to rescue her? Would Mamma have rescued her anyway? What if, after all, she could not finish her education? What if everyone was right, and no one but her cared about Mamma? What if the war was never over? What if?

Then one September night her fears were confirmed when there was a terrible scene right after supper. Poppa and Tante Tillie and Tante Sadie all seemed to fix her with the awful look they shared when they had been conspiring against her. (Uncle Franz, sitting in the corner, was avoiding family matters the way he always did.)

"Shayna," Poppa began, "the decision has been made. I have decided that you will go to work in November, after your birthday."

"Please, Poppa," she had started to plead, but she was immediately engulfed in tears.

"You must listen to the man in the family, young

lady,'' said Tante Sadie. David was in her lap. He was going home with her now, because there was no one home on Orchard Street in the daytime since school had started. Unlike last June, now Tante Sadie said it was too hard for her to keep coming over to help. Things were changing. The children were even losing one another, Shayna felt, now that Mamma wasn't coming home.

"You have no choice now, miss," said Tante Tillie.

Shayna pleaded with them and wept and knew it was no help, had known actually for weeks that it was going to come to this, all the weeks she had scrubbed and Poppa had shouted she had known. Even with Mamma and Rachel gone, so two less (no—two fewer, she corrected herself) mouths to feed, there was need for more money. Yakov was on strike and wasn't bringing in anything. She had known she would have to go to work. All right, she was hopeless for a minute, she would have to go to work; there was no way out of it.

No! There had to be a way. All night long after Poppa told her his decision she lay in bed and thought about it. She had to find a way.

The next day came, a bright September day. It was on the way to school after that gloomy night that she said to herself, "Never mind what if. There has to be a way. Even if Mamma can't come home, there has to be a way. No matter what my dumpy, beaky old aunts talk to Poppa about, there has to be a way for me. Even if the whole world is against me, there has to be a way. Because God is good, no matter what Yakov said about His not caring one way or the other, there has to be a way. Because President Wilson will rescue all American citizens, of whom my mamma, Sarah Klugerman, and my sister, Rachel Klugerman, are two, however Jewish, however poor. Poor doesn't matter—they told me in school. Citizenship matters. And . . . and even if they don't come home, I *will* finish high school, I *will* go to college. There has to be a way." Even if she'd thought to give up last night, this morning she gathered up her failed courage and reshaped it to find a way. There was a psalm that fitted that day after the fight with her father and her aunts: "Weeping may endure for a night," it said, "but joy cometh in the morning."

She dreamed her way to school, all the way to Latin class. She barely said a word to Cassie when they met.

"The principal parts of the verb 'to bear,' please. Shayna Klugerman?"

*"Ferō, ferre, tulī, lātus,"* said Shayna, standing up hurriedly beside her desk. "And may I see you after school Thursday, Miss Barton?" she asked quickly before she sat down. There—she had asked it. There had to be a way. She ignored the curious stares of the other girls and looked determinedly out of the window at the house across the street.

Cassie gazed at her in amazement, but she was finding it harder and harder to explain about things to Cassie. Cassie's being away in the mountains with her family had stretched to all summer. And these days Shayna could only remember how Cassie's mother was home in her gaily colored clothes in the big, bright flat on East Broadway. How could Cassie imagine Shayna's charred existence on the fifth floor of #40 Orchard Street without a mother? How could Cassie understand?

At least Shayna had actually asked to see Miss Barton, at least she had done something. Thursday, when the last bell rang, she would have someone to tell—someone who could help. There had to be a way. Thursday was the day she could do it this week, because tomorrow and Wednesday were Rosh Hashanah, the beginning of the High Holidays, those holidays for which Mamma wasn't home. She'd had to brave up today, and thank God she had spoken. If only Miss Barton would say yes and see her right after that last class Thursday, she'd be home in time, and no one would notice if it was only a little later than usual. Anyway, she could run.

Miss Barton hesitated only momentarily before she replied to the girl's query. "Yes, Shayna," she said, and she went on with the class.

Usually Miss Barton herself was the one to ask a student to stay after school; she didn't remember that it had ever been the other way around before. When the bell rang she gathered up her material for the Cicero class and thought about Shayna Klugerman.

Easily the best student in Caesar, that was obvious already. Clean and neat. Young for the class—the register said that she would be fourteen in November. Must have skipped in grade school. Oh, well, probably another bright one going. When they reached that magic fourteen and could get their working papers, so many of the bright ones left. Such a pity with one like this too, she thought—so young and so bright. Young did make her different. Usually the fourteen-year-olds left in first-year Latin, not in Caesar, if they even got that far. Mostly they were fourteen in eighth grade, so Miss Barton didn't teach some of them at all. Little Shayna Klugerman—was she small for her age, too?—was the best pupil in second-year Latin, and she wasn't even fourteen yet. Did she do as well in her other classes?

Shayna herself was surrounded by remarks and questions the minute she left the classroom.

"Teacher's pet, teacher's pet," said Karen Berkowitz, her nose in the air as she purposely bumped into Shayna, making her drop her math book.

"What's it about, Shayna?" asked Cassie, squeezing in beside her as they went toward biology. "What on earth are you going to see Miss Barton about?"

"Oh, Cassie, I can't tell you now—I'm sorry." Her eyes filled with tears as she said it. She picked up the book. "I'll tell you later if it works out, but I can't tell you now."

"Oh, so what!" Cassie expressed her resentment. "But I thought you were my best friend and we didn't have any secrets. Anyway"—she decided to hurt in return—"I'm going with Mitzi's family to *shul* for the holidays, so there!"

Cassie's anger only added to Shayna's misery. She knew it was no way to talk to her best friend, but what could she say? Cassie would never understand. And Shayna's springtime love for Cassie's brother, Ari, with its aches and dreams, had to be hidden no matter what.

As she waited for Miss Hallaby to start the biology class she thought again about what she had to say to Miss Barton. If only she could stop thinking about it and concentrate on the work in front of her! Instead she mused on about how maybe Miss Barton could be her way. Maybe she could finish her high school courses by going to night school somehow. And if Miss Barton could give her the assignments for the rest of the term . . .

Miss Barton was her hope. Latin was her favorite subject, but she had achieved scores in the nineties in all her other Regents exams as well the past spring. Oh, she wished there weren't still two more years to go, though, two whole years!

"I asked—Shayna Klugerman do you hear me—I asked what the order of the phyla is." Miss Hallaby's voice was hard and metallic. Shayna sat up and then rose quickly from her desk. She couldn't allow herself to dream any longer; it was the time for answers.

"Yes, Miss Hallaby," she said, and she recited, "protozoa, porifera . . ."

\*     \*     \*

On Thursday, as soon as the dismissal bell rang, Shayna hurried to Miss Barton's homeroom. The building was oddly quiet at that hour as the last of the students clattered out. When she walked through the halls her steps echoed. She clutched her books tightly to her and couldn't help thinking in the quiet about how much she loved the building itself. It still smelled somehow of its newness, less than four years since it was built. The light-colored brick outside and the huge windows flooded with afternoon sun seemed to Shayna the very embodiment of the enlightenment she had found within these walls. Breathing itself here was comfort.

And now, in only her second year, would she have to leave? The thought was so terrible, yet it was no longer a question but a finality. Poppa had decided. The answer had been given—yes, she would have to leave on November thirteenth, her fourteenth birthday. No one could make her leave before then, but on that day she would have to leave.

She knocked timidly on Miss Barton's door. The sound was even louder in the empty hall than her walking had been.

"Come in," came Miss Barton's voice.

Shayna opened the door and at first walked only partly through it, seeing Miss Barton bent over papers at her desk. "Miss Barton?" she said. "I'm Shayna Klugerman. I asked if I could see you this afternoon."

"Yes, Shayna," said Miss Barton, putting a book on top of her papers with a sigh. "I've been correcting homework. But tell me, what can I do for you?"

Still hesitating by the door, Shayna said, "Perhaps there would be a time that would be more convenient. I can come back another time if you prefer. . . ."

"No, no, come right in and close the door. I don't mean to put you off. I'm always correcting papers, it seems to me, and I forget that there are any things in life beside Latin conjugations. Please, tell me what I can do for you." She pointed to a chair in the front row. "Sit down, sit down, and tell me what it is you want."

"Actually, in a way it is about Latin, Miss Barton," said Shayna, slipping into the seat and looking up at Miss Barton behind her desk on the raised dais in the front of the room. Miss Barton's eyes gleamed out from metal-rimmed glasses that seemed to rest not so much upon her insignificant nose as upon her chubby cheeks. The glass winked at Shayna, who still clasped her books in front of her as she spoke, as if books could offer some protection against the coming talk, stand in some way between her and the words she had to say. "I need to know if there is any way you could give me a schedule of the assignments for the rest of the year, starting in November, so that I could do them on my own." She hurried on. "And whether you know any way I could have a key to the answers, so that I could correct them myself. I think if I can do the Latin, and read the history books Miss Adams has planned for the year, and finish my geometry book if Miss Catesby has an answer key, too, I will be finished with nearly all the work for the sophomore year. Then, if I can take the Regents—"

"What's this? What do you mean, Shayna? I think you are not really starting at the beginning of what you have to say. Why do you want to do this work on your own? Are you planning to go away, or will you be ill?"

"I'm sorry, Miss Barton," said Shayna, blushing because of her own confusion. "I started in the middle because I think I am in the middle all the time, but I guess I'd better explain."

"Perhaps that would be wisest," said Miss Barton dryly. Since she knew what was probably coming, she took the next few minutes, while Shayna talked, to look carefully at her best student, sitting there in that shiny, worn brown dress, so carefully neat. It was the same dress Shayna wore every day. The child's face was pale, as it always was, and the dark eyes seemed ringed with even darker circles, the circles of a sleepless night. But as Shayna talked bright pink spots appeared on her cheeks, and at last she lifted her head and seemed to blaze forth with a defiance never apparent in the daily Latin classes.

". . . so I have to find a way to finish school if I possibly can. My father doesn't think it's important, I know, for a woman to be educated, but I do. And when my mother comes home . . ." She stopped, sighed, and the head dropped a fraction, the eyes lost their sparkle for a moment. "I mean if my mother can come home," she continued, "I want to have lost as little time as possible, because I know she'll say I can come back to school then and finish."

"And you'd like me to give you some assignments so that you can continue your work," mused Miss Barton, unconsciously rolling a pencil up and down between her hands as she often did in class.

Shayna watched her, simply nodding her head in agreement, and listening to the familiar click, click as the pencil went back and forth between Miss Barton's rings, back and forth, back and forth. She and Cassie and the other girls had often joked about the way Miss Barton's click, click of that pencil punctuated the third conjugation -io verbs. It had actually helped them to memorize: *capiō, capere, cēpī, captus* (click, click), *capiō, capis, capit, capimus, capitis, capiunt* (click, click), *capiēbam, capiēbās* . . . Her mind drifted into the familiar pattern with which she had spent so much time, walking back and forth to school testing Cassie and saying "click, click" between the tenses. Now that click, click held part of the key to her whole future, she thought, and she made herself pay attention so she could hear what would come next.

"You want me to find a way for you to continue

your education. . . ." Miss Barton was obviously speaking mostly to herself. Miss Barton's vague dialogues with herself were another source of her students' amusement. Now, however, she turned to Shayna and looked her full in the face. "Shayna Klugerman, you are my best student. I would like to help you find a way to continue to read Latin. I will do what I can."

Sarah knew, after she reached her decision, that each thing she did now was a last thing. She had read a newspaper Pinchas had received from his buyer. The American consulate's notice was in it; they had to go to Budapest in person. They could not simply write. They could not prove their identities except in person, and there would be papers they must sign. She discussed it with her brothers and knew she must go to Budapest.

"All right, Rachel," she told her daughter as they wound their way between rain puddles on the streets from her sister Chenny's house one September afternoon, "we will go immediately after the High Holidays. I understand now what we must do."

"Can't we go sooner, Mamma?" asked Rachel. "Can't we start before the holidays? I have missed so much school. We were supposed to be home. . . ."

But the holidays were too close by then, and it was unthinkable that they should ignore them, begin their journey so that they were actually traveling at the most holy time of the year. There would be one last time for Sarah.

First there were the round loaves to bake for Rosh Hashanah, round with the endless promise of the new year that the holiday signaled. There were apples to pick, too, newly ripe on the tree at the back of the house. Yet the dipping of the apples in honey and the ritual wishes for a sweet year were nearly unbearable to her. *I will never do this again with my own family,* she thought. It is the last time. Besides, she felt she couldn't know if it would be a sweet year for her; maybe there was no promise in the future she had chosen—a future in which she would never see her mother and her sisters and brothers again. Always before, from the time she had gone to America, she had promised herself a visit someday. Now the visit itself was over. This was the last of it.

On Yom Kippur, at the end of the month, when she sat in the *shul* behind the curtain repenting her sins, the familiar catalog seemed to apply not to all the Jewish people, but to herself personally. Yes, she had been stiff-necked; yes, she had strayed from her duty to a singing and dancing of the spirit her real life would not allow. She ached for a true repentance, knew she must settle herself simply for acceptance of her life as it really was. She was still stiff-necked, perhaps she would always ache for something else, but she must try to accept what was. Besides—and this was her comfort—there were always her children.

The heat was stifling. She smiled to think of Shayna's saying to her just last year (could it be only a year ago?) that if Yom Kippur came even on December twenty-fifth it would be the hottest day of the year. In the women's section of the little *shul* the curtain cut off any hope of circulating air. At the *Yizkor* remembrance service, though, she forgot the heat for a little while and thought not only of her dead father whom she had never known, as she had mourned for him dutifully at all the years of *Yizkor* services of her life, but found herself thinking again of Isaac and the children. Were they even alive? There had been no letters for so long. Did they know that she was alive? Or were they mourning for her on that day, thinking that she and Rachel were dead to them? Who would be dead, what would be dead, by the next year?

A relapse in her mother's condition delayed Sarah for the week until *Succos*, but it turned blustery and

285

cool midway through the holiday, making it a real problem to eat outdoors in the special booth with the cold as company. With the change in the weather there came a desperate feeling of necessity to Sarah. Her mother improved again, and she knew the end had come; she could get away, get home, take up the life she had chosen. She began to pack her few garments before *Simchas Torah* was even upon them. That was truly the last thing. Suddenly she and Rachel were both desperate to leave, tickets or no tickets, money or no money. "We have two feet, Rachel," she said. "If we have to, we can walk to Holland and swim." She smiled as she said, "And we may have to," not knowing how close to the truth her words would become.

On the day Sarah and Rachel left Rivka stood in the road to wave them off, then stared into the distance at the last place she had seen them. Pinchas and Mendel had come, and Chava, of course. When the travelers were completely out of sight Rivka's sons tried to take her hands. They would have led her away, but she resisted, not letting them take her, not yet.

"Let me stay a little," the mother said, "just a little."

When she pulled her hands back her strength surprised them into acquiescence. They looked at each other, shrugged, and let her stay a bit.

I hope she can manage, Rivka thought. No, I know she can manage. I will never see her again, but she will manage. She doesn't need me anymore. She needed me still this summer, but she found what she needed by coming here. I'm glad I could give her that last gift. Now she can manage. I wish she loved her husband Isaac the way I loved her father, but that is one thing I cannot have to give away. My love is gone; my Sarah will never have a love of her own.

286

Oh, God, she whispered within her, take care of my baby, I will miss her now forever.

She stood there, and her sons could see the shaking of her shoulders with her silent weeping as they came back to her side. Finally she let them lead her away with Chava sobbing beside her, no longer full of strength, now an old lady who was shaking with weeping for her lost child. The cold rain of that autumn of 1914 fell on her and on her sons, and the road began to turn muddy beneath their feet.

When Sarah and Rachel descended from the train at the Eastern Station in Budapest the sky was still cloudy, but no rain was falling. Pinchas had written to his correspondent firm in the city, which had sent a man to the train to meet them. The man was easily recognizable to Sarah by his beard, earlocks, and long black coat, so different from the garments of the *goyim* who thronged the station.

"How do you do?" he said formally when she approached him. And he named her brother's name when she replied. He did not take her suitcase. He was not a man who carried women's burdens. He did, however, take the two of them to his home in the old Jewish district in Pest, where his wife was voluble and kind.

"We go immediately to the American consulate," explained Sarah. (It was clear to her that a woman having such a business was a marvel to her hostess.)

"But you will stay with us?"

"Thank you; you are very kind," said Sarah as Rachel smiled uncertainly beside her. "We will stay at least tonight. After that"—she shrugged her shoulders—"it depends how long it takes to do our business in the city."

As they walked along toward the bridge that crossed the Danube to Buda Sarah and Rachel marveled at the sights. They were no longer used to such crowds, and their life in New York was very far away. But here, too, the streets were thronged with people, although the people seemed much more prosperous after they left the closely packed streets of the Jewish district. The spires of the parliament building reached up to the sky beyond the trees of the boulevard on which they walked, competing, it seemed, with the churches for height. Marvels were everywhere, and soon the sun came through the clouds to bathe the yellow stucco facades with brightness. Even the severity of the few stone buildings was pleasing to the eye.

"Oh, why isn't it pretty like this at home?" asked Rachel when they had crossed the Danube and stood gazing up toward Castle Hill.

"Razele," teased her mother mildly, "I thought nothing was as wonderful as New York for you."

"Oh, Mamma." Rachel squeezed her arm. "You know what I mean."

"Yes, *zies kind,* I do," said Sarah, whose eyes had been drinking in the sights as well, "but now I want to go to New York, not to stay here." She was grateful, if surprised, to realize that it was true at last. So, holding onto each other, they turned in to the door to the gray building with the American flag and were afraid suddenly that their journey might end before it had really had a chance to begin. Perhaps they would be thrown out the door, two poor Jewish women who were not worthy of the sparkling cleanliness of that building in a foreign land. Perhaps it would not be possible for them to go home to New York after all.

But their fears proved groundless. When next they stood outside that building, barely two hours later, they both were weak-kneed with relief. They found a bench on which to sit in the square and looked in disbelief at the money they had received.

"That is surely more than we will need," said Sarah.

"Why did they give it all to us now?" asked Rachel.

"It is the money for the ship's ticket," her mother replied. "I think there is even enough, though, for a little extra. But perhaps they are right and it costs more now than it did."

"Because of the war," agreed Rachel.

Suddenly Sarah felt very tired. It was over so soon, this visit to the consulate, but she had dreaded it for weeks. Thank the Lord it had not lived up to any of her nightmares. When they had arrived, the consul—Mr. William Coffin—had seen them after only an hour's wait. Even the waiting had not been painful. Once they had stated their business they had been escorted into a large room with tapestry-covered tables and Turkish rugs. They even had comfortable chairs to sit in. It had reminded Sarah of David Nathan then, seeing such furnishings. But so many things reminded Sarah of David Nathan. He was rarely far from her mind, especially these days when she was at last starting home—home, she also forced herself to remember, to Isaac.

The forms they had signed, the number of times Sarah had written her name and her address in America, were reiterated emphases that she was returning to the place where she belonged, doing the right thing. Rachel had been a wonderful help, reading the small print, asking respectful questions in her unaccented American voice.

Sarah promised to pay back the money, of course, as soon as she returned to America. She willingly signed her name to the document, amazed that there should be any questions. Of course she would be glad to pay them back; it was such a miracle that Americans were helping them in this way, that it really was her country and would reach out its arms all the way to Hungary to help her come home.

"Is there anyone who should be notified that you have registered with us?" asked the bored official in the stiff white collar as he counted the forms to be sure they were all properly completed.

"Notified?"

"If you would like to telegraph home, that can be arranged," he said, looking beyond them at the next people in the line.

Sarah thought. She knew that the right thing, the logical thing, would be to contact Isaac, to telegraph him that she was safe, that she was coming home. It was logical, but nevertheless she couldn't do it. It had been so long since there had been any letters, any communication in either direction, that the idea of sending him some word now was obscurely frightening. Sufficient unto the day . . . Besides, she told herself superstitiously, it was a long way yet to Holland, to the ship, and she did not know when they would actually arrive, actually leave. When she knew, then she would telegraph, she told herself.

"I think we will do that when we have the ship's tickets actually in hand," she told the official.

He shrugged. Many of the foreign-born returnees had said the same sort of thing in the last weeks. Still attached to old-country ways, he supposed.

The official—even Mr. Coffin himself—would have been surprised at what Sarah and Rachel Klugerman did that evening. They planned it as they sat on the bench. It was Sarah's idea, but Rachel was easily persuaded to it. She, too, had enjoyed the piano on Orchard Street, had looked forward to starting lessons with Mr. Nathan when it was her turn. Why not hear some music in that beautiful concert hall they had passed on the other side of the river? It would be just a little of the money, and it would be a treat for both to remember, being in Budapest and going to a real concert. Planning it, for the first time on the whole journey they had a taste of being world travelers, tourists—Sarah said the word with a smile—on their way. She looked at the money again and then put it away. It would be enough.

"It's an orchestra from Vienna, Mamma," declared Rachel, who had run to the kiosk on the corner to look at the poster announcing the concert. "They will play Beethoven's Third Symphony, and there will even be some Strauss waltzes. I figured out the sign."

"When I was young," Sarah reminisced, "I danced to Strauss waltzes. I met your father at such a dance," she added.

"Did Poppa dance, too?" asked Rachel, amazed. She had never heard that story before.

"Yes," replied Sarah, smiling, "even your poppa danced in those days."

Rachel shook her head. "But you and Poppa would never let us do that now," she insisted. The Law said that men must dance only with men.

"Of course, Poppa would object," said Sarah. "But you are too young even to think of dancing in any case." She avoided the implied question carefully.

Rachel could not imagine old people like Mamma and Poppa dancing. Was it because she had been so long away from home? She tried to think, as they walked back across the river to Pest, if she knew of dances at home, but she did not. Perhaps it was just that she had been too young to know of dances? She decided to ask Yakov, when she got home, if he went to dances. But weren't Poppa and Mamma too serious for dances? It was another puzzle, and she was tired of puzzles. Now she could go home to America at last and grow up safe in New York City where she belonged, grow up to no more puzzles, to being sure of things like Poppa and Mamma.

"I think it is a lovely idea to go to hear the music," their hostess surprised them by saying when they informed her of their evening plans in the narrow house in the Jewish quarter. "My husband and I often go to concerts on Sunday afternoons in winter."

Sarah and Rachel looked at her, nearly choking on the supper she had kindly provided. It was beyond their imaginings—a husband and wife together—Isaac at a concert!

"We did not mean to trouble you," they said to their hosts yet again when the couple decided to walk along with them through the brisk evening streets.

"Not at all, not at all," they insisted. "We will enjoy the walk."

Sarah and Rachel couldn't think of a time when Isaac had walked anywhere to enjoy a walk. The kindly couple, the cool evening air, the anticipation of the evening's pleasure gave them a sense of hope about what lay ahead of them as they crunched through the drifting beech leaves in the gathering dark.

At last they crossed Concert Hall Square and passed through the large doors beneath beckoning stone angels strumming on lyres. They followed the line to purchase two of the cheapest seats in the last row of the top balcony. Once there, they found that they did not need to feel embarrassed by their poverty. The people around them were also poorly dressed. Some of them carried bags of food, and it seemed that they, too, regarded the occasion of hearing a real orchestra as a cause for celebration. There were even Jews among them, they noticed, comforted by the familiar dark garb, the long beards, and the Yiddish words. The two of them smiled and nodded as they settled into the hard seats.

When the conductor came out the applause was deafening. He turned around in his wonderful black and white suit and bowed toward the audience. It seemed to Rachel that he bowed especially to Mamma and herself, high up there "in the gods," as she had heard one of their neighbors describe such seats. They applauded with the rest. At last he turned back to the orchestra, and there was silence for a second; then the music began.

And what music! The first piece was "Tales from the Vienna Woods." The horns started, then came an oboe. Finally the violins and the rest of the strings joined in. There was even a flute that sounded exactly like a bird in the woods. It was a sea of sound, a sea of joy that made Rachel close her eyes in delight. No one wrote waltzes like Strauss waltzes, and there must be no orchestra that could play them better than a Viennese orchestra, Mamma had always said.

Tears were running down Sarah's cheeks when Rachel glanced at her, and for a moment she was embarrassed by her mother. She looked around to see if anyone had noticed Mamma's tears, and she saw that Mamma was not alone in her reaction. All around her were people with smiles on their faces and tears in their eyes. She closed her own again. What a wonderful thing to be able to tell about when she got home— Strauss waltzes in a Budapest concert hall, played by an orchestra from Vienna. And if Poppa objected, she would even have the courage to tell him that it was the music to which he and Mamma had danced when they were young. Because Mamma had said so. When the Beethoven symphony began Rachel looked again at Mamma. She was not crying anymore, and the look on her face was all joy, as if she was part of Beethoven's music.

It came to Rachel, sitting there, that she loved her mamma very much; she wanted always to see that look on her mamma's face. If it had been this long journey that had produced that look, then Rachel was even glad of the journey. She reached for her mamma's hand.

It was Leah, the mother, who reached for her daughter's hand on the train to London. She squeezed it, but there was still no response from the silent Ethel.

"Our travels will soon be over," she tried saying to both the girls.

"Thank God," said Diana in her newly practiced world-weary voice. Ethel said nothing.

They had come far. After several weeks at the Ritz in Paris they had cashed checks on the credit with which Aaron had provided them and crossed the Channel to England. They ignored the war. There was no war to interfere with them in England, just some young men marching to ships for France (the very ships that might have taken them home across the Atlantic); but luckily—at least Leah viewed it as luckily then—there were no ships yet making the journey to America. She still thought, at that point, that a little more time might be all Ethel needed, just a little more time. . . .

Because of the delay they could have a long, delightful time in Scotland with some charming people they met, at something the English called a shooting party. They stayed in a great house that was like a castle; Diana charmed several stiff young men and went out with them every morning in tweeds to shoot grouse—or was it pheasant? Leah had trouble understanding the clipped way these people spoke. Their manners were charming. They chattered so constantly in their brittle fashion that Ethel's silences were not remarkable.

Diana noticed, one morning, that her sister looked at the shooting party's guns very peculiarly, with a kind of hungry gaze, but she did not discuss Ethel's peculiarities with her mother.

She did try again to talk to her sister, though.

"I've made up my mind" was all Ethel would say, however. At least she did say that much, but it was unclear to Diana what her sister had made her mind up about. She found herself afraid to ask. There was no way to get through to Ethel.

It was shortly after that abortive exchange that

they had taken the train to London. The ocean crossing must be faced, whether or not Ethel was better. It was too soon, Leah said to her younger daughter Diana, but ships were moving again, and they would have to go.

Ethel was not consulted by her mother or her sister before the train wound down the length of England. Leah just held her hand. It had all become a matter of vast indifference to Ethel where she was or who held her hand. She had seen the guns and thought her thoughts. It must be possible, somehow, to end this pain she could no longer bear. James was lost to her, and with him had gone her hope of a life with love. He had not even written to her. There had been no communication, and she had begun to realize what any less innocent girl would have thought of long before: Maybe he had not really cared. Maybe it had all been talk, his courting of her. Maybe—and this was the hardest to bear—it had really been about her money, as Diana had once suggested, and even when he had touched her body it had been about money.

The weeks in Europe had passed in a fog of silence, because why should she talk to anyone if she could not talk to James Olson, whom she loved, if she could not have love? She did not want to live without that love she had fleetingly tasted. That taste had made her know for certain that she had been starved all her life until then. Now she must die of her new hunger.

Leah telegraphed to Aaron that as soon as they could arrange it they would be taking passage home. She still said nothing to him about Ethel's terrifying silence.

On the day Aaron received his wife's cable, his office was busy with a conference about the striking workers in some of his shops. His secretary, George, signed for the cable, glanced at its contents, and decided not to interrupt the meeting for it. He went back to his notepad instead.

"Tell them my exact words: I will not speak to them, and that is final," Mr. Morgenstern was concluding his speech. The words concerned the striking workers, of course, but it was the shop bosses who smiled with relief when they heard them.

"Yes, sir," said George, writing down Mr. Morgenstern's exact words.

"And I have told the newspaper people who came this morning as well: There will be no negotiation with the strikers. None. I will be perfectly happy to get through the height of the season without manufacturing a single garment, if necessary. They will not break Aaron Morgenstern." It was irrelevant that the height of the season was over, that the strike, in fact, was nowhere near coming to any such pass. Actually, the union's membership seemed small; not everyone was out at all. He was clearly enjoying his own rhetoric, enjoying his power. He would gladly use any means to break these criminals.

Right now Aaron Morgenstern needed a stage on which to enjoy power. Too often in the last few weeks he had felt it slipping out of his hands. His relationship with Tina, so ecstatic and passionate only a little time before, seemed to him to be changing.

It had started the night he had taken her back to her old club for a special treat. She was no longer dancing there, but some of the regulars recognized her. A man with a big cigar, whom Aaron did not know, came up to their table and said, "Where have you been, doll?"

Tina had smiled but had not answered directly.

The man had seated himself with them without being asked. It turned out he was a producer putting on a revue on Broadway, and Tina had smiled at him far more than Aaron had liked. He had been powerless, somehow, to get rid of the man. Ever since that day he had been worried, wondering where Tina was, what she was doing, in the hours when he could not be with her.

Was she seeing anyone else?

Somehow he could not ask her, but Aaron could feel his power over her slipping away. He was happy for any chance to feel his old self again, and he could feel that in his office. He would use scabs, if he had to, to break this strike.

"Do you want us to do anything about the picket lines?" asked one of the shop bosses, speaking tentatively.

Aaron considered a moment. "How many of you have lines in front of your shops every day?" he asked.

Only four men raised their hands.

"Good," said Aaron to their surprise. They understood, though, when he continued, "That means it has not spread enough so that they have pickets to cover all the shops. Probably the rest of you have not got to deal with the union itself—only with sympathizers. They'll come back to work in a few days, don't worry. The others of you—the ones with the picket lines—must just be sure that the good workers, who have not joined the strike, can still get to work. But I don't want any violence," he added in a pious tone, knowing full well that if he had to, he would be perfectly willing to use violence, too, as part of his "any means necessary."

Saperstein, the small, sweaty man who smoked cigars and ran a cloak-making shop, spoke with his strong Yiddish accent. "I have found that I can clear a path for the workers who are still coming," he said, "if I arrange with them to come a little early. That seems to throw the pickets off a little—there is not as much organization among them as it first appears. The older members don't like having the young organizers yelling at them and telling them what to do all the time, and while they argue I get my workers through. Actually, Mr. Morgenstern"—he warmed up in his boasting—"we won't even miss that much in our quota, never mind the strike."

Aaron nodded absently at him. The man was a bore, he thought.

"Maybe you won't," said Yankelman, also sweating in the Indian summer heat of the conference room. Aaron remembered that Yankelman ran a shirtwaist shop. "But for some reason my girls have really held the line. I can't get anyone through. I don't know how I'm supposed to produce anything under these conditions," he grumbled. He always grumbled.

"Well, speak to each other—get ideas from each other," said Aaron. The boasters and the grumblers did not interest him. He did not want to get mixed up in any of the petty details of how they worked out ways to beat the strike; he just wanted to be very clear with them—he was not going to negotiate, and he was going to win. *He* was going to beat the strike. He didn't care how.

"Mr. Morgenstern," interrupted George, "perhaps we should get to the design requirements of the spring lines while this meeting goes on." It was George's job to remind Mr. Morgenstern of the agenda items still to be covered. Autumn duties included the planning of the spring lines.

"Spring?" said Aaron. "My heavens, gentlemen, time has been flying by while we have been dealing with this little worker uprising. My designers are prepared to discuss the spring lines. By the way, Saperstein"—he decided to favor the man with some attention, since he *was* helpful—"is that cutter ready to do the samples as soon as we get the patterns to you? I hope he isn't on strike?"

"He's in the shop every day, Mr. Morgenstern," said Saperstein, holding his head high. "But he has missed the High Holidays, of course," he added.

"Yes, yes, of course," agreed Aaron. It would not do for them to get any notion he was neglecting any of the religious duties. He always wanted to set the correct Jewish example for all the people under him. He used that to consolidate his power over them all. (Part of his uneasiness about Tina was that she was not Jewish.)

But thinking of the correct Jewish example brought his mind suddenly to his family, and to the duties that rankled him in that sphere of his life. Damn Leah for giving him any worry! And now Tina? Damn women for causing trouble!

Abruptly, caught up by such thoughts, he dismissed the meeting. "I have decided we will discuss this next week," he said. "Meanwhile I want the strike to end before our next meeting."

The men sitting around the polished conference table in that fancy room looked at him with apprehension. By the next meeting? For a moment his face had darkened dangerously. What had caused his sudden dismissal? Whatever it was that had upset Mr. Morgenstern, each one felt that perhaps it was his fault. But they filed out of the room without a word. The sun was getting ready to set over their lofts, and there was much to do if they were going to stay on the good side of Aaron Morgenstern.

When the last of them had left the room Aaron turned to George. "I saw you sign for a cable," he said shortly. "Was it anything important?"

"Your wife just sent word that she and your daughters have returned to London to try to book passage home," replied George.

"London?" Aaron pursed his lips. "I read in the paper that while people wait for ships home they are sleeping on the floor in the dining room of the Savoy Hotel in London." He smiled then. "I wonder how Leah will like sleeping on the floor!"

George was careful to say nothing in reply.

The thought of Leah having to taste the reality of a war-ready capital was somehow comforting to Aaron. He would look forward to the next days, he felt, with some equanimity, if it weren't for his nagging worry about what Tina was up to. It would be a while, but his family would be coming home. At least the strike had not gotten out of hand, he thought. His power in the strike was his comfort.

On Wednesday he heard about the riot.

Wednesday at #40 Orchard Street began as usual. Isaac prayed, gulped his bread and tea with the rest of the family, then hurried off to work. Yakov was already gone, as was his custom since the strike began, leaving before anyone was up to man his picket line before the rest of the working world had started.

Shouldering his placard, Yakov wished again that there were more people on his line, that he did not have to spend today, of all days, on the line. Today was the day the secretly hired strikebreakers were supposed to come to Dora's line, he knew, and he ached to have his own duty done, the day over, and his fears stilled at last. Moish came running up to him on his way to another line. Moish was running messages for the organizers.

"Everything okay?" he asked breathlessly. "You talked to her? She understands? And the *Tribune* guy is supposed to come?"

"Everything is okay," said Yakov. "Let me know what happens," he called after the running figure. He knew that Moish would head now for Dora's line just three blocks away. If only he himself could be there.

"Morning," said Edelmann, meeting him at the midpoint of their patrol. "Stop looking so glum," the older man went on. "It's a beautiful fall day—better to be out here enjoying the air than in there working today."

It was indeed a beautiful, clear day. Yakov could

see the brightness of the early morning sky above the buildings. He tried not to think of what was going to happen in an hour or two at Dora's shop. It was all organized; it would go like clockwork; Moish had said so.

Actually, the organization of the strike had impressed Yakov and Dora as they had gone to the meetings and taken part in their section of the planning. A meeting room had been arranged for each of the shops separately, where they could see one another and get their orders as the strike went on. And every night there was a speaker one place or another urging them not to give up, telling them of the importance of the Cause. A strike fund, had, of course, been set up, so that there was at least a little money coming in for the people who were not working. It wasn't much, but it was better than nothing.

Yakov had resolved not to draw his full strike fund entitlement, however, because he knew that others needed the money more than he did. Why should he give to Poppa and impoverish the Cause? Money was beginning to run short, and it had to continue to stretch until the Morgenstern enterprises at last gave in. As they would, Yakov reminded himself. As they would.

He thought about the exhortations of the member of the Speakers Committee who had addressed last night's meeting. He had stressed the importance of picket lines again, likening their job to that of missionaries among the unenlightened. It was an odd simile for the mostly Jewish group, but they had listened attentively. Pickets had to try to convert those who did not yet understand the value of the Cause, to preach what was really a new religion of the working classes. Pickets had to understand the problems of the unconverted but reject their excuses for scabbing and strikebreaking. If reason did not work, the pickets must hold to their convictions and use their bodies to stop the scabs. The pickets marching in front of each shop were the legionary standard-bearers for the union at that shop; they must not give in.

Yakov had thought that was fine and inspiring talk, but when his father came walking up the street—the only consistent strikebreaker at Saperstein's shop these days—it was not easy for him to put the speaker's words to the test. Other mornings he had yelled, "Scab, strikebreaker!" at Poppa and the other men, but today it was just Poppa, and Yakov found he could not yell at him today. He looked at him, but Poppa looked back wordlessly, and then Yakov turned his back and walked in the other direction, as if he had not seen him. Today he let Edelmann do the yelling. He could not.

Of course, as he had every other morning, Poppa simply ignored the shouting and walked into the building. Yakov could not feel that Poppa was the kind of heathen last night's speaker could have converted, either. He smiled to himself. Some heathen.

After his father had entered the building Yakov strained his ears to hear if there was continued shouting at any of the other shops. Would some of the scabs be frightened and turned away today, as they had been on other days? (But those had been scabs hired by the bosses—today's would be their own, however secret.) Was Dora's line being challenged even now by the scabs of whom Moish had talked? Was there trouble? The morning noises of the working city were all around him, and he could not distinguish between the yelling of delivery men, the wrangling of early marketers, and other sounds, sounds for which his ears were straining above the traffic noises that blanketed all with a constant rumble as he walked back and forth, back and forth in front of the building.

Suddenly, though, there was Moish running up the street toward him, calling, "Drop everything, drop everything—we need help to hold the line at Yankelman's! Hurry! Hurry!"

Yakov did not need to catch all the words. Before Moish had reached him he had laid his placard on the ground and begun to run. His fear made the three blocks seem like three miles, as if he was running under water, choking to death as he ran. What had happened? Didn't their own hirelings understand it was just for publicity? That it was for the papers today? What did Moish mean they needed help? He had to get to Dora. He had to help his dear love.

When he rounded the corner near Yankelman's shop he could not believe his eyes—there seemed to be hundreds of people in the street. The noise of their shouts was confused to his ears, but it appeared that after weeks of inactivity the pent-up furies of the workers and the strikebreakers had been let loose, and they were rioting like mad dogs before him. Men with long beards and black hats were hitting other men with rough trousers and peaked caps. There was more than one set of strikebreakers here. There were clubs in the hands of many of the men. Policemen on horses were riding through one end of the melee, swinging their nightsticks and trying to bring some kind of order, but even the horses could not stop this milling, flailing throng.

Yakov waded into the fight immediately, his fists swinging. He had to find Dora, he kept thinking, kicking smaller men out of his way. Where were the girls who had been picketing in the midst of this crazy, men-filled scene?

His elbow connected with someone's rib cage just before his right fist smashed into the stomach of a strikebreaker who crumpled before him. Pushing him aside, he bent his efforts on a man with a club who was facing the other way. He hit him such a blow in the middle of his back that he, too, staggered to the side. If blows were falling on Yakov himself, meanwhile, he did not feel them. He had only one thought as he moved desperately but steadily through the fighting, heaving crowd toward the building. If he knew Dora, she was still near the building; they would not have managed to move her. Indeed, when a way cleared briefly for him to catch a glimpse, there she was.

They saw each other at the same instant. Dora had just brought the wooden stick of her placard down with a bang on a square man who had approached her from the front; she raised her eyes and saw Yakov and smiled.

"I'm coming," he shouted to her, but he could not tell if she heard him, because suddenly a policeman was behind her and had knocked her to the pavement. Would she have seen that policeman if she had not been smiling at Yakov? He would never know the answer to that question. The sight of Dora lying on the pavement turned him into more of a madman than he had been before; maybe it was the wild look in his eyes as much as the force of his fists that brought him to Dora's fallen figure in the next moments, but he was instantly there.

In that same moment he saw Kalinsky nearby and shouted, "Clear a space, give her some air, Dora's hurt," and he knelt beside her. Later he realized with a numb gratitude that at that moment Kalinsky had obeyed him, not the other way around, as it had always been before. Kalinsky's fists had swung, Kalinsky's deep voice had cleared the air around Dora.

Dora's head must have struck the pavement as she had fallen. The profuse blood of a head injury had started to flow immediately, and Yakov's hands were covered with it when he attempted to turn her over.

"Dora," he shouted, "Dora, can you hear me?"

Her eyes fluttered once and she smiled again, but she didn't speak. She was silent, worse in her silence than in the worst of Yakov's nightmares. Her red hair was matted with blood as it had been in those terrible dreams. He knelt there beside her and shouted and held her and wondered if there was anything worse in the whole world than the stillness of that still form in his arms. "Dora," he wept. "Dora."

He did not know how much later it was that the police reinforcements finally restored order. He did not hear them asking their questions of the others who were left. He did not see the policeman who had hit her standing silently a little way off. It was only when some stretcher-bearers came and lifted Dora's body and put a sheet over it that Kalinsky could move him away. There was no way he could hold her any longer. He went with Kalinsky then, to the flat with the slogans on the walls.

For years and years after that day there was some part of Yakov that still held Dora's silent, bloody form in his arms. He asked himself over and over if she might have escaped the policeman if she had not been looking at him instead. And he tried to remember whether they had actually put the sheet over her face as they had taken her away on the stretcher, but he could not remember, and he could not ask such a question aloud. Kalinsky had helped him on that day, that much he knew, and he would follow Kalinsky through hell if need be from then on. Or was hell where he already was?

He did not see Aaron Morgenstern in the window of a building across the street, nodding his head. If he had, would his heartache have increased at the knowledge of Aaron's thoughts as he watched?

Yes, the boss was saying to himself, I can break them now. I've used those scabs well this time. I can crush them now.


"Shayna, Shayna!" Harry burst into the room, startling his sister from her book. "There's someone downstairs who is asking for you."

305

"What do you mean asking for me?"

"He is asking for Miss Shayna Klugerman. He says he is a photographer. He's asking Mrs. Goldstein, who is sitting down there on the stoop. I heard him when I was running bases, so I came up to tell you. Come down quick! He's asking for you." He pulled her arm to get her up from the chair.

"A photographer! Oh, thank heavens Poppa isn't home!" Shayna jumped up and ran after Harry down the stairs. She nearly bumped into a young man she recognized as Henry C. Jones at the bottom of the second story.

"Oh, there you are, Miss Klugerman," he hailed her. "But where are you running in such a hurry?" he had to ask as she seemed ready to continue her downward progress.

"Hello, Mr. Jones." She struggled for politeness despite the fact that she knew that neighbors were listening at their doors all around. In fact, Mrs. Goldstein had come into the hall downstairs and was standing there to catch the conversation.

"I hoped I would find you at home," he said. "I've left my equipment outside with a woman who was sitting there. Do you think it's all right while we talk?"

"Perhaps not," said Shayna, glaring at Mrs. Goldstein as they passed her. "Let's talk outside so you can watch it yourself. Harry, you run and play," she added, not wanting her curious little brother to hear any more of her conversation with a stranger. "And don't blab everything to Poppa," she whispered.

When she and Mr. Jones were on the sidewalk she knew they would be stared at from all the windows if people wanted to stare, but at least they would be unlikely to be overheard in all the noise of an October Wednesday afternoon.

"What do you want?" Shayna was blunt now.

"I wanted to give you the picture I took a couple of

months ago—the picture of you and your brother. I knew he would be working today, but I had to be in the neighborhood, and I thought you'd be home from school."

"I told you that day—I don't want the picture," she said, determined to control her curiosity about it. "I can't pay for a picture." She didn't correct him by telling him Yakov was on strike.

"Oh, Miss Klugerman," he teased, "why don't you smile the way you did the day I came before? Don't be so grumpy. I never meant you to pay for it—it's a gift. Come on," he urged, holding out a package.

"I don't think I should." Shayna hesitated. She was remembering the new ways he had taught her to look at things on that long-ago day.

"You must take the picture," he insisted, "because your brother will want to see it. You can show it to him when he gets home from work. Then you can give it to your parents."

"Well"—she summoned up her courage—"I guess no one needs to know what day it was taken. Maybe when my mother comes back . . ."

"Good for you." Henry C. Jones smiled. "And now," he said, after he handed her the large brown envelope, "I have to be off to work. I'm actually doing some regular work for my paper in your neighborhood today."

"Where?"

"There's been a strike of garment workers. I imagine you've heard about it."

"I guess Yakov said something." She was casual, not giving away family business to strangers. "He's always talking about strikes these days, though, so I didn't pay much attention."

"Well, this one may achieve higher wages, but it has also had terrible consequences. I was supposed to get there this morning, and I couldn't come when I said. Now I hear there was a riot when the owners brought in scabs, and some women were hit and injured. One of the people on the picket line—a woman, a Miss Dora Schneider, they told me—was severely injured in the fight, and they think she's going to die. You didn't know her, by any chance?''

Shayna shook her head. "I never heard the name. Was anyone else hurt?" she asked.

"Several women were, apparently," he said. "And now I'm going to take pictures for my paper." He frowned. "I've never taken pictures of that kind of thing before, and I don't know what will be left when I get there, since I'm late as it is. Frankly, I came by because I hated the whole idea of pictures of something like that."

"What an awful thing!" said Shayna. "I wonder if my brother knew that woman." Well, she thought, at least it was only women who were hurt, so Yakov was safe. "Yakov seems very involved in all this striking," she went on. "I will tell him to be more careful," she added. "Now thank you very much, Mr. Jones. I do appreciate your thoughtfulness in stopping by. I know my brother Yakov will appreciate it, too."

Upstairs Shayna took a moment to look at the picture before the family came in. The likeness was good, she supposed, but it surprised her how different the young people in the photograph looked from herself and her brother now. She felt as if that innocent girl in the picture who'd had all those questions for her brother that *Shabbos* afternoon was a very different girl from the one whose mother wasn't coming home from a war in Europe, who would have to quit school and go to work in November.

And when next she saw Yakov he looked very different also. When he came home that night it was very late, and she didn't see him because she was already asleep. She awoke once in the night and thought she heard sobbing from his room, but then she thought that was impossible, and she was very sleepy, so she turned over and plumped up her pillow and went back to sleep.

Yakov left early in the morning as usual, before anyone was up, so that even Poppa didn't see him go. As a matter of fact, the whole family didn't see Yakov more that week because he came in so late and left so early, unless Poppa saw him at the shop. But, Shayna reminded herself, Yakov was on strike, and Poppa was working, so they wouldn't have spoken anyway. She wondered once if her brother took time from his picketing to attend the memorial service for the strikers who were killed in that riot—there were long articles in the *Forward* about the memorial service—but she forgot to ask.

By the time Yakov did come back to the family he seemed to Shayna very different indeed from the way he looked in the picture. But then, it was a time in her life when everything was more and more different. He was much thinner even than he had been, and his eyes seemed bloodshot and sunk into his head. He didn't speak.

Then, when the strike was finally broken and Morgenstern had won, there was a way he looked that made her afraid. It was as if he had forbidden her to ask him any more questions. She tried to put it out of her mind. With Mamma gone forever, with her own life so troubled, she tried not to think about it for as long as she could. A day would come when she could not put her brother out of her mind, but that was in the future. She had long since hidden the photograph away, and she never did remember to show it to Yakov. Luckily Harry didn't tell Poppa, so no one found out about Henry C. Jones.

# ❦ 11 ❦

*None calleth for justice,*
*nor any pleadeth for truth. (Isaiah 59:4)*

I won't be home right after school tomorrow," said Sophie. "Don't forget, Shayna, tomorrow is the day."

Shayna raised her head from *The Count of Monte Cristo* and looked blankly at Sophie.

"I knew you'd forget," Sophie accused her. "You're the only one who would forget, but I knew you would."

Shayna frowned, trying to think what Sophie was talking about. Then it came to her.

"Oh," she said, "the trial."

"Poppa's even taking the day off from work." Sophie's voice was awed as she reached for her embroidery. "He's going to come with me. He says I can't go alone to a courtroom."

There was a place inside Shayna that hurt all the time. Poppa wouldn't let Sophie go alone, but she felt that if it had been herself, he probably would have shoved her gladly out the door even if it was to feed her to lions. Poppa cared about Sophie, even if he hated the rest of his children.

Then she was ashamed of herself for thinking like that about him, even at the same time she felt so hurt. "I'll wash and iron your dress after supper," she offered guiltily. "I do want you to be as clean and neat as possible. You mustn't disgrace the family."

"Disgrace the family, disgrace the family, that's all you ever think of," Sophie returned, still annoyed that Shayna hadn't remembered. "And reading," she added.

"Well, I don't see why I shouldn't read," said Shayna. "I've done what I was supposed to for today, and there's hardly anyone home anymore. Why shouldn't I read?"

"Well, Tante Tillie won't like it when she finds out," Sophie threatened.

Everyone else was being special about Sophie these days, and Shayna guessed her little sister wanted her to join that world of admirers. Well, she wouldn't. "I don't care what Tante Tillie likes and doesn't like anymore either," she declared. "What more can she do to me?"

It was true, she felt, but even as she talked defiantly she was cold and miserable inside herself again. Most days it seemed Tante Tillie had won. Poppa had said that she was to quit school on her fourteenth birthday, November thirteenth. Tante Tillie was going to take care of the house then while she, Shayna, went off to work instead. Then, they said, little David would be able to be at home instead of staying at Tante Sadie's house. Harry wouldn't be running back and forth there so much either, Shayna admitted. So unless she found another way (she crossed her fingers), Tante Tille had won.

"Is it true," asked Sophie, changing the subject, "that Tante Sadie is going to have a baby?" She bent and picked up a dust ball as she spoke.

"Where did you hear that?" asked Shayna, surprised. "And throw that mess away—honestly, I think it flies in the window."

"I was listening when Tante Tillie was talking to Mrs. Goldstein on Yom Kippur. She said that Tante

Sadie is going to have a baby next spring. How do they know?'' Sophie put the dust in the trash bag. It was so nice to have two hands again since her cast was finally off. She could even embroider.

"I don't know. She isn't fat or anything, like Mamma was before she had David.'' Shayna considered. Her own ignorance upset her. "How am I supposed to know something like that? They just know, I guess. Tante Tillie seems to know everything,'' she added bitterly. Mamma should have told her about things like how you know about babies.

"Well, Tante Tillie said that Uncle Franz and Tante Sadie were going to have this baby, so Tante Tillie would have to take care of us, because she told Mrs. Goldstein Mamma had disappeared in Europe. That's the way she said it—disappeared in Europe—and wasn't coming back. 'I will have to take care of my brother's family,' she said, 'so I won't be marrying that fellow after all.' What fellow, Shayna? Who was going to marry Tante Tillie?''

Shayna looked blank.

Clearly Sophie liked being a reporter. "And then Tante Tillie said, 'If Isaac's wife had come back, I would not have stayed with her in that house. There's not room for the two of us. I would have married him. But now,' she said, 'I will stay and take care of my brother's family.' Shayna, do you think Tante Tillie would leave if Mamma came back?''

"Questions, questions, questions. I don't know the answers to your questions, Sophie, and that's that. Anyway'' —she turned back to her book—"you'd better start thinking of answers for your witnessing at that trial tomorrow, not questions.''

"Oh, I know the answers to what they'll ask me,'' said Sophie positively. "I saw the thieves. I know what happened.''

"Well, just make sure you don't embroider any

extras onto your answers," said Shayna. "Just tell the truth, without extras."

"I know, I know." Sophie clearly didn't feel she should be told what to do. After all, she was the heroine, not Shayna.

Shayna knew, the next afternoon, that she had to try to talk to somebody, and the somebody she still wanted to talk to was Cassie, so she went over to Cassie's house after school. She knocked at the door, expecting her best friend to appear, counting on Cassie to talk to about some of Sophie's questions, which were also her own.

But it was not Cassie who answered the door. It was Ari Rose.

"Hello, Shayna," he greeted her with a smile.

She felt her last spring's weakening at the knees at the sight of him, so she stammered when she asked, "Is Cassie home?"

"No," he answered, "the whole family had to go over to my aunt's house this afternoon. I'm the only one here. But come in, please."

"Oh, no," said Shayna, backing away. "I don't want to disturb you. Will Cassie be home soon, though, do you think?" she asked. She wanted so much to talk to a friend.

"Probably she won't be long," Ari said. "Why don't you come in and wait? I have a new book with pictures of Palestine I can let you see while you wait."

"Oh, well, if you don't think it will be long . . ." She allowed herself to be persuaded.

He led her into the bright living room with the bookshelves and pointed to the sofa on which Mrs. Rose was usually perched. The room seemed strangely empty without her. "I'll just get the book," he said.

Shayna found herself unable to resist doing anything that Ari Rose suggested, so she plopped herself in a corner of the couch, smoothed her skirt, and waited.

He was back in a moment with a large book. "I remember when we talked about Palestine," he said. "I thought you might like to see these pictures of what we talked about." He sat down beside her.

With his body so close to hers, their thighs actually touching as he spread the book out between them, Shayna could not concentrate on the pictures. She held one side of the book while Ari held the other. He pointed to a picture of the Wailing Wall, then to one of some workers on a farm, but all she could think about was how close he was, how warm his body was next to her. She felt the way she did when she had drunk some Passover wine, all weak and slithery.

Then something completely surprising happened. Without saying anything about it, Ari leaned over to the page that was more on her lap than on his own, supposedly to point something out, but as he leaned it seemed that somehow he had put an arm around her waist. Shayna was most surprised by the fact that she did not draw back from his arm, but actually found herself snuggling into it. It was as if the wine in her feelings was making it so she was dreaming some wonderful dream, and Ari Rose was hugging her in the dream. It could not be real.

She looked toward him to see if he realized what he was doing, and at the same time he looked toward her. With their faces so close to each other it was perhaps natural, she told herself later, that he kissed her.

Shayna had never been kissed by a stranger in her life, and even as she lifted her arms to push back his shoulders the book slid to the floor. But what she could not think about later was that then she found herself beginning to kiss him back. And that was only the beginning, before the thing happened that frightened her most of all.

One of Ari's hands touched her breast. She did not know—refused later to think about—whether it was deliberate, but when he touched her Shayna's whole body tingled in a way that terrified her and somehow woke her up from her winey dream so that at last she could push him firmly away. She jumped up from the couch and heard herself saying polite words that had nothing to do with what she was feeling or what had just happened.

"I'm sorry, but I can't wait for Cassie any longer" was all she said as she fled. "I'll see her in school tomorrow." With those few words she was out the door and onto East Broadway, running home.

She couldn't even imagine how those few minutes had happened, and she couldn't think about it. If only Mamma were home. Had anything like that ever happened to Mamma? Had Mamma ever felt that winelike feeling with a man? With Poppa? It seemed impossible. Was this indeed what led to people having babies? She was terrified, and she knew she could never tell Cassie about it, so there was truly no one to talk to. What had she done?

When Poppa and Sophie came back to the house that night Sophie was full of the story of her day in court, still the heroine. Even Poppa seemed a little indulgent as he let her describe the scene to the family. Tante Sadie and Uncle Franz came over, so everyone was there together to hear the tale. It certainly gave Sophie her attention.

"I had to swear first," she said. "They gave me an English Bible, and I had to swear that I would tell the truth. I was going to anyway, of course, but they made me swear it. Then they started to ask me questions."

"Who asked first?" Shayna wanted to know. Anything to distract herself from her newest fears.

"The lawyer who was on our side," said Sophie.

"I could tell because he was very nice to me. He wanted to know about my arm and the cast and everything. He had me show him which arm it was and tell him about it. And he wanted to know when the cast came off, if it was before or after that day."

"Yes, yes, Sophie, but what about the thieves?" interrupted Harry. "Didn't they ask about the thieves?"

"I'm telling you, I'm telling you—just wait a minute," said Sophie. "First," she went on, "they asked exactly how much money was in the till, and they wanted to know how I knew. So I told them about you counting it out, Harry."

Harry squirmed with importance. "Then what?"

"Well, I told them that there was the eight cents more because of the lady who bought the blue wool. I think the jury believed me that I knew because I told them so carefully." She smiled with pride at that point, drawing the story out.

Even Poppa nodded at her.

"It matters that it was less than twenty-five dollars," broke in Tante Tillie, obviously wanting to share some of the limelight. "A woman at the shop today told me that if it's under twenty-five dollars it's just petty larceny. More money than that is grand larceny. They're different charges. The criminals get more punishment if it's grand larceny." She smiled.

"Well, I told them the right amount," said Sophie, "and they knew it anyway, so there!" she pouted.

Shayna noticed that no one rebuked Sophie for her little show of temper.

"Well, then, didn't they just send the thieves to jail after they heard you?" asked Harry.

"That's the bad part." Sophie hesitated. "They didn't even go to jail," she finished in a rush.

Everyone was stunned to silence.

"Because I didn't see them," she explained then.

"What do you mean you didn't see them?" asked Shayna. "You told us you saw them."

"I did see them, really, but when the judge asked me if I had seen them actually taking the money, I had to tell the truth, didn't I? I was up on the chair getting the shirts when they took it, and I didn't see them actually doing it. I mean I identified the men and everything—no one argued with that—but I couldn't lie and say I had seen that one with his hand in the till when I hadn't, could I? You said not to lie, and anyway," she added with self-conscious virtue, "I swore to tell the truth. It didn't even seem to matter that Harry caught them when they ran away! They said stuff about all that being only 'circumstantial evidence,' not enough 'to convict on a criminal charge.'"

"So they just got away with it?" asked Shayna, her voice horrified. But she knew the answer before she asked.

"Yes," Tante Sadie answered for Sophie. "They got away with it." Her voice was flat, as if she had expected it.

Shayna saw Yakov across the room just staring at his plate. Then he said, "The police and the courts don't help people like us."

"But it wasn't Sophie's fault," insisted Uncle Franz, trying to cheer his little niece. He patted Sophie's head. "She did the very best she could," he said.

The best she could. Shayna guessed she knew that Sophie had done the best she could, so why wasn't the best good enough? Mamma had always said that the best was what you should do, that cream rose to the top, that the right side would always win in the end. So why didn't it win this time? Had Mamma been wrong again? Why hadn't the court done the right thing and punished the thieves? The judge must have known that they did it—Sophie even identified them. So why did the bad men win?

For Shayna it was, somehow, the last straw. Who was that girl she had been, that girl who believed that

Mamma was always right? She felt as if she were two people, and the new one was sitting there looking at the other, the younger, stupidly innocent one, the one who had been in the photograph Mr. Jones had taken, the one who had thought she wouldn't make so many mistakes. The self who knew more now was terribly, terribly sad as she looked. She was older now; she might even have a baby after what had happened that afternoon with Ari. No one understood.

And for some reason she didn't want to look at her older brother Yakov at that moment. Tears came to her eyes. Why hadn't she understood before? Why hadn't she understood what Poppa and Tante Tillie had tried to drum into her head, that the happy endings were only in books, not in what really happened? Why had she kept hoping?

When the rest of the family saw Shayna's tears they thought that she was simply being sympathetic to poor Sophie after the little one's terrible ordeal. No one was surprised when Uncle Franz dug into his pocket and produced a shiny quarter and gave it to Sophie.

"You did the best you could," he said. "It wasn't your fault."

Shayna thought then that her new self who understood the bad things would have to tell Sophie, too, someday, that despite this evening of getting praise and a quarter, there were no happy endings. And then, as she sat thinking her sad thoughts, the evening suddenly erupted in a way that she hadn't expected, an awful way that threatened to make all their lives even worse.

It started because Poppa seemed to want the lesson pushed further, and he turned on Yakov, of all people. "It's like that stupid strike of yours!" he said. "You didn't win a thing by it, did you? Nothing at all was accomplished, was it?"

"Oh, for God's sake," Yakov said at first, pushing

his chair away from the table even though he hadn't quite finished. He drew in his breath as he rose, making a sound that was enough like a sob so that Shayna looked at him sharply through her own tears.

"Don't you use the Lord's name in vain in this house!" Automatically, Poppa quoted the commandment. He must not have heard the sob.

For a minute Shayna really thought that her older brother, too, was going to weep. He stood suddenly tall above them, and his face seemed to crumple as she looked at him. What had happened to take away the hope from Yakov?

"I'm leaving," he said, and at first he wasn't even shouting. Then he repeated himself, and there was no sob now. This time he was shouting, and his voice was terrible and final. "I'm leaving this house, and I'm never coming back!" he shouted.

What had happened? It couldn't be just about Sophie; Shayna knew that. Was it something about the strike?

"Yakov . . ." Shayna began, putting out her hand as if she could detain him, "don't . . . wait . . ." She had stopped crying, but suddenly she couldn't find words that might make her brother stay with them. His troubles seemed bigger than her need for him to remain.

He turned his sunken eyes toward her, and he looked at her with a terrible, lonely sadness to which she couldn't put a name, a look she knew she would store in her for the rest of her life and never forget, a look that made her suddenly know that although she loved Yakov, she would never again reach him, not really. Her brother was lost to her.

"Don't touch me," he said to her. "I'm sorry, but I have to go."

Then he just walked out.

Poppa didn't say a word, and the rest of them were too appalled to speak, too afraid of Poppa to speak, too sick and hurt to speak. Even Sophie was silent then, as if she had forgotten her new quarter.

Shayna knew, looking at the closed door behind her brother, that even if he ever came back to them he would be different. He was lost, more lost even than Mamma.

Yetta Garfinkel looked down with surprise at the little girl tugging at her skirt on Sunday afternoon. She was a pretty little one, Yetta thought, but she had better speak up if she wanted to be heard. "What do you want?" she asked again. She was still her impatient self. "I haven't got all day here. What do you want?"

"I want to buy a dress," said Sophie.

"Nu? Buy!" said Mrs. Garfinkle shortly, turning back to her friend Esther Schenckman, with whom she had been talking. Really, children! Thank God she had none of her own at home anymore.

"My sister bought a dress here last spring," insisted Sophie, tugging again. People kept pushing up against her. She looked up momentarily. What if it rained and they covered up all the dresses and took the pushky away? "I have some money," she said, holding out her quarter.

Yetta Garfinkel turned back to look at the money, then threw up her hands. "Her sister bought a dress, she says," she addressed the group crowded around the pushcart. "Her sister bought a dress, and she has money." She looked at Sophie's open palm again. "She thinks she can buy a dress with only a quarter."

"Don't pay attention," her husband called across the cart to her. "Just mind your business and put those wool cloaks on the left with the others," he directed, "without all this gossiping. We don't have children's dresses," he said, turning to Sophie and shaking his head.

"My sister bought a dress Mrs. Morgenstern brought,"

said Sophie, ignoring Mr. Garfinkel and still addressing his wife.

"Hear that, Nachman?" said that lady, sounding glad of an excuse to needle her husband. She obviously did not like his orders any more than those of her little customer. "Your fancy friend's fancy dress is what the sister bought. So she comes today with only a quarter, and she wants to buy, too?" She glared at him. "See what comes finally of that nogoodnik Leah Morgenstern? See? Like the Americans say it, she 'raises the expectations.' Now what does your royal highness direct me to say to this child?"

The customers were standing back, watching the exchange with amusement. The Garfinkels' fights were legend on Hester Street. Half of the pleasure of shopping from their pushcart, the women always said, came from watching the two of them arguing all the time. And there was a quality in the argument people always knew was safe, as if there was an underlying core of something between the two Garfinkels that was never touched by the superficial bickering. One could enjoy it without being in any way distressed by it.

"Is it my fault Leah Morgenstern hasn't shown up in a long time? Am I supposed to be a magician I should make her appear out of thin air? Is it abracadabra I'm supposed to say for you, princess?" Nachman Garfinkel roared. Then he took a ragged parasol from the cart and actually waved it in the air like a magic wand. "All right, there, abracadabra," he said, "abracadabra!" Then he snorted. "Well, princess, will my magic make the automobile appear? Will it?"

Sophie's eyes were round.

Suddenly Esther Schenckman said, *"Oy veh,"* and she pointed her finger up the street. She grabbed Yetta's sleeve. *"Oy veh,"* she repeated.

Sophie looked in the direction in which Mrs. Schenckman was pointing. So did the rest of the customers. What they saw made them all stand there silent and somehow alarmed.

*"Oy veh,"* echoed Mrs. Garfinkel. "Look, Nachman, look." She, too, pointed up the street. "This can't be happening." She turned to her old friend Esther and spoke in a low tone Sophie overheard. Then she shook her head and moaned, "I can't stand it—he'll never get over it. All I'll hear from now on will be abracadabra, abracadabra. Why should God do this to me?"

There it was—the Morgensterns' Daimler, appearing magically around the corner of Hester Street as they all watched. As Sophie told Shayna later, it was really there, right when Mr. Garfinkel said it would be, right when he said abracadabra. It didn't matter to Sophie that she hadn't been able to buy a dress after all, not after that magical moment. She still had her quarter, didn't she? So she'd buy something else. So what? At least she had been there to see Mr. Garfinkel waving a magic wand.

It hadn't been Mrs. Morgenstern in the car, either, Sophie had told Shayna; the passengers had actually been Mr. Morgenstern and his little boy, who looked like he was just her age. He was sort of a chubby, self-important little boy, but then, in Sophie's eyes, little Norman Morgenstern had a right to be important, just like she did. And when Mr. Morgenstern had stepped from the car and spoken to Mr. Garfinkel Sophie had heard him say something about his wife's not coming because she was still in Europe. Had Mrs. Morgenstern disappeared in Europe like Mamma?

If she had, Shayna did not seem to think that any abracadabra from the pushcart man, Nachman Garfinkel, could bring her back. Sophie's story just seemed to make Shayna sad. Oh, well. She shrugged her shoulders. Anyway, she had seen the magic with her own eyes.

Even if the little ones did not seem so fazed by it (except for Shayna), Isaac was deeply shocked by Yakov's departure. It was as if his son's going was Sarah's going all over again. He had no real idea, either, of what it was about. How was he to cope with this from his eldest son without Sarah? Surely this was not something that she had left Shayna to deal with. This was for him, Isaac. And he had no way.

Something had happened to Yakov since he had been working, Isaac saw, something that had moved him irrevocably away. Isaac had thought he knew what was happening, had thought it was the union, the Cause, that had turned his son against him. Yet he always knew he was not merely the boy's enemy; he was his father, too, and now there was something in Yakov's eyes that was not the union or the Cause. Now there was pain. When Isaac allowed himself to think of it, he knew his son was in pain, and the pain of his son was worse, much worse than just his leaving.

When he turned to his holy books Isaac found little comfort even there. Only the story of David and Absalom gave him words for some of his own pain. He read over and over again the story of King David crying, "Absalom, my son, my son, Absalom, my son," and he thought of his own son and wept alone in the night for Yakov, his own rebellious son.

But he dried his eyes in the day and glared at his family and went to the shop as usual. For Yakov was no longer working there; he had been fired after the strike. Even to his friend Tanchun Isaac said nothing about Yakov's departure. In the evenings he just sat reading the same story over again, willing the pages to tell him an answer they did not reveal.

One evening he looked up from his book in some

surprise when there was a knock at the door. For a moment he had forgotten that the rest of the family had gone up to the roof again. He himself paid little attention to the weather, and the discomforts of Indian summer were significant only to those members of the family who were not already bowed down with the trouble he felt weighing on him. Up on the roof then, were they? Well, he supposed he could put the book down and answer the door, though it was probably a mistake. Who would want to come to their flat on a hot October evening, after all?

To his surprise the music teacher, David Nathan, stood in the hall.

"Come in, come in," said Isaac. "I haven't seen you in a very long time." It had been so long, in fact, that there had been a second when he wasn't absolutely sure who the man was. He had visited them on and off over the years, always at Sarah's invitation (but with his permission). Since they had had the piano David Nathan had come and played a few times in the evenings. It had pleased Sarah, as Isaac knew, so he had given the permission. He himself did not particularly care for music, but it pleased him (although he had never said so) to please his wife. He was proud of her that she liked such things, even though Tillie said it was foolishness.

"I wondered," David Nathan said abruptly, "I wondered if you'd heard from Sarah. When Shayna did not come for her lessons"—he hesitated—"I wondered if something had happened. With the war in Europe, I mean. I knew that your wife was in Europe. . . ."

"Shayna is too busy for the lessons," Isaac said, looking at him in surprise. Did the man think everybody had time only for piano lessons? It was strange that this man should ask after Sarah. "With her mother gone, Shayna has to take care of the house more. She has no time for lessons!" He was short and final.

"If it is the money . . ." Mr. Nathan began, then he stopped at the look on Isaac's face.

"It is not the money."

"Well, perhaps when her mother comes back . . ." Mr. Nathan tried again.

"When her mother comes back we will see," said Isaac. He could not bring himself to say more.

"Then you've had no word since the war started?" the music teacher persisted.

"No," Isaac said, "there have not been mails from Hungary."

David Nathan nodded, twisting his hat in his hand. "I hope that all is well," he said awkwardly. "Let me know if—"

"Certainly," Isaac interrupted him.

It was only later that it occurred to him that the man might have meant to let him know about Sarah, not about the lessons for Shayna. David Nathan was a strange and awkward man for his Sarah to have befriended, he thought as he showed him out the door. It must have been her liking for music that had caused it. Perhaps the man's rough edges would have been smoothed over if he had ever married. But who, Isaac asked himself, shaking his head, would marry a music teacher?

He had barely settled himself back in his chair with his book when there was again a knocking. Had Mr. Nathan forgotten something? But when he opened the door this time, it was a small woman who stood there and said, "How do you do, Mr. Klugerman?" as if she knew him.

He stared at her. Her blue serge dress was worn, but carefully proper. She wore a small felt hat on her head, the kind of hat worn by impoverished Christian ladies, the kind he had seen on the heads of the ladies who worked at the settlement houses. It was not, he thought wryly to himself, because his family didn't know he noticed such things, the sort of confection

*Janet C. Robertson*

worn by the uptown ladies of fashion who sometimes
came down to the neighborhood on errands that had
always been obscure to him. This woman also had
steel-rimmed spectacles pinned to her lapel, ready, as
anyone could see, for instant use.

She held out her hand to shake his, but he did not
take it, because she was a strange woman, and according to the Law he could not touch her. He spoke
reluctantly, using careful though accented English.
"How do you do, miss?"

Since he had not invited her in, she had to stand in
the foul-smelling hall to tell him who she was. "I am
Miss Helen Barton, your daughter's Latin teacher."

He still looked doubtful.

She insisted, "Your daughter Shayna, Mr. Klugerman,
is my student. May I come in?"

He could see no way around it that made sense of
the odd situation, so he stepped reluctantly aside. "If
you wish," he said. "Has Shayna done something
wrong?" he asked. "My wife isn't at home, I'm
afraid."

She passed him as he spoke, and he turned to face
her, still standing, after he closed the door.

"Perhaps if we sit down," suggested Miss Barton,
ignoring his question. She took on the role of the
absent hostess as a possible way in which to win this
formidable man's confidence. "Perhaps we might talk
about it."

"You sit down, please," Isaac preempted her and
was courtly for a moment, holding a chair for her at
the kitchen table. "But I prefer to stand to hear bad
news."

"Oh, please, Mr. Klugerman, I do not intend to be
the conveyor of bad tidings," she said. "In fact, what
I come to tell you is quite the opposite. Your daughter Shayna is my best student. Truly she is."

She caught a glimpse for a second of a pleased light
in Isaac's eyes and a smile of pleasure, but it was

326

instantly suppressed, because what difference could it make to him how Shayna did in a Latin class in an American high school?

"Shayna is also first in her class in English and in history, and she does very well in biology." Miss Barton hurried determinedly on. "Since she is one of the youngest pupils at her grade level, these are particularly outstanding accomplishments."

"I have seen my daughter's report cards in the past, Miss Barton. I know she has done well before. But I do not recall ever receiving a report on her work in October, nor one delivered in person. So I do not think that is why you have come."

"Actually"—she tried smiling—"it *is* why I have come, in a way." She was determined to keep the discussion on her own ground as long as she could.

He remained silent. Whatever the woman was there for, apparently she would have to come out with it on her own. He did not know what he could do to help her. And he did not see what possible reason he could have to help her in any case, but he decided to try. "Why exactly have you come, Miss Barton?" he asked.

"Because Shayna is my best student," she countered, trying still to go through her points in the order she had planned. "I looked up her record in all the rest of her classes. I have it here with me if you wish to see it." She opened up her large purse, brought out a piece of paper, and adjusted her spectacles on her nose to read the record, but Isaac stopped her.

"I do not wish to hear it if there is no reason," he said with impatience. "Frankly, Miss Barton, I do not feel it is even proper for Shayna to be studying these things at her age. Her place will be in the home, and I think it strange that American schools teach some of these subjects. At home she has learned Hebrew, as befits a bright Jewish girl. But"—he relented for a moment—"I am glad she does well and is a credit to herself and to us."

"Well, Mr. Klugerman, I do think it is important to be learning what you call 'these things' at Shayna's age. And it is Shayna's age that I am here to talk about."

Isaac's brow darkened briefly. "What has she been telling you?"

Miss Barton lied composedly in her answer to him, aware that it was the only course open to her. "She has told me nothing, Mr. Klugerman, but every girl's age is listed in our records. It was natural that I look up the age of my best pupil. Anyway," she hurried on, "I find that she will be fourteen very soon."

"Yes, she will be fourteen very soon," said Isaac, "and on her fourteenth birthday she will leave your school and go to work. As you can see, Miss Barton"— he gestured toward the room as he spoke—"we are not rich enough to afford the luxury of unnecessary school for a girl. She will go out and get a job. One of the other classes in which she has done well, I'm sure your records have told you," he added with sarcasm, "is her typing class. She types sixty words a minute. When she reaches her birthday she will go out and get a job as a typist and help to support the family."

"But surely you can see that she has a bright academic future before her if she continues in school."

"A bright academic future is not something I care about for my daughter. Please understand, though"—he held up his hand to stop her instant objection—"it is not that I do not respect learning. But in this case, there is no way to further it. We do not have the money. If Shayna were a boy, it might be different. A bright boy who did well—he could go on in the path of learning, and it would certainly be worth the sacrifice." He stopped suddenly with the thought of Yakov, then went on. "But a girl—well, she has a duty to the family."

"Mr. Klugerman, I was once a bright girl, and my family allowed me to stay in school in difficult times. Now I am a Latin teacher in a high school."

"I am sure that is a respectable achievement, Miss Barton. But it is not what I have in mind for my daughter. Besides which, there are other problems. If Shayna goes to work and makes a decent wage, it will, perhaps, be possible for my sister to stay at home and . . . but I do not want to bore you with family matters."

Miss Barton decided to press her advantage. If he was going to impart some confidences, then perhaps her way might be easier. "You said your wife was not at home, Mr. Klugerman?" she hazarded. She thought it was a way for him to think that he had told her, not Shayna.

He sighed. The woman was remarkably easy to talk to, even if she was a Christian, a schoolteacher, and clearly opposed to his decision about Shayna. "My wife went to Europe in May, Miss Barton, to visit her mother. Now, with the war, we have not been able to get any word of her, and it does not seem likely that she will be able to come back—come back soon, I mean. She was in the war zone."

"I'm sorry to hear of your trouble, Mr. Klugerman. Have you written to anyone in the government about the problem? If she is a citizen, then they will try to trace her for you. Every day I have been reading lists in the *Times* of people whose whereabouts have been determined, and—"

"I, too, read the *New York Times*," said Isaac in a bitter tone. "But I think that the lists are not lists of poor Jews who have been caught behind the lines in Eastern Europe. There are too many people named Astor or Morgan on those lists for me to think that Sarah Klugerman's name will magically appear there as well. No, Miss Barton." For the first time he was speaking his bitter truth aloud, and to a stranger. "I think my wife is not coming home."

"I'm sorry." She spoke quietly.

"So"—his head came up, refusing any sympathy— "someone must care for the home and the little ones. Shayna is not trained for it. She has never been good in the home, my sisters tell me, and she is plain as well. It would be best if she went to work as soon as possible so that my unmarried sister can do the work at home. I see no other way."

"But perhaps that is just why she should go on with her education," said Miss Barton, at last seeing a possible opening. "For a woman who does not marry, like myself, Mr. Klugerman, it is good to have a profession that will support her. Teaching is a respectable profession, as you yourself have said. If Shayna is educated, she can be a teacher. Besides which, I do not think of her as plain." She smiled briefly. "Have you ever read the fairy tale about the ugly duckling, Mr. Klugerman?"

"I do not read fairy tales, miss," he replied with asperity. "And I do not think that I wish to support my daughter's education for the faint hope of a possible future income when my family needs the income now. I do not want to argue about it, either, with a stranger. No, Miss Barton, Shayna must bring money into the home when she reaches the age when she can work."

Sighing, Miss Barton decided the only hope was the way she had planned as a last resort. "I see that it is the money that is the problem here, Mr. Klugerman. Therefore I would like to make you an offer. To me it is Shayna's education that is the problem, that makes the difference. So I would like to pay you, every week, the money that your daughter could make on a job. I think she would have to start in an office at seven dollars a week. That is the standard rate paid to an office worker who is just beginning. So I will pay you seven dollars a week if you will allow your daughter to continue in high school after her fourteenth birthday."

Isaac sat down at the table suddenly, unable to stand above this astonishing woman for another moment. "No!" he said. It was stark, but he was so shocked by her proposal that he could not think of any other way of expressing it.

"I thought that would be your first reply, Mr. Klugerman." She smiled her brief smile again. "But I will not take it as your last." She stuffed the list that had lain open before her throughout their conversation back into her purse and snapped her spectacles shut on her lapel. "I know that I have surprised you. But I also know that you are a Jew, and you care about learning. You have said so yourself. You may also care about it even if it is for a girl. I was once a girl who loved to learn, who nearly could not continue. I would like this opportunity to help someone like myself—to help your daughter Shayna." She stood up. "I will come back nearer to the time, and you will have thought about my proposal. Seven dollars a week for Shayna to continue in school. Think hard. I will be back soon, before the middle of November, Mr. Klugerman." She was at the door, and Isaac was still seated, unable to move. "Good-bye," she said, then she opened the door herself and went out.

He sat thinking about what she had said without moving for the next half hour, until Tillie and the children came back into the flat.

"I have had a visitor," he said then, to their astonishment. Somehow he had forgotten David Nathan and remembered only one visitor.

"Oh, Poppa, was it something about Mamma? Was there news of Mamma?" Shayna spoke the hope still uppermost in her mind.

"No," said Isaac, turning to look closely at her. "It was about you."

"About me?"

He could tell that her surprise and confusion were genuine. At least she had not known about Miss Barton's plan to come to the house. Then an irrelevancy surfaced in his mind, and he looked at her even harder. Could Shayna be pretty? Were his sisters wrong? "Your teacher, Miss Barton, was here just now."

"Miss Barton? What was she doing here? Was it something about my schoolwork?" Could it be (she hardly dared to hope) about staying in school?

"Yes, it was."

"But Poppa, I have been doing well, honestly I have. I have passed all my tests, and—"

"Huh, schoolwork! Teachers! Tests!" broke in Tante Tillie. "I never had a chance at such things. What you need, young lady, is—"

But Isaac's firm voice drowned out Tillie's words.

"Miss Barton," he said, "thinks that what you need is to stay in school."

"Oh, Poppa—"

"Miss Barton is willing to pay this family seven dollars a week to have you stay in school!"

"What?" squeaked Shayna, completely confused now, "Miss Barton said that—that she would pay seven dollars a week herself?" She closed her eyes, feeling faint. "Oh, my gosh, I've never been so embarrassed in my whole life. You mean Miss Barton came here, to this house" —Shayna opened her eyes and looked around frantically at the bareness of the room, feeling that the very smell of her family's shame was in that room with her—"and offered you money? Oh, Poppa, how could you?" She sank into a chair and covered her face with her hands.

"How could I what? How could I what now? How could I let her in the door? How could I converse with her? How could I hear what she had to say? How could I what?"

"But what did you tell her, Isaac?" interrupted

Tillie. "I mean, maybe it is a good idea, because the money might be the same as what she could earn at first, and she wouldn't be always complaining. . . . But on the other hand, I still feel—*we* still feel"—she clearly meant her sister Sadie was to be included in the feeling—"that Shayna should not go longer to that school." Tillie never mentioned her own marriage as one of the possibilities to be terminated or not terminated by his decision. If Sarah was not going to return, Tillie did not want to leave her brother, not ever. She clung to that.

"I told her no, Shayna," said Isaac, ignoring Tillie. He was still looking at his daughter as if he could somehow will her to understand him, this daughter who had the temerity to shout at him whenever she did not agree with him. "I told her just that. No."

But Shayna wasn't really listening to him. She still sat at the table with her face covered, certain that in the next moment or two she would die of shame. She would never be able to tell anyone, certainly not Cassie, about this. No one could understand how she felt. She was alone in an impossible world.

"Oh, Poppa, how could you?" she repeated.

"How could I what now? How could I turn the offer down? Or how could I even think of accepting money from a stranger? Because that is what I am doing, Shayna, I am thinking about it. It is, after all, a way for you to continue your education and a way for us still to have the income in the house. Now that your brother is gone . . ." He stopped, then went on. "And there are other reasons she mentioned why it might be useful for you to continue. Besides, she said that she was coming back in time for my final decision."

"Oh, no," Shayna groaned again. Had her hopes come to this humiliation?

Sophie came and stood next to her and took one of her hands and held it. For once Sophie was simply silent and a comfort. Maybe she understood what it would be like to have a teacher from school come and see their flat, how ashamed a person would feel.

"Now," said Isaac, suddenly too tired to think or argue further, "we will go to bed. We can always talk about this tomorrow. Everything always looks better in the morning. Oh, by the way," he suddenly remembered, "Mr. Nathan came by, too. I told him you weren't taking any more piano lessons."

"Oh, Poppa, how could you?" Shayna wept into her pillow later. Of course she cared about the piano lessons—they were a way she and Mamma had been close in their love of music. Now even that was gone. And how could she face Miss Barton in school the next day? "I wish this horrible war never happened," she moaned, "I wish this whole year never happened and I was never going to be fourteen."

Could they be lost? Of course Rachel knew they were lost, had known it for days, even though Mamma hadn't said so. It seemed as though they had been walking forever, and to look at their clothes, torn and gray with mud and dirt, it might have been the truth.

Rachel tried to remember back to her grandmother's, to Budapest, even to the train to Vienna. But all that seemed to have taken place in another life. The thought that only a few short weeks ago she and Mamma had looked at the money from the American consul and congratulated themselves that it was so much—it was impossible to believe. And it wasn't that the money was too little. It was just that since then money had simply stopped mattering.

What did money help after their train had waited two days on a siding in Germany while trains full of soldiers and horses, long trains of cars and cars, had gone by endlessly to the war? Money could not buy a train ticket to Holland when the trains just didn't go. Money had stopped meaning anything. So they had finally climbed down from that railway car with the other hungry, bewildered passengers, and they had started to walk, to walk toward a nightmare. A few times a passing cart, already loaded with people and bedding, had stopped and given them a short lift, but mostly they had walked, a journey of endless walking, Rachel thought, stopping to shake her aching feet, first one, then the other. Her feet hurt so much. But the walking continued no matter how much her feet hurt.

And now they were lost. The thumping of guns had been getting louder and louder all day, she could hear, but still they had gone toward it, always toward the sound, never away.

"Mamma, are we supposed to be going toward the guns?" Rachel had tried asking. She asked it more than once, but then she had stopped asking that question, too. She had not asked any more after Mamma's face had somehow not made it possible to ask again. And now, Rachel thought, all the rest of the world was going in the opposite direction, a steady stream of people that seemed never to stop, going away from the sound of the guns.

Louder and louder came the guns, and still they went toward them, ever toward them, never away from the booming of the guns, the thudding of the guns, finally even the crackling of the guns. And then the soldiers had come along, going the same way she and Mamma were going, but going faster, forcing them off the road so they had to stop as their train had stopped. Some days they were only able to go a very little way because there were so many soldiers on the road.

"Move off, please," said the military policemen, and then she and Mamma would move off the road and sleep—sometimes in the great hollow areas left where the shells had come—sleep where they stopped, because they were so endlessly tired. They tried walking through fields beside the road, but the fields had not been planted with any cover crop after the hasty harvest in that autumn of war, so there was no footing for them in the mud.

Now the guns were off on a ridge to their left, and they were cowering in a steady rain in an abandoned trench. The intermittent flashes of light from the gunfire served only to illuminate the endless pelting raindrops. They were hungry, but there was no food, and they could not move until daylight came. In the dark the barbed wire round about was treacherous, and they could not move. Sometimes the soldiers who had been in the trenches before them had left some food, and if the rats had not found it, Rachel and Sarah would stuff the stale bread in their mouths and sleep better. Stale bread, mud, rats, and this endless cold rain.

It was time to get going when there was a grayness in the sky and they could see the wire at last. There was usually a lull in the gunfire just before true daylight. It was time to move again, to walk again out of the trench, but Rachel, knowing that they were lost, couldn't bear to rouse Mamma to trudge again toward the renewed booming of the guns. At night Mamma had coughed fitfully in her sleep. Then she woke herself without Rachel's aid. "Come, *shaynheitel*," she said, and they moved on.

That morning they saw the American woman. She was obviously American from the cut of her clothes and the way that she moved, but when they stopped to talk to her she talked strangely. It was as if she was possessed, possessed by a *dybbuk*, not there herself, but with a strange spirit speaking inside her. She carried a large, heavy bundle that she put gently by the side of the road and left while she started to dig in a crater. Digging and mumbling, and her little girl standing numb beside her watching the digging, not hearing the mumbling. She did not respond to their words at first, just went on with her digging.

"Mamma," Rachel whispered to Sarah, "what is she doing?" Her own voice had emotion in it for the first time in days—horror, not just hunger and exhaustion. She could easily see what it looked like, but she could not believe it, right here on the road, with the people and the soldiers passing unheedingly and unceasingly, passing and passing, and the boom of the guns now steady from the ridge.

"You are right, Rachel, she is digging a grave," Sarah replied in the level, dead tone in which she had spoken for days, and then she coughed again. "What else can she do?" she asked, and she pulled Rachel to come on. They had talked like that for so long, in a kind of shorthand, with the unnecessary words left out. Sarah could see through the bundle next to the woman by the side of the road as if it were transparent, she could see that it was a little child lying there dead by the side of the road. Surely Rachel could see it, too. Why should it need more words?

But Rachel in turn pulled her mother toward the woman, and they listened for a while to the woman's vacant talk about the dead child as she dug. She had been visiting her sister in Germany for the summer. She had brought her two children. All of a sudden the little boy had become sick, and then he did not get better, and the people in her sister's village heard that the war was coming and the soldiers were coming, and they left. Just left. The sister, too, from what the woman mumbled. So the woman had tried to leave, but she had lost her way and had gone toward the battle, not away from it, and the little boy was sick still, and then he died in the rainy night, and the woman was digging this muddy grave in which to bury him.

She told them, mumbled it all to them, and then started to walk away, this time in the direction away from the battle, leaving the grave with a dead child. And now she stopped being possessed by a *dybbuk* but turned hollow, it seemed, before their eyes, as if the *dybbuk* was in the hollow grave with the dead child.

"Don't go that way," she said softly to Sarah and Rachel as she prepared to resume her journey. She pointed north, in the direction they were going. "Don't go that way." Then she went on down the road away from them, and Sarah's eyes glazed over, and she coughed and coughed.

But they went on. On north. Rachel was sure then that they were truly lost.


Days later, when the party of Belgian nuns found them by the side of the road, at first the nuns had trouble understanding what had happened to the delirious woman lying on the ground and the weeping girl who was tending her, her tears mixed so hopelessly with the cold of the autumn rain. Gradually, however, between the German they knew and the child's Yiddish, they were able to piece together the story of their wandering. It seemed that the pair of them had been going toward the war, toward the battles, toward the booming guns.

It became clear to the nuns that Rachel had not understood about the war, despite her mother's explanations. The war was being fought in the north of France, she thought, and it was being fought in the middle of France, and it was being fought by the Russians in the north of Germany, or was it Prussia? she asked, her eyes wide. Or were they both the same? Anyway, she had pieced together from what must have been less and less coherent explanations by her mother that the Russians were the ones to fear the most, that the cossacks would find them unless they fled to the west. So—the nuns shook their heads at the horror of it all—they had headed both north and west through the increasing cold and rain of October.

Perhaps the good health with which the two had started the journey, the result of a summer spent in fresh air, had saved them thus far. They were toughened by the physical labor of life at the grandmother's—the walking to get water, walking to get everything, carrying buckets and baskets and children for longer distances than had ever seemed necessary in their home in New York. After all, Rachel proudly told the nuns, on Orchard Street there was water in the tap. On Orchard Street one did not have to pick food in the garden in the sun. (She did not add that one instead bought it rotten from the pushcart on the street in a hotter sun. And only if one had the money.)

But their health could not hold in the rain. To hear Rachel tell it, there was no time when the rain had stopped in the last weeks. The aeroplanes no longer appeared in the sky above them then, no longer dropped bombs near them, no longer strafed the patches of roads they had seemed to haunt when the sun had shone. But the rain did the work the bombs had failed to do. It was a cold, unceasing, northern European rain, and it turned the clay fields and the unpaved roads into a sea of mud. Even the paved roads were covered with a layer of slick mud that made them slip with the bags they carried, that made them turn their ankles on the cobbles, that penetrated their shoes and stockings and hems, that crawled up their skirts both inside and out, that soaked them and muddied them and, of course, eventually made them ill.

Rachel told them her mother was sick first. She coughed and coughed until she had to stop each time the fit came on her, waiting for it to pass, had to stop more and more frequently with the coughing. When Rachel started to cough in turn her cough just stayed the same—it got no better, it got no worse. It rained, and Rachel coughed. But it rained and Sarah coughed and coughed and coughed. And stopped. And grew feverish. And did not know where they were. And somehow took them in the wrong direction until they were not going to Holland at all but were in Belgium in the rain by the side of a road, and Sarah could not go on any longer through the fever and the delirium and the mud. That was where the nuns found them.

The nuns were going on a short journey to their mother convent in Bruges, and they had a cart on which they put the woman and the girl and brought them to that ancient city as the bells in the great square tolled the angelus. The sky was just darkening after a rain-washed sunset over a battle still heard faintly in the west.

Across the North Sea and across England Americans were gathering in Liverpool, because that was the port from which the likely ships would go to America. Ethel Morgenstern and her mother and sisters, after seven sleepless nights on the floor of the Savoy dining room in London, had left that crowded city with tickets in hand and journeyed by crowded train at last to Liverpool.

The crowds did not bother Ethel. She had come out of her silence at last on the train, because at last she had made up her mind about how and when to do what she had to do.

Her feverish conversation from then on seemed not to bewilder her mother as it might have done. Leah seemed only grateful to have words from her daughter; she did not know to look beneath them. They talked of the weather, they talked of the crowds, they talked of the discomforts they endured. Only once did Ethel say something about what had passed and had never been spoken of before.

"Mother," she said, "I want you to know that I understand it was not your fault."

It was in the midst of a harangue by Diana on the impossibility of their trunks of new clothes catching up with them in time for the ship's sailing. Diana stopped in midsentence and looked confused.

"Of course it's not Mother's fault about the trunks," she said. "How could it be? You didn't think she could carry them personally, did you?"

"I didn't mean the trunks," said Ethel, looking at her mother.

"I know you didn't," said Leah, who understood that they were speaking of the girl's lost love. "I tried, my darling, honestly I tried, but you father is not someone against whom I could win. I am truly sorry."

"I know that, Mother," Ethel replied.

The girl felt as if this little conversation at which her sister had looked so perplexed, and which neither of them explained, had been a necessary step before the end. The end would come in the sea, and although the others did not understand it, they were going to the sea for Ethel's end. She had decided, so she did not have any more questions. She had been wrong at every stage of her life before—even being born a girl had been wrong, she knew that now. Now she would be right, because now she knew a way and a time to end her life in the sea.

On Orchard Street Shayna struggled with Caesar's *Gallic Wars,* her dictionary propped beside her against the biology book. She could not know that some of the terrain of which Caesar wrote was terrain her mother and sister were at that very moment knowing all too intimately. And despite all her own troubles, Shayna still loved the daily contest with Latin translation, still found some cheer in the small daily triumph of forty more lines of Caesar's opacity survived and bested. If only there were a way she could stay in school! If only she could promise herself this pleasure every day, then she might survive all the rest, she sometimes thought.

After her father had shamed her she had expected Miss Barton to look at her with pity when she went to Latin class, which would have mortified her past bearing. But she had been wrong. Miss Barton had clicked her pencil and looked at Shayna just as she had before she had been to Orchard Street. She looked at her expecting the correct translation of Caesar and nothing less. If Shayna could not erase the shame of Miss Barton's offer, at least a correct translation of Caesar was something she could produce, which she did, and she received the reprimand she had always received on those rare occasions when she missed a word. So Miss Barton was always the same, Latin was always the same. Shayna felt Latin was work she could do, and it was done. Yes—done, finished, over.

Latin was not like taking care of a family. Taking care of a family was never done, never over, never finished—it was always there to do, no matter how much had already been done. There were always the meals to get, there were always the beds to make, there was always the washing of the clothes, there was always the marketing, there was always the climbing up five flights of stairs with the packages, there was always the scrubbing of the floors and the walls, there was always the endless battle with the char and the dirt that was never done. About some parts of things, then, Mamma had been right; the making of beds and the baking of bread were not the hard parts, for instance, even though Shayna still could not do them well. She chewed her pencil on the thought.

The hard parts had been the parts Mamma had not really told her about, and they had been harder than Shayna had ever dreamed they could be. The endlessness of it all, stretching forever and forever into a bleaker and bleaker future if Mamma did not come back—that was the hardest part. Before Mamma had barely been gone, too, some of the other hard parts had started, like when she lost the little ones. The kind of fear she had felt then—Mamma had never told her about that. Or how she would feel so helpless when Sophie was hurt. Or about what would happen in a fire. And had Mamma ever been beaten with a strap while she was learning? No, she hadn't, because Mamma grew up in a family without a poppa in the old country; so she hadn't ever talked to Shayna about the strap. Or about Poppa. Certainly not about the mystery of what happened between men and women that made a woman like her mamma marry a man like her poppa.

And then, with Poppa, endlessly and always with Poppa, were her aunts, who hated her. Mamma had stood between her and her Tante Tillie and Tante Sadie when Mamma was home. When she had left had come the hard part. As a matter of fact, her aunts were maybe the hardest part. She would have a hard time even thinking of how she could win against her aunts.

As Shayna sat there going over so many things besides her Latin translation she deliberately did not think about her brother Yakov. It was a thing she couldn't think about—his leaving—because she couldn't understand it. Angry as she had often been, she had never thought of leaving the family, and she could not understand Yakov's leaving. She had finally told Cassie about it, finding at last a topic on which she and Cassie could regain a little of their lost closeness, but even Cassie had not understood how such a thing could be—Yakov's leaving like that.

"Didn't he explain at all?" Cassie had asked. "You mean he just walked out?"

Of course Cassie didn't understand; in Cassie's family people talked to one another. Cassie's brother Ari talked about how he disagreed with his parents. And his parents listened to what he said and talked back.

(She refused to think of what had happened between herself and Ari, because that was a hard part with which she absolutely could not deal.) And Cassie's mother, the one who somehow held it all together with her bright scarves, Cassie's mother had not left their family.

That was it, Shayna thought, her eyes glazing over as she turned back to the Latin; Mamma's leaving was the hardest part. And what she herself wanted was to hit out against all of it—against all the hard things that had happened and kept on happening no matter how she did her best. What if they really kept on for the rest of her life? Oh, why couldn't her mamma just come home and rescue her? Why couldn't taking care of the family just end? Were endings, happy or sad—it didn't matter which sometimes, just the fact of endings—only in books?

But her life was all still there to be lived, and Mamma was not coming home. Would there ever be a way now for Shayna? Could she find a way?

## ❧ 12 ❧

*I said of laughter, It is mad;*
*and of mirth, What doeth it?*
*(Ecclesiastes 2:2)*

Isaac sat in the silence of an early November *Shabbos* afternoon alone in the house, clutching the paper in his hands, staring at the headlines. Shayna had taken the little ones away for a walk in the crisp fall air that sang over the Saturday quiet of the neighborhood. Away was better, away was always better than here. Away . . .

Why didn't I go with them? he asked himself. If I were a good, dutiful father, I would have gone with Shayna and the children on a *Shabbos* afternoon. Even Tillie went along this time. And if I had gone with her, I would not have been here when Yakov came in. And if I had not been here, I would not have seen that look on my son's face when he walked in the door, that terrible look that surely I was not meant to see.

If I had gone with my children I would not have compounded Yakov's sin by taking this paper from his hands—this paper he had obviously bought with money on the Sabbath. How did he know to buy it? After all these weeks, why did he come back

345

today of all days, and with this newspaper and its terrible headline?

Yakov slammed out onto the street and cursed his own stupidity. What made me do it? he asked himself. I said I would never go back or speak to the old man again; why did I? He knew that his only hope lay in the blankness he had carefully built around himself. When he saw Poppa rage came, and with rage came pain. He could not bear the pain. Yet he had gone. Why?

He had gone out to get a paper for Kalinsky, and instead he had bought a paper for his father. Kalinsky wanted the paper; there was news these days of the uprisings in Russia. Yakov had volunteered to find one. It was a way to fill the blank time. And what did it matter that it was *Shabbos* and a sin to spend money? He didn't care about *Shabbos* anymore. What did *Shabbos* mean, what did it matter, when there was no God?

Because he knew now, as Kalinsky had told him before, that it was true that there was no God. He had mouthed the words before the strike, but he hadn't known the truth of them. Since what had happened to Dora, the truth was obvious. No one had ever said to him that she was dead, but he knew it. No one ever mentioned her name to him.

He stopped his walk down the block when he thought that, stopped absolutely still. He had learned that was the way to deal with it. Every time he thought of her he had to stop absolutely still and take the thoughts away from his mind, make his mind blank. He could not think of Dora. Could not. If he let himself think of her, he wept, and did that help? Did his agony bring her back? No. So he stopped.

The worst times were when he saw her. The first time it happened was when he was walking back from the shop with Kalinsky, back to the narrow bed

Kalinsky had set up for him in that flat with the slogans on the walls they now shared. He saw her down the street. Since it was the first time, he said something. "Who was that?" he asked.

Kalinsky looked where he was pointing. "Someone you know?"

"I thought I saw . . ." Yakov began, but then he realized he couldn't say it, couldn't even say her name. "But it can't be," he finished lamely.

Kalinsky didn't say a word one way or the other.

Still, Yakov had been sure that it had been Dora; he had seen her with his own eyes, and it took all the small strength of character that he could still muster not to run down the street, weaving through the crowd looking for her.

Because of course it wasn't Dora, just like there was no God. He knew because he had held her still body that real day after all, screamed his pain aloud over her real body, had begged her to come back, to live. But she had just lain there in his arms, silently dead, he was sure of that. If he had seen her dead, why did he still see her alive?

So he stopped still now and told himself the truth, reminded himself of the deadness of her, didn't let himself walk on. The pain went then, the sharp, shooting pain in his stomach, and instead he had only a blankness and a dull thump of a headache. But a headache was nothing—he knew a headache was nothing, nothing to compare with the pain of letting himself think about Dora, about still holding Dora in his arms.

So of course there was no God.

There was only the Cause, the work he had to do for the Cause. Nothing else mattered. He could lose himself instead in the Cause, in doing Kalinsky's bidding. If there was any hope in the world, even if there was none, Kalinsky was his friend.

Then why hadn't he done Kalinsky's bidding today? He had gone to do it, gone to get the paper. For Kalinsky. He had turned from the newsstand to head back to Kalinsky's flat. She had been there suddenly again then, and he had stopped, and she had gone away.

But he had taken the paper to Poppa, to Orchard Street. What about that paper had driven him to his father? He did not know. There had been some headline about a ship coming from Europe, but that had meant nothing to him. It was just that when he had picked up the paper he had known he must take it to his father. Why?

When Sarah opened her eyes and looked up at the white plaster ceiling above her bed she moaned. She felt as if every bone in her body ached. Then she coughed. All the muscles in her chest rebelled as if they had contracted for a cough too many times and refused to move again. The cough was weak, but it was loud enough to be heard by Rachel in the next room. Her daughter was at her side in a moment.

"Mamma," she said, "here, take a little water," and then she stopped in surprise, because Sarah turned to her with eyes that were comprehending at last, no longer the blank, delirious eyes of fever.

"Mamma," Rachel asked timidly, "are you better?"

Sarah smiled a little and said, "Yes, *mein kind,* I guess I'm alive. Where are we? What is that?" and she gave a slight motion of her head toward the cross she could see on the white wall.

"It's all right, Mamma. Thank God you're better. We are in a convent in Bruges—in Belgium. Some kind nuns found us when you were so sick, and they have been taking care of us. Oh, Mamma, thank God, thank God." Rachel sank onto Sarah's bed and put her arms around the thin form lying so quietly there. "I didn't know what to do, Mamma, and they were so very kind. . . ."

Rachel heard the soft sound of a skirt brushing the narrow walls of the corridor outside their rooms, and she opened the door to a small nun in a large black habit with a white headdress like a linen butterfly about her head. "My mother is better," she said in Yiddish to the nun.

The nun smiled with pleasure and put her candle down beside the bed, for the late October afternoon sun was fast fading from the small window. The shadows cast by Rachel and the nun confused Sarah briefly as they darkened the white wall, but when she closed her eyes she felt peaceful, grateful for the skillful hands that eased her pillow and the voice that clucked at her in German. The German had a different accent from what she was used to, but she could answer it nevertheless. She opened her eyes and thanked the nun for her care in her best *hoch Deutsch,* though spoken in a wispy, quiet voice.

When Sarah stopped speaking the little nun grinned broadly. "Ah," she said, "we can talk with ease. I have had trouble understanding the words of your child." She turned toward Rachel and spoke slowly, asking her to get some broth from the refectory.

Momentarily confused by the words, Rachel hesitated, but then her mamma repeated them in Yiddish, and she smiled with relief as she left the room.

"We will have you up and about in no time now," said the nun. "I told Sister Lachteld that the crisis had passed last night. I see I was right."

Sarah tried to sit up, but she was pushed easily and firmly back.

"Not too much yet, please; we do not want a relapse. It will take a little time for you to regain your strength." Instead she propped Sarah carefully with pillows. "Now," she continued as Rachel entered with a bowl of broth whose steam escaped from under a linen napkin, "you will have some broth to recover your strength."

Janet C. Robertson

The face that leaned over Sarah, framed as it was by that white butterfly of a wimple, was soft, with faint lines that defined years of smiling at and cajoling patients with kindness, a kindness for which Sister Agnes was known throughout the convent, as Rachel had already discovered in her timid explorations.

"I will help you," said the nun as she dipped the lovely silver spoon with its ornately fashioned handle into the bowl.

"What is it?" asked Sarah before she could eat. "What is the soup made with, please?"

Rachel and the nun looked at each other with distress, but Sister Agnes replied forthrightly, "It is a beef soup."

Sarah turned her head away.

"Please, Madame Klugerman," Sister Agnes went on firmly. "We know it was not prepared according to your Jewish Laws"—she hesitated only momentarily when Sarah nodded her head with finality—"but we also know that your Law says that in a matter of life and death it is all right to accept this gift from a stranger." The words were put with a courtesy that could not but be appreciated.

"Drink the soup, Mamma," said Rachel. "We must eat, and surely refusing their kindness would be as wrong as anything else. There is nothing else we can do now."

Sarah still sat immobile.

"Please, please," begged Rachel. "You have been nearly dead from sickness, and surely God does not want you to die, but to live and to get home," Rachel wept. "Please, Mamma, eat and don't die."

The nun looked approvingly at Rachel and patted her on the shoulder, then faced Sarah again with a question. "Will you eat, Madame?" she asked. "The child is right, you know; a God of mercy will help us all, Jew and Christian alike."

"I thank you for your kindness from the bottom of

350

my heart," said Sarah, and she allowed herself to be fed a few spoonfuls before she sank back, exhausted, onto her pillows.

When a week had passed she asked to see a newspaper and walked to the cloister entrance, leaning heavily on Rachel's arm. The newspaper told of sailings, and she needed to know where the next ship would leave from for America. To her relief, the *Noordam* was sailing in five days from Rotterdam. She felt that she would have regained enough strength by then so that if a train could get her to Rotterdam, she and Rachel would be on the *Noordam*. Even with the war, inquiries provided the information that here the trains were running.

Her determination overcame her weakness, so that on the following day she was able to go without help into the town to the shipping office and pay for their passage. The funds given her by the American consul in Budapest all those weeks before, which she had sewn into the hem of her dress when they were useless for so long, had been husbanded for this purpose, and now they answered her needs. There was even enough to go to the telegraph office next door and send a telegram to Isaac, the first communication to him since they had left her mother's house. She included the ship's name—the *Noordam*—and the date it was due in New York. Then, barely able to support herself, she made her way through the cold streets back to the haven of the convent.

While her mamma had been out Rachel had spent the afternoon helping the nuns in the kitchen, then watching some of them make lace in the large garden room lit by the low afternoon sun from the west. When Sarah got back she was so exhausted that she only showed Rachel the tickets. She did not have the strength also to tell her that she had sent the telegram to the family. Anyway, it was surely less important than the fact that they were finally going home. The beginning of November, but they were going home at last.

"Do we really sail on Thursday, Mamma?" asked Rachel with delight.

"Yes, Thursday, *zies kind*, on the *Noordam*," said Sarah, lying down exhausted on her bed. A weakness seemed to be enveloping her again, and she was covered with a film of sweat.

"Rest, then, Mamma. I will bring your supper to you here," said Rachel. "You must conserve your strength. And I will tell Sister Agnes what a wonderful thing you've done," she added, encouragement flavoring her words.

But Sarah's eyes were already closed with exhaustion and returning fever. She didn't open them to see Sister Agnes's look of concern when she came back with Rachel because she was already deep in sleep, too tired for any food.

"She went out too soon," said Sister Agnes. "I hope she will be all right."

"Oh, she will, don't worry, she will," replied Rachel with the buoyancy of wishes and her own youth.

But late that night Sarah woke in terror to find herself lying in a pool of blood. She knew it was not time for her regular period, and she knew that she was bleeding a great deal. She was determined, however.

I must get to that ship.

No matter what, I must sail on the *Noordam*.

I telegraphed to Isaac and told him, and he will expect me. I cannot be sick again; I must go.

I must see my little ones.

Rachel will help me. The nuns will help me.

I must go home.

Yakov wasn't here last night when the telegraph came, Isaac reasoned, so Yakov did not know what it was when he brought the paper. It had only been a chance that he had brought it today of all days. But I had to be here this afternoon, sitting here and hugging my happiness to myself, hugging to myself the words on the telegraph, the news at last that my Sarah was coming home. I had to be here on *Shabbos* to take the paper from him and learn the truth.

It was my sin.

He smiled wryly to himself, because no one was here to see him smile, as no one had seen him weep. But God has punished my sin now in ample measure. He looked at the headline again.

SHIP WITH AMERICAN REFUGEES SUNK BY GERMAN MINE.

More than ample measure.

NO SURVIVORS.

More than ample measure.

Such a punishment for such a small sin? The brief smile left his face, and he put the paper on the table and put his head in his hands and wept again. Long, wracking sobs with no one to hear them.

Oddly, then, he thought of what he had read that Jesus said on the cross: "My God, My God, why hast Thou forsaken me?" and he shuddered and cursed himself for the thought but cursed his God (that same Christian God?) for the deed.

Even Yakov is gone now, he thought. I am alone here, and I will be alone here for the rest of time. I have sent my eldest son away in his own pain. Did he come to help me? No. He could not know. And yet somehow, young as he is, he has suffered, too. He must have wanted to see me, that he came with this newspaper, knowing I would be angry, but somehow knowing something in his heart as a man of my trouble and wanting to help. How could he have known? Only God could have put into his head to come here today. And now he is gone.

I have lost him now, as I have lost his mother. I

have let his mother go, and I have sent him away now, too. My God, My God, why hast Thou forsaken me?

Isaac beat his head on the table and nearly screamed then as he thought also of his little daughter, the gentle little Rachel, and his pain mounted. He was forgetful then of anything but the pain that seemed to fill his whole being, that tore at the center of him with a wrenching he could not find a way through without sound. He was still sitting there and rocking in the chair and hitting his head against the table, sobbing alone, when Tanchun opened the door and walked into the room.

"Isaac, Isaac, my old friend, what for are you weeping?" Tanchun burst out. "You didn't even hear my knock, but I heard your weeping on the stairs already. What has happened, my friend? What has happened?"

For a while Isaac continued to rock back and forth, weeping and not answering.

Tanchun saw the paper then in front of him and came and picked it up, looking at the headlines about the ship that had blown up. After he looked he closed his eyes a moment, then opened them and asked with one word, "Sarah?"

Wordlessly, still rocking and weeping, Isaac nodded.

Tanchun lifted his head and breathed a short prayer. Then he looked again at Isaac. "I have said the prayer, Isaac. Have you said it yet?"

Now Isaac did not merely shake his head. He stopped his weeping and looked directly at Tanchun for the first time. "Why should I pray now?" he asked. "I have been praying for weeks, for months. What good is praying?"

It was Tanchun's turn to sit without words quickly on the chair across from Isaac. He tried to keep the shock out of his voice and to answer gently, but his voice sounded harsh in the small room now that the air was thick with silenced sobs. "There is a prayer for the time when we hear evil tidings, Isaac," he prodded. "Say it with me."

"*No!*" Isaac had stopped rocking now, and stood up instead, glowering in his place. "The paper does not say that she was one of the passengers. Maybe the telegraph was wrong." A half-crazed smile lit his face. "That must be it—that is why I cannot pray. I cannot pray because she is not lost. She wasn't on that boat." He sat down again and looked at Tanchun with a simple look. "That's it! The telegraph was wrong, everything was wrong, and now you are wrong—I cannot pray because God hasn't done this to me—she wasn't on that ship! I do not need to bless God as the true judge, like it says in the prayer, because He has not judged in this case—it did not happen."

Now it was Tanchun who swayed briefly in his chair before Isaac's blazing eyes. "What telegraph, Isaac?" he asked. "Tell me from the beginning."

"It came yesterday," said Isaac. "You know we have not heard from Sarah in months—since this war began. Yesterday, just before the beginning of *Shabbos,* a boy came to the door with a telegraph. I had not heard for so long that you know that I thought it was bad news?" He smiled a mirthless grimace at the irony. "But it wasn't—it was good news at last! Sarah and Rachel were on that ship—the *Noordam*—or rather"—he stopped, and the hope filled his eyes—"not that they were already on the ship, Tanchun, not that they were on it. The telegraph only said that she and Rachel would be on the ship. It was sent last week, but it took a long time to find us, because they aren't used to looking for telegraphs to come to Orchard Street." He reached for Tanchun's hands then, as if to touch him would be to make him share this new truth. "Tanchun, Tanchun, don't you see? Doesn't it sound as if she wasn't on the ship? Doesn't it sound as if she wasn't among the dead?"

Tanchun shook his head and detached his hands. "Isaac," he insisted, "you know she was on the ship, because you have received the telegraph. You must face it, and you must bear the truth, my friend. Your wife and your little girl were on the ship, may they rest in peace. Do you hear me, Isaac?" He raised his voice because Isaac was shaking his head and twisting away. "Do you hear me? These are indeed evil tidings, Isaac, but you must hear them. Your comfort will begin to come with prayer, Isaac. *Say the prayer!*"

Then suddenly Isaac turned his whole body toward his friend and gazed at him for a while with a cold and stony expression, all traces of his recent weeping erased from his face. When he spoke at last his voice was what was dead. "No," he said, "I will not say a prayer, because I will not pray to a God who would kill Sarah and Rachel, if such a God exists at all. Anyway, I cannot pray as a mourner for those who *are not dead.*"

"Oh, Isaac—"

"Her name is not listed in the *New York Times* among the dead. She is not dead. I do not believe she is dead." He stared sightlessly for a moment at the newspaper, then put it down and spoke as through a glass curtain. "It is *Shabbos,* Tanchun. That is why you are here—let us study as we do on every *Shabbos.*"

Tanchun saw the futility of further talk and thought that perhaps the balm of study would ease his friend's burden. Anyway, he said to himself, it is traditional, too, to study in a house of mourning. So they turned to the books. The two of them were still mumbling over the large tomes when the family came home from their walk. Tanchun left as soon as they came in the door; they looked so happy, it did not seem there was any way he could help.

They all had bright eyes and rosy cheeks, and even

Tillie spoke cheerfully. "Well, Isaac, we had a lovely walk. The air is beautiful outside today, and . . ." She stopped short in the middle of her description, however, because even Tillie could see it in his face. "What has happened?" she asked.

"Nothing has happened. We do not know that anything has happened," he said, a steely determination in his voice belying the ravaged look on his face. If Sarah was truly never coming back, then he knew the rest of his life would be spent with his sister Tillie. Sarah, although she had never known it, had rescued him from the bitterness of his sister.

"Poppa, why is the newspaper here?" asked Shayna. A sudden flash made her ask also, "Did Yakov come home?" It seemed impossible, it had been weeks, but . . . "Oh, dear, he didn't buy a newspaper on *Shabbos,* did he, Poppa? Is that what's wrong?" She tumbled the questions out.

"Why do you say something is wrong?" he shouted. *"Nothing is wrong!"*

Shayna stood still in amazement and sudden fear, the color fading from her cheeks. Even when Poppa was angry it was not usually so sudden, so totally unreasonable. The one thing she had always felt about Poppa was that he was a reasonable man. She didn't see how she had provoked him now. She could think of nothing to say.

"Nothing is wrong." He spoke only slightly more quietly and then turned on the one he too often turned on. "But I have finally made a decision about you, Shayna. I have decided that on your fourteenth birthday you will, after all, leave that foolish school. I had thought about taking your teacher's offer, but that is clearly not right. You know it isn't right, don't you?"

"But Poppa," she protested, "now that Mamma's coming home, surely that changes everything, doesn't it? I know it would be wrong to take Miss Barton's offer, but now we don't need to. Now everything is different, isn't it? Why do I need to quit school now?" Somehow as she spoke she started to feel all cold, as if everything wasn't as different as it had seemed since the wonderful news of last night. It was like the nightmare was settling in again, like the good news of Mamma's coming home had been the dream, but the nightmare was still going to be the reality. Why?

"No, it is not different. You will do as I say," he replied shortly, seeing Tillie's smile and nod of encouragement. It was as if Tillie would want Shayna to suffer too. "You will find a job and earn money to help with the family. When you are settled in the job Tante Tillie will stay home and take care of the family. I have decided now, furthermore, that you will go into a shop, not an office." Why did he feel this rage toward Shayna? "I will speak to the boss tomorrow to see if there are any vacancies. I am sure he will have a suggestion."

"Tante Tillie take care of us? But Poppa, what about Mamma?"

"No," he interrupted her. "I have decided. Perhaps your mother is not coming home. So you must quit school. That is all that there is to it."

"Not coming home?" The terrible chill of fear was wider now. "Why do you say now that perhaps Mamma is not coming home? Yesterday we got the telegraph, didn't we? I didn't dream it. And we know she will be home now. The *Noordam* will dock on November eighth. Isn't that what the telegraph said? So why are you saying that perhaps she isn't coming?"

Isaac turned away from her. "I just said *perhaps* she won't come home. I didn't say she isn't coming for sure," he mumbled now.

"But look in the paper, Poppa—look where the dockings are scheduled. You have today's paper," she insisted, picking it up from the table. "It will say in the paper—why should you say 'perhaps' at all? Come on, Poppa." For a moment she thought she might be able to jolly him out of his mood. After all, she had nothing to lose by the effort. "It's a beautiful *Shabbos* afternoon, and we know that Mamma and Rachel are coming home on the *Noordam* on November eighth. Come on, Poppa, it's all going to be okay now."

But Isaac turned on her in such a fury that she didn't even resist when he grabbed the paper from her hands before she had a chance to look at it. "They were not on the *Noordam*. The telegraph was wrong. They will not be coming home on the eighth," he shouted.

Even Tillie was taken aback at the sudden return of his rage. Her life had gone in circles in the last twenty-four hours, and she did not know what her brother could mean. First had come the telegraph saying that Sarah was returning. That had meant that she, Tillie, would have to leave. And now he was talking as if he wanted her to stay, as if somehow Sarah was not returning. What was going on? She looked up, walked across the room, and took the paper from him before he could continue. She glanced at it briefly, and then spoke in a matter-of-fact voice without a trace of emotion to color it. "It says here that the *Noordam* was sunk yesterday by German mines, and all the passengers are feared lost." She looked at her brother. "Is this what you mean when you say Sarah will 'perhaps' not be back? It looks as if it is more than perhaps, Isaac." She stood waiting for his answer. When none was forthcoming, she went patiently on. "The ship she said in the telegraph was the *Noordam*, wasn't it, Isaac?"

He still did not answer her.

"Isaac," she asked, "is there a reason you know Sarah was *not* on the ship? Tell me what has happened." She waited again through a silence that seemed ridiculously long in the little room. "Isaac, what has happened?" she repeated.

Throughout this exchange Shayna was standing where she had been, frozen to the floor. Sophie and Harry were in the other room playing. David was with Tante Sadie at her house. They had left him there on their walk. She could hear the grownups' voices with the back of her mind, but she could not really hear anything consciously after that headline Tante Tillie had read out loud. The *Noordam* was sunk. All passengers feared lost. She heard that word "lost," and then the whole center of her was full of a terrible pain. She actually groaned aloud from the hurt in her stomach as she sat down, bump, on the chair.

"No," she said, not hearing her own voice. "It isn't true. Nothing has happened." She clutched at her stomach and bent double over the pain, saying again, "Nothing has happened, has it, Poppa?"

"No," echoed Isaac, "nothing has happened because they are not on that ship." He held up his hand to silence the words Tillie seemed ready to say. "I don't care what the telegraph said, Tillie, because Sarah is not drowned. She is alive. Rachel is alive. They were not on that ship."

"Oh, oh, oh," moaned Shayna, her arms across her stomach, because she could not bear to believe the paper, and there was still a part of her, no matter what, that could not bear to doubt her father. "Why did you say perhaps she isn't coming back, Poppa? Oh, I have a terrible pain. Why didn't they telegraph again if they are alive? Oh, Mamma and Rachel can't be dead. I can't bear this, I can't, oh, oh, oh." It seemed to her that Sarah and Rachel couldn't be dead, and that at the same time they were dead, and that she, Shayna, was dying, too, at that moment.

Isaac lifted his hand from the table as if it weighed with a terrible weight and put it awkwardly on his daughter's shoulder. Was this part of what Sarah had taught him—this inability to bear his children's pain?

"They are not dead, Shayna," he said gently. "The paper is wrong. Stop it, they are not dead."

Afterward, when she thought about it, Shayna thought it was the only time her poppa had ever touched her with his hand in her life. There was a way to forgive him a lot of things after that day he touched her to comfort her.

Tillie looked at the two of them in disbelief, her doubt clearly etched in her frown. She read the paper to herself, standing there, and shook her head. For once she couldn't think of what to do. It was frightening to see Isaac look the way he was looking.

Then she found a reason to open her mouth again. "Where did this paper come from on *Shabbos*, Isaac?" she asked. Maybe the very illegitimacy of the bought paper on the Sabbath could explain the inexplicable.

"Yakov was home and brought it while you were gone," he answered, grateful for any distraction. "He should not have bought the paper on *Shabbos*, of course. I reprimanded him, don't worry." But the memory of Yakov's eyes after the reprimand, of the sound of the door slamming behind him, was very terrible to Isaac.

"But he bought it because he must have seen the headline," began Shayna, excusing her brother. "He hasn't been home for weeks," she dared to say. It was all so strange. "He must have known somehow about the telegram, and he must have known that Mamma and Rachel were dead." She bent double again. "Oh, Mamma," she moaned, "I hurt so." She rocked back and forth with her knees drawn up, moaning aloud.

Sophie and Harry finally heard the sounds and came in from the other room. "What's wrong with Shayna?" asked Sophie. "Why is she crying?"

"Mamma is dead," wailed Shayna before Isaac or Tillie could furnish another answer. "Her ship sank, and she and Rachel are dead. Oh, oh, oh."

Sophie and Harry were shocked into immobility for just a second, but the wailing was contagious, and they, too, burst into tears.

Then Isaac roused himself again from his silence. "No," he said, so firmly that they all stopped to listen. "Your mamma is not dead. Rachel is not dead. They are alive. Shayna, the story in the paper may be true, but your mamma was not on that boat. I will not believe it. Stop your crying immediately, all of you. Mamma will be home. I will not allow you to believe otherwise. Mamma will be home."

Tillie shook her head. "But Isaac—" she began.

"No!" he said. "This is final. *No!*"

Somehow the little ones believed him, because they had always believed him. Shayna, in their experience, could be wrong, but their poppa could not.

Shayna tried to believe him. She made herself stop crying and told herself that she believed Poppa, but the terrible pain in her stomach continued, and she had to stay in bed for two days. She missed two of the last precious days of her schooling because of the pain.

When she went back on the following Wednesday she heard herself explaining to Miss Barton as if she were hearing somebody else talking to another person beyond a thick wall, "I will have to leave school. My father told me to tell you that was his decision."

"I will speak to him again," Miss Barton, startled, said firmly.

"Never mind," Shayna heard herself answer. "My mother was on that ship that was blown up by mines. He's right now—now there is no way." She left the room without waiting for a reply.

If she had told Miss Barton, did that mean that she believed it herself? She would not let herself say to the rest of the family that she believed it. She didn't even tell Cassie about the telegram or the ship. That somehow left things undecided still, didn't it? It meant that Poppa might still be right, even if she had to quit school, that there still might be some hope. Nevertheless, after she had told Miss Barton, somewhere inside her Shayna knew that Mamma and Rachel were dead and would never return.

She kept remembering, too, the conversation Tante Tillie had had with Tante Sadie on that walk they'd all taken the afternoon after they'd received the telegram with the good news. Tante Tillie had made a bargain with Tante Sadie that afternoon about marrying.

"I will marry that man after all, Sadie," she had said. (Shayna had been ashamed of eavesdropping, but she could not help herself.) "I cannot stay in Isaac's house," Tillie had said, "now that his wife is returning. But otherwise I would not do it."

Tante Sadie had nodded her understanding.

"But there is one condition," Tillie had continued. "It is about my dowry. I bring the dowry to the marriage, but if I should become a widow, the dowry money comes back to me. The man can leave what he pleases to his own children, but I insist that I receive my dowry back—I have heard too many tales of what happens to a wife's money in a second marriage, and this will be his second marriage."

"I will tell Franz what you have said," Tante Sadie had promised. "It will be arranged."

Now, of course, Shayna knew that it had all been unarranged again, because now Tante Tillie would not marry. Now she would be staying always in the Klugerman household, just as she had always wanted. Because Mamma and Rachel were dead and would never return. No matter who was told or not told, the facts remained. Mamma was dead, and there would be no one to rescue Shayna.

On the afternoon of Sunday, November 11, 1914, Shayna Klugerman sat on the stoop of #40 Orchard Street in New York City and idly watched her sister

Sophie playing hopscotch with some other little girls. Sophie doesn't realize that Mamma is dead, Shayna thought. But I know it. I know my mamma is dead, even if Poppa won't mourn for her or for Rachel, even if the little ones can't understand about it. Mamma and Rachel have been gone so long, it's as if they've forgotten. I haven't forgotten, she thought.

Mrs. Goldstein came out with her knitting and sat beside her. "It is surprisingly warm for November, isn't it?" she said, more kindly than usual. "I thought I'd sit for a while outside before I do my potatoes." She glanced sidewise at Shayna, who seemed deep in thought and had not replied. "Shayna," she went on, coming to her point, "I thought your mother and Rachel were coming home before now. Then, when your Tante Tillie told me what happened, I was very sorry to hear of your loss. Will your family sit *shiva* for them? I cannot understand why you will not show your mother and your sister respect."

Shayna closed her eyes briefly and took a deep breath, feeling much older already than the fourteen she would be on her birthday in two days. Her voice was hollow and without emotion when at last she replied. "We do not sit *shiva*, Mrs. Goldstein, as undoubtedly my Tante Tillie has also told you"—she could not resist the bitterness for a moment—"because my father does not believe Mamma and Rachel were on that ship. My poppa says they are not dead, and you do not sit *shiva* for someone who is still alive. He says—"

"But you heard they were coming on that ship," insisted Mrs. Goldstein. "You know—"

"I know, Mrs. Goldstein, I know."

Her voice was so sad that it silenced even Mrs. Goldstein.

"I will be leaving school on Tuesday," said Shayna, suddenly needing to tell someone the whole of her misery, even if that someone was Mrs. Goldstein.

364

"It's my fourteenth birthday, so I can go to work then, and later Tante Tillie can stay home and take care of the house. If my mamma had not been killed because of the war . . ." But she could not continue. All of a sudden all the tears that had been pent up inside her for the last few days came rushing to her eyes, and she wept. First quietly, and then with great long sobs, she wept.

Mrs. Goldstein put down her knitting and came close, sitting awkwardly beside her on the stoop. She even put her arm about her to comfort her. Even if she was not a nice woman, Mrs. Goldstein was a woman, and she could not let the child cry like that for her dead mother without some comfort.

It was starting to turn cool, and the sun was already setting when Shayna looked up and her eyes found the two of them—the pale older woman and the thin young girl—walking up the street, carrying their suitcases, pushing through the crowd toward her.

"Mamma? Rachel?" she said in a small voice, unbelieving.

They kept on coming, even if they didn't hear her.

Later, even years later, she thought she would never bring herself to believe in the miracle of it. Certainly that afternoon she could not. There was, of course, hugging and kissing and hugging again, real touching of real people, but still it was not to be believed. Just when she had given up completely, she told herself, just when she had been sure that they were dead, here they were walking up Orchard Street alive. She looked at her father with new respect after that, because she knew he hadn't given up. Not Poppa. Not ever.

It seemed that the miracle had many parts. First they had ridden and walked across all of the continent of Europe, all the way from Hungary, through the war lines even, and the trenches. Rachel told her later about the trenches, trembling in their bed as she told it in whispers after Sophie was asleep. And then, Rachel said, they had been terribly sick, and Mamma had nearly died. She had been scared out of her wits that Mamma would die. The Roman Catholic nuns who had rescued them cured Mamma, but Mamma went from her sickbed too soon to the steamship company to buy tickets for the *Noordam*.

The worst time, Rachel said, was when Mamma became sick again, and they couldn't go on the boat when they planned.

"No," insisted Shayna. "That wasn't the worst time, because you would have been killed—you would have drowned like we thought you did. Oh, why didn't you telegraph us that you missed that boat? Why did you let us think you had drowned?"

When she asked the question that first afternoon, Mamma hugged her yet again. "I'm here, Shayna, I'm here," she kept saying. "I didn't telegraph . . . because I didn't telegraph. I had sent that telegraph once, and look what happened! I was afraid to do it again. And anyway . . ." But she never did explain *and anyway*.

Rachel said then, "Oh, Shayna, we were so scared and so sick, frankly we just thought of ourselves; we didn't think of you."

It was hard for Shayna to bear that part of it. She had thought only of them, but they had not thought of her. It was hard to understand what it had been like for Mamma and Rachel; she tried to bury her hurt when she could not understand.

But all that came later. On that first afternoon there was only the miracle of it.

"Go," Mamma said to her at last, laughing when she hugged her again, reaching around Sophie and Harry, who clung without cease. "Go to the shop and get Poppa and Yakov." She practically pushed her out the door. "And buy a chicken," she added. "Tell

Poppa to buy a chicken on the way home. We will celebrate." She smiled her old smile. "Thanks be, we will celebrate." She had tears running down her face with the smile.

"And I want my baby," she said. "Where is David?"

Harry and Sophie went for Tante Sadie and Uncle Franz and little David. Shayna went to the shop for Poppa. She had not told Mamma anything about Yakov not being there.

She walked right past Mr. Saperstein's office and told Poppa that they were home. And she saw the miracle of her father, in front of all those men there in the shop, putting his head down on the cloth he had been cutting and weeping. "It's true, Poppa," she had to repeat many times. "It's true they're home." The other men stopped their machines and came over then and touched Poppa on the back, patted her head, smiled with tears in their eyes.

Finally Mr. Saperstein came from his little office at the back. "Why are you not working?" he shouted. "Get back to work."

Poppa ignored him, beginning instead a prayer in which the other men joined, all of them together in Hebrew blessing the Lord "who has kept us alive and sustained us, and enabled us to see this day."

"I'm going home," Poppa said to Mr. Saperstein then, putting his knives and scissors away as the other men went back to work.

What could Mr. Saperstein do but nod to a man like Poppa?

"Now find your brother," Poppa said to Shayna. "Find your brother and bring him," and he walked out of the shop.

So Shayna did what her poppa told her. She found Yakov. It wasn't hard, really. First she remembered he had been friends with Mr. Edelmann in the shop; Edelmann still worked. He told her about Kalinsky, and when she went to the shop where Kalinsky was he told her where her brother was. He looked sharply at her, and at first she wondered whether he would tell her.

"Why do you want him?" Kalinsky asked.

She told him about her mother's return.

He nodded once, then asked, "Your mother?" in a puzzled tone. Who else did he think?

She repeated her news.

"Yes," he said then, seeming relieved. "Tell him his mother has returned," he said. As if she would see Yakov and somehow not tell him? But Kalinsky was supposed to be Yakov's friend.

The surprising part was that when she found Yakov, he came home without protest. He looked at her after she told him what had happened, and he said what seemed to Shayna a peculiar thing. "Maybe there is a God," he said. "If there are miracles, maybe there is a God—at least for you, Shayna," and he went home to Orchard Street with her.

When they came up the stairs the chicken was already in the pot, and Mamma was back in charge. For a second Shayna felt a strange surprise to see Mamma in charge, but she felt a great relief as well. It was a surprise to her that she could regret, even momentarily, that she was no longer the one in charge. She hurried to help with the preparations.

Sophie stood beside her and whispered, "Shayna, when Poppa came in the door he went up to Mamma and hugged her. And he kissed her—honestly, right here in front of us he hugged her and he kissed her."

In all the rest of her life Shayna remembered that party. It was the first of the series of parties on November eleventh that marked all the years until her mother's death. After the war, of course, they all thought it strange that the rest of the world celebrated November eleventh, which turned out to be Armistice Day in 1918, as well, but peace and Sarah's return were easy to intertwine. Even for the woman Shayna became, it was always a glorious party.

On the first evening they ate the chicken and they drank wine and they sang songs. Not *Shabbos* songs, but Hanukkah songs, the songs of the Feast of Lights that was still a month away. The songs about wonders and miracles (if you sang them in English, Shayna pointed out, you had to say "wonders and mirACKles" to fit the tune) that seemed so appropriate to the way they all felt. The whole family was there—Tante Sadie, not yet fat with the baby inside her (Shayna had whispered the news to Mamma, who had wept again when she heard it, wept again with a smile on her face), and Uncle Franz beaming when he patted Harry or Sophie on the head, and a friend of Uncle Franz's who sat with Tante Tillie while they ate, even smiled at her while she looked at him sidelong and seemed to frown just a little less than usual.

Sarah is home, thought Tillie, and she knew now for sure that she would marry this man, this widower who did not want children. Her sister Sadie had indeed provided the solution to the impossibility of her living longer under Isaac's roof. If she could not have her brother, she would have to take this man. She had made her bargain. It was a life.

One of the loudest voices singing the songs at the party was the voice of Mr. Nathan, the music teacher, who sang as he accompanied them on their piano. Shayna had been surprised when Mamma had sent her out yet again that afternoon for Mr. Nathan, but Mamma had insisted. When he came in the door with her and saw Mamma in the crowded room he, too, had smiled and wept. He had reached out both his hands, and Mamma had taken them, even though he was not a relative, she again smiling and weeping.

The grownups certainly seemed to Shayna to be full of tears for such a happy time.

After dinner, when they all sat close together in the small room, Mamma and Rachel told some of the stories of their journey. Shayna had thought that the travelers must be exhausted, but they weren't too tired to tell.

"I will be tired, later, *shaynheitel*," Mamma said, holding the baby David, who had not quite recognized her when he first saw her and had fallen asleep on her lap with his thumb in his mouth. "Now I am home, though," she said, "so now when I am tired I will sleep."

"Didn't you sleep on the boat, Mamma?" asked Sophie from across the table.

"Mostly not," said Sarah, shaking her head. "We were so frightened on the boat, you see. We had heard of the mines, of the boats that were blown up. We didn't sleep much."

"I did," Rachel contradicted in her gentle way. "I was so tired by then and so relieved to be coming home, I slept. Especially after we left England," she added.

"England? But you said the boat left from Holland," Mr. Nathan put in.

Sarah took the sleeping baby into his room and tucked him in before she replied. "We stopped in Liverpool to pick up more passengers," she said, coming back into the expectant room. She spoke as if it was the most natural thing in the world for her to be a traveler who speaks of stops on a voyage. This was a new mamma since her journey. "After that," she said, "I walked the decks every night anyway. I walked the decks and looked at the water." She laughed. "Maybe I thought I would see a mine and save the boat. But," she added, "it was lucky I did not sleep, because one night I saved a person, even if it was not the whole boat."

"What happened?" asked Yakov, the first time he had spoken. "How did you save a person, Mamma?"

"It was one of the passengers who had boarded in Liverpool," she said. "As a matter of fact, Shayna, it was a young woman named Ethel Morgenstern, the daughter of the Mrs. Morgenstern you saw that day you bought Rachel's dress." Sarah knew nothing of any other connection between her family and the Morgensterns. Had Isaac ever told her of such a connection? She just remembered the name of the uptown lady from whom Shayna had gotten the dress all those months ago.

"She was a very sad young woman," Sarah went on. "Every night I would pass her walking as I was walking. I cannot imagine what a person like that was doing in the part of the ship we were in. Oh, well, the war made strange things happen. I could see often that she was crying as she walked, but I never spoke to her. After all"—she brushed her hair back where it had crept from under her *sheitel*—"it was not my business why a strange young woman cried on such a ship.

"But one night I saw her standing by the railing looking at the water. You know how beautiful the water is when you're on a ship? It gleams so white in the moonlight sometimes, and near the ship it sometimes glows with many colors; it is always different—you never become tired of looking at the water," she went on.

"I did," said Rachel, interrupting.

Sarah smiled at her, then continued. "I went and stood with the young woman, since we both seemed to be doing the same thing—staring at that water. I said something about how cold it looked, I think.

" 'Cold,' she said. 'Yes, maybe cold, but it will be so restful.' "

"It was only when she said that that I realized she was starting to climb over the railing, that she was actually thinking of jumping in. I felt so terrible for her then, such a young person to think of such a thing. I grabbed hold of her and held her back. She did not have much resistance in her after all. When she climbed down I held her hand still and tried to understand how it could be that she could think of it." Tears filled Sarah's eyes as she told the story. Her tears and the sadness of the picture of that young woman climbing over the ship's railing brought tears to other eyes as well.

"She was so sad because there was a young man she loved, and she was not allowed to marry him. I never learned the reason why. She had not heard from him for months; perhaps he did not love her as she loved him. She was so desperate with her sadness that she could even think of killing herself in the sea. I held her hand and tried to understand how she was so fallen into sadness that the sea could be an answer for her."

"What did you tell her, Mamma?" It was Yakov again who asked. "What did you tell her to save her?"

Sarah squared her shoulders as she looked at her son. "I told her you don't die for love," she said. "I held her hand and told her just that. I had seen enough dying in the old country on my journey. You may think you will, but you don't die for love." She looked around the room at the others, her eyes resting briefly on Mr. Nathan, and unexpectedly she smiled. "It seems there are many things you don't die of," she said. "So we lived."

She hesitated before finishing the story: "I took the girl down to her mother, that Mrs. Morgenstern, and although I did not tell her mother what had happened, I think she knew. The girl ran to her and hugged her so fiercely that I think the mother knew at least that something had happened and was over." Sarah looked at Yakov as if she had fashioned her answer just for him.

I make it sound so simple.

Well, what has happened is past; I am here now.

Isaac, you see I have kept my promise and come back.

David, there will never be a promise, or even a word, between us. I cannot even thank you aloud for music.

My life, my children for whom my heart has ached, are here.

My girlhood was where I have been, and it is over.

That evening they all drank more wine, and they sang more songs and asked for more stories. Mamma was home, they all felt, to show them the world.

In the morning Shayna went to school smiling the whole way. Maybe, she thought, she could stay in school now. Nothing was sure—she had found out how wrong things could go. But there were miracles— she'd learned that, too. So maybe.

# Acknowledgments

My grandmother's stories were my beginnings. She never told me a word, however, about the summer of 1914, when she was caught in Europe by the beginning of World War I.

Without my mother's recollections of her childhood on the Lower East Side, my life and this book would have been the poorer. Younger than the Shayna of this story, she nevertheless remembered the details for which I asked.

*The New York Times* and Barbara Tuchman's *The Guns of August* helped my research immeasurably, as did other books too numerous to name. When I started to delve into this past I was aware, as always, of the pleasure of being married to a historian. He gave without stint.

My writers' group, Bernice Buresh, Diane Cox, Helen Epstein, Phyllis Karas, Diana Korzenik, Caryl Rivers, Sally Steinberg, Carolyn Toll, and Barbara Ehrlich White, supported my efforts. Jill Steinberg prodded when I needed prodding. And without Frances Ackerly and Elizabeth Gregg, I might never have had the courage to write. E. Diane Kirkman's help has been crucial.

Elaine Markson believed and helped, as did Joanna Cole. Jane Chelius read and understood. Thanks.